"Doreen Birdsell's humor, resilience, and indestructible spirit shines through this gripping story of her journey from an early childhood of neglect and abuse to eventual triumph, prosperity, and spiritual salvation. Riveting, sensitively written, and even at times funny, this story will bring inspiration to anyone who has ever faced tragedy, or found themselves on a path toward self-destruction."
—Jessica Bram, *author of Happily Ever After Divorce: Notes of a Joyful Journey, Westport Writers' Workshop founder/director*

"Doreen has been my spiritual guide for over a decade. Her faith is the strongest I've ever witnessed in a human being. Having read and loved *Without Faith*, I now understand the source of her belief and spirit. I couldn't put the book down and continue to marvel at Doreen's ongoing journey of discovery, faith and passion."
—Jane Pollak, *Speaker, Coach, Author—Soul Proprietor: 101 Lessons from a Lifestyle Entrepreneur*

"It was my pleasure to know *Without Faith* during its gestation. Birdsell peels off her skin without anesthesia to reveal the wounds of abandonment, family betrayal and resulting addictions. I held my breath while I turned her pages and followed her journey to hell and back. Hers is a testimony to God's grace and will give hope to all who struggle in this life."
—Lucy Hedrick., *Author, publishing coach*

"Look up the word *integrity* in the dictionary and you just might find the name Doreen Birdsell in the definition. Her story is one that challenges every reader to think again about his or her own relationship to God."
—The Rev. Dr. John H. Danner, *Senior Pastor, Sanibel (FL) Congregational United Church of Christ*

Copyright © 2011
Cover design and interior by Jennifer Cole
Author Photo © Kate Eisemann
Make-up, Faces Beautiful
Printed in the U.S.A.
Don't Push Press – Westport, CT

No part of this publication may be reproduced or transmitted in any form or by any means, electronic or mechanical, including photocopying, recording, or any information storage and retrieval system now known or to be invented, without permission in writing from the publisher, except by a reviewer who wishes to quote brief passages in connection with a review written for inclusion in a magazine, newspaper, online publication or broadcast.
Although events herein are true according to author's recollection, many names have been changed to protect privacy and identity.

All rights reserved.
Library of Congress Control Number: 2011926196
ISBN 978-1-4507-6982-2

Without Faith: a memoir/Doreen Birdsell

1. Biography 2. Spiritual 3. Addiction

WITHOUT FAITH

A Motherless Child Redeemed by a Determined Spirit

Doreen Birdsell

DON'T PUSH PRESS
Westport, CT

Contents

1.	When A Mother Dies	3
2.	Denny's Garden	9
3.	Port Chester to Ridgewood	16
4.	A Visit Back Home	21
5.	Blondie and Dagwood	26
6.	Kindergarten	31
7.	The Lighthouse	37
8.	Adele	42
9.	Day Camp	47
10.	Traffic Street	57
11.	Birdie	59
12.	Cowboy Boots	64
13.	Ice Cream	67
14.	Community Center	71
15.	Tracks	78
16.	Kents	90
17.	Hitting a Wall	103
18.	How Lucky	111
19.	A Proposal	116
20.	A Baling Hooker	120
21.	48th Street to Flushing	129
22.	Womyn	135
23.	New Building, New Me	139
24.	Donna Visits the City	144
25.	Chumley's	154

26.	Private Clubs	164
27.	The Fat Farm and the Model	172
28.	Cherry Grove	175
29.	After Dark	179
30.	Parallels	189
31.	Blue Nun and Harleys	200
32.	First Days Sober	206
33.	No Will of My Own	209
34.	Personal Development	211
35.	Oracles and Addictions	213
36.	Pain and Suffering	218
37.	Alternate-Side-of-the-Street	220
38.	Anthony Quinones	225
39.	Within My Means	229
40.	Moving On	231
41.	Loving and Available	234
42.	You Call Yourselves Christians?	240
43.	Peekskill	248
44.	Westport	252
45.	Meeting Mary	254
46.	Saugatuck Shores	260
47.	Mary's Ageless Birthday	264
48.	Our Primary Purpose	267
49.	What a Predicament	272
50.	Probate	276

Acknowledgments

Thanks be to God — without whom I would not have been thought into being or kept alive to overcome tremendous odds.

Lisa, my life partner, sister in Christ, and best friend, sacrificed her time and patience to give me the time and space necessary to write. Most importantly, I am grateful to her for believing that telling my story would help others and be a witness to God's love and presence.

Thanks for the love and courage of my Aunt Hazel and Uncle Ted, who fought to keep me from being given to Catholic Charities after my mother, Faith, died after my second birthday. God bless them for surviving my adolescence in the 1960s.

To my sister Donna, the one I often ran away from home to be with; for loving me so much she couldn't help but notice even after I tweezed my eyebrows — more importantly, for never letting me forget how important it is to have a family. In your heaven home I know your spirit sings.

Jane Pollak was my muse. Having heard bits and pieces of my story, she said, "Have you ever thought of writing a book?" She never stopped encouraging me after I said, "Yes."

Then there was Jessica Bram, founder of the Westport Writers' Workshop, whom Jane knew I needed. Jessica gave my words legs to stand on and then the ability to walk through each page of my memoir. I would also like to thank Jessica for bringing the Westport Writers' Workshop Retreat to the Inn at Cook Street for five consecutive years with her mentor, and remarkable teacher, Suzanne Hoover, affectionately known as Yoda by many of her students.

Thanks to my good friends Gemma Tummolo and Betsy Krobot, who volunteered to read the final draft — especially to Gemma (a.k.a. Carol) for her good influence and tenacity, and being with me when I crossed the bridge to recovery.

I could not have arrived at this destination without the ongoing help and support of Lucy Hedrick, my coach throughout the process, who taught me about the business of being a writer and publishing. She is pure energy and enthusiasm.

To complete the process was Marggie Graves, my editor. God continued to connect the dots leading me to Marggie. More important than correcting grammar or being on the lookout for continuity, Marggie "got" my story and inadvertently became another encourager in the process.

God knew I needed a lot of encouraging and surrounded me with these talented, spiritual, loving supporters as I walked the narrow path to write *Without Faith*, giving me the opportunity, for the first time in my life, to publicly thank my mother, Faith — without whom I would not have this title … or the opportunity to have inherited a rich and constant faith.

Foreword

Coming out of my office in the church one morning, I bumped into Doreen who was leaving a twelve-step meeting. In those days, there were sixty such groups that met weekly in this section of the church. Therefore, it was usual that I would say hello to some of the people who were about to pass my office each day. But one day, something unique, inspiring, Spirit-led, random or coincidental happened. There was a spark, and I introduced myself to this woman who was leaving the meeting. Although that was now 15 years ago, I recall where I was and where she was. Not all the conversation is remembered other than the gist. I wanted her to know that our church is a welcoming place, that the God of inclusion is alive, present, and engaging. Right off, Doreen indicated that in her experience churches had been exclusive, judgmental, and even condemning of people who are part of the GLBT community. I said forthrightly, "We are open to all, to everyone regardless of their sexual orientation."

Doreen and I stood in the hallway talking for a long time about the hurt and pain she and her partner Lisa endured when they were stripped of the privilege to teach the Bible in their church community because of their sexuality. I saw no contradiction in being Christian and gay and I hoped that in helping them speak their truth, their own convictions would be affirmed. In fact, while there was a huge wall between the twelve-step meetings and the church sanctuary itself, I was sensing that at least here, right then, Doreen was willing to take the risk to see if indeed the congregation would welcome her and Lisa.

It was their courage, their spunk, their willingness to open the wound of exclusion just to see if the balm of our church's faith could help and heal. As a result of their God-based live-out-loud faith, they became members of our church community that was led to the process of becoming an Open and Affirming church.

Through their stepping out on their faith in the Christ who welcomes and affirms all, that local church plunged into the discernment process of how their Christian witness would declare the power of inclusion. Thank you, Doreen and Lisa, for being led by the Holy Spirit in your courageous, loving actions. You were vanguards of helping at least that one church embrace the truth of the gospel of Jesus.

—Rev. Alan Johnson, *Author, Encounters at the Counter*

WITHOUT FAITH

Chapter 1
When a Mother Dies

Hall & Oates was blaring on the radio of our eleven-year-old 1972 brown Corolla fastback. Lydia was behind the wheel and ready to admit that we were lost. She rolled down her window, hoping to spot a passerby to get directions. Her short, cropped blond hair blew in the cool night breeze. Little Carol and her Irish curly-haired girlfriend, Maureen, huddled in the back seat under Carol's black woolen cape, swigging Tango out of a brown paper bag.

I reached over the passenger seat and grabbed the bottle from Maureen.
"Hey, you guys, don't hog it all," I said.
"Aw, c'mon, Doreen. That's all we got till we get to the bar," Maureen said.
"You've always got a stash. Pass it up."
Maureen clutched the paper bag tighter.
"I need more than you — I'm a lot taller."
Nobody could drink as much as Maureen, and she never drank unless there was enough to get stoned. She'd go directly from straight to passed out, so you would never know she was wasted until it was too late. Little Carol was always there to clean up her mess and carry her home. God help anybody who got in Carol's way. Her Sicilian temper made up for her size.

My girlfriend, Lydia, was a UPS driver and most often had a pretty good sense of direction, but not tonight. The four of us had left New York City an hour earlier and were drinking kamikaze shots before we hit the road. I thought the farther we were from the city, the farther I was from myself.

That morning, I had been jolted out of sleep by the telephone. "Who'd be calling so early on a Saturday morning?" I thought.

I pulled the pillow over my head, counting the rings until the machine could pick up. One, two, three, four … click. "Hi, Reenie. This is your cousin Ann …." I straddled Lydia's unconscious body, lying next to me, and reached for the receiver. The water bed swooshed and rolled. Lydia still didn't move.

Ann never called unless it was my birthday or a major event. We were never close. Secretly, I thought she was jealous all these years because her mother, my

WITHOUT FAITH

Aunt Hazel (whom I called Tazel for short), had raised me as her own since I was two years old. Ann had just gotten married when Tazel replaced my mother.

"Hi … Ann …. It's me …. I'm here."
"I'm calling to tell you that your Aunt Hazel is no longer in remission. You might want to come and see her. She's going to die."
"Die! But I thought …. She was OK for so long …."
"I don't believe it. I can't believe it. You can't plan dying. She'll be fine," I told myself.

Disbelieving, I wrote the words that Ann recited: Calvary Hospital, 1740 Eastchester Road, Bronx.
"I'll come when I can get up there. She'll be there for a while … right?"
"What's going on? Your aunt?" Lydia asked.
"I have to go see her. Can you take me tomorrow?"
"How about we go shopping? Get some new clothes. I heard there's a new band at this club in Nyack. Getting out of the city will be good for you."

Lydia would have been driving all night in the woods of Rockland County if we didn't find somebody soon to point the way. Parallels, a gay bar that catered mostly to women on Saturday nights, was somewhere on Route 9W in Nyack.
It was a still, autumn night that was unusually warm for late November. A thick fog haloed the country streetlights, making the pavement slick and even the straightest hair turn wavy. At last, a lone, dark figure appeared out of the mist walking toward us. We pulled over to ask directions. "Hey, mister. Can you tell me how to get to 9W in Nyack?" I asked.
The white-haired old man with sunken cheeks leaned into the window and filled our car with his smoky breath. His finger shook as he pointed down the road. He said, "You see that road? You take that road till you can't take it anymore." We all laughed and sped away, imitating him in our own old man's voice.

This is where the road began …

DOREEN BIRDSELL

My Aunt Hazel and Uncle Ted had raised me since I was two years old. We all lived together in a rented two-family yellow house with red trim windows on Edison Place, a dirt road off Main Street in Port Chester, New York.

March 18, 1953, was my sister Donna's fourth birthday. Daddy's older sisters — Hazel, Marion, Elizabeth, and Violet — were having a birthday party for Donna that came to an end after the alarming ring of the Edison Bell telephone.

I was 25 months old and know only what Aunt Hazel and Donna remember about that day.

A year later, my Aunt Hazel told me this:
"It was wintertime and the furnace went out. Your daddy was at work, so Faith, your mother, went down to the cellar to stoke the furnace with coal like your daddy does. Her belly was big with the baby coming soon. She tripped and fell on her way down. The cellar steps were steep. That's probably how the baby died. She didn't tell the doctor or go to the hospital until she thought she was having labor pains a week or so later. That poor girl … she was only 33. You would have had a brother. They say the baby poisoned her blood system. … Her heart was broke from losin' that baby. I think that's what killed her."

My mom had had a baby boy ten years earlier. Aunt Hazel told me that she lost custody of him because she had fallen in love with her first husband's best friend who was my Dad. She gave birth to that baby at home alone on the living room couch. Tazel said my mom was a good seamstress, and although her sewing room was a mess of pins, spools of thread, and pieces of cloth, she could always find any little thing whenever she needed it.

I'm glad I was only two years old and can't remember that day at Donna's birthday party when the telephone rang and Tazel burst out crying when my daddy told her that my mommy had died. I was protected by my infancy from the pain my sister had to bear that day, her fourth birthday: not understanding why everyone started to cry at her party and why her mommy couldn't be there; and when she found out our mommy would never come home again.

WITHOUT FAITH

Daddy's four sisters closed in quickly to try to fill the empty place left by the loss of our mother.

It was not long after supper, about a year later, that my whole family was gathered in our big, yellow kitchen.

The black iron, wood-burning stove gave us heat and cooked our food. Every day, Daddy put some pieces of wood under the heavy black lid on the stove, crumpled up a piece of yesterday's news, scratched a wooden match, and got a fire going.

As always, Nana shared her tea with me, drinking out of a dainty chipped English teacup. I loved to sit on her lap, watch her sip her tea, and wait quietly for her to share a piece of her golden brown, buttered toast that she dunked in her tea just for me.

I sat in the corner of the yellow kitchen on Nana's bony lap, and everything and everyone else seemed so far away. Uncle Ted and Uncle Bert leaned against the large white porcelain sink while Tazel and Aunt Marion sat in the wooden chairs next to the icebox near the back door. Uncle Frank pulled up a chair for Aunt Violet to sit at the brown and red-trimmed metal table with Nana and me. Little Uncle Henry and his portly wife, Aunt Elizabeth, crowded into the kitchen in front of the black iron stove.

Daddy walked in with Donna trailing behind him and holding his hand. Two brown striped suitcases were open on Nana's bed just outside the kitchen door. Golden Ballantine beer cans and half-filled foamy glasses were scattered everywhere. There was lots of talking and laughing, and then it got quiet for a moment until my daddy yelled, "No, God damn it."

It was hard to just be there with Nana and that tea and toast. They were all talking at the same time, yelling louder and louder. Then my dad yelled the loudest, and everything stopped.

All my aunts and uncles had their eyes on Daddy.

"None of you can afford to take Donna and Reenie together … and I can't afford it either. I don't want to split 'em up. I'm gonna give them to the Catholic Charities. The nuns can take care of them."

"What were nuns? Why were they all yelling? Why was Daddy so mad?" I thought.

Uncle Frank got up from the kitchen stool next to Aunt Violet and said, "I'm going to take Reenie outside."

He lifted me off my nana's lap and carried me out into the dark night to the backyard behind the kitchen. Uncle Bert had made our barn-like garage into a repair shop, where he fixed TVs and all kinds of electric gadgets. The building carved a black edge into the starry sky on top of the hill, and I hoped Uncle Frank was taking us up there to explore. The loud voices behind us faded as we walked up the long, sloping hill. "Lightning bugs!" I said.

"Shush, Reenie. We have to be quiet," he whispered. Then he scooped me up to lay me down on the grass. He loosened the tie around his thick neck. The ground was cool and wet. He lay down next to me. He was so close that I felt his round belly press against me. His heavy breath stunk of the big, fat cigars he smoked.

He reached down and opened the zipper below his belt and pushed my hand inside. The zipper scraped my wrist. His round belly was wet and hairy. He pushed my hand farther down until I felt this smooth, fat thing. He said, "His name is St. Peter. You have to hold it and just rub it. This is what God wants, and it is very, very special for you and me alone, and nobody else can ever know, because it is just between you, me, and God. You have to promise, Reenie. You have to keep it a secret."

I didn't understand, and I didn't know what I was supposed to do. He pushed and pulled my hand, rubbing against that fat thing. "It's hurting me, Unka Frank," I said.

He wouldn't stop. I closed my eyes tight to make it go away. I felt like I was choking, like there was no air. I couldn't even swallow. Everything felt so big, and I was so small. I couldn't move. Then something wet and sticky came out of that thing, and he let go of my hand. He took a handkerchief out of his pocket and wiped my gooey hand and then the thing he called St. Peter.

"You can't tell anyone what we did. This is very special and just between us. This is what God wants. Do you understand what I'm saying? You can't tell anyone."

When he took me back through the kitchen door, everything was different from when we had left. My daddy was walking away through the living room toward the front door. Donna was holding his hand, almost running to keep up. Aunt Violet was following, yelling something at them. Uncle Frank hurried away and left me standing alone. There was more yelling. I got scared and began to cry, "Daddy, Daddy!"

I ran to follow them out the door. Tazel and Aunt Marion grabbed me and held me back from running after my daddy. I screamed and I cried, "Daddy, please don't go! Where are you going, Daddy?"

Aunt Hazel and Aunt Marion held me down in my nana's bed, pressed between the two of them, crushed in their bosoms. They tried to keep me quiet, to hold me, to control me, to calm me. I fought so hard to get loose to run after my daddy, but it was useless. I couldn't get out from under them. He was gone, and I cried myself to sleep in their arms.

Chapter 2
Denny's Garden

It was springtime the night Daddy left and took my sister, Donna. After that, the days started getting warmer and my first summer adventures on my own began. After breakfast, Tazel would send me out to play in the backyard.

My bedroom was next to Tazel and Uncle Ted's. I could see right through to the front porch because there was no door between the rooms we shared. My bedroom had one window covered with long, lacy see-through curtains, with a shade behind them drawn halfway down. Hanging from the bottom of the shade was a crocheted string with a knitted circle at the end just big enough to put two of my fingers through to pull it up or down.

The only door in my bedroom was connected to the big bathroom that led to the rest of the house. The bathroom, its white porcelain tub with clawed feet, was big enough for Donna and me and all our toys to take baths together. If Tazel didn't pick us up, we'd have to reach up and slide over the rounded edge into the warm, soapy water. A window high above the tub overlooked the backyard. Next to the bathtub was a sink that was taller than I was. I climbed up the cold, white toilet seat every morning. My feet dangled over the black-and-white checkered floor.

"How long will it be before my toes can touch the floor?" I thought.

I stretched my toes toward the floor to see if I had grown just a little more from the day before. When Donna and I lived together, I'd race her to the toilet; if she got there first, I'd jump up and try to push her off. She pushed me back to keep her seat, and we found out it was big enough to hold us both to sit and pee. Then we'd laugh and stretch out our legs together to see whose toes could reach closest to the floor without falling off.

Mornings were quiet without Donna there anymore, and I was really lonely without her to play with.

Tazel was in the kitchen wearing a flowered housedress and apron. She scraped the burned toast and spread my favorite grape jam over it. The rumbling teapot whistled, and Tazel poured tea for Nana and me. Nana drank her tea and dunked her toast to make it soft because it was hard for her to chew without her teeth in. Most of the time she let me sit on her lap while I had my breakfast. I always wanted her toast with melted butter and jam more than mine, and she always gave in.

"Leave Nana alone, Reenie, and eat your own breakfast or you'll have to sit in your chair," Tazel said.

Donna and I had our own chairs that our mother had bought for us. They were just the right size for Donna and me to sit on so we could be up high like everybody else. Both chairs had a yellow duck painted on the back, and underneath the duck were our names, painted in yellow letters that stood out against the black metal background. Underneath one duck was the name "Donna," and underneath the duck on my chair was my name, "Reenie."

I felt very special because my name was really Doreen but my mom gave me another name too: Reenie. Donna didn't have any other name. She was just Donna.

Sitting on my nana's bony lap, staring at the name on my chair, I tried to imagine my mother and how she looked. What was she thinking when she had my name put on that chair? Did she think I was special? How many times did she get to pick me up and put me in that chair?

Donna would take me through our family photo book and tell me stories about how Mommy loved shoes and that she was just like Mommy because she loved lots of shoes too. My favorite picture was Mommy with lots of makeup and a big, wild, toothy smile; under the picture, she wrote "Catwoman." What would it have been like if Mommy was still with us?

Daddy, Donna, Mommy, and I would all be together. Donna told me she was really fun. I loved Donna's stories. I knew I could remember Mommy if Donna told me more. She wasn't here anymore to ask about Mommy, and I really missed playing with her.

I couldn't read yet, but I knew which chair was mine by the shape of the letters. It was the only thing that I knew I had especially for me from my mom.

I asked Tazel, "How come Mommy gave me two names?" Tazel was drying the breakfast dishes. The water dripped off a dish onto her apron as she waited to answer me.

"Well, Reenie, your mommy gave you a nickname. She took the D and the O off of Doreen and added I, E — that spells Reenie. Your mother always said she liked the name Reenie."

"Then why'd she not just name me Reenie?"

Tazel paused for a moment. "Maybe she liked the name Doreen too." Whatever reason my mom had, I bet she loved me even more than Donna, because she gave me what Tazel called a nickname.

After breakfast, Tazel gave me a sponge bath before putting on my play clothes. She pulled my arm through the T-shirt, zipped up my shorts, and gave me another lesson on how to tie my sneakers.

I played in a narrow dirt driveway behind the kitchen. Uncle Ted had built me a swing set and given me a tricycle that we kept under the back stairs. My playground was bordered by a stone wall that held back a grassy yard that went way uphill to Uncle Bert's repair shop. The wall was high enough that I couldn't climb over it, and Uncle Ted had put a lock on the wooden gate to be sure I couldn't get out. I swung so high to see to the other side that I thought I could fly right over the wall that led to the rest of the world.

I rode my bike for a little while, back and forth, kicking up dust as I went along. I wanted to explore. I wanted some fun, and I wanted a friend. The wall was too high, so I tried the fence. There was nowhere to stick my foot to climb over. I pulled and pushed, but the lock held it tight. I shook it and pulled and shook it some more until finally the whole fence broke off the hinges and I was free. I ran and I ran and I ran - Up the hill and across the yard, through the hedges, and then into the neighbor's yard.

Some days, Tazel took me next door to play with Denny when she visited his mom, but she never let me go by myself. Denny was a little bit younger than I was, but he was the only one on the block I could play with. He lived with his mom, dad, grandpa, and so many brothers and sisters I didn't know them all.

For the first time, I was at Denny's all by myself. I ran up to the front of the house and stood beneath the long wooden staircase, hoping to find Denny.

WITHOUT FAITH

One of Denny's big brothers called me, "Hey, Reenie, ya wanna see something? C'mon. It's in the shed."

"No. I want Denny."

"Denny's not here. C'mon!"

He grabbed my hand and took me into the woodshed under the house. It was dark and smelled like dirt. He closed the door so only a slice of light came through. His bright yellow hair and white T-shirt stood out in the darkness.

He took my hand and put it on a thing that felt like Uncle Frank's and said, "Go ahead ... touch it."

The wooden door creaked open and in the light of the doorway stood Denny's sister Marcy.

"Bobby! What the ...! Reenie — you all right?"

"I want Denny."

"Get out, Bobby! You ever go near Reenie again ... I'll, I'll ... tell Ma and Pa, and you'll really get it."

He fumbled, fixed his pants, and said, "OK. OK, Marcy," as he pushed past her out the door.

Marcy kneeled down and held both my hands in hers.

"Look at me, Reenie. You tell me if Bobby ever comes near you again. You promise?" she asked.

"I just wanna play with Denny," I said.

Marcy squeezed my hands tighter.

"You gotta promise, Reenie."

"I promise, Marcy. I'll tell."

She let out a big breath and said, "Denny just got back from the store with Ma. I think he's over there ... by the rabbits."

I ran across the dirt yard past the garden fence to the line of tall trees where the wooden rabbit cages were. I loved the rabbits.

Denny was picking pink stuff off his gray zippered jacket and sticking it in his mouth.

"What you eating?" I asked.

"Ma bought me bubba gum."

"Bubba gum! You got more?"

"No, just this. I saved it on my jacket after the taste was gone."

He had chewed up the whole pack and then stuck the pieces all over the front of his jacket.

"Why'd you do that?"

"So I can have some later."

"Can I have some?" I asked.

"All right," Denny said, and I began picking the gum off his jacket piece by piece until I had a big wad in my mouth.

I loved playing at Denny's.

He was much littler than I was. I was 3 1/2 and he was only 3. His shorts were always puffy because he still wore diapers. His yard was a lot bigger than mine, and his skinny, old grandpa had a garden as big as a farm with lots of rabbits in cages along the edge. Denny's grandpa was always in his garden dressed in suspenders that held up baggy pants. He walked hunched over with a walking stick, poking things as he went along. If he saw us, he'd chase us out, hollering and swinging that wooden walking stick.

At first, I was happy to just put my finger through the square holes of the screened caged door to touch the bunnies' fur. I liked the touch of their soft pink noses and the smell of hay at the bottom of their cages, but I really wanted to hold one in my hands and hug it. I wanted to feel its warm fur against my face and to love it. They were all locked up in that dark cage with no room to play.

"I want the bunny," I said.

Denny tugged my sleeve and said, "Reenie, Reenie. The rabbits will run away."

"I'll take just one."

I slipped my finger under the hook that held the door shut and reached into the cage. One leapt out, then another, and another. They all ran in every direction, hopping past Denny and me. They ran through our legs and into the garden and then into the woods.

Marcy was hanging clothes on the line with her mom when a rabbit ran right by them.

"Ma! Ma! The rabbits are out again!"

WITHOUT FAITH

"Get 'em!" her mom yelled.

Suddenly, the whole family was running everywhere, in every direction, trying to scoop up bunnies. White ones, brown ones, spotted ones. There wasn't one bunny that stayed behind.

I knew we were in trouble, so we ran away with the bunnies and into Denny's grandpa's vegetable garden. It was so big that when we hid behind the corn, *nobody* could find us. Kids were yelling in the distance, "I got one!" and "There goes another one!"

We were crouched down in the garden, hidden by the tall cornstalks.

"Denny ... Reenie ... where are you? ... I know you're in there!" Marcy said.

We didn't move. I hoped that if we stayed quiet long enough, they would all go away and forget about us. Denny's grandpa was watering the tomatoes not far away. He had a watering can in one hand and that big walking stick in the other.

I put my arm around Denny and squeezed him close so his grandpa wouldn't see Denny's puffy pants sticking out between the cornstalks.

Just when I thought we had gotten away, a loud, deep voice yelled, "Reenie! ...Reenie!" It was Uncle Ted.

Uh-oh. I was really in trouble. I couldn't hide anymore. No cornstalks or anything else was going to protect me now.

We slowly got up and walked down the row of corn.

"I'm over here," I said.

"Oh, no! He's with Tazel and Marcy too. I'm really gonna get it," I thought.

Marcy grabbed Denny by the arm and led him up the hill, taking steps bigger than Denny could keep up with.

"Please don't hit me, Uncle Ted. I'm sorry," I said.

Tazel looked down at me with squinty eyes, and then all of a sudden her expression changed as she asked, "*What* are you chewing?"

"Bubba gum," I said, with my eyes so wide I felt like my eyebrows disappeared into my scalp.

"Where did you get bubble gum?" she demanded.

"Denny. I picked it off his jacket and chewed it."

"Off his jacket?!?" she yelled as she held out her hand for me to spit it out.

I spit out the gum, and they marched me home.

DOREEN BIRDSELL

"I'll fix that fence so you'll *never* get out!" Uncle Ted said.
But he never said a word about the bunnies.
"What's so bad about chewing gum off Denny's jacket?" I thought.

WITHOUT FAITH

Chapter 3

Port Chester to Ridgewood

Tazel nudged me gently. "C'mon, Reenie. Time to get up," she said in a low whisper. I was still so sleepy. Tazel never woke me when the windows were still black. The ceiling light hurt my eyes. Nana's bed was covered with my clothes, neatly folded in little piles, next to two large brown striped suitcases lined with a silky maroon textured fabric. A smaller boxy suitcase was filled with perfume bottles, jars, and hairbrushes that had been on top of Tazel's dresser.

Nana had broken her hip and gone to live in a nursing home. It seemed like such a long time since I had sat on Nana's lap, dunking toast in her tea.

"Where we going, Tazel?"

"Today's moving day."

"Already?"

I knew that we would be moving, but I didn't understand when. When Tazel said tomorrow or a week, it all felt the same — like forever. Uncle Bill told me I was going to be a Brooklyn Dodgers fan because we were moving to Ridgewood. He said, "It's Queens, but it's close enough to Brooklyn." I wore the Dodgers baseball cap he gave me every day.

Aunt Hazel buttoned up my blue and white sweater while Uncle Ted marched out the door to put the suitcases in the trunk of his '49 dark green Pontiac. We left in the still dark morning without any goodbyes. I wondered where Daddy was, but I felt safe with Tazel and Uncle Ted. I stood on the back seat and watched as our house and the two big pine trees got smaller as we rumbled down the gravel road and finally turned the corner onto the smooth pavement of Main Street. I wondered what it would be like where we were going and when I would see Daddy and Donna again. I curled up into a tight little ball, with hands clasped under my chin to keep warm, and nuzzled my forehead up to the back wall of the cold and slippery shiny seat and drifted off to sleep.

When I woke, it was daylight. We were driving down a wide black paved empty street. Not at all like the gravel road on Edison Place where we lived.

Identical brick houses that were three stories high opposed each other on both sides of the street. Dark brown steps with black iron railings led to the doorways. The only signs of life were all the parked cars that lined the curb.

"Is this where we're going to live?" I asked, almost jumping over the front seat.

"No. No. This is where Ann and Billy live," Aunt Hazel said. "We're stopping here first to have some breakfast and see the baby. We live nearby."

Ann was Aunt Hazel and Uncle Ted's daughter who was married to Billy. She was very pretty with long dark wavy hair and reminded me of the ladies I had seen on television. She wore bright red lipstick that pronounced her white-toothed smile. Billy had licorice-black hair and a round smooth face that matched his body. Whenever he kissed me, his skin felt soft, not like Uncle Ted's, which was always scratchy when he came home from work to give me a kiss and rub his face on my cheek. Billy always played with me and laughed at the things I did.

Eager to explore, I jumped to the sidewalk and started to run down the block. I didn't get more than a few steps before Aunt Hazel was yelling, "Come here, Reenie. You're not staying out here by yourself. We're here to see Ann and Billy and the baby … not for you to get in trouble."

Hand in hand, we walked up the stairs. Aunt Hazel called it "a stoop." I had never heard that word before. Uncle Ted pushed open a large dark oak windowed door that led to a little room he called a vestibule.

He pressed one of the buttons on the row of brass mailboxes, and almost instantly the door in front of us that looked the same as the one we had just come through started buzzing. Uncle Ted pushed, and the door opened. I wondered why we had to push buttons and wait for buzzes in order to open the door.

In the shadowed hallway was a long staircase with a wooden railing. This I learned was called a banister. Holding tightly to Tazel's hand, I started climbing the long staircase through the dark hallway. Uncle Ted led the way up the creaking stairs. The only light came from the ceiling way above us. Uncle Ted told me it was a skylight. We reached the top of the first staircase and walked

WITHOUT FAITH

down a hallway and around to another long staircase, drawing us closer to that window in the ceiling. At the very top and at the end of another long hallway were two doors on each side. An odor that was sour and unfamiliar became stronger as we came to the end of the hall.

Uncle Ted knocked on the door to our right. The door swung open. The light from inside poured into the hallway, and there Ann stood smiling her big wide smile, so happy to see us. I was so glad that the smell wasn't coming from her apartment.

"C'mon in! I'm so happy you're here! Let me take your coats. Hi, Reenie! How are you?" she said, almost singing. She bent over, squeezed my cheek, and shook it with a pinch that made me hurt. I knew it was coming. She always did that. So I closed my eyes and scrunched my face until she let go.

(I didn't think she liked me very much although she pretended to be happy whenever she saw me. Sometimes when Tazel asked her to take care of me, she'd wash my face and scrub so hard that I thought she'd rub my nose off with the washcloth. One night we were all sitting around in our living room on Edison Place. I was sitting between Aunt Hazel and Uncle Ted on the couch, and Ann was in the overstuffed armchair. Ann reached over and said, "Reenie, c'mon, sit on my lap." I tried to pull away, but she grabbed me and sat me on her lap anyway. I sat there while she bounced me side to side on her knees. I had to go to the bathroom really bad and I couldn't hold it any longer and I was afraid she wouldn't let me get up to go, so I wet my pants. She got really mad and threw me off her lap, screaming. My Aunt Hazel told me she'd never forget that.)

"Hi, Ann," I said, after she finally let go of my cheek.

"Come here! I want you to see Sarah," she said.

We walked into a long, narrow kitchen that was as bright as the sun that shone through the window at the far end.

"Wow! She's so tiny!"

"Shhhhh ... don't wake her," Tazel whispered.

After breakfast, Billy asked, "Hey, Reenie. Wanna go outside and play some catch?"

"Yeah. Can I?" I asked Aunt Hazel.
"OK, go ahead. No rough stuff," she said.
So off we went, down the staircases. I had never run down so many stairs at once. I wondered how fast I could go racing to the daylight at the doorway.

I was so excited to be outside and to play ball on the sidewalk with Billy.
He had a brand new Spalding that we tossed back and forth. After a while, Billy made it a little harder to catch by throwing the ball high up in the air. I was a pretty good catcher and liked the chance to show off. Billy threw one up and said, "OK, Reenie, catch this one!"
I ran, keeping my eye on the ball the whole time. I was stopped cold. I heard a loud bang and felt the vibration of the metal light pole run right through me. We didn't have light poles on Edison Place — we had trees! I stood as firm as the pole, dazed at what had just happened, but I didn't cry. I was afraid to touch my forehead and maybe make it hurt worse. Billy stood there laughing.
"Boy, are you going to have an egg," he said.
"What does he mean — an egg? What is he talking about?" I thought.
Then I put my fingers to my forehead and felt the lump and pictured an egg growing out of my head. Now I really wanted to cry but knew it wouldn't help.
"Let's go inside and take a look at that."
He took me back inside, but instead of going upstairs we went downstairs to a dark cellar with gray stone walls and a concrete floor. It smelled like a wet cave. We walked toward a lit doorway to a little room in the back. The light was coming from a dirty broken window that was high on the wall. A sunbeam filled with floating particle dust shone on a rotting wooden workbench. Billy pushed aside a rusty hammer and saw, picked me up, and sat me on the table. I touched the lump on my head and asked, "Is it as big as an egg yet?"
"Yep. But you'll be OK."
I heard a zipper open.
"I just want you to hold it," he said.
All I could see was his navy blue jacket, the gold zipper almost touching my nose. I felt this big thing in my hand. He wrapped his hand around mine.
I thought about how Uncle Frank did this too, and I wondered if somehow Billy knew that. Suddenly there was a noise from the back of the cellar. He

WITHOUT FAITH

jerked away and put "his thing" back in his pants and scooped me up off the table.

"Don't tell anyone what we did."

Some old man was putting a bag in a garbage can at the other end of the cellar.

Silently we went upstairs, and Billy told everyone what had happened to my head. They all seemed to think it was really funny. They laughed, and Aunt Hazel touched me gently and said, "Don't worry, Reenie. You'll be OK."

Chapter 4
A Visit Back Home

The aroma of bacon and eggs drove me from my bed straight to the kitchen table. Uncle Ted always cooked breakfast on Sunday, and I knew there'd be a white bag from the bakery filled with pastries on the kitchen table. More than bacon and eggs ... more than jelly doughnuts ... more than the Sunday comics, I couldn't wait until breakfast was over. We were going to Port Chester today to see Donna and Daddy.

After breathing in the sugary dust and devouring the jelly doughnut, I pushed my eggs around the plate and asked, "Are we leaving soon?"

Uncle Ted dropped the funny papers and, with a raised brow over the top of his reading glasses, said, "Reenie, we're not leaving here until you eat all your breakfast."

I ate as fast as I could, choked down my milk, and was ready to go. I ran into the bedroom to check on Tazel. I sat in the overstuffed chair that used to be in our living room on Edison Place. Tazel picked out a light blue dress and slid it over her head. I knew that if I sat still and didn't make a peep, she would get ready even faster.

Tazel had wavy, silvery hair and eyes that were blue and gray like her hair. She put powder on her nose and then couldn't decide what earrings to wear. She turned from side to side, looking in the mirror, and put her hands on her belly, pushed it in and said, "I don't know if I like this dress. This brassiere doesn't make me look good."

"Oh, no!" I thought. "We'll never leave."

I said, "Tazel, you look very pretty."

She looked at me with her head half-cocked and said, "Oh, you just want to get out of here."

I didn't understand why everything had to take so long but knew I would be in trouble if I said another word. So I waited, I watched, and I thought about the long drives home at night from Port Chester when I would lean over the front seat and ask if I could come sit up front. I loved to climb over the big seat and sit next to Tazel and lean my head against her. If she was humming a song,

I put my ear against her fleshy smooth arm. It was like I could hear her singing inside, and I was happy and sad all at the same time.

Finally, we were ready to go. Uncle Ted packed the green Pontiac with a plastic lunch bag of food and extra play clothes for me. We were on our way.

Tazel said Ridgewood wasn't very far from Port Chester, "only an hour and a half away." I only knew that I could never get there on my own, and that made me very sad.

On the back seat of the old Pontiac, I sat quietly, mesmerized by the sameness of houses and brick factory buildings whirring by. Approaching the Whitestone Bridge, I lay on the back seat to see the design of the giant bridge and metal cables that soared to the sky above. When only blue sky filled the back window, I knew we were near the tollbooths. I sprang to my feet behind Uncle Ted, and he handed me a quarter. I was so excited. I reached out the window, cheek to cheek with Uncle Ted. His Old Spice after-shave scented the breeze. The husky uniformed man at the tollbooth smiled and took the coin. I watched the bridge fade in the distance. It wouldn't be long before I'd see green trees again, houses with backyards, and Daddy and Donna.

Tazel and Uncle Ted got very mad when I got too excited and called me "rambunctious." Sometimes I'd get Uncle Ted so angry Tazel said she was afraid he'd drive off the road. I waited until I couldn't stand it anymore.

"Are we almost there yet?"

"Almost, Reenie. In a little while," Tazel said.

"How long is *a while.*"

"You just be *patient,*" she demanded.

"*Please.* How much longer, Tazel?"

I tried as hard as I could to sit still and be good, but it felt like there were ants crawling up and down inside me and nothing I could do made them go away unless I knew how soon we would be there.

So I started jumping up and down on the hump of the back floor until Uncle Ted turned around, with one hand on the steering wheel. With the other, he pressed his finger right in my nose and said, "If you don't stop, I'll pull right over, and you know what that'll mean!"

I sat back down in the middle of the big green leather seat with both hands clenched between my knees. I squeezed tight to keep me still. I shut my eyes and thought, "I won't look up until we stop. ... I won't look up until we stop."

That didn't last long. I just had to open my eyes and see where we were. We turned off Main Street onto a bumpy road. The gravel crunched under the tires, full green maples waved hello. We slowed past the high hedges and long driveway that led up to Denny's house until we came to the red farmhouse that I used to call home.

"Why can't Uncle Ted get a job near home? Why'd we have to live so far away?" I wondered.

✶✶✶✶✶✶✶

Tazel helped me write letters to Donna every week. I would tell Tazel what to write, and she taught me how to sign my name. I was four years old. Whenever Tazel called Port Chester to talk to my dad, I would wait patiently, standing alongside her, leaning into her apron. Waiting for the moment just before I thought they'd say goodbye, I'd tug on her apron, pleading, "Is Donna there? Pleeez, lemmee talk to Donna."

"Hold on, Walter. It's Reenie — she wants to talk to Donna, and she won't let up. Is she there?"

I knew Donna was standing right there next to Daddy, just like me, waiting for us to have a chance to talk.

Tazel handed me the big black receiver and said, "OK, Reenie. Not long ... remember this is a toll call, and toll calls cost a lot of money."

Tazel held the phone to my ear until I could steady it with both my hands, and then I heard Donna's voice.

"Hi, Reenie. ... It's *me!* ... When are you coming up?" she asked.

I was so excited to hear her voice. It was like she was right there with me. I wanted her to see everything I saw and know everything I knew.

Tazel was putting her hand on the receiver when I pulled it even tighter to hold it to my ear.

WITHOUT FAITH

I said, "Donna, Tazel's taking the phone. ... Why don't you and Daddy come here?"
"Say goodbye," Tazel said. "We'll see Donna soon."
I said, "Bye, Donna. ... See you soon, Tazel says."
It was always soon, but never enough for Donna and me.

I wanted so much for my friends to meet my dad so I could show him off. His smooth, slicked back, shiny copper-brown hair, lean slim figure, and sharp facial features made him the handsomest man I ever saw.
He did come once, for the day of my first Holy Communion.

✵✵✵✵✵✵✵

I already had my hand on the long silver handle inside the back door, not to waste one second once we came to a stop at the grassy curb.
Tazel said, "You wait a minute. Don't you and Donna go wandering off. You're going with Uncle Frank today."
"Do I have to?" I begged. "I want to stay here and play with Donna."
"Donna's going too," she said.
I ran inside the house, through the living room, and into the kitchen, to find Daddy drinking beer with Uncle Frank at the table. Donna came running out of the dining room and tried to climb up on Daddy's lap with me. I hugged him with all my might and never wanted to let go.
"OK, Reenie. That's enough," he said, holding me by my wrists. "Yeah, I'm happy to see you too. Now go on. ... Play with Donna, and I'll see you later."
Donna said, "C'mon, Reenie. Let's play tea in the dining room."
"What is tea?" I wondered.
Uncle Frank stood in the doorway of the dining room, chewing on a big, fat cigar.
"Don't take too long. We're going to be leaving soon," he said.
"I want to stay here with Donna. ... We just got here. ... *I don't wanna go,*" I pleaded.

I wanted to stay on Edison Place with Donna and play all day. I didn't want to go with Uncle Frank to *his* house. I knew what he would do. Maybe this time he wouldn't do anything because Donna was there. He told me that what we did was special and no one else knew; so if Donna was there, maybe that meant nothing would happen.

    Donna showed me her new tea set, four tiny little teacups just our size with a teapot. When she poured the tea, it was only clear water. I had to pretend that it was tea and I had come for a visit. Daddy and Uncle Frank were laughing in the next room, drinking their beer. We sat in the corner of the dining room at a table Donna had made from cardboard boxes. The white sheer curtains swayed as a cold breeze found its way through the cracks of the old windows. Donna and I cuddled up and shivered, sitting on the cold linoleum floor. There wasn't anywhere else I'd rather be than sitting with her, sipping the water that we pretended was tea.

WITHOUT FAITH

Chapter 5

Blondie and Dagwood

"OK, kids. Time to go," Uncle Frank said, standing over us in the doorway.
"Just a little while longer?" I asked.
"Come on. We'll have a good time," he answered, smiling. "I'll buy you both an ice cream."
Ice cream sounded pretty good.

Donna put on her coat, and Uncle Frank helped me put on mine. We got in his gray round-shaped car that always stank like old cigars.
He made us both sit up front, and he told me to sit in the middle. I wanted to sit in the back with Donna so we could play. There wasn't any room in the front. Uncle Frank was too fat and crowded us in. We both sat quietly, propped up on the front seat with our bare legs sticking out from under our long Sunday coats.
Uncle Frank lived in Greenwich, Connecticut, just across the New York state line. Uncle Frank's car had a handle on the steering wheel that he pushed and pulled to shift. I liked Uncle Ted's car so much better. It didn't have that shifter thing, and it didn't smell.
A fat cigar hung from the side of Uncle Frank's thin-lipped mouth; and when his hand wasn't on that shifter thing, it was on my leg. I didn't like that either. Donna just sat there staring out the window, and we were both very quiet.

He pulled into a dirt driveway and parked alongside a hardware store. We climbed up the outside wooden staircase to the apartment above the store where Uncle Frank lived.
It was a lot smaller than Edison Place and very crowded with furniture. A big-cushioned couch had doilies on the bolster arms, and lots of rugs were scattered on the floor. A round table with swooping clawed feet in the middle of the room separated the large bed from the rest of the room. The kitchen had a door with another staircase on the other side of the house. Uncle Frank said,

"OK, Reenie and Donna. Let's take off all our clothes."

What was Uncle Frank doing? He never did this with Donna and me. He told me this was something special only between him and me. Why was he telling Donna to take off her clothes?

I stood motionless, unable to understand.

Donna began to unbutton her frilly, pink blouse. "C'mon, Reenie. Your turn," she said.

"Uncle Frank does this to you too, Donna?" I asked.

She just nodded her head.

I was so surprised. I thought this was just between Uncle Frank and me. That's what he told me. It was special just between him and me.

Uncle Frank was still wearing his jacket and loose necktie.

"C'mon, Reenie. You're old enough now. We can have this special time together."

I looked at him and then at Donna. She was almost all undressed except for her black patent leather shoes.

I unbuttoned my blouse, just like Donna had done, and then took off all my clothes and even my shoes.

Uncle Frank just stood and watched. When we were all undressed, he said to Donna, "You stay here for a few minutes. I have to go to the store. ... Watch Reenie. I'll be right back."

"OK," Donna said, like she was going to be in charge.

As soon as Uncle Frank left, I started to explore the rest of the room.

Here and there, dark, fringed throw rugs were scattered over the wooden floor. The fully drawn paper shades were illuminated by the afternoon sun, and the thin white curtains drooped to the floor. On the other side of the room was the big bed with a wooden headboard and posts on each corner. It was so high up I had to stand on a stool to climb on. I started jumping up and down, flailing my arms in the air.

"Ya-hooo! Ya-hoooey! C'mon, Donna!" I yelled, jumping higher and higher.

"No, Reenie! Get down. You'll get us in trouble!"

She was standing near the big claw-foot table looking at some funny papers, so I decided to get down just to see.

WITHOUT FAITH

I recognized the people in the pictures of the funny pages, but they had no clothes on.

"It's Blondie and Dagwood," Donna said.

Blondie was standing in one of the cartoon squares talking to Dagwood. She had bumps on her chest and fur between her legs. Dagwood had no bumps, like me, but he had a long skinny thing between his legs like Uncle Frank's.

I looked down at Donna and me and said, "How come we got no hair?"

"We will. When we grow up."

I couldn't read the words in the captions, so I asked Donna if she would read to me.

"We'll ask Uncle Frank," she said.

Uncle Frank hurried in the door holding a brown paper bag, looking at us with a big smile on his face, sucking on his cigar.

"What are you two kids doin'? Readin' the comics?" he asked.

"Reenie wanted to see Blondie and Dagwood," Donna said.

Uncle Frank took a bottle out of the brown paper bag and went to the kitchen, got a glass, and poured a drink.

"Can I have a sip, Uncle Frank?" I asked.

"Sure, here," he said with his cigar-faced grin.

It burned my mouth and set fire to my tongue.

I pushed it away, shaking my head and spitting.

He drank it down in one big gulp and unloosened the tie around his neck.

After he took off his jacket, he threw it on the back of the kitchen chair and unbuttoned his shirt.

He opened his pants and pulled down his zipper and stepped out of his pants.

Donna and I just stood there and watched, and I wished I hadn't asked for that sip of his drink because I could still taste it in my mouth.

I had never seen a man without all his clothes on before, except the comic of Dagwood just now. Uncle Frank was fat and hairy, and his stomach hung over the white underwear with a slit in front. He said, "Donna, put your hand in and take it out."

Without a word, she walked across the cold linoleum floor, reached up into that slit in his shorts, and pulled out that big fat thing.
"Put your mouth on it, Donna." And she did.
He put his hand behind her head and pushed it in and then told me to come over so he could press me next to him.
"OK, Reenie. Now it's your turn. Do you want some of St. Peter too?"
I really didn't want to. My mouth already didn't taste good, and I didn't want to taste that thing, so I backed away.
Uncle Frank pulled me toward him and pushed me into his belly and said, "You have to, Reenie. This is what God wants. You just have to lick it."
It was so big, and he pressed it against my lips. As soon as I opened my mouth, he pushed it in.
There was something wet on it, and I thought I would throw up. I pulled away and said, "I don't want it. It tastes bad. It's got a wet thing on it."
Uncle Frank reached behind him, took the sugar bowl off the kitchen table, and sprinkled sugar on his thing.
"Here, Reenie. Now ... lick it off."
"I don't want to," I said. I looked at Donna, but she just stood there silent.
"It'll taste sweet. Like candy," he said, and he pushed my head in between his legs again to make me lick it off.
"We're going to go in the bed now and play a game."
"What kind of game?" Donna asked.
"You'll see."
He lifted Donna up first and tossed her onto the bed, and then me. He climbed in and lay on his back. His hairy chest and big belly were so big that I couldn't see Donna lying on his other side.
"OK, Reenie. I'm going to take you for a ride. Get on."
I crawled over him and sat on his round hairy belly.
"Oh, no ... not there ... down further," he said.
I moved down a little bit farther, trying to avoid that thing.
"No. That's not far enough."
He lifted me up by my waist and sat me down on his big fat thing pointing upward and pushed me down on it until I screamed because it hurt.
"I can't," I yelled. "I can't. ... I don't like this game."

WITHOUT FAITH

"C'mon. Donna plays all the time," he said.

Donna said nothing. She just lay there. She probably didn't want to play this game either, I thought.

"OK. We'll try it different."

He flipped me over onto my back and said, "I'm going to rub St. Peter on you but not so hard that it hurts. You just lay there. Donna, I want you to climb on my back and hold on. This will be fun."

Uncle Frank pushed his thing on me, but I covered up my hole so he couldn't hurt me. His eyes were closed. He was pushing, and I was holding myself as tight as I could so it wouldn't hurt. Then I felt something wet come out of his thing. He let out a big sigh and almost crushed me. I had to push myself out from under him, and he just lay there breathing heavily. Donna climbed off his back and off the bed. I ran to the bathroom.

Uncle Frank came in and wiped himself and stood over the toilet to pee.

He said, "This is how men pee."

When he was done, he wiped himself and left the room.

I said to Donna, "Let's try to pee like that too."

She said, "OK, let's try."

I was too little to stand over the toilet, so I climbed up on the seat and stood over the toilet and started to pee. I laughed and said, "Donna, look. I'm peeing just like Uncle Frank," but it went all over the seat and onto the floor.

Uncle Frank must have heard us laughing and came in. When he saw the mess I had made, he yelled, "You can't do that. You're girls. Only boys pee like that. Don't ever do that again."

That was the only time I saw him get mad.

Chapter 6

Kindergarten

Grove Street between Forest Avenue and 60th Place in Ridgewood was the block where we lived. Although it was Queens, we lived only a few blocks from the Brooklyn neighborhood of Bushwick. Our neighbors were mostly Irish, German, and Italian. On Sundays, the hallways would reek of garlic or be overpowered by the stinky-feet odor of sauerbraten.

My bedroom window was fortified with white iron bars. Tazel told me that was to keep me from running away. I had made a friend whose name was Bobby. We were the exact same age, four years old. When I wanted to cross the street to see him, Tazel would look out the side door in the alleyway and watch me as I went to the curb. We didn't have any front windows, so Tazel waited until I got to the curb. She couldn't see the street, so she'd ask, "You see any cars?"

Even though it was a one-way street, she'd make me look both ways. As soon as it was clear, I'd yell, "No cars, Tazel!"

"OK, Reenie. Run!"

Bobby's mother would help me cross back over again.

I ran down Bobby's driveway to the backyard. It was huge compared with our concrete square yard. The trees and long grass weren't the best part. It was the abandoned wooden garage way in the back.

Joey the Italian kid and red-headed Brucey the butcher's son were big kids from the neighborhood. They were about seven years old and went to the public school on Forest Avenue. Bobby and I hadn't even started school yet. Joey and Brucey treated Bobby OK because it was his yard.

Me, they pushed around, and cheated me out of my Mickey Mantle card when we flipped baseball cards. One Halloween, they cornered me when I was walking down the block. They shoved me up against the garage doors while

WITHOUT FAITH

Brucey held me back. Joey had a new bow and arrow set, and they were going to use me as a target. Joey took aim and let the arrow fly. The rubber-tipped arrow bounced off my chest. Joey was mad that it didn't stick and yelled at Brucey to hold me still. I struggled so hard, the buttons on my blouse popped off, exposing my bare chest.

My screams were heard by a lady, who came running out of her house and threatened to call the cops. Brucey the butcher's kid let me go and followed Joey the Italian, who already was fast around the corner. I was in hot pursuit right behind them, heading up the block. They ran into the vestibule next to the butcher shop where they lived. I flew by, hoping they weren't thinking about me, and ducked into my alleyway to be safe at home.

When I walked in the door, I was panting hard and crying. Sniffling, I lifted my blouse to show Tazel and Uncle Ted the red marks the arrows had made on my chest, and I told them what Joey and Brucey had done. I couldn't wait for Uncle Ted to march down there and tell their parents the awful thing they did to me.

"You shouldn't be playing with those kids," he said.

"They weren't playing — they tried to hurt me."

"I'm sure you had something to do with it," Uncle Ted said.

That was always his answer when I asked him to stick up for me. Aunt Hazel went back to reading her paper.

Brucey and Joey were laughing as they jumped one by one from the edge of the garage roof onto a mountain of dried leaves piled high on the grass below. It was Bobby's backyard, so they had to let us play. I couldn't wait to take my turn and told Bobby I'd try it first. I climbed up a rickety old ladder and slowly walked across the black tar roof to the edge. The mound of leaves seemed a lot farther from up there.

"Go on. Chicken!" Joey the Italian kid yelled. The tips of my blue PF Flyers hung just over the edge. I was about to jump when I heard a crack. The wood beneath me snapped, and I fell straight to the ground and hit hard. The leaves were no cushion at all. I landed on my feet, but my left ankle turned over. A ripping pain shot through my foot. I fought to hold back the tears. I didn't want to cry in front of those boys, and that hurt almost as much as my ankle.

Bobby's mom, Mrs. Hunt, ran toward us to see what all the commotion was. She picked me up in her arms and carried me across the street. She knocked on our kitchen door and told Tazel and Uncle Ted that I had gotten hurt playing on the roof. I sniffled back the tears while Uncle Ted soaked my swollen foot. That's when I found out what a sprained ankle was. Tazel told me to calm down while Uncle Ted wrapped my ankle tight with strips of cloth he cut up from one of his old T-shirts. "Don't favor it. It'll take longer to heal if you do."

He taught me never to let anyone think I was afraid. Uncle Ted always pushed me. "It'll toughen you up," he said. I tried hard not to limp in front of him.

It was three whole days before I could go to Bobby's again, but now the ladder to the roof was gone and the garage door was nailed shut.

✸✸✸✸✸✸✸

With my brand new pink Spalding handball I raced from my bedroom toward the kitchen door.

"Wait a minute," Tazel said. "We're going shopping for school clothes."

"School clothes — do we have to?" I hated shopping.

"We're gonna use the money your daddy sent to get you some new clothes."

"Do I have to go? Can't you go? Please?"

"Oh, no, not this time. You have to try things on."

"Try things on. Oh, no ... I really hate that," I thought.

We got to the store, and I had to try on scratchy wool skirts, with things called accordion pleats. All I wanted to do was go home and play.

"Stop squirming, Reenie. Be patient."

I didn't know what patient was — just that I must not have been it.

Tazel bent over, pointed her stubby finger in my face, and in a slow, steady whisper, so the saleslady couldn't hear, said, "You — Just — Better — Cooperate. Reenie Birdsell."

I straightened up when I heard that tone.

WITHOUT FAITH

Tazel was always afraid of what other people thought. When Uncle Ted came home drunk, she always said, "Oh, my God. What will the neighbors think!"

"Who cares about the neighbors?" he'd yell back, and Aunt Hazel would cry because she knew they could hear.

So, I tried my best to be quiet, but I couldn't help myself. I hated these clothes.

"Why do I have to go to school? Why can't we just go home?"

It was the first day of school. Tazel woke me up and got me dressed in the new scratchy skirt with the accordion pleats. This was worse than going shopping. I had never been to school before, and I didn't like going anywhere that made me dress like this. I was fidgety and cranky; and when Tazel tried to put on my shoes, I curled my toes. When she couldn't push on my new saddle shoes, she slapped the ground with the sole of my new shoe and yelled, "If you don't stop it, Reenie, I'm calling Uncle Ted!"

"Uh-oh," I thought. "Uncle Ted. If he has to come home from work, he'll hit me good if I don't stop."

I uncurled my toes, and the new shoe slipped on my foot over my new white ankle socks. Tazel stuck her finger behind the heel and told me to stand up so I would get my foot in right. After she tied my shoes, she had to go put powder under her arms because she said I made her sweat.

She took me by the hand, and together we walked down the three steps from our kitchen, through the side door, and down the brick-walled alleyway. Uncle Ted had hammered steel taps into the heels and toes of my new shoes the night before. They clicked like dance shoes on the concrete when I tapped my feet. Tazel squeezed my hand and jerked me back.

"We're not here to play, Reenie. We're going to your first day of kindergarten."

I didn't have any friends except Bobby Hunt across the street, but he went to public school. I didn't know what it would be like, and Tazel didn't make it sound like fun. We walked around the corner to 60th Place, past Menahan and Bleecker streets, to the big stone church, Our Lady of the Miraculous Medal. There were lots of other kids with their grown-ups pulling them down the hill to the school behind the church.

When we got inside the building, it smelled sour, and all the voices echoed in the long hallway.

"Tazel, I gotta go to the bathroom."

"Can't it wait?"

"No, Tazel. ... I gotta go," I said.

She looked around to find someplace for us to go and took me into this big room with little toilets lined up on both sides of a long white-tiled wall.

"They call this a lavatory," Tazel said.

This made me very scared. Even the bathroom had a funny name, and there were so many little toilets with no doors. She pulled up my skirt, and I pulled down my panties, but I couldn't go.

"You don't have to go. ... You're just stallin'. ... Let's get out of here."

She jerked me off the toilet seat, pulled up my panties, pulled down my skirt, out the door, up the stairs, and into a classroom.

Kids were taking off their coats and kissing their grown-ups goodbye. Tazel walked up to a lady with a long black dress, wearing a black hat that went down around her shoulders. She had wooden beads and a cross that hung from her waist. A black cloth tightly framed her chubby pink cheeks, dark brown eyes, and thin, tight lips. She tilted from the waist to peer down at me, with arms folded across her waist, hands hidden in black hollow sleeves, and said, "I'm Sister Jan. Your Aunt Hazel is going to leave you with me today."

I grabbed Tazel's hand as hard as I could and wrapped my arm around her leg. I held her so tight, she couldn't pull me off. Sister Jan was pulling me from behind, and Tazel was tugging on my arms to pull them apart, but I wouldn't budge. No way was she going to leave me here with this lady with just a face and all these kids I didn't know. I started to scream,

"No, Tazel. Please don't leave me. Please don't leave me."

I heard their voices, but I didn't know what they were saying. I wouldn't stop crying, "Please don't leave me. Please don't leave me."

"OK, OK. I'll take you home. It's OK. I'll take you home."

I was so afraid. I wouldn't let go. She had to carry me out the door with my arms still wrapped tight around her. I just wanted to go home and be where I was safe.

WITHOUT FAITH

When Uncle Ted got home, I wasn't afraid, because there was nothing he could do that would be worse than staying at that school with that lady in the black dress with the beads and the cross they called a nun.

"I was shakin' like a leaf," Tazel told Uncle Ted, with her voice quivering.

I thought about the trees we had seen that day, and what she said didn't make sense.

"You're taking her tomorrow. I'm not taking her again!" she said.

Uncle Ted didn't yell at me. He didn't hit me. He just looked at Tazel and said, "OK, I'll take her."

The next day came, and I didn't put up a fight. I knew I'd never win.

Chapter 7

The Lighthouse

After I had survived kindergarten and first grade, Sister Catherine Timothy became my second-grade teacher at Our Lady of the Miraculous Medal School, or O.L.M.M., as signified by the golden initials sewn over the heart of the jumper of my navy blue uniform.

My starched white blouse with Peter Pan collar was worn with a clip-on navy blue tie. I liked to think of it as a Roy Rogers tie. Woolen navy blue patterned knee socks and white and blue saddle shoes completed the outfit.

On Sunday night before school, Aunt Hazel would take great care to iron each of the accordion pleats of my jumper while Uncle Ted sat at the kitchen table polishing the whites of my saddle shoes and even the soles, so I'd always look my best for school.

I was assigned the last seat in the first row. I was far enough away to doodle and daydream undetected. One of my doodles was a note to Patricia Farris, who sat across from me two rows over. One of the boys I played with had taken out his thing and shown it to me, and I wanted to know if she had ever seen one. She passed a note back asking me what it looked like. The silver clip on my ballpoint pen was broken, with a very sharp edge — sharp enough to scratch the clean wooden surface of my desk. I proceeded to carve a picture of a penis on my desk.

Patricia passed back my note, and suddenly Sister Catherine Timothy, slamming the chalk down on the ledge of the blackboard, stormed down the aisle, her habit rustling and rosary beads shaking, to see what we thought was more important than paying attention to her lessons. She snatched the note from my hand and read it. Red-faced and furious with her hand raised to give me a wallop, she stopped and gasped.

"What is that?!"

"It's a lighthouse, Sister," I answered.

"A lighthouse! Show me how that's a lighthouse!" she said, shaking the note in her fist.

WITHOUT FAITH

"Well ... there's the lighthouse, and that's the light on top."
"And what's that at the bottom?"
"Those are rocks. ... With grass growing out of them."
"And what is that ... coming out of the top of the lighthouse?"
"Uh ... water?" I said.
Without another word, she grabbed me by the arm, pushed me down the aisle, and threw me into the hallway, where she ripped the school tie from my neck. With cold and piercing eyes, she leaned over, squeezing the tie in her hand and shaking it in my face.
"You don't deserve to wear this," she said and shoved me down the hall to Mother Superior's office.

I had never been to her office before. It was what I imagined the inside of a palace might resemble. An Oriental carpet covered the highly polished stained wood floor. Large, dark oil paintings of old men in clerical robes peered down at me from the walls above. Sister Catherine Timothy told me to take a seat in a dark wooden chair that had lion's head posts and four clawed feet for legs. I held onto the curled wooden arms as if this beastly chair might come to life. Nothing felt real, and I was so afraid as I sat there waiting to hear what they would do to me.

A huge mahogany desk with ornate carved moldings was centered between two tall burgundy-draped windows on the far end of the room. Statues of Jesus, Mother Mary, and other saints bordered the desk blotter where Mother Superior's folded hands rested. Sister Catherine Timothy handed Mother Superior the note, showed her my tie, and whispered so I couldn't hear. Mother Superior nodded her head and waved Sister Catherine Timothy away.

Mother Superior's gentle smile quietly embraced me, easing my tension. Her complexion was smooth, and although I could tell she was an older woman like Aunt Hazel, she did not look worn or tired. Her blue eyes had a silver glint, and she spoke softly.

"Doreen ... we are *not* going to punish you. Tell me, dear ... where have you seen what you drew on your desk?"

I told her about Uncle Frank ... what he did to me and to Donna.

DOREEN BIRDSELL

Mother Superior picked up the heavy receiver of the telephone on her desk; and shortly after, Aunt Hazel was sitting across the room from me. She took care to put on lipstick and wear her Sunday coat. She sat quietly glancing back and forth at Sister Catherine Timothy and Mother Superior.

"Doreen, will you tell your aunt what you told us?" Mother Superior asked.

I pointed to my crotch and said, "Uncle Frank tried to put his thing in there."

Aunt Hazel gasped, and she covered her mouth with her hand.

"She's been telling me this, but I didn't believe her. ... You know how children are?" she said to the nuns. "They make up the darndest things. ... I just couldn't believe it."

Suddenly I felt free. Mother Superior believed me and, because she believed me, Aunt Hazel had to believe me. The next thing I knew, we were driving to Port Chester with Uncle Ted, who came home from work early when Aunt Hazel called him.

Donna was sledding down the driveway (on the sled that Uncle Frank had made her) and was so excited to see me so we could play together. She ran up to the car, and Aunt Hazel quickly stole her joy and laughter when she said, "We're here on business, Donna."

Donna's face went white, and I knew that she knew why we were there. Aunt Hazel and Uncle Ted told my dad what had happened at school and what Frank had been doing to Donna and me.

That was the one and only time I saw my father react to protect us in any way. He picked up the telephone and began to dial. I could hear the phone ringing on the other end through that huge, heavy black receiver.

A voice said hello, and my usually meek and timid father screamed into the phone in a voice I'd never heard before or since, "If you ever go near those kids again, I'll get a gun and shoot you."

There was a brief silence, and in that moment I wondered, "Where would Daddy get a gun?"

Then he said, "You know what I mean!" And he slammed the phone down.

WITHOUT FAITH

Aunt Marion's face turned red, and she started panting. Holding her throat, she said, "Oh, my God. What if this gets in the *Port Chester Gazette*?" Donna ran into the closet next to the telephone table, screaming and crying. The door had a latch on the inside that could be locked. My daddy tuned the knob, but she wouldn't open the door. She was screaming, "No! No! No!"

Donna was nine years old, and I think she felt that she would be held responsible because she was two years older than I was. Uncle Frank had her convinced that what he was doing was right; and when the truth came out that day, something in her just snapped. She was never again the same Donna I knew.

I felt so calm and free of any blame, almost as though I had done something to be rewarded for by carving that penis in my desk and telling Mother Superior where I had seen it.

Eventually, Donna was coaxed out of the closet by Aunt Marion, but she wouldn't say anything. She just stared at the floor.

Uncle Frank's name was never mentioned again.

After that day, my Uncle Ted became more distant toward me. I wondered if he was angry with me or if he thought what happened was my fault.

At school, I had become Sister Catherine Timothy's favorite. She gave me the first seat in the third row, so I could be right in front of her desk. Leaning over, she would often quietly ask me if everything was all right at home, and she told me that I could come to see her at the convent anytime I wanted. She treated me like a mother, and I loved her. I missed her so much when I went on to third grade.

Sister Mary St. Francis, my new teacher, had a narrow, bony face with a long nose and a sharp chin. She used her wooden pointer to direct us to our seats and warned us that she wouldn't hesitate to correct us by poking us with the long pointed rubber tip. Pointing to the metal golden ruler on her desk, she said, "The pointer is for you to pay attention and to sit up straight. The golden ruler is for bad behavior, and I'll crack the back of anyone's hand that misbehaves."

I got that pointer stuck in my shoulders all year long for not sitting up straight, but I never got the golden ruler. I was too afraid to do anything wrong in *her* class.

WITHOUT FAITH

Chapter 8
Adele

It was a school night, and as usual I had to be in bed by nine o'clock.

"C'mon, Tazel. One more show, pleeez."

"Don't make me get off this couch," Uncle Ted said. "Now get in that bed."

I lay in bed staring at the dark ceiling. "Oh, God. Please take me. Please take me." I wanted God to take me to heaven. I couldn't stand it anymore. The kids at school had moms and dads and brothers and sisters they lived with. Their parents felt sorry for me because I didn't have a mother. Kids didn't know what I was talking about when I told them about my Uncle Frank or my cousin or the boys who showed me their thing. I didn't like dresses, dolls, school, or homework. Why was I so different from everyone else? I couldn't fit in anywhere, and every day when I woke up, it would still be the same. I missed my dad and Donna and living in Port Chester — the way it used to be.

The muffled sounds from the distant living room TV drifted into my bedroom. The dim light from the kitchen that separated my bedroom from the living room cast a sliver of light through my doorway and illuminated the white Blessed Virgin Mary statue on my dresser.

I had been the runner-up for selling the most raffle tickets in my fourth-grade class. As a prize, Mother Superior let me choose from among the many statues that decorated her desk. She treated me special, and I felt as if she understood me because she believed me when Aunt Hazel could not. I chose the Blessed Virgin Mary, the mother of Jesus.

I stared at the statue in the grayish light as I drifted off to sleep, hoping that God would answer my prayer and I would wake up in heaven.

"C'mon, Reenie. Time to get up! Don't make me come back twice to get you out of bed."

I thought that if I prayed hard enough, God would perform a miracle in my life like He did for those girls at Fatima who saw the Virgin Mother. Everyone in the whole school got to take off and go see that movie together because the Pope said it was true.

One day after school I went to the convent. When I reached the dark wooden doorway, I froze. I couldn't ring the bell, and I couldn't run away. Against my will, I lifted the heavy metal door knocker and let it drop.
"Hello, Doreen. What can I do for you?" Sister Marie asked.
"Mother Superior said I could come by anytime I wanted."
"Well … please come in. Is there any particular reason?" she asked.
"No, Sister."
Secretly I hoped that I would find them without their habits on and see if they had hair under those bonnets. I saw a piece of the sister's earlobe, but not one hair stuck out. Sister Marie had some black hairs on her chin, but nothing else.

She gently guided me down a long, barren hallway. The floorboards squeaked with every step. The room we entered was as bare as the hallway. Two nuns were sitting on stools in front of easels, painting what looked like was going to be a garden. These nuns were wearing habits too, but they were white, not black like those of our Sisters of Notre Dame. I wondered if they were visitors, but I didn't ask. It was all so foreign to me.
Sister Marie said, "This is Doreen Birdsell, and she's come for a visit."
Putting down their brushes and with eyes that smiled, they nodded politely.
"They probably know all about me," I thought.
One of the painting nuns turned toward me and asked, "Would you like to learn to paint, Doreen?"
That didn't interest me at all, but I knew I needed to mind my manners so I said, "No, thank you. I think I'll leave."
I could tell that she knew about me.
Patricia Farris, who sat near me in second grade, said that because the nuns took vows of chastity they could never get married. One of the other kids said some of them kissed each other. Maybe these two nuns were like the ones Patricia told me about, I thought.
I was very curious about their life inside the convent when they weren't being teachers.

WITHOUT FAITH

Sister Marie appeared in the doorway with a tray.
"Would you like some tea and cookies, Doreen?"
"No, thank you, Sister," I said.
She held me in her gaze. The room was silent except for the boards that creaked when I shifted my weight from one foot to the other.
"Do you know Adele the cleaning lady?" she asked.
"I think I've seen her after school, Sister. But I don't know her."
"You know …," she said, "I heard she pays the boys and girls that help her a quarter a day to help her clean. She's probably in the classrooms now. What do you think?"
That sounded good, I thought — and Christmas was coming. I could add that to my fifty-cents-a-week allowance.
"I think I'll go see if I can help Adele."

It was a cloudy, cold, and damp November day, and there was no one out to play with anyway. I walked from the convent across the garden and ran down the steps through the chain-link fence and into the deserted school. The smell of furniture polish led me to where Adele would be cleaning. Up the frosted-glass staircase to the second floor, I followed the sound of her mop swooshing across the dark red painted hallway floors, clattering back and forth. There was Adele making her way backward down the hall one swoosh at a time.
"Hi, Adele!" I said. "Sister Marie said you might need help?"
"And who might you be?" she asked.
Her hair was gray like the cold, concrete-colored clouds and pulled back in a bun. Her dress hung like a sack tied in the middle by a thin black belt, and thick ankles bulged over the sides of worn, black, fat-heeled shoes. Her feet turned outward when she wobbled down the halls pushing her mop and rolling the bucket alongside her.
"My name's Doreen, but you can call me Reenie," I said. "That's what my family calls me."
"OK. I'll call you Reenie."
"Sister Marie told me you pay a quarter."
"Only if you earn it. … All right then. You can start by emptying the garbage cans in all these classrooms and dumping them in here," she said,

44

pointing to the big rolling trash can in the hall.

After emptying the trash, Adele let me use the big, stringy mop to clean the floor in my old second-grade classroom, Room 2A. I mopped, dusted, and emptied all the trash. I did everything she asked me to. When we had put everything away, Adele put on a long tweed woolen coat and we walked through the dark empty hallways down the stairs together.

Adele locked the school door behind us, and I waited for my quarter. She snapped open a little brown-and-yellow-speckled corduroy purse and with her thumb and forefinger reached inside to fish out a shiny quarter.

"Thank you, Reenie," she said, handing me the quarter. "You can help me anytime you like, and I'll gladly pay you."

Smiling down at my quarter, I said, "I'll be back tomorrow."

"I'll see you then," Adele said, and I watched her wobble down the alleyway to the street. I hurried up the stairs and ran all the way home, clutching the quarter in my hand.

I couldn't wait to tell Tazel I had a job with Adele and got paid a quarter. I burst into the kitchen breathing hard, but it was all very quiet. Uncle Ted didn't even look up, and Tazel was busy stirring the pot on the stove. "Reenie, get inside and do your homework until I call you," she said.

At supper, Uncle Ted read the newspaper and Tazel just stared at the wall in front of her as she slowly put each fork of food into her mouth. She didn't even eat our favorite dessert, Jell-O mixed with vanilla pudding.

I thought about Christmas and decided I would hide the money I saved and surprise them with their presents.

Dinner continued without a word, and I wasn't about to say anything that would get Uncle Ted mad. Whatever had happened, I hoped it didn't have anything to do with me. I quietly finished my supper, and my Jell-O with vanilla pudding, and went to my room.

I waited until the six o'clock news was over before I went into the living room to lie down in front of the TV and watch my favorite show in the world. "Look up in the sky. ... It's a bird. ... It's a plane. ... No! It's Superman!" the announcer said.

WITHOUT FAITH

"Hey, was your father a glazier?!" Uncle Ted yelled.

"What do you mean?" I asked, swiveling my head from the TV screen to see his expression.

"What do you think! Your head is made of glass and I can see right through it?" he yelled. "Move over!"

I moved over, feeling that his question about the glazier was not fair. I knew I just better keep my mouth shut if I was going to see whom Superman would rescue. *I Love Lucy* was on tonight too. I loved hearing Tazel laugh when Lucy did something funny, but tonight I was the only one who laughed.

After the show, Tazel said, "OK, it's a school night. Time for bed —you."

"Oh, please. One more show, please?" I asked.

"Don't push it, Reenie," she said.

I kissed Tazel and then Uncle Ted's scratchy cheek. He didn't look up but just nodded his head, and I went to bed.

I lay in bed wide awake and thought about what Mother Superior had taught me. She said that because I was baptized I would go to heaven and how much God and Jesus loved me and that I was very special in God's eyes. But thinking about Superman made me feel better. I prayed that I would dream about Superman and that I'd be flying over Metropolis with him and he would protect me. ... But how would I hold on? I wondered. I'd be safe if he tucked me inside his tight pants, I imagined.

Then I prayed, "Oh, Lord, please take me ... please take me," and again I hoped I would wake up in heaven.

Chapter 9
Day Camp

After running down the alleyway and up Grove Street, I slowed to a controlled pace. I was free. It was a hot, steamy early summer morning in July as I walked to Our Lady of the Miraculous Medal School swinging the brown paper bag with the tuna fish sandwich that Tazel had made for my lunch. Playing a game to see how fast I could walk without actually breaking into a run helped to contain my excitement.

Big yellow school buses were lined up in front of my school. Only two blocks more down the hill and I'd be there. Unable to hold back any longer, my legs burst into a sprint as I ran down the long slope of the concrete hill past Our Lady of the Miraculous Medal Church to the front of the school. Hundreds of kids crowded the sidewalk, spilling into the street. They were all clamoring to get on the buses for C.Y.O. Day Camp.

Counselors held clipboards and hollered out grade numbers to organize the masses. I pushed through the sea of kids moving in every direction and almost lost my bagged lunch. Then I saw "Grade 4" on the window of one of the buses. I squeezed to the head of the line and made my way to the school bus door. Parents were kissing their children goodbye and telling them how to behave. I had just been promoted to fourth grade and was no longer one of those little kids who needed a grown-up to see them off to camp.

One of the organizers, with short blond hair and wearing tan pants and a black-and-white checkered short-sleeved shirt, stood in front of a bus holding a clipboard. A big number 4 was written on the back in red paint. I stood underneath the clipboard waiting patiently for my name to be called. The sun reflected the yellow hairs on his pudgy arms. I thought, "Wow — a whole entire week at summer camp." It was the first time Aunt Hazel and Uncle Ted were able to afford to send me. The kids closed in around us, one by one pushing their way onto the bus as their names were called.

WITHOUT FAITH

The bus was getting full. Fearing that I might have missed hearing my name, I reached up and tapped the counselor's hairy arm. " 'Scuse me. ... 'Scuse me!" But he didn't pay attention.

I reached up and poked him again — this time in his side. My finger sunk into his mushy waistline.

I yelled, "EXCUSE ME!"

He made a teeth-sucking noise and spread his arms above me, holding the clipboard over the heads of the other kids around me. Looking down, he said, "You gotta wait like everyone else. ... Did I call your name yet?"

"Doreen Birdsell, fourth grade. I don't know. ... I just got here and maybe you did and I wasn't here and I'm a 'B' so I figured you did ... and ..."

"Quiet," he said. "Do you know it's not polite to poke people?"

"I'm sorry, but I did say, ' 'Scuse me.' "

I felt afraid and excited at the same time as his pencil ran down his list and stopped.

"Birdsell, Doreen. This is your bus," he said.

"Oh, boy!" I yelled and jumped up the stairs in my brand new blue PF Flyers sneakers that Tazel had bought for this special day. I ran down the aisle to the back of the bus and sat down with some other kids from my class in the last row.

The bus filled up, and the man with the clipboard stood in the front and said, "Hi, everybody. I'm your camp counselor. You can call me Wally. Anything you need to know, you ask me. When we get to Alley Pond Park, don't go anywhere at anytime without your group — or telling me first. Have a good time and remember: We're from Our Lady of the Miraculous Medal."

The bus driver pulled back a big black metal handle that shut the door. With a roar of the engine, we pulled from the curb and we were off. This was my first time on a school bus and my first time going to camp. Wally walked down the aisle all the way to the back of the bus where I was sitting. Unable to find an empty seat, he said to me, "Hey, why don't you sit on my lap so I can have some room to sit down?"

"Tut-tut," I said and turned my head and pretended to look out the window.

"Tut-tut?" he asked. "What is that supposed to mean?"

"Tut-tut is what you say when you don't want to be bothered. That's what Topper the Englishman says to George and Marion Kirby. Don't you know … the ghosts on the TV show?"

"OK. Tut-tut," he said and picked me up from my seat, spun me around, and sat me on his lap. Before I could get out another "tut," he had taken up almost two seats and we all were squeezed in together on that long seat in the back of the bus. I was glad that I had poked him. He probably liked me, I thought.

The bus pulled away from the curb and headed down Fresh Pond Road past the Oasis movie theater, up Metropolitan Avenue and onto the Interboro and then to the Grand Central Parkway. Somebody started to sing, "A hundred bottles of beer on the wall …" Then another kid: "A hundred bottles of beer …" Then me: "If one of them bottles should happen to fall …" We were all singing and bouncing our way to Alley Pond Park.

When we exited the parkway and drove down the pretty tree-lined streets, the singing stopped. The homes were in neat little rows with gardens and driveways, and grass lined the sidewalk. We all craned our necks to see out the windows. A forest in the distance grew nearer. That must be it.

"Settle down, everybody," Wally yelled, pushing me off his lap to get to the front of the bus.

We drove around a corner and into a lot that was filled with yellow buses that stretched all the way to where the trees of the park began. We pulled into spaces that were marked O.L.M.M., for our school name, and came to a stop.

We were all wooo-hoooing, and a couple of the boys were whistling through their fingers, when a whistle blew that was louder than all of us put together. With the silver whistle hanging from his neck and his balled fists glued to his hips, Wally blocked the head of the aisle and stared us down until we didn't make a peep.

"OK, everybody. We're not moving until you stay calm and be quiet. Whenever you hear this whistle, you stop — and you listen."

WITHOUT FAITH

Like soldiers, we waited for our orders as we lined up in rows of twos, to follow our leader, Wally.

We marched across the parking field over painted white stripes and cracked asphalt, between school buses with names of schools I had never heard of before, and then stepped onto the soft green grass of Alley Pond Park. A tent village was set up just for C.Y.O. Day Camp. Wally announced as we passed, "This is the Kool-Aid tent. We have recess here at ten o'clock, and we'll all be back for refreshments. We're going to arts and crafts."

Long benches with paper and crayons, Elmer's glue, wooden sticks, silver and gold stars, and all kinds of things were lined up for us. A girl camp counselor with a long brown ponytail helped us make key chains by braiding plastic strings, but mostly she kept us from wandering off or from fighting with one another.

After recess, we played horseshoes and then ran a three-legged race before it was time for lunch back at the Kool-Aid tent. The shade of the park and the Kool-Aid weren't enough to cool me off and I wished we could go swimming, but there was no swimming at Alley Pond Park.

(Some of the kids in my class had gone to sleepover camp. I found an ad in the *Daily News* and read it to Uncle Ted. I would have done anything to go to a dude ranch and be the cowboy on the bronco in the advertisement. Uncle Ted said, "Reenie, I don't make that kind of money to send you to one of those camps."

"How about you and Daddy put your money together to send me? ... Or maybe I could give something up ... like Catholic school?"

"No way, Reenie," he said. "We've already given you more than we ever gave our own kids. You should be grateful.")

I was happy to be at Alley Pond Park, even if it didn't have horses or a lake to swim in. Whistles started blowing all over the park. It was time to leave. Our fourth-grade tanned girl counselor shooed us like chicks toward Wally's whistle.

We lined up and marched back to our bus behind Wally. Standing at the bottom of the school bus steps, he made checkmarks on his clipboard as he called out our names. I ran to the back to get the last seat next to the window; and, like before, Wally came to the back of the bus and said, "Would you like to sit on my lap again or are you going to give me that *tut-tut*?"

I knew it was useless, so I surrendered the seat and he hoisted me up onto his lap.

This time I started the song: "A hundred bottles of beer on the wall ..." Another kid started to sing, and everyone else joined in, including Wally. We were all bouncing and singing our way back home until there were almost no more bottles of beer on the wall. I felt something funny, like when Uncle Frank used to make me sit on his lap. It felt like skin against my bottom beneath my shorts leg, and I knew that Wally had taken out his thing. I didn't say anything. I stopped singing, but Wally kept on singing along with the rest of the busload of kids. His hands were on my hips, pressing me down. I didn't know what to do. I liked his attention, but I knew it was wrong. I just sat there and didn't say anything for the rest of the way home. It seemed like a very long time before we reached Our Lady of the Miraculous Medal.

Wally reached under me, fumbling to put his thing in his pants. He lifted me off his lap and said, "Don't go away. I want to talk to you before you leave."

I wondered if he was going to keep me and do something in the empty bus. I was excited, I was afraid, and I was ashamed.

All the kids were running home or to their parents' cars. Wally and I were left on the sidewalk alone, standing alongside the school bus.

"Where do you live?" he asked.

"59-22 Grove Street," I said.

"How about I drive you home? My car's over there," he said, pointing to a dusty, black sedan.

"I'll get in trouble if my Aunt Hazel and Uncle Ted see me come home in a car."

"Where's your mother and father?" he asked.

"My mother died when I was two. My father takes care of my sister with my other aunt and uncle. They live in Port Chester. That's in Westchester," I said.

WITHOUT FAITH

"OK. I understand. I'm sorry. Do they let you go out and play after dinner?" he asked.
"They let me go out as long as I'm home by eight o'clock," I said.
"Ernie's Delicatessen is right near you. Do you know it?" he asked.
"Yeah, I go there sometimes. My Aunt Hazel says Ernie looks greasy and so does his store."
"Ernie's my friend. Why don't you meet me there tonight after supper, and I'll take you for a ride."
"I don't know. I guess I can."
"Let's go. I'll drop you off at Ernie's now. Your aunt and uncle will never know you were in a car."
Maybe he'll let me steer his car, I thought.
We pulled up past Ernie's Deli. I jumped out of the car and said, "OK. See you later ... *tut-tut.*"

I ran home and went straight to my room. Every time I had told Aunt Hazel something had happened to me with Uncle Frank, she never believed me anyway; and even if she did, she probably wouldn't let me go back to camp. I told her how fun camp was and showed her the key chain I had made for her. Uncle Ted came home for dinner and said, "How was camp today? Did you make any friends?"
"Oh, yeah, it was great. I have a camp counselor named Wally, but I didn't make any friends yet."

At dinner, I just pushed the food around my plate.
"You're not getting out of here until you finish your dinner. What did you eat today that you're not hungry?" Tazel asked.
I lied and said, "I filled up on milk before dinner."
I knew I wouldn't get out, so I forced down the mashed potatoes, peas, and Monday night meatloaf and said, "OK, I'm done now. Can I go out?"
Tazel looked at my empty plate and, making dots in the air with her finger, said, "OK, you know you have to be home here by eight o'clock, and no wandering down to Fresh Pond Road — that's too busy a street for you on your bicycle."

"I won't," I said, as I kissed her on her soft cheek.

I ran out the door and down the alleyway to the backyard to unlock my bike. I wondered if Wally would really be at Ernie's. I rode my bike down the sidewalk and stopped when I got to the end of the block near the gin mill and peeked around the corner. Wally's dried-mud, dusty car was parked in front of Ernie's Deli. I told myself that Wally thought I was so special that he picked me out over all the other kids on the bus. Nobody had ever treated me like that except Uncle Frank and cousin Billy.

If Tazel and Uncle Ted found out, I'd probably get in trouble, but Wally was my camp counselor, I thought. I didn't want to miss out on riding in his car and maybe being able to steer.

I hid behind the corner so that only my bicycle wheel protruded beyond the edge of the gin mill's rounded staircase. The sour smell of beer-soaked wood poured into the street when my neighbor Mr. Nielsen came out with a bucket of beer. Blocked by my bike at the end of the railing, he was forced to stop, and the white foamy head of beer splashed over the rim and onto the steps.

"Hey, move that bike before somebody breaks their neck," he said. I gripped the handlebars and pedaled one rotation forward, coasting toward the deli; any slower and my bike would have stopped and fallen over. Beyond the doorway, Wally was leaning against the ice cream freezer chest and talking to Ernie behind the counter. He saw me from the doorway and said, "Hey, Doreen. How are you? This is one of my kids, Ernie, from camp."

Ernie popped his head over the counter.

"Yeah, that's Reenie. … How ya' doin', Reenie? … What can I get ya?" he asked.

"Nothin'. Thanks," I said.

"Reenie?" Wally asked.

"That's my name too," I said. "That's the name my family calls me."

"Can I call you Reenie?" he said.

"All right, I guess so."

"How about an ice cream sandwich, Reenie?"

I didn't really want it … my heart was racing. I knew Wally would take me

WITHOUT FAITH

for a ride in his car. He said he would, and I didn't know why, but I said, "OK."

Wally gave Ernie a dime, and we walked outside.

"Well, you showed up. I wasn't sure if you would," he said.

"You said you'd take me for a ride?"

"Oh, you can't go in cars. ... You told me you'd get in trouble."

"Oh ... tut-tut," I said.

"OK, I'll take you, but you have to promise you won't tell anyone you were with me. Do you promise?"

"Tut-tut," I said.

"Don't give me that tut-tut, Reenie. No promise, no ride."

"OK, I promise," I said. "Let's go."

I locked my bike to the railing of the stoop next to Ernie's Deli and hopped in the front seat. I sat on my hands to prevent the cracked and torn leather seat from scratching my bare legs. It was so exciting being in a car all by myself with Wally.

"Where do you wanna go?" he asked.

"I don't know ... just around."

As we drove by Our Lady of the Miraculous Medal Church, I made the sign of the cross, as always. Cruising down the hill on 60th Place, passing Metropolitan Avenue, we went all the way to Flushing Avenue. I had been that far only with Aunt Hazel and Uncle Ted or my cousins Ann and Billy. Beyond the factories, Wally turned down a dirt road to the back of a big warehouse and stopped.

He looked at me and said, "Do you want to sit on my lap?"

"Tut-tut," I said.

"If you say 'tut-tut' one more time, I'm going to spank you."

"Tut-tut," I said, unable to resist daring him.

He pulled me on his lap and pulled my bumblebee-striped polo shirt up over my head and covered my eyes.

"Don't look," he said.

I thought about the yellow and black key chain I had made Tazel that morning ... that seemed so long ago. I felt that big warm thing beneath me, and Wally was bouncing me up and down. He told me to put my hand on it.

"This is your spanking," he said.

My shirt was thin, so I could see through it, but Wally didn't know. He was holding his thing and pulling me up and down.

He suddenly stopped and pushed me across the seat. He reached under the seat and pulled out a crumpled rag and wiped himself. "OK, you can pull your shirt down now. We're gonna go."

Wally didn't say anything all the way back to Ernie's, and neither did I.

He stopped a block before the deli, leaned over me, jerked back the silver door handle, and pushed my door open. He looked me in the eyes and said, "Remember. Don't tell anyone." Nodding my head, I got out, ran to my bike, and rode it home.

Uncle Ted was lying on the couch reading his newspaper. I stood in the doorway between the kitchen and the living room without saying a word. He put down his paper and said, "What are you standing there for? Huh? ... What's wrong with you, Reenie? ... Answer me! Where were you?"

My lips trembled. "I saw my camp counselor, Wally, at Ernie's, and he bought me an ice cream. He took me for a ride in his car ..."

Before I could finish, Uncle Ted jumped off the couch and was unbuckling his belt. "In his car! ... In his car! ... You know you're not supposed to go in anyone's car. ... I'm gonna kill you, Reenie!" And he started to beat me with the belt.

I cried and yelled, "Nothin' happened, I swear ... nothing happened. ... He just took me for a ride."

Tazel ran in from the bedroom, screaming, "Stop it, Ted. Stop it." And then he yelled, "Where is he? I'm going to kill him. ... Where is the bastard? ... Where does he live?"

Tazel was crying. I was crying, and I couldn't breathe without shaking. I tasted the snot running in my mouth. "I don't know ... I don't know ... I swear I don't know!"

Uncle Ted ran to the phone and said, "I'm calling the rectory. They'll know where he lives."

Tazel held me and said, "What did you do, Reenie? ... Reenie, what did you do?"

WITHOUT FAITH

"Nothin' ... Tazel ... nothin' ... I swear. ... I only went for a ride."

When Uncle Ted came back in the living room, he had on his jacket and shoes. He grabbed my hand and said to Tazel, "We'll be back. We're going to that bastard's house."

He dragged me down the alleyway, threw me into the back seat of the car, and slammed the door.

He sped past Forest Avenue toward Brooklyn, a few blocks down and then over. Uncle Ted stopped the car on a street with brick houses three stories high that all looked the same. With a quick stride, hand in hand, silently we walked up the staircase and into a vestibule with a line of doorbells. His hand shook as his grease-stained finger moved across the names on the many doorbells. "That's the bastard," he said, and he pushed the button.

The large wooden door buzzed. I stayed back, but he yanked me in the hallway. From the top of the long dark staircase, a man's voice asked, "Who is it?"

"Is your name Wally? ... Are you the camp counselor? Do you know this girl?" Uncle Ted yelled.

A yellow-haired, chubby, wide-eyed face peered over the banister. "Why?"

"You son of a bitch" — Uncle Ted's veins were popping from his neck. "You know you know her, you son of a bitch. ... If I ever catch you near her again ... I'm going to kill you. How can you go near little girls? ... You sick bastard. ... Taking them in your car. ... I told them at the rectory what you did. ... You son of a bitch. ... How can you be a student in a seminary? ..."

"I'm sorry, sir. I'm, I'm really sorry," he said from the top of the dark staircase.

Uncle Ted called him a son of a bitch one more time, until he jerked me back outside the door and into the car.

I didn't know what seminary was, but I knew that there'd be no more camp for me that summer.

Chapter 10

Traffic Street

I never liked playing with dolls, hated wearing dresses, and only tolerated playing "tea" with my sister, Donna, because I loved her and never had enough time with her. Shorts and sneakers, riding my bike, Roy Rogers six-shooters, playing cowboys and Indians — I was in heaven. Donna, on the other hand, was all about pink dresses, scratchy petticoats, and Mary Jane shoes. Yuck. I hated Easter. It meant getting dressed up and not doing anything that might get me dirty.

Joanne Angelino sat next to me in fifth grade. She was the first girl I met that liked all the same stuff I did. Joanne was square-built with a mop of curly reddish-brown hair that matched the color of the freckles on her cherub cheeks. She liked to wrestle and always won. The best thing about Joanne was that she owned real army helmets that had belonged to her father. On cold days, we'd play at her apartment because her mother was at work until suppertime and her father no longer lived with them. We played army, wearing the real helmets, and ate pork and beans right out of the can in our sheet-draped camp behind the living room couch.

When Joanne and her mom had to move away, I really missed my best friend. There were no other girls like her, and the boys wouldn't include me in their ballgames or flipping sports cards. If they did let me play, they always took advantage by ganging up on me. They'd steal my baseball cards, knock over my bike, or throw me a ball that was too hard to catch and laugh at me because I was a girl.

A couple of weeks after Joanne had moved away, on a cold, damp Sunday, I rode my bike down to Traffic Street. It was a few blocks from where I lived but was in a desolate neighborhood with the Long Island Rail Road tracks on one side and garages on the other.

WITHOUT FAITH

I had stolen a book of matches from Aunt Hazel's dresser drawer and was very excited about finding a place to light them. I slowly rode into a courtyard of garages. There was no one on the streets, and the apartment windows that overlooked the courtyard seemed vacant. The enclosure of the courtyard blocked any possible breeze — perfect for striking a match. The November winds had gathered a pile of dried leaves in a corner between two of the connected garages.

I lit my first match and threw it into the pile of leaves. I watched as the match light turned into a flaming leaf that caught another, and as a twig crackled and burned, catching the rest of the pile. One match had turned into a blaze. Flames licked the glossy dark green wooden garage doors. I looked up to the windows and hoped no one saw me. I jumped on my bike and stood on the pedals to get out of there as fast as I could. By the time I got to Fresh Pond Road, I heard the sound of fire engines. I pushed the pedals as hard and fast as I could to get home. I raced home and ran into my room.

Aunt Hazel and Uncle Ted were reading the Sunday papers in the living room. I was so glad they didn't ask me any questions or see me when I came home. My pounding heart and cold sweaty face would have said, "I was up to no good," as Aunt Hazel always used to say.

When I felt like I was safe, I came out and slipped in front of the TV, not even aware of what was on the screen. The excitement of the afternoon, lighting the fire and not being caught, was exhilarating. The secret made me feel stronger and smarter than the stupid boys who wouldn't play with me. "They could never do what I did," I thought.

Chapter 11
Birdie

My cousins Ann and Billy were able to move from their three-story walk-up apartment and buy a one-family home in Glendale on 65th Place to house their growing family. Unlike Ridgewood, Glendale had lots of one-family homes. Because Aunt Hazel and Uncle Ted were Ann's mother and father, we visited often. I became friendly with the next-door neighbors' daughter Karen. We were the same age, eleven years old and in sixth grade.

Glendale was the parish for St. Matthias. Ridgewood, the border town where I lived, was the parish for Our Lady of the Miraculous Medal. Our parishes and our neighborhoods were different worlds; each had its own gang. The teenage gang in Glendale was the Saints. They controlled Old Farmers Oval Park, directly across the street from Ann and Billy's new home. The Drifters, in Ridgewood, ran Junior High P.S. 93 on Forest Avenue. They spray-painted their names on their playground walls, under the overpasses of the railroad tracks, and on the pavements. No member dared go into the other gang's territory alone.

The Saints wouldn't let me join because the guy who was their leader said I was too young. Although I was eleven years old, I lied and said I was thirteen. I thought my black marshmallow leatherette jacket and tight jeans would help me pass for older and make me look tough enough so they'd want me in their gang.

I hung around P.S. 93, hoping the Drifters would let me in. I circled the edge of the playground, slowly getting closer to where the gang of silver-zipped, black-leather-dressed guys and red-lipsticked girls hung out. A skinny, big-teased redheaded girl pointed in my direction when a leather guy with a cigarette dangling from the side of his mouth flipped open a switchblade. He shot me a look that stuck me as though it were the knife. I got on my bike and took off. Laughter broke out behind me, but I wouldn't turn around and show that I cared. I thought they weren't laughing at me. Who did I think I was that I could fit in? So I kept riding. I wasn't like those girls, and I wasn't a guy.

WITHOUT FAITH

None of those girls rode bikes, and they'd be the first ones to run if they saw trouble coming. There was no way I was going to tease my hair, and I loved my bike. It was a black three-speed Royce Union English racer with brakes on the handlebars, not the kind you had to push back on the pedals to stop.

I borrowed Aunt Hazel's hair gel and tried to comb my hair like my friend Teddy's. He'd comb his hair straight back and, with a flip of his wrist, bring the front down over his forehead to make this cool dip. Aunt Hazel would have killed me if she saw me combing my hair like that. She hated that I wasn't like other girls and always wanted to know what she did to deserve me.

I raced my bike to Glendale to hang out with Karen. Karen didn't care about being cool. Her jeans were loose and long like the blond untamed curls that bounced on her shoulders.

Karen's cousin Debra was at her house. She was a year older, in seventh grade. Debra was more than a head taller than me and had a real leather jacket that was belted at the waist and fell to her knees. She knew how to crack gum and smoked Parliaments that she stole from her mother. I wouldn't dare make fun of *her*. Debra had met a girl at school who had just moved to the neighborhood. She said the girl's mother worked and she didn't have a father, so we could have a real place to hang out all to ourselves during the daytime.

We got on our bikes and rode down 65th Place alongside the tracks to where she lived. It was a two-room apartment next door to a boarded-up gas station near the railroad overpass. Debra said it used to be a store before they moved there.

A girl with long brown scraggly hair and tight calf-long jeans like mine answered the door.

"Hey, Brenda. I came over — like you said," Debra said.

Brenda kind of grunted at Debra, and with a quick jerk of her head she motioned us inside to a whitewashed high-ceilinged room with a skylight. It was half empty with only a purple couch, a chair, and a TV. The painted concrete floor and walls were bare except for a couple of shaggy throw rugs.

A redheaded guy with a freckled face who was about the same age as me sat at a small kitchen table that was pushed against the wall at the far end of the room. He was rocking back and forth on the rear legs of a red vinyl chair, checking us out. The wall next to the front door was a store window painted white except at the very top, where the light from the street came through. Telephone poles with sagging parallel wires between them cast a shadow on the painted glass.

Brenda looked me up and down, making sure she wouldn't catch my eye.

"This is Reenie. I mean Birdie," Karen said. She knew that only my family called me Reenie.

(On the first day of school that year, my sixth-grade teacher, Sister Mary St. Charles, was doing roll call. "Doreen Birdsell ... Birdsell? What kind of name is Birdsell?" she asked. Before I could answer, she laughed and said, "With a name like that, they should call you Birdie." The whole class cracked up, and from then on my name was Birdie. At first I was embarrassed, but then I thought it was cool that now I had a street name.)

"Birdie, huh?" Brenda said.

"That's right. That's what everybody calls me."

"Say hi, Keith," Brenda said to the freckled redheaded kid sitting in the chair.

"He lives around here and hangs out with me. He's a guy, but he's cool," she said.

He nodded hello, with nothing else to add.

"This is cool. Where's your room?" I asked Brenda.

"This is it. I got the whole living room to myself. My mom sleeps in the other room."

"You sleep on the couch?" I asked.

"It's a convertible sofa, you jerk," she said.

She reminded me a little of my friend from fifth grade who wore her dad's army helmet when we played war together.

"You ever sniff Carbona?" she asked.

"No. What's that?"

"Cleaning fluid. My mother uses it. You can really get a buzz. Wanna try?"
"Yeah. How?"
She reached under the kitchen sink, took out a plastic bottle, and poured the clear liquid onto a Kleenex.
"Put this under your nose. Don't touch it. Just sniff it ... slow."
She poured some for everyone, and we sat down and sniffed.
Wow. Everything started to hum. It was like I could hear all the voices traveling in the telephone wires outside the window all humming in unison.
This was great — and all I needed was cleaning fluid.
"How can I get this stuff?" I asked after I came down.
"You can buy it in the store," she said.
I couldn't believe Karen and her cousin Debra knew somebody as cool as Brenda.

The five of us of us hung out together every day after school. It was a cold, gray, early December afternoon, and we were hoping to find an open freight car where we could hang out and stay warm. One by one, we stepped through the hole of the chain-link fence and walked up the embankment to the string of freight cars parked on the hill above.
Keith spotted a car that wasn't sealed. He was able to release the latch on the thick black iron bar and slide the heavy metal door open. We hoisted ourselves up into the car and onto the splintered wooden floor. It was half filled with stacks of flattened corrugated cardboard. Brenda sat back in a corner of the car surrounded by the cardboard piles. She reached into her jeans pocket and pulled out a book of matches. Ripping one of the cardboard matches from the pack, she slid the red head on the striker with her thumb and flipped the flaming match.
"C'mon, Birdie. You got some matches?" she asked.

I flipped a match for fun just to see if it would catch. Brenda was still lighting matches in her corner until a small flame grew on the edge of one of the pieces of cardboard. Karen, Debra, and Keith sat against the wall rubbing their hands together like they were warming themselves at a campfire. When I saw Brenda's fire, I was determined to get one going too. We both struck matches that flew aimlessly through the air.

DOREEN BIRDSELL

Within minutes, the flames grew up one side of the wall, devouring the dry cardboard, with small flames rising in every direction.

We rushed to the open door and jumped onto the slate railroad stones below and scattered. I ran to my bike in the nearby playground and pedaled furiously. The sky behind me was black. Flames shot out from the open door of the red metal freight car. Multiple sirens screamed in the distance. I was really scared this time because I wasn't in this alone and I knew the cops would be asking questions.

When we saw one another the next day at the park, we made a pact that, no matter what, we wouldn't tell.

One afternoon after school, I was riding back to the park when a car pulled up alongside me. A man in the passenger seat wearing a fedora that shaded his face asked, "Is your name Birdie?"

"No," I said and kept pedaling. I wanted to move as fast as my racing heart.

When I turned the corner, the car turned with me. The same man showed me a badge and this time asked, "Is your name Doreen Birdsell?"

The next thing I knew, I was at the 104th Precinct police station. This wasn't going to be like the day my aunt got called to the principal's office.

It turned out that all the girls had kept their mouths shut. I knew that it was Keith who caved in.

I told Aunt Hazel and Uncle Ted that the whole thing was Brenda's idea. "We were just trying to stay warm," I said.

We were in Juvenile Court a few weeks later. The papers said there was $10,000 in damage to the freight car and its contents. If we pleaded guilty and didn't get in any more trouble by the time we were eighteen years old, the case would be expunged.

I didn't get hit for starting that fire, and I usually got hit for a lot of things I did. Punishment always started with getting hit.

After the fire, I couldn't go out or ride my bike for a long time. I loved my bike. It was how I got away.

Chapter 12

Cowboy Boots

I liked Linda Connor. She went horseback riding every weekend at Parkside Stables in Forest Hills. I loved horses. I still get excited about the idea of riding, even though I never did get to go to a dude ranch when I was younger. It cost $2.50 an hour to ride, and Aunt Hazel gave me the money to go. Linda had her own boots. We rode together every week. When Christmas came, Aunt Hazel asked what I would like as a gift.

I didn't hesitate.

"Riding boots!"

Because Aunt Hazel didn't know anything about horseback riding, she took me shopping before Christmas to pick out the boots. I was thrilled when we got on the Metropolitan Avenue bus to Jamaica, then went to the tack shop that sold riding gear. I chose the most beautiful black and red Western riding boots. They were sixty-five dollars. Aunt Hazel told me that was more than she had planned to spend, but if my father chipped in, we could make it. I couldn't wait for Christmas, but was even more ecstatic about the day after, when I'd wear them riding.

I waited for Linda at the bus stop at Fresh Pond Road and Metropolitan Avenue. My heart was pounding. I was so proud to be wearing my new riding boots and couldn't wait to show Linda. I didn't say a word. I waited for her to notice. When we sat down on the bench seat behind the driver, she busted out laughing.

"What are those?" she asked.

"What do you mean? My boots?"

"They're Western! We ride English, you dope."

"So what! I don't like English boots," I said.

I was so embarrassed. Linda wore black stirrup stretch pants that fit inside her brown leather flat-heeled riding boots, while I wore blue jeans tucked into my beautiful Western square-toed boots.

Would they laugh at me at the stables? I wondered.
"What difference does it make?" I asked her.
"It's not proper," she said.

I never wore them riding again. Whenever Aunt Hazel asked me why I didn't wear them, I told her that I loved them so much I didn't want to wear them out. (I kept those boots for twenty years, and one day they became very stylish. I wish I still had them, but the leather cracked and I had to give them up. Aunt Hazel and I definitely got our sixty-five dollars' worth.)

Besides horseback riding, Linda Connor introduced me to Linda Meehan. We were in eighth grade, and Linda Meehan was in sixth. Although she was two years behind us in school, she was only one year younger. Her long blond wavy hair, blue eyes, ever-rosy cheeks, and prematurely developed breasts made her appear much older. Suddenly, I no longer cared about Linda Connor or horses. I found Linda Meehan much more fascinating. The boys in school fell all over her, and so did I. The big difference was that it was easier for a girl to be her friend than a boy. Linda Meehan had decided there could only be one Linda, so now we called Linda Connor, "Connor."

On my first day home from vacation with my aunt and uncle, I ran to Linda's house. I couldn't wait to see her. She was all I thought about when I was gone. I lied and told Linda and Connor that I had tongue-kissed with a boy named Ricky while I was away. I wanted them to think that I knew something they didn't and that I had become more grown up.
"Really. What was it like?" Linda asked.
"I can't explain it," I said.
"Show me," she said.
I couldn't breathe.
"What do you mean? I can't show you here ... on the stoop?" I asked.
"Connor. Go home," Linda said.
"Let's go down to the basement, Doreen."
I couldn't feel my body. I only noticed that I was moving toward the front door and down the basement steps.

WITHOUT FAITH

Linda sat next to me on the yellow leather couch in the finished basement. "OK. So show me."

She tilted her head to one side, closed her eyes, and lifted her chin ever so slightly, waiting for me to kiss her.

My lips tingled, and the air between us felt magnetic as I leaned over and touched her lips with mine.

I had never tongue-kissed and didn't know what to do. I pushed out my tongue and found my way between her lips, licking more than kissing.

She pulled away.

"That's it? That can't be it. Let's do it again," she said.

This time she put her lips on mine first and slowly moved her tongue across my upper lip, then my lower, and then into my mouth, more gently and surely.

"That's probably more like it," she said.

"Yeah, that's a little more like it," I agreed.

That was my first kiss, and I was in love with Linda. I didn't question how I felt or that Linda was a girl, and we never talked about it.

I slept over often, and we experimented much.

Chapter 13

Ice Cream

Marie Addamo and I were walking down the street, 60th Place in Ridgewood, when a car pulled to the curb and stopped alongside us.

"Hey, girls. Where's 69th Street?" The guy had a bulging Adam's apple and curly, greasy black hair.

When I leaned into the passenger window to give him directions, I noticed his hand jerking back and forth, pulling on his penis. "Get the hell out of here!" I yelled.

Marie, who stood beside me, spit at him, yelling, "Yeah! You bastard!"

I was so angry. The memories of all those damn penises men kept exposing me to came rushing back.

As he sped away, I absorbed the numbers on his license plate, as well as the make and model of the car.

"Let's call the cops!" I said.

We ran to a telephone booth on the corner.

"Marie … you call."

"Why me?"

"Because I got the license number. You make the call."

"Oh, all right, I guess."

"C'mon … dial 0 … ask for the police. But — no matter what — don't tell them your name. Remember — just tell them 'A man exposed himself, and his license number is 6R6312 … black Ford Falcon.'… No names!"

She did exactly what I said.

"Great," I thought. "We got him." Finally there would be some vindication, and he would be the one accused.

There was some hesitation. She was nodding her head and still hanging on. "Marie Addamo, 61-32 60th Drive, Maspeth, New York, and Doreen Birdsell …"

WITHOUT FAITH

"Oh, no!" I thought. "Aunt Hazel and Uncle Ted are going to kill me because I did it again."

✶✶✶✶✶✶✶

The previous summer on a very hot, breezeless night, the fan would not give us any relief. Aunt Hazel went into her bedroom and brought out her change purse. She gave me sixty cents to go to Wilkens Ice Cream Parlor on Fresh Pond Road and buy us a quart of chocolate-and-vanilla fresh-packed ice cream. It was after dark, but Wilkens was only two streets away. One of the blocks was a long sloping hill with two-family brick homes on either side. Huge maples lining the sidewalk formed a dark tunnel that led to the lights of Fresh Pond Road below.

As I was walking up the hill on the dark, tree-lined street, a beige Volkswagen pulled over and a man said, "Excuse me." I walked over to the car and saw his arm moving rapidly. When I looked down, I could see that his hand was between his legs and he was pulling on himself. I got his license number, turned around and ran back to Fresh Pond Road and into the phone booth at the back of Wilkens to call the police.

Aunt Hazel and Uncle Ted were waiting for me when I walked into the living room with a quart of melting ice cream and two detectives.
The taller of the two detectives asked my aunt and uncle if anything like this had ever happened to me before, because nothing turned up on the license number I had given them. Uncle Ted told them about Uncle Frank. I couldn't believe it. Now I was being doubted for what really happened. That was it. I swore to myself that I'd never do that again.

✶✶✶✶✶✶✶

"Marie! I said, 'NO NAMES!'"
"They're the police. They asked! And I couldn't lie."
I was jumping up and down on the sidewalk screaming, "That's not what I said to do!"

DOREEN BIRDSELL

"What a jerk," I thought.

Later that afternoon, we both identified the man in a lineup at the 104th Precinct police station. I felt as though Aunt Hazel and Uncle Ted were silently angry with me. They never spoke to me about what happened or asked me how I felt about any of it.

Marie and I spent the entire summer going back and forth to Kew Gardens Criminal Court for an arraignment, a hearing, and finally the sentencing. After all of that and cutting summer vacation short to be at court, to be questioned and cross-examined on the witness stand, and finally to be asked if what I saw might have been an ice cream cone, we heard, "Case dismissed on the grounds of insufficient evidence."
I felt so defeated and so wasted. Worst of all, I felt as though I had ruined the summer and disappointed Aunt Hazel and Uncle Ted again.

Later that year, I started smoking regularly, about a pack a day. I'd steal the cigarettes from Herman's Delicatessen when I didn't have fifteen cents to buy them. Herman was pretty naïve for a store owner. I'd order a quarter pound of potato salad, and when he'd walk down the aisle I'd grab a pack of whatever promotional brand of cigarettes was displayed on the counter. Mostly it was Carlton's with the charcoal tip.

****

Aunt Hazel and Uncle Ted really gave me everything they could — more than they were ever able to give their own kids, which they told me often. They sent me to parochial school, took me on summer vacations, and gave me the choice to go to Catholic high school or get braces to straighten my teeth. The tuition for school was about the same as the cost for braces, but I had to choose which I thought was more important. Uncle Ted would always remark to Aunt Hazel, "She'd be really attractive if she just didn't have that front tooth overlapping the other one."

The following September, I was enrolled at St. Nicholas High School for

WITHOUT FAITH

Girls in Greenpoint. I could graduate in three years. I would be sixteen years old, be able to work, and finally get my own place. That's what I wanted most.

I walked ten blocks to the bus that went down Metropolitan Avenue to Greenpoint. St. Nick's was in an old building with creaky stairs and small classrooms. I didn't know anyone, and I felt like I didn't fit in. Three more years of nuns? I thought.

Within a week, I transferred to the local public school, Grover Cleveland High School. I didn't care about Catholic high school or braces.

Chapter 14

Community Center

The community center was open on Tuesday and Thursday nights at P.S. 153 in Maspeth. It gave me a place to hang out with my friends and stay warm on winter nights. When the center was closed, we'd hang out at Jack & Dot's Candy Store, on the corner next to Herman's Delicatessen, where I stole my cigarettes. Jack and Dot, the gray-complexioned, silver-haired owners, would give us a ten-minute limit on our fifteen-cent egg creams. Jack swished a wet rag across the counter, brushing past my almost-empty glass. An eight-ounce egg cream lasting ten minutes became an art of a hundred sips when it meant being in the warm store or freezing outside in the cold doorway.

Herman's Deli was a better shelter from the bitter wind, with its deep vestibule. My feet throbbed from the cold, but there was no way I was going home before my 9:30 p.m. curfew and miss out on something. One by one, our small group thinned out. Chicky, who was the tallest fourteen-year-old in our crowd, was always the last to leave. He was six feet tall and skinny and had orangy-red hair and freckles. "Nobody cares what time I get home," he said.

(I thought it was great that he had freedom to stay out as late as he liked. He wasn't like Eddy, The Twins, or Bee-Bop, whom I could never trust. At Halloween, they would bombard the girls with eggs and chase us down the street, hitting us in the back or on our legs with socks that were filled with flour. Eddy would try to con me with his big brown eyes and tell me it was all just a joke. I wanted to believe him. When none of the other guys were around, we'd talk and play Ace-King-Queen against the smooth brick wall of Kennelly's Bar & Grill. I always had a pink Spalding ball in my pocket.

(When Eddy got with the other guys, he'd turn around and betray me. At a party in Stevie's basement, Eddy peed in a bottle of Thunderbird. He tried to pass it off as wine and offered me a sip. When I fell for it, I was the big joke for them, except for Chicky. He didn't laugh, and he never participated in the Halloween pranks or the other things they did to make trouble for me or

WITHOUT FAITH

anyone else. We both lived in Ridgewood, at least a mile from where we hung out in Maspeth. Sometimes he walked with me because his house was on the way. His stride was so long, it was almost a running walk to keep up with him.)

I couldn't wait to get home and stick my bare feet under the hissing iron radiator in my bedroom, being careful not to burn myself on the steaming pipes. My toes and feet were so red and itchy from the cold that I scratched them sore. Long red marks striped my legs from toes to thighs. Frozen, aching feet were still better than spending a night at home.

****

Izzo was our counselor at P.S. 153 Community Center. We often heckled him because of his tall, scarecrow frame. One thick caterpillar eyebrow with even thicker black-framed glasses hung on a long pointed nose. How could someone bald be so hairy? I thought. Rug-like black hair swept the sides of his head around his ears to his neck, framing his shiny dome. His eyes darted in every direction, keeping tabs on our every move. During the day, he was one of the teachers at the school. His attention to our activities never ceased, as he made sure we weren't destroying the games or vandalizing the property with chalk or spray paint.

I was hanging out and shooting bumper pool with Sara and Elaine when Eddy came over to the table with The Twins, Dale and David. They huddled together, whispering to one another. Dale, the bigger twin, had a small brown envelope in his hand. David kept his eye on the counselor. Eddy grabbed the envelope and said, "Be cool. Don't let Izzo see it."

Izzo was standing next to the brand-new ping-pong table, punching it with his hairy-knuckled finger as he yelled at Sara and Elaine. Whenever one of them missed a shot, they hammered the table edge with the side of their paddle, splintering the edge.

I had to know what Eddy and The Twins were up to.

"What's happening, man?" I asked, trying to include myself.

"Me and The Twins bought a bag of pot, and we don't know how to roll it."
"I do. Let me," I said.
"You smoked pot before?" Eddy asked.

Before they could think about it, I said, "Give me the pot. I'll go in the girls' room and roll it. We'll all get high."
Eddy and The Twins looked at one another, not saying a word.
I continued: "It's better if you let me do it. Izzo can't come in the girls' room. If you try to roll it, you might get busted."
"OK. All right …," Eddy said, and he handed me the small manila envelope of pot and a pack of Bambu rolling papers.

"C'mon, Sara. Come with me," I said. Uninvited, like a puppy dog, Elaine followed Sara and me into the girls' room.
Sara was tall, with dark eyes and charcoal black hair that turned slightly under and fell just below her shoulders. I wanted to be her best friend, but Elaine always got in the way. She lived near Sara and got to spend more time with her on their walk back and forth to Middle Village.

Taking refuge at the far end of the long, white-tiled bathroom between the rows of toilet stalls, I used the deep windowsill as a counter. Elaine hovered so close that her stiff, Just Wonderful hairsprayed reddish nest of hair brushed my face. "Give me some room!" I said, making space with my elbows.
I pulled out a sheet of the thin white paper with a glue-lined edge. I had never seen rolling paper before. I tapped the manila envelope until tiny green specks of stalks and a few seeds fell into the paper crease. I gently pushed it down, smoothed out the weed, and folded the paper over the dry grass, then licked the edge and twisted the ends. It looked more like a fat piece of Mary Jane candy than a slim joint, but I was sure it would work and the next one would be better. Sara sucked her teeth and, with her hand on her hip, asked, "Did you ever do this before?"
Without looking up, I said, "They'll never know," and went on to roll the next joint.
"This better work, or they're gonna kill you," Sara said.

"Don't worry, man." And I twisted the ends of the next joint and could already see my progress.

There was a knock at the door. I scooped up everything and ran into a stall. It was Dale, one of The Twins.

"What's goin' on, man? … Hurry up."

Elaine, who had tiptoed to the door, said in a loud hush, "Get away from the door or you'll get us busted."

"All right," he said. "But hurry up!"

When I was finished rolling, I put six joints in the bag and two in my pocket. When we got outside, Dale asked, "How many joints did you get?"

"Six. That was a good bag of pot, man," I said.

David and Eddy barely took notice. They just wanted the bag with the joints so they could go outside in the schoolyard and get high.

"Hey, you're not gonna get high without us!" I said.

"OK. C'mon," Eddy said, and we sneaked down the back stairs when Izzo wasn't looking.

We stood close to one another in a tight circle outside the emergency exit door.

Eddy lit the twisted end, took a long drag, held his breath, and passed it on to Dale, who did the same. We each took a turn until it got to Sara, who choked but was better at holding it the second time around. I didn't feel any different, and I knew I had those two extra joints to myself, so I went back inside the center, where it was warm. On my way up the stairs, I got an idea. I thought I'd have some fun with them. I turned around and quietly crept back down the stairs. I heard them talking and knew they had no idea I was behind the door. I pushed the heavy door open as hard as I could. It swung open, slamming the brick wall and startling all of them. I yelled, "Izzo's coming! Run!"

They scattered so fast that before the door swung back and I could say I was only kidding, Eddy, Dale, and David, with Elaine close behind, were already through the gate. Sara was sashaying way behind them, her pocketbook swinging back and forth. When she came to the large frozen puddle just before the gate, her foot slipped out in front of her, laying her flat on her back. She

didn't get back up. I ran across the schoolyard.
"Are you all right?"
"Where's Izzo!?" she asked.
I lied and said, "I don't know. ... Maybe he ran back up the stairs to the front of the building to catch the guys coming around. ... Can you get up?"
She grabbed my hand, and I pulled her up. She stood on one foot, and I helped her hop out of the schoolyard."
"What am I going to do? My father will kill me if he finds out."
"I'll help you get around to the front of the school. We'll say we went outside to hang out — and that's when you slipped on the ice."
Her ankle blew up so big that she had to take off her shoe. Izzo called Sara's father, who came to take her home.

I called Sara the next day. When her mother answered, she told me that Sara had fractured her ankle in three places. She was in a cast and would be home for at least six weeks.
I never told her that it was a prank, but I was really glad that I'd be able to visit her every day and have her all to myself.

One afternoon while I was visiting, a snowstorm-turned-blizzard prevented me from getting home. I was awake most of the night, thrilled to be lying next to Sara. The next morning when I woke, the weatherman on the radio said it was eight degrees with a twenty-mile-per-hour northeast wind. I walked three miles facing the wind, wearing a wool miniskirt and black tights, to Grover Cleveland High School. I clutched my school binder to my chest to help block the icy wind. The thought of Sara made it all worthwhile.

Her cast finally came off, and we were back in school together, hanging out and partying again.

✷✷✷✷✷✷✷

Elaine threw a party when her mom and dad went away for the weekend. Three guys from Middle Village whom I had never met before were there

WITHOUT FAITH

with the friends from Maspeth I usually hung out with. Little John, who was seventeen and looked the oldest, had a phony draft card. We all chipped in fifty cents each and waited for the wine to get the party started. Minutes later, Little John came down the basement steps, arms filled with two brown bags of clinking bottles.

After guzzling a pint of Gallo burgundy and dancing to a few songs, I followed Sara, who had now become my best friend, into the knotty-pine basement bathroom. The stereo played The Mamas and The Papas, "Monday Monday." We were both really drunk and stumbled into the tiny bathroom together.

Sara leaned against the knotty-pine wall, smiled, and then closed her eyes. I couldn't help myself. I took her chin in my hand, tilted my head slightly, leaned into her, and our mouths touched. At last, I had finally kissed her. I closed my eyes and felt her tongue. I wanted to touch her and feel even closer. I reached under her blouse to touch her breast, when suddenly she pulled back, pushed me away, and stumbled out of the bathroom, wiping her mouth.

"What's the matter?" Elaine asked.

"Doreen tried to kiss me," Sara said.

Try! I didn't try. ... We both kissed. ... We tongue-kissed. I felt so betrayed. I know she liked it. She must have gotten scared when she realized she liked it. Me ... her best friend ... it's only because I'm a girl, I thought.

Before Elaine or Sara could tell everyone what they thought had happened, I split and went home. I stayed in all day Sunday and didn't go out until it was time for school on Monday morning.

I was a defenseless sophomore at Grover Cleveland High School, rushing down the hall to my homeroom, seeking asylum from anyone who might have recognized me from Elaine's party.

Trying to make myself invisible, I walked head down, chin tucked into my chest, hoping to recede like a turtle into my red woolen jumper. I clung to my blue three-ring binder like a shield.

DOREEN BIRDSELL

Someone yelled, "Hey, lezy!" I kept walking. I didn't look up, pretending I heard nothing. I picked up my pace just enough so it wouldn't be obvious that I was really running away from what I could no longer hide.

Chapter 15

Tracks

After Sara, I didn't try to kiss another girl again. My first love, Linda, had long forgotten me and was on her way to becoming engaged to her beautiful, blond, blue-eyed boyfriend, Robbie. They looked like male and female copies of each other.

I no longer had a "best friend." Something had changed in me. I didn't care about girlfriends or boyfriends. My only desire — and ambition — was to get high, and I wasn't going to give anyone a reason, ever again, to call me "lezy."

I wasn't afraid to go to Bedford-Stuyvesant in Brooklyn, even though it was a bad neighborhood, to buy heroin. The dealers got to know me; and because I was really tan, they sometimes spoke to me in Spanish. My "friends" trusted me to buy their drugs, and I made sure I skimmed my share off the top. It got to the point where I didn't need my own money to get high. Technically, I had become a drug dealer. After that day in the girls' bathroom at P.S. 153, I quickly graduated from pot to ups, methamphetamine, and LSD. Too many bad acid trips led me to heroin, so I could "normalize." Too often when I tripped on acid, I got paranoid and felt like I was losing my mind. Carmine Pergosi found me in Maurice Park in Maspeth. I was desperate to come down. He handed me a glassine bag that contained heroin. "If it gets really bad … take it. You can snort it," he said and left. Short black curls pasted flat to his head in the misty air. Even though he was only a year older than me, maybe seventeen, he seemed old to me. He walked hunched over, shoulders up, and hands buried deep in his jacket pockets. Carmine was a loner and used very few words when he spoke.

Having the bag of heroin in my hand was all I needed. It was enough to know that there was a way out. When I came off the trip, I opened my hand that had held that bag tight in my grip for hours. It was soaked from sweat and now probably useless, but it had been enough to know it was there if I needed it.

The next time I tripped on acid was worse. I was in Grover Cleveland Park, and the acid was bad stuff. Carmine was there again to give me a bag of dope. This time he had works, (that's what he called a needle and eyedropper), and he showed me how to mainline. Carmine popped the needle into the biggest vein in the crook of my right arm. Blood mixed with the cooked heroin and water in the syringe. He squeezed the eyedropper. The liquid mix pushed into my vein.

I was so stoned on acid. Sitting on the park bench, I glanced up at the street lamp. The glow of light around the lamp appeared as rays that shot out like stars. Everything was vivid and over-exaggerated. Then the heroin kicked in. The rays surrounding the street lamp were literally sucked back into the globe of the lamp and reduced to a soft warm glow. The browns and greens of the park were subdued, no longer luminescent. I was calm … calmer than I had ever been in my life. I felt safe and warm. I wanted to feel like this forever.

****

Most of the guys I had gone to high school with were drafted and served in Vietnam. Carmine had gotten drafted too. When he came home on leave, he was too sick to leave his parents' house. His best friend, nicknamed "Crazy Pete" partly because of his stutter and partly because of his wild frizzy Italian Afro, would visit Carmine with me every day. The three of us became good friends and got high on dope in Carmine's basement. When Carmine passed out we thought he might have OD'ed but he wasn't frothing from the mouth, so we figured it was just because he was sick. He never did get well enough to leave his parent's house.

He went back to boot camp a week later and never came home again. The word on the street was that his liver burst from untreated hepatitis. I got stoned and then attended his funeral. We reminisced about what a good guy he was and said he was brave not to tell anyone he was sick. Crazy Pete said he was too proud and didn't want anyone to find out he was a junkie.

The same year Carmine died we were all yellow at one time or another.

WITHOUT FAITH

One night I was desperate to get high and didn't have works. When I saw Richie coming up from the railroad tracks I asked him for his.

"I got hep man," he said.

"I won't get it. C'mon, lend me your works," I insisted.

Three months later I was yellow. I had found out that hepatitis had a three month incubation period and that it had to have been the night I used Richie's works. It was the only time I knowingly used dirty works.

Eventually, I knew I'd have to see a doctor to get help. I didn't want to wind up like Carmine. I had tracks on my arm and knew the doctor would see them, so I copped two bags of dope to get good and stoned and devised a plan. I went to the triangle near the end of Fresh Pond Road and sat on the park bench alone. When I was really stoned and partially nodding out I lit two cigarettes. I dragged hard on both until they were branding-iron hot. I pressed the red-hot ends into the tracks in the crook of my right arm. I watched the passing traffic and counted slowly to three. When I was sure the tracks were burned off, I checked out my new scar. It was black from the burnt skin and ash, but I hadn't felt a thing. I mostly used the vein in my right arm to shoot up, so the much smaller scar on the vein in the crook of my left arm I thought wouldn't be questionable.

I made an appointment with Dr. Jacobsen in Maspeth. He was a white-haired old man that some of the guys in my senior class at Cleveland High School went to. I thought he would be less likely to figure out that I was a needle user than my family doctor who was much younger. I told his receptionist that I was feeling queasy and needed a checkup. I taped white gauze on the burn. Of course, the doctor asked me what the bandage was all about.

"Oh, yeah ... that. I was ironing, and when I reached for the spray bottle I bumped the ironing board. It tipped the iron over right onto my arm."

He looked at the burn and retaped the bandage without question. As part of the examination, he pressed my abdomen with his fingertips.

"You have swelling here. Does it hurt?" he asked.

It hurt a little bit, but I lied and said, "No."

He looked me in the eye and asked, "Do you know anyone with hepatitis?"

"No. ... No. ... What's that?" I asked.

Without answering, he turned out the lights in the examination room and opened the blinds. Pulling down my lower eyelid, he verified his suspicions. "Yellow," he said. "Hepatitis."

Two weeks in Kew Gardens Hospital in a private room all to myself. It was great. I was in quarantine, diagnosed with hepatitis A because there was no evidence that I was a needle user. The only remedy was strict bed rest and a high-protein, low-fat diet.

It became really boring day after day in that hospital room alone. My room had a window overlooking the street next to the Interboro Parkway. I called Crazy Pete for help. The plan was that I'd leave my window open so I could hear him when he called my name from the street below. Crazy Pete threw a ball of heavy twine up to the window. He made it on the first try. I took one end and tossed the ball to the street, where he stood holding a box of pizza. He secured the box with his end of the twine, and I hoisted the pizza up to my room.
Crazy Pete also brought me pot. That really gave me the munchies, so I asked him to bring me butter cookies from the bakery. I never had to worry about hiding them, because there were never any left. The only thing I had to worry about was the smell of pot in my room and timing the nurses' visits. I smoked out the window, and no one ever suspected. When my friends visited, we blocked the door, opened the window, and smoked pot. Crazy Pete always brought the cookies.

When I finally got out of the hospital, Aunt Hazel and Uncle Ted went to Bohack's supermarket to get all the special food I would need. I was still on strict orders: bed rest and a high-protein, low-fat diet. As soon as they left, I had my chance. I needed to get to Kathy Dixon's house, ten blocks away, where I could get some dope. I ran all ten blocks in the rain. I shot up, got stoned, ran home, and was back in bed before Aunt Hazel and Uncle Ted got back from Bohack's.

Six months later, I relapsed, but this time I wasn't going to a hospital. It was summertime, and when my eyes turned yellow, I went to the beach to get tan, so Uncle Ted wouldn't find out. But he did. He came into my room one morning and said, "I want to look at your eyes. You don't look good."

He was smart now and knew that he could see the yellow in the whites of my eyes only in daylight.

He opened the blinds, turned my head toward the light, and pulled down my eyelid.

"I knew it! They're yellow! That's it. You're not getting out of here until you're finally better."

"I'm not going to that hospital again!"

"Fine. ... They didn't do anything we can't do. You'll stay right here. But you're not going out until you're better. I'm calling that doctor."

I couldn't believe it. I was a prisoner, and I was going to be sick if I couldn't get high. I had bars on my window, and Uncle Ted heard every sound, so I couldn't get Crazy Pete to help me.

Uncle Ted called the doctor, who agreed to treat me at home, and Aunt Hazel was off to the grocery store for the special diet I'd need again.

I had a habit and was going to be crawling out of my skin soon.

"I have to go out!"

"There's no way you're getting out of this house!" he said.

"I'll only be a little while. I just want to see my friends!"

"Get back in that bed, Reenie, or I swear ...!"

I was standing in front of my dresser, putting my jeans on.

"I'll go to bed when I get back."

He snapped and put his fist through the frosted glass in my bedroom door. Blood poured down his arm from the gash in his knuckles. I had never seen him like that.

After he broke the glass, I threw myself on the bed and covered my face with my arms to protect myself.

He was in such a rage that he wiped the blood all over me, screaming, "Look what you've done to me! ... Look what you made me do!"

He held himself back from hitting me probably because I was so sick, but I had to get out of the house to get some dope. He wouldn't let me go, no matter what I said. Aunt Hazel walked in the door and saw the broken glass, the blood dripping down his arm and hand, his blood all over me.

"Oh, my God, Ted!" she screamed.
"It's my blood. ... She made me do it!" he said.
"What did you do, Reenie? What did you do? You know, you can't push him to get your way!"
"I have to go out. I just have to go out," I cried.
"He's got a heart condition, Reenie! You're going to kill him ... and me too!"
I didn't care. I needed to get high, but there was no way I was getting out. I surrendered, knowing I'd be sick and not sleep for days without dope.

✲✲✲✲✲✲✲✲

Finally, I was allowed out again. I knew it wouldn't take much to get high, because I had been clean and on bed rest for two weeks.
"I'll see you later. I'm going out for a little while," I said after dinner.
"Don't come home late and wake us up," Aunt Hazel said. Uncle Ted didn't look up from his newspaper.
"I won't. I'll see you later," I said, backing down the stairs and out the side door into the early September night.
My skin was damp and my hands were clammy. I couldn't wait to get high.
I met Crazy Pete in front of the deli on the corner of 60th Drive and 60th Street in Maspeth near the Long Island Railroad tracks. This deli had become our new hangout. "You got any dope, Pete?" I asked.
"No, man. No dope, no dough."
Louis from Forest Hills Estates drove by in the new white Cadillac his father had bought him for his birthday.
"Lookin' for some hash. You got a connection?" he asked.
"Yeah. How much?" I asked.
"I'm lookin' for a pound."
This is it, I thought. We'll be getting high tonight.
I knew that twelve hundred dollars would be a good price and that he had the money.
"Meet me back here at seven o'clock, and I'll have it for you."

I had an idea. Sometimes we'd shoot up on the embankment of the railroad tracks, and I remembered seeing some broken pieces of tar that looked just like hunks of hash. I even made a joke once about selling it.

"I gotta taste it first," Louis said.
"No problem."
Marty always had hash, and he was constantly asking me to go out with him. I knew he'd give me some if I asked. Pete and I called him from the deli phone booth, and within half an hour he was on the corner. I promised to pay him back for the nickel of hash he agreed to give me.

At seven o'clock sharp, Louis was back, this time with his friend Nick.

Louis deserved to be taken. He had ripped me off once for a bundle of dope when I was dealing with Frenchie. Frenchie had a rental car, and when Louis took off without giving us the money, I told Frenchie to chase him. When Louis realized that he and his friends outnumbered us, he stopped the car and they got out. I told Frenchie to smash his car with ours. After all, ours was a rental. Louis never blamed me. I wasn't driving.

Louis and Nick got out of the Cadillac, and Crazy Pete and I met them halfway between the deli and their car.
"You got it?" Louis asked.
"Yeah. Let's make this quick before the cops come. The dicks have been watching us," I said.
"Wait a minute. I want my hit first."
"Sure. ... Here," I said and handed him Marty's nickel of hash.
It was as black as the tar that Crazy Pete and I had wrapped in tinfoil.
Louis lit up and took a hit. Then Nick did the same.
"See ... it's ... it's good shit, right?" Crazy Pete asked.
"Yeah, it's good. Where's the pound?" Louis asked.
"Where's the money?"
"I got the money. Show me the hash."
I pulled the tinfoil wad out of my burlap shoulder bag and peeled away a small piece of foil so he could see the "hash."

"Give me the money. Let's do this before we get busted. Hurry up, man."
Louis reached into his pocket and pulled out a wad of hundred-dollar bills and handed it over. I counted twelve bills and gave him the tinfoil tar ball.
"Let's get out of here before the cops come around again," I said.
Louis and Nick ran to their car and took off.
Crazy Pete and I ran to his house. Pete got his mother's car keys, and we drove to Brooklyn to cop a bundle of dope. I gave Crazy Pete a couple of bags and told him to drop me off at Old Farmers' Oval Park in Glendale. I didn't want to be anywhere near the deli in Maspeth when Louis found out that he had gotten ripped off.

I walked up the hill to the railroad tracks behind the park to find a place where I could get off. There was just enough bluish light from the park's street lamp for me to see. I tapped the white powder from the glassine bag into the bottle cap, added a few drops of water, lit a match, and watched it bubble and dilute. I put the needle into the cotton and released the rubber bubble to suck back the liquid. I pressed the 26-gauge needle into the vein of my right arm. The blood mixing in the dropper revealed that I was in the vein. I squeezed the dropper empty.

My feet were moving, but I wasn't walking. I heard someone talking very far away, but everything was dark. The voice got closer. I was being dragged by a guy with blond hair.
"Hey, man. Stay up. Keep walking. Keep walking," he said.
"Lemme stop. I wanna sit down."
"No, man. You have to keep walking. I was walking the tracks, and I found you OD'd. You're foaming from the mouth. You have to walk. If you pass out, you won't wake up!" he said.
I just wanted to stop. I just wanted to sit down and nod out and be left alone.
"Keep walking, man. If you don't, you'll die. You're lucky I was up here, man."
He dragged me down into the light of the park. It was Jackie.
I had met him a few times at the deli. Mostly, I'd see him walking the streets.

WITHOUT FAITH

He always said hello.

"I ain't leaving you until you're OK. What's today's date?"

He was really ruining my head. I wanted to get rid of him so I could nod out.

"OK. OK. ... September 8th. It's September 8th.

"What year!"

"1969. September 8th, 1969. Oh shit! It's my cousin's birthday. Shellllives across the street," I slurred.

He would not leave me and insisted on walking me across the street to my cousin's house.

"All right, man. Are you sure you'll be cool?"

"Yeah, man. I'm good. I'm real good. Thanks, Jackie. I'll see ya. You can go."

I knocked on the front door, and when it opened I fell in — right into the middle of Ann and Billy's living room.

"Hey, Ann. Happy birthday," I said, picking myself up. "I was in the neighborhood and remembered September 8th is your birthday."

A man and woman were sitting on the couch, and Ann nervously introduced us.

"Reenie, these are our friends Tom and Rose. ... Tom ... Rose, this is my cousin Reenie. ... My mother and father raised her since she was two."

Ann asked, "Reenie what are you doing to yourself? I'm in my thirties and you look older than me. You're only eighteen!"

I couldn't take it anymore. I wasn't safe in my own neighborhood. I knew Louis would be looking for me. I had more than a thousand dollars in my pocket. I almost overdosed and died. Maybe I will die next time, I thought.

"I'm shooting dope. And I can't stop," I said.

"My father was a heroin addict," Tom said.

No one said a word. Ann and Billy seemed to be as surprised as I was.

"He couldn't stop either. He went to a place called Odyssey House. He stopped for a while, but eventually he shot up again and died."

"He died?" Ann asked. "From shooting heroin?"

Billy just shook his head, looking at the ceiling, and let out a big sigh.

"Would you be willing to go to Odyssey House?" Tom asked. "It didn't work for my father, but a lot of people get straightened out there. It could work for you. My father was old and wouldn't change. You got your whole life ahead of you."

All eyes were on me. I looked at Ann and said, "I'll go … if you take me. But you can't make me see Aunt Hazel and Uncle Ted. I don't want to see their faces after you tell them."

Ann called Odyssey House. Ann and Billy said they'd take me the next day. I slept on their couch. We stopped on Grove Street at Aunt Hazel and Uncle Ted's, but I waited in the car. Ann and Billy returned with one of Aunt Hazel's best blue suitcases. She must have packed some things she thought I'd need. I couldn't face Aunt Hazel and Uncle Ted and was grateful Ann and Billy kept their promise not to make me face them.

Odyssey was on East Sixth Street between First and Second avenues in Greenwich Village.

It was September 9, 1969. We drove down Second Avenue through a canyon of brick tenements. Storefronts and fruit and vegetable markets dotted the sidewalk. Fire escapes and high-noon shadows zigzagged up the front of all the tenements. Second Avenue was aglow in the hazy September light. We passed the Fillmore East and turned left onto Sixth Street. I had been there many times before, but it never looked like this. I had spilled my morning coffee and had a big stain on the right leg of my brown tweed bell-bottoms that I had shoplifted from Clothesbug on Continental Avenue in Forest Hills the week before. I wished I looked better for this thing they called induction.

The large institutional building had a wide double staircase to the front doors, resembling a school. A wooden sign for Odyssey House Induction on the sidewalk pointed us to the basement entrance.

WITHOUT FAITH

A few metal folding chairs were lined up against the basement wall near the entrance. Beyond that were long tables with the same kind of metal chairs on either side, where people were being interviewed. An attractive black woman in her late twenties welcomed us and asked Ann and Billy to take a seat against the wall. A white guy about my age, with a crew cut and sharp creased trousers, handed me a questionnaire to fill out and walked away.

I looked over the list: What was the first drug you used? How old were you? What other drugs did you use? How often did you use?

It was easy to answer:

Cleaning fluid, airplane glue, cough medicine, pot, downs, ups, speed, LSD, and finally heroin.

I had nothing to lose, so I answered each question honestly. Then I came to a question about sex: "Have you ever had intercourse?" My answer was "No." I was proud of that ... so far so good ... no problems with this test.

"Have you ever had sex with the same gender?"

There was a notation underneath: "Sexual experience with the same gender does not necessarily mean homosexuality."

That's where my pen stopped.

The crew cut guy walked over when he saw me staring into space.

"Is there a problem?" he asked.

I was tapping my pen, not knowing how to answer.

He picked up the questionnaire, scanning the answers.

"You never had intercourse?" he asked.

"That's right," I said.

"Why is this question blank?"

"Well ... because ..." I looked across the room to where Ann and Billy sat on a bench near the door, making sure they were out of earshot. ... "Because I did have experiences," I said.

"How old were you?"

"The last time was when I was fourteen. I was drunk."

"Oh, well. ... Look what it says. You were an adolescent."

I paused to think about it.

"But I really liked her," I said.

88

"Don't worry about it. You can deal with it in treatment."

He walked over to Ann and Billy. They were nodding their heads and looking over at me. Then they just walked out the door with Aunt Hazel's suitcase.

"Hey," I yelled. "Wait a minute."

The black woman who had greeted us said, "Don't worry. You'll be OK with us. We're going to induct you today."

"What about my clothes?"

"Oh, we got clothes. We got everything you're gonna need."

WITHOUT FAITH

Chapter 16

Kents

"Doreen Birdsell, report to the supervisor's office." It blared and crackled over the PA system in the old East Village former public school building now called "Odyssey House, a Therapeutic Community for the Treatment and Prevention of Drug Addiction." I learned later that the short form for my temporary home was "TC." It was one of the few TCs in existence in the 1960s, along with Daytop Village and Samaritan House. My new address was 308 East Sixth Street in Greenwich Village.

****

I felt like an alien in this concrete institution shared by sixty other addicts of mixed ethnicity, age, criminal records, and so-called abnormal sexual orientation — definitely not the crowd I had grown up with. At least Donna Pearlman and Jeanette Bernennardi were somewhat like me — white girls, eighteen years old, and fairly new in the program. I would have bet by Donna's round freckled-face complexion and red curly hair that she was as Irish as any of the girls I had gone to Catholic school with, if it were not for her name.

I had met only one other Jewish girl when I was in grammar school — Myra Rothkersch — and at the time I thought the only thing that separated us was Holy Communion. The nuns didn't like us hanging out with kids who weren't Catholic. They said Jews weren't going to heaven because they didn't believe that Jesus was their Savior and hanging out with them could lead us astray. I brought Myra to church one Sunday and thought that would make it OK to hang out with her. It was when I was forbidden by the nuns to visit her synagogue that we had to stop seeing each other.

Jeanette was a skin-and-bones Italian girl from Scotch Plains, New Jersey, with scraggly dark hair that draped her long, droopy face. Donna and Jeanette were heroin addicts, like me. Donna had been inducted into the program from jail a month earlier and fit right in. She laughed easily and was friendly toward me. She informed me that cigarettes were free but there was a limited supply of brands handed out each morning on a first-come, first-served basis according to seniority. She asked me what kind of cigarettes I smoked and told me that if I ever got stuck with a bad brand like Kent, I could usually trade two Kents for one Marlboro.

Without drugs, it was difficult to talk to people I didn't know. Heroin made me feel sure of myself. Everything about this place was foreign, including the language. "You can't be laying in the cut," Donna said. "If you don't do as they say and try to fit in, they'll blow you away and accuse you of trying to hide out. … You know … 'laying in the cut.' … Get it?"

Donna had been serving time for possession of heroin when she found out about a program that allowed drug addicts to be released to a TC if they expressed a desire to get help. Donna, as well as many others at Odyssey, thought a TC would be much easier than jail. I had never had any friends who were black or Hispanic — only drug dealers. It didn't matter here. I quickly learned that we were all the same and that it was essential for survival to remember that. Dr. Judianne Densen-Gerber, the founder and program director, called it a bureaucracy that worked. I was too scared to talk to anyone except Donna.

She took me to the Girls' Dorm and pointed to the community closet, where she said I had to pick out an outfit every morning. I was assigned a drawer and given two nightgowns, underwear, and socks that I was responsible for washing by hand. The outfit of the day would go to housekeeping to be laundered and ironed by the residents assigned to that department. The community closet held dresses, skirts, blouses, and shoes in all sizes, which were donated by outside sources. There were no pants for lower-level girls.

"You have to give up your clothes and take a shower," Donna said. Silently, I gave up my coffee-stained bell-bottoms and stripped down to shower.

I didn't sleep all night, and I couldn't stand lying in bed going through withdrawal. Kicking off the covers, I slid from the top bunk and wandered the halls in my cotton nightgown, even though I knew it was against the rules. I needed to get a feel for where I was. I was careful to stay close to the walls and keep to the shadows.

I made my way down three flights of a chicken-wire glass stairway. The glow from the lampposts on East Sixth Street was enough to illuminate the hallway. The only other light was from the front hall office where a resident called "the night man" kept watch and answered the phone that occasionally rang. When I reached the front door, I knew there was nowhere else to go. Carefully, I made my way back to my bunk. I tossed and turned until the bell rang for the community to wake up and shower before breakfast.

A woman with a short-cropped pixie haircut jockeyed for first pickings in the community closet, but no one seemed to mind. She squeezed out a solid black cotton dress that was jammed so tight between the other clothes they could have stayed suspended without the help of hangers and a pole. Her skinny white legs were scarred from the ankles up to her thighs.

Donna said Judy Katz had been on crutches for a month while she was kicking dope. She had blown all the veins in her legs — that and dirty needles caused abscesses, which became infected, leaving the disfiguring circular scars.

After breakfast, I was assigned to the kitchen and introduced to my department head, Nadine Thompson. She had a flattop Afro like an inverted triangle and a tiny belted waistline. I had to work in the kitchen scrubbing the underside of a wrought iron commercial stove with a steel wool pad.

Who the hell would care about shit under the stove top? I thought. *And no Brillo or S.O.S. pad? Just steel wool?*

"Oh, yeah ... and another thing," Nadine said. "No looking out those windows. I don't care what you think you hear out there. You don't look. It's against the rules. If you do ... you get your privileges taken away each time."

What privileges? There are privileges? I thought.

I don't know if she read my mind or my expression gave me away.

"For starters ... there'll be no dessert. Keep it up ... there'll be no cigarettes."

That got my attention. I turned to the huge greasy stove armed with a steel wool pad and an army-size soup pot filled with soapy water.

DOREEN BIRDSELL

Sweating in the hot, glossy yellow kitchen and finished with my task, I leaned back against the wall, staring at the clean matte black metal monster. Nadine came behind me and reached under the stove top, submerged up to her shoulder, and scraped the farthest corner with her fingernail to make sure I had done my job thoroughly.

She stuck her black grease-crusted fingernail in my face and said,

"You'll be cleaning this all night until you get this right, girl."

What a pain in the ass. I never did shit like this in my life. The most I ever had to do when I lived at home was make my bed and once in a while dry the dinner dishes.

✳✳✳✳✳✳✳

After three weeks, I finally slept through the night without waking up kicking, sweating, or getting sick. I was still assigned to the kitchen to clean that damned greasy stove when I heard my name called over the loudspeaker: "Doreen Birdsell, report to the supervisor's office." I didn't care what it was for, as long as it got me out of that greasy, burned-bacon stinking kitchen.

I closed the door behind me and stood in front of a tawny-complexioned man in his early thirties whom I hadn't met before. He resembled a young Nat King Cole.

He told me his name was Lamont Champlain and he was a Level Four supervisor. I knew that he had to be in the program at least a year to get that far.

"Doreen, I have good news for you. You're going to the Bronx to be in the new core group of the Adolescent Treatment Unit. You leave tomorrow with some of the other young residents. How do you feel about that?"

"I don't know? Good ... I guess."

Anything was better than this, but I wasn't going to tell him that. I wasn't going to tell anybody how I felt about anything. I figured I was better off if I kept my mouth shut as much as possible and did what I was told. As long as I didn't get accused of "laying in the cut."

WITHOUT FAITH

I hadn't been outside since the day I was inducted, September 9, 1969.

It had been four weeks since I had looked out a window, except for an occasional stolen glance. Looking out a window was a Level Two privilege that took about three months and good behavior to achieve. I wasn't even a Level One yet, and I was going out! In the East Village! And then on a subway ride all the way to the Bronx!

Nadine, who was a Level Three, would escort Donna, Jeanette, and me to our new home on Bruckner Boulevard in the Hunts Point section of the Bronx. The only place in the Bronx that I knew was the Whitestone Drive-In, off the Hutchinson River Parkway. Aunt Hazel and Uncle Ted had taken me there on hot summer nights when I was little. The playground at the foot of the giant screen and the cartoons during intermission were my favorite parts. I wondered how far the drive-in was from where I was going to live.

I braced myself against the cool October air as though it were the first time I had felt an autumn breeze. We were hustled so quickly down the block and down the stairs under the street to the screaming subway trains that all I saw were feet, concrete sidewalk, and faceless storefronts along the way.

In the Bronx, I was quickly ushered up a dank, dark subway staircase that stunk like piss to the street above. I was blinded by sunlight. Cars quickly passed one another going in opposite directions on Hunts Point Boulevard. One side of the street was lined with three-story brick tenements. Iron girders, trucks, and smokestacks rising from the decks of oil freighters lined the water's edge on the other side. Cars whirred and trucks rumbled on the Bruckner Expressway overpass high above the boulevard.

The four of us walked down a vacant sidewalk, passing boarded-up tenement buildings, some with signs that read, "Condemned." None of us spoke, although we were allowed to.

"This is it. The ATU," Nadine said.

It was a lot smaller than the mother house of sixty residents in Greenwich Village. Here there would be only about twenty of us, including staff.

The only person older than me was Lillian Flores, the new Level Four supervisor. Probably in her late twenties, she was attractive and had an athletic figure, short brown side-parted hair and a smile that welcomed us.

Donna, Jeanette, and I shared a room in the back of the house on the third — top — floor. The beds were covered in terry cloth spreads, and the walls and ceiling were painted bright celery green. Donna claimed the single bed because she was a Level One and had seniority. Jeanette and I shared the bunk bed. That was fine with me. I got the top. We shared two dressers and a closet filled with clothes that would be our new wardrobe. It would take about six months for me to become a Level Three. Then I'd be able to get my own clothes from home.

Jeanette, who had always kept to herself, started to talk more freely.
"My mother and father busted me with a bag of pot and some tabs of acid. They made me go to a shrink. Then they found my works and knew I was shooting dope. That's when they sent me here. I should have been more careful, but I was so fucked up ... I didn't know," she said.

That was the most she had said to me in the four weeks I had known her. I wondered how long she would last. A lot of people split the program. In the short time I had been there, I had heard stories about people who split, overdosed, and died. In group therapy, I was told that if I took all my negativity and turned it into positive use, I could be very successful. I thought about that a lot and wondered, "What would I do?" I could do anything if I didn't get high. I didn't want to split. I wanted to graduate from that program as fast as possible.

Unlike Jeanette, Donna *never* stopped talking. Her curly red hair bounced around her face when she got excited. She nudged me every time she said something to make sure she had my attention or until I would agree with her. I had no choice, because she had Level One seniority, which she always made sure to remind me of.

The morning after we got there, we had a general meeting and met the rest of the residents. They were all male, mostly African-American and Hispanic.

WITHOUT FAITH

One kid, Benedito, was only fourteen years old. I couldn't believe he was already a junkie.

I was in group therapy every day and was assigned to the housekeeping crew. One day melted into the next. Breakfast, morning meeting, group therapy, lunch, clean the house, iron shirts, coffee break, iron more shirts, dinner, group therapy, hang out in the community room with Clayton, who taught me to play congas. We beat Latin Percussion congas, while Jose played along with a drumstick on the cowbells and we sang "Chinko…Chinko-Bah-Bah" until bedtime.

One evening after supper, Nadine sent me to the supervisor's office. I had become a Level One. Lillian, the house supervisor, had never had a conversation with me directly, but there was something I had liked about her from the first day she welcomed us, and I felt that I could trust her. Lillian always looked like she had a tan and kept her hair cut very short and sporty. When I walked into her office, she was standing behind her desk facing me. She leaned over, palms flat on the desk and said, "Doreen, it takes people about eighteen months to get through this program. If you stay here in the Adolescent Unit, you'll *probably* graduate in about a *year* and go right back out there and use again."

"What do you mean?" I asked.

"You're too smart. You get away with too much here with these kids. Your peers don't challenge you. I'm sending you to the Garden State house in Newark, where you'll live with adults. It's for your own good. Those people will read right through your games, and you'll get what you need to stay clean."

"I don't understand. … What games? … I'm not smarter than anybody here."

"You don't need to bring anything. They'll have what you need at the Garden State house. Get a coat. Jose will take you tonight on the subway and then to the PATH train."

For a moment, I felt her sincerity in the warmth of her brown eyes, and I wanted to cry. But I girded myself until the muscles in my neck and throat ached, holding back the tears.

"This is for your own good, Doreen."

She drew her attention back to the papers on her desk and dismissed me: "That's all, Doreen."

DOREEN BIRDSELL

My hands had turned into balled fists, with my fingers curled around my thumbs. Jose was already standing outside holding my coat.

I couldn't even say goodbye to Donna and Jeanette. I had to leave immediately with Jose. With his hands tucked in his leather waist jacket and head down to the wind, we walked side by side, arms brushing, in the darkness to the subway. His burgundy iridescent pants were so tight that his thigh muscles bulged when he walked.

Newark was as foreign to me as Hunts Points in the Bronx had been. Lincoln Park appeared to have once been an upscale neighborhood, judging by the brownstone mansion that seemed to take up the entire block. On the side streets were wooden two-story houses with peeling paint and black windows. Jose said some rich doctor had donated the brownstone to the program. I knew I wouldn't be seeing the outside of this house for a long time.

The next morning after the general meeting, I was given a job in housekeeping and tried to blend in.

Walter Taylor was in his late thirties and was from New Jersey — transferred from prison to Odyssey House, just like Donna Pearlman, my first friend in the program. I wondered when I might see Donna again. Franchot Jones had been busted for grand larceny and came from the same prison as Walter. They were both in my group therapy. I was now the youngest, not the oldest, except for another state prison inductee, Furman Greene from Trenton, who was also eighteen. He and I measured about the same height, five feet six inches, although his flattop Afro added at least three more inches. Furman was the first guy my own age who ever complimented me on my appearance. I did my work and learned how to get by without getting in trouble, and after six months I made it to Level Three.

One Sunday afternoon while I was leaning back on my bed, flipping through the pages of a magazine, Leslie Mascaro, a new resident, sauntered into the Women's Apartment. She threw herself on top of me and tried to kiss me. I flipped her over on the bed and pinned her down. "What are you — fucking crazy? Don't you ever come near me, or I'll turn you in for breaking a cardinal rule. You'll get thrown out. Do you understand?!"

"I thought you were a lezy," she said.

"I'm not! Don't ever come near me again," I said, releasing her.

She didn't come near me after that and didn't dare look at me, not even during group. Within a week, she split the program.

I hadn't seen Aunt Hazel and Uncle Ted for six months. Because I had worked my program, I was allowed a visit from home. My palms were wet. What would it be like to see them? Could they still be angry with me? I hoped they knew I was trying to change.

We met in the wood-paneled conference room. They were already sitting at the long table when I entered the room. Their hair was silver-gray. It wasn't that silver when I left, I thought. Was it my fault? Did I make them worry so much their hair turned silver?

"How do you like it here? Do they treat you all right?" Tazel asked. "Ted painted your room," she added.

Painted my room? I thought. They must be waiting for me to come home.

Our visit lasted only half an hour.

In the hallway, we said goodbye. Aunt Hazel hugged me and said, "I love you, Reenie."

That was the first time I had ever heard her say that.

Our eyes held each other's for a moment, and then they were gone.

After eleven months of group therapy, working in the kitchen, housekeeping, and the business office, I had made the Garden State Odyssey House my home. It didn't matter that we were all different colors and ages, where we came from, or what we did. We were all the same — trying to live without drugs.

Furman and I both made it to Level Three. He was appointed house coordinator, the highest possible position for a Level Three. I was made department head of the business office. At Level Three, men and women were allowed to talk to each other without a third person being present. He and I had become good friends.

I was sitting at a small desk on the landing outside the Women's Apartment when Furman pressed a tightly folded piece of paper into my hand and walked away without a word. The note read, "I think about you all the time but not as a friend. I had to tell you — Furman."

My heart raced like I was on speed. I liked him too. He had a button nose on a big brown shiny face like a teddy bear. Mostly what I liked was that he thought of me so much that he took a big chance telling me. "If I told anyone he could be busted down for doing this … and so could I," I thought.

I made a decision not to tell.

A week later, the staff decided to transfer Furman to Gramercy Park in New York to be the house coordinator there; I would be promoted to the house coordinator in the Garden State house. The house coordinator was in charge of the entire facility. It was the highest position I could get before becoming a staff person and graduating.

Furman was the only friend I had, and he was leaving. I couldn't believe they were doing this to me. Every time I got close to someone or began to feel at home, it was taken away from me. I couldn't stand it, and I didn't know what to do.

"Who gives a shit about being a house coordinator. Who will I talk to? Who's going to be my friend?" I thought. I felt so alone.

When I saw Furman, he didn't speak to me. Instead, he passed me a note: "Meet me in the second floor bathroom after lights out."

I couldn't wait for eleven o'clock to see him privately before he left for good.

When I was sure everyone was asleep, I slipped into the bathroom that was in the hallway outside the door of the apartment. There was a tap at the door. "It's Furman," he whispered. I quickly opened the door, and he slipped inside. Before I could say a word, he pressed himself against me, put his arms around me, and put his tongue inside my mouth. The next thing I knew, we were on the floor and he was unbuckling his pants and pulling at my panties.

Even though I was no stranger to male parts, I had never let a guy have sex with me before. I lay there wondering, "Is this what making love is?" It felt awkward and uncomfortable. The excitement about meeting each other in

WITHOUT FAITH

secret was much better than lying on this cold floor with his full weight on me.

His pants were open, and he thrust himself into me. I felt only pain, not pleasure. I pulled away. "It's all right. ... I'll be gentle," he whispered. I tried to relax. He pushed harder, and I told myself this felt good even though it didn't. He pushed harder again. I put my hand between my legs, grabbed his penis, and felt it bend in my hand. He moaned in what I think was pain but still pushed, trying to get inside me. There was a knock on the door. "Who's in there?"

Furman pulled back in retreat. It was James, the night man, making the rounds. I just lay there stunned and silent. Furman lifted his head and said, "It's just me. Furman. I'll be right out." We rose to our feet, careful to not make a sound adjusting our clothes. I knew we were in trouble. Furman slipped out and closed the door behind him. I heard James and him talking but couldn't make out what they were saying. I kept my eyes squeezed shut with my body pressed against the wall, wishing I could crawl under the wallpaper to hide. The door opened again. It was James.

The next morning, a special staff meeting was called because of our actions. "Furman Greene, report to the conference room" came over the house PA system. I had resumed my duties as usual and waited. At least an hour ticked by. "Doreen Birdsell, report to the conference room."

Furman wasn't in the room, and I wondered what had happened to him, but I didn't dare ask. Dr. Judianne Densen-Gerber had come all the way from New York. She was with the house supervisor, the house nurse, and my group counselor. I was too afraid to lie, so I told them about the notes and meeting Furman to say goodbye. The nurse asked, "Doreen, do you think you could be pregnant?"

"No. We never really had intercourse."

"You are a disgrace," Dr. Judi said, sitting at the head of the table. "You're being discharged. You can reenter the program as a boarder at the Gramercy Park house and start over from the bottom."

I went to the office and was given one dollar for the train. I couldn't go home to face Aunt Hazel and Uncle Ted. They'd be so ashamed of me. I was ashamed of myself.

DOREEN BIRDSELL

I went directly to East Twentieth Street. When I got to the brownstone in Gramercy Park, I was told that I'd have no privileges. I would be given no cigarettes for thirty days and could talk to no one except authority figures. A cardboard sign hung from my neck to my knees and in big red letters read, "Do not talk to me. I broke a cardinal rule." I was assigned to the housekeeping crew and given a rag to start dusting the banisters. Strangers brushed past me without making eye contact. I was ashamed and alone and I really wanted a cigarette.

I lasted three days. I went to the office and said, "I have to leave. I can't hack this." I was given a subway token, and I asked for a pack of cigarettes. The guy behind the desk handed me a pack of Kents. They were always the leftover brand. As soon as I got outside, I was free but in a cold and strange place. I lit up one of the Kent cigarettes and inhaled deeply.

I got on the subway and then took the orange Triboro bus from Queens Boulevard back to Ridgewood — back to Tazel and Uncle Ted. I was so ashamed, and I knew I had disappointed them again.

I hadn't seen them for months, and now I had to see them like this. I knew that someone from the program would have called them to say I had left.

It was a damp, gray morning that chilled me like autumn, even though it was early September — almost a year since I had overdosed and left them without a word. I slowly walked down the alleyway. I knew Uncle Ted would be at work. The side door was unlocked, as always. I stepped on the familiar black-rubber-matted steps that led to our kitchen.

Aunt Hazel was standing in front of the stove, wearing an apron and holding a dish towel. Her grayish-blue eyes filled with tears when she saw me. Her lips trembled, and the towel dropped to the floor. She rushed toward me with her arms open wide. Hugging me and crying, she said, "I'm so glad you're home. I'm so glad you're home. I'm so glad you're not in that place anymore."

"I'm so sorry, Tazel. I'm so sorry." I couldn't believe she wasn't angry.

Suddenly, I flashed back to being twelve years old when Uncle Ted drove by the corner where I hung out with my friends and saw me smoking a cigarette.

WITHOUT FAITH

He whistled and yelled, "Get home!"

I expected to be beaten to a pulp, have my bike taken away, and not be able to go out for who knows how long. Instead, he said, "If you're going to smoke, do it here and not behind our backs. Now eat your dinner."

Chapter 17

Hitting a Wall

For the first time in my life, Uncle Ted sat down with me at the kitchen table and actually talked to me. "Reenie ... life is hard enough. You cannot go out with a colored. Not while you're living in this house!"

"It's not fair. His color doesn't make any difference. I lived with all kinds of people in the program. We all got along ... "

"This is not Odyssey House. This is how the world is." He didn't yell or insist but instead was trying to reason with me.

My sister, Donna, had her own place in Port Chester, and I knew she'd let me stay with her until Furman and I figured out what to do.

Good secretarial skills enabled me to get a job right away at the Economist Intelligence Unit. My bosses made the mistake of giving me a key to their offices, which were conveniently located one block from Grand Central Station at Third Avenue and 42nd Street. I commuted from my sister's apartment in the south end of Port Chester.

It was a three-story gray clapboard tenement. A dilapidated wooden staircase on the back of the building led to the kitchen door. The gas oven burned most of the day, with the door open to heat the small living room and two small bedrooms behind it.

Donna had been living on welfare with a black guy named Lucky, who had gotten her pregnant when she was twenty years old. They named the boy Stanley, Lucky's real name. Donna said she had what she always wanted — "a family." When Lucky wasn't home shooting dope or cocaine, he was usually in jail for stealing to support his habit.

Furman had started shooting dope again, and I went on a methadone program. No matter what, there was no way that I was going back to Odyssey House. I would save up my doses of methadone so I wouldn't get addicted to methadone and still be able to occasionally get high on dope.

My job at the Economist Intelligence Unit lasted only a few weeks. My

WITHOUT FAITH

tardiness got me fired, but I didn't turn in the keys to the offices. I made good money, but it was never enough to stay high and live.

The following Monday before 8 a.m., I let myself into the Economist Intelligence Unit and found the checkbook in the top desk drawer, where I had seen my former boss put it.

I tore out two checkbook pages from the back of the book, then grabbed a few pieces of office stationery and put it in my pocketbook. I pressed the elevator button, my pulse throbbing in my throat, and walked through the marble lobby to the revolving doors that seemed a mile away.

Furman was waiting for me on the corner. We ducked into the nearby coffee shop, where I wrote out a check for $300, and took it to the check-cashing place near Grand Central on 45th off Lexington. I used the office stationery I had stolen to verify my employment, which gave authorization to cash the check under my false identity, Delores Ward.

The small check-cashing office was only three blocks away, next to Grand Central. I hoped the cashier wouldn't sense that I was scared shitless.

Keeping my eyes down, I slid the check across the steel-barred glass-enclosed counter with the authorization letterhead. The white-haired man started counting out twenty-dollar bills, and my pulse quickened. Furman, who was waiting outside, ran with me to Lexington Avenue to catch the double L to Canarsie, where our connection lived. We copped our drugs and got off at the dealer's house.

We drifted in and out of a drugged stupor all the way home on the New Haven Line to my sister's place in Port Chester. We arrived with a bundle of dope and some money left over to give Donna.

My sister didn't like to shoot or even snort dope — maybe an occasional line of cocaine — which was fine with me. There was more for us. I speedballed a combination of cocaine and heroin and mainlined it for the rush of coke and then the downward slide stoned on dope.

It was too easy and too tempting, and the drugs were gone so fast that we went back to the city to cash another check the next day.

What the hell. The company's not going to know I passed a bad check yet, I thought.

Another check, another round of speedball, and another trip back to the city, and then another. Three days passed by, and I knew that if I tried to cash another check it might be the last.

"Look, Furman. If we get busted, don't say we're drug addicts. I don't want that on my record."

"OK, man. Don't worry. You're not gonna get busted."

I passed the check across the counter, through the barred window, to the white-haired man. He lifted the check off the counter to get a closer look. "It's her! With the bad checks! Get her!"

As I turned to run for the door, a giant Swedish-masseur-sized woman grabbed me by the hair and pulled me into the doorway through the metal partition. I struggled with every ounce of strength I had, swinging my arms, kicking her shins; but no matter what I did, I couldn't break her grip. The white-haired old cashier threw himself in there too. I was frantically flailing my arms and legs to tear out of their grip. I was jammed in the doorway. The old white-haired cashier slammed the metal door against my back over and over because I wouldn't give in.

Several police officers ran into the store, and it was all over. They cuffed me and took me outside to the street, where they held Furman handcuffed next to a patrol car. A cop read me my rights, and they took us away in separate cars to the local police precinct, where I was fingerprinted, photographed, and locked up to wait for night court.

I thought for sure I'd be home in a few hours, because it was my first offense. I used up my one phone call to call my sister to tell her we were busted.

"Donna, no matter what, do not tell Aunt Hazel and Uncle Ted that I am arrested," I said.

"Are you sure, Reenie?"

"Don't tell them, Donna. I'll get out of this. I don't want them to know. Promise me."

"OK. OK. Oh, Reenie. What are you gonna do?"

WITHOUT FAITH

The cop pulled the phone from my ear. "That's enough."

The charges were grand larceny, forgery, and fraud.
Because I had no previous arrests or convictions on record, the public defender asked the judge to let me go on my own recognizance.
The district attorney rose to his feet. "Your honor, she cashed three checks, not one. Three. Totaling $1,100."
"$5,000 bail!" the judge said and slammed the gavel.

That was it. I was off to the Women's House of Detention in Greenwich Village.
I couldn't believe it. I should have gotten away from that lady at the check-cashing place. I should have been let go without bail. I shouldn't be here at all!

It was late at night when I was transported from the courthouse holding pen to the Women's House of Detention on Greenwich Avenue. First, I was stripped and body-searched; then I was put in a cell in solitary until the prison doctor could check me out before I was admitted into the general population.

When I took off my clothes, the black-and-blues had already swelled up on my arms and legs from my resisting arrest. The doctor asked me how I had gotten so bruised. I told him about the cashier who kept slamming a steel door against me to stop me from running away. The doctor nonchalantly resumed the exam, and I was brought upstairs to a different cell.

On the elevator ride, I was with two guards and half a dozen other inmates. We stopped on one floor, and when the doors opened there were inmates walking back and forth in a hallway. They were mostly black and Hispanic women, but there was also a guy who looked to be in his twenties walking hand in hand with a brown skinned woman about the same age. "I thought this was the Women's House of Detention and there are no men here?" I asked. The guard and the elevator operator laughed. "Those are women."

I hadn't been issued clothing yet. I wore only the examination robe I had been given after I had been stripped of even my underwear. A prison guard put

me in a cell, and the steel door bolted shut.
I felt something warm and wet on my leg.
Oh, shit. I got my period!
"Guard!" I yelled down the hollow, shadowy hallway.
"I got my period. I need a sanitary napkin."
What a fuckin' day. It's not going to end, I thought.
The guard came back with an industrial-size pad as big as a hammock.
She handed it to me between the bars, and then I realized I couldn't attach it to anything.
"How am I going to hold this up?"
"With your hands."
The other inmates on the hall were beginning to understand that I was a virgin to the jail system — a virgin with her period.

"Hey, white girl. What you doin' in there?!" an anonymous voice called out.
My instincts said, "Be tough, and don't let on that you're scared shit."
"What the fuck do you care, bitch?" I yelled back.
"I'm going to kick your fuckin' ass, you punk!"
"You ain't gonna do shit in here," I yelled back.
What can they do? I'm behind bars, and my mouth is the only way I know how to protect myself, I thought.
Down the hall, somebody was heaving like she was throwing up; across from my cell, someone was sobbing.
I couldn't think past my current predicament. How would I survive the night?

I pressed my head against the bars to get a better view of the hallway. A rat ran back and forth between the shadows on the gray concrete floor.

I lay down and tried to sleep, but sleep would not come. It had been too long since I had had a fix, and I was beginning to get sick.
The girl down the hall who was throwing up called the guard, "I'm puking blood, man!"
A guard came, opened her cell, and took her away.

WITHOUT FAITH

A short while later, there was activity in the hallway. The puking girl was being brought back. One of the inmates in a nearby cell asked, "How ya doin', man?"

"They fixed me with some meth 'cause I was puking blood."

I was going out of my mind in that cage. I was sick and began to panic.

If I could only sleep, but I can't. ... If I could just get knocked out. Maybe if I bang my head against the wall, it'll knock me out.

The wall of my cell had large tiled squares. If I hit it hard enough, it should work. I braced myself on the edge of my bunk to back up as far as possible. I thrust myself headfirst into the wall with as much force as I could from the short distance between the bunk and the concrete wall.

I was more conscious now of the pain in my forehead. A fear ran through me. I was out of control, and there was nothing I could do to stop it. I trembled and my knees shook. There was only about two feet between my bunk and the wall. I backed up again and pressed myself into the bunk for more force and sprung off both my feet, headfirst, and lunged into the green wall. My fear and frustration outweighed the throb of my forehead.

Then it occurred to me that if I bit the inside of my mouth and spit blood in the toilet, I could say I was puking blood and maybe I'd get some methadone. I didn't care anymore if they found out I was an addict. I just wanted to sleep. All I wanted was the peace there was in sleep. I bit hard on the inside of my mouth and sucked out the blood and spit in the toilet. I gagged, coughed, and spit. "I'm puking blood! I'm puking blood!"

The guard opened my cell and stepped past me to verify that there was blood in the toilet.

Five milligrams of methadone in a pink liquid solution administered in a paper cup was all I was given. I had taken as much as a hundred milligrams when I was on the methadone program. Five milligrams was barely enough to do anything, but it was enough to take the edge off and to stop me from thinking about ramming my head against the wall.

Curled up in my bunk, with my hands clutched between my thighs partly to keep the huge sanitary pad from slipping, I waited for the night to end.

The next day, I was released into the general population and sent to the community shower. I was naked standing in an open shower stall in a room about twenty by thirty feet with four shower stalls, a couple of sinks, and a heavy metal door with a window to the outside hall, where the matron kept guard. Four or five women stood a few feet away. They were talking about me while I showered as though I wasn't even there.

"Let's see what that white girl's got."

"I bet she got somethin' good," said another.

Holy shit. How am I going to protect myself? What can I use besides my fists? I thought.

I was naked with only a bar of soap. I reached up to the round metal showerhead and tried to rip it out of the wall. I pulled it with all my might, and at that moment, out in the hallway someone yelled, "BIRDSELL, BAIL! BIRDSELL, BAIL!"

I screamed, "That's me. That's me. I'm in here." The shower room door opened, and the guard stood between us as a barricade, protecting me from those girls. Looking around, she said, "Who's Birdsell?"

"Me. ... I'm Birdsell!"

"You got bail. Get out of here."

A guard took me back to my cell, gave me my clothes and told me to get dressed.

As I passed through the gate at the end of the hall to freedom, I yelled out to those bitches, "By the time your face is in your lunch, I'll be cooking up my dope."

I had no idea who posted bail for me and figured maybe it was Furman's family. But when I got downstairs, Aunt Hazel and Uncle Ted were waiting for me. I thought they'd be so angry, but Aunt Hazel's eyes were wet and bloodshot, and she asked, "Are you OK?"

"I'm fine," I said, and Uncle Ted breathed what seemed to be a sigh of relief.

They put up $500 for my bond. I knew that was their vacation money. Donna didn't listen to me. She called Aunt Hazel and Uncle Ted and told them

WITHOUT FAITH

I was in jail, and I was so glad she did.

Being outside seemed like a new world. I hadn't known when I would be out again or what would happen to me. Two days felt like a lifetime. I drank a Coca-Cola, and it tasted like I hadn't had one for years. My aunt and uncle didn't yell. They really just wanted to know how to help.

"I'll go back to work and pay you back and never do anything so stupid again."

On the drive back to Port Chester, I asked, "Can you give me twenty dollars so I can get my work clothes out of the cleaners?"

Aunt Hazel reached over and handed me a twenty-dollar bill. They dropped me off on Main Street. I waved goodbye and headed down South Main to the dealer in town to cop a bag of dope.

Chapter 18

How Lucky

Lucky was arrested for burglary on the same day that I was arrested for grand larceny, forgery, and fraud. However, he didn't get out and had to serve time. I was exonerated on the condition that I would attend six months of group therapy for drug addiction, once a week, and make restitution to Irving Trust Bank, which honored the checks that I had cashed. The company whose checks I had stolen and the bank agreed to drop charges upon my meeting the court's conditions.

Donna and little Stanley moved to a better neighborhood in Port Chester with her high school friend Beverly. I went back home to live with Aunt Hazel and Uncle Ted.

Life at home would never be the same. I couldn't believe that my aunt and uncle put up with me. They were in their sixties and were still willing to take me back if, as always, I lived by their rules, and now the rules of the court.

Group therapy was in Brooklyn, where I went directly from my temp job in the city once a week. My secretarial skills always enabled me to get work and for what I thought was decent pay. Every Friday after my temp assignment, I'd cash my paycheck and go to the offices of Irving Trust Bank at Third Avenue and 42nd Street. Every week, I had to return to the bank that was in the same building as the company I had stolen the checks from. Eleven hundred dollars in restitution, fifty dollars a week. The same mustached banker, the same questions — "How are you doing? Are you going to your groups?" — and me pretending to know better.

I took methadone almost every day. I wasn't a kid anymore, and my life took on a more serious tone. I had to pay bills, go to group therapy, and work every day. I only wanted to be with Furman, but it would be impossible while living at home.

How in the world am I going to live my life like this? I'm not on drugs anymore. I make a decent living. I'm not going to give up Furman just because

WITHOUT FAITH

he's black. Something's got to change.

Living in New York made job hunting easy. There were many jobs for people with my skills. I chose companies in fields that seemed to interest me. I thought I could combine having fun and a future with where I worked. The interviewer always perked up when I asked, "Is there opportunity for advancement?" I had temped as a secretary for CBS Music, ABC, and United Artists. I would always imagine that one day I would have a secretary, not be one. All I wanted now was to make the most possible money and get out from under my aunt and uncle's roof.

The Muscular Dystrophy Association had a position open in the research department, and a prominent Madison Avenue architect was looking for an administrative assistant. I had no aspirations, so I took the first job offer, in the unglamorous gray offices of the Muscular Dystrophy Association. It was one of the most boring, tedious assignments I had ever had — typing grant applications most of the day and then filing correspondence — but I was paid $225 a week.

Methadone helped me to stay clean. I knew I couldn't do it on my own, and there was no way I was ever going to start over again at Odyssey House. The methadone program, like this job, was the first thing that came along and also offered the easiest solution.

In 1971, methadone was a brand new band-aid for the problem of heroin addiction. Although it was a federally regulated substance, the doctors who prescribed it were liberal in how much they dispensed. They gave me a seven-day supply of methadone in 100-milligram doses. And if I said I was going on vacation or I had "lost" it, they'd give me more or replace it.

This was potent stuff. The first time I took a dose, I was riding the bus and nodded off. I came to when the bus hit a bump, and I was afraid that if I passed out again I would overdose like I did on heroin. I got off the bus before my stop and called Wyckoff Heights Hospital from the corner telephone booth and asked if I could overdose. The woman on the other end asked how many milligrams I had taken and told me that I had nothing to worry about.

DOREEN BIRDSELL

I spent a lot of time in the stall of the ladies' room at the Muscular Dystrophy Association. Every day, I'd be in there throwing up, nodding out, or trying to have a bowel movement. Methadone made me so constipated I'd push, grab onto the toilet dispenser, squeeze, and pray to pass that brick. I saw a doctor because of rectal bleeding and was relieved to find out that it was only what he called a broken fissure from straining.

The people in the office were so lax that by the time I did sit down at my desk and get some work done, I'd churn it out so fast that it made up for all those toilet sessions.

The interview for the company that didn't offer me a position was at H.R. Mezzer & Sons at Madison Avenue and 59th Street on the third floor. The firm consisted of three generations of architects — grandfather, son, and grandson —plus an engineer, six or seven draftsmen, a mailroom boy, and two administrative assistants.

My new interview outfit consisted of a corduroy cocoa brown hot-pants suit with matching suspenders and a burgundy turtleneck sweater. The first-generation architect, a frail-figured eighty-or-so-year-old senior partner, briefly monitored his son's interview with me. The grandfather never looked me in the eyes. The entire time, he stared at my legs and never shifted his gaze while his son, Harold Mezzer, dictated a letter.

I had forgotten about that interview until two or three weeks later. I received a phone call at home one night. "Hello, Doreen? This is Laurie from H.R. Mezzer & Sons. If you are still available, Mr. Mezzer would like to know if you would like to accept a position as administrative assistant."

The thought of another day in the bathroom stalls at the Muscular Dystrophy Association was enough for me to accept the position.

The drab West Side office building I had been in couldn't compare to Madison Avenue and 59th Street, and it was an easier commute.

This place was first-class and paid for lunch every Friday. The delivery boy from the restaurant we ordered from wore a white jacket, bow tie, and white

WITHOUT FAITH

gloves. The Reuben sandwich was my Friday favorite.

While going through my desk drawer one day I came across a folder that contained the records of all the interview appointments for my position. There were dozens of pages about applicants who had been interviewed.

Who interviews more than sixty people for a job like this? I thought.

It wasn't a particularly demanding position — receive clients, make appointments, answer telephones, write letters, take dictation.

I was getting a little suspicious. Every time I would go in to take dictation, Mr. Mezzer would close the door but leave it partially ajar. One day, when he was done dictating, he got up from behind his desk and walked over and closed the door. He walked over to me, leaned over, and kissed me. I was stunned but not too surprised. He was a terrible kisser. With his mouth closed tight he pushed his tongue between his lips. It felt more like a wet crayon than a tongue. My first attempt at tongue kissing with Linda when I was twelve years old was better than this. I pushed him away, walked out of his office, and left for home.

I sneaked off to Trenton, New Jersey, every weekend to see Furman, but I would tell my aunt and uncle that I was visiting Donna and Stanley in Port Chester. I thought Furman might be getting high again, but he swore to me that he wasn't. I didn't know how he could stay straight. I was on methadone and still thought about getting high all the time.

Within a week, I had another job, this time at Park Avenue and 47th Street for a mutual fund company. It was the same pay and all business. I made friends with a cute twenty-year-old Italian girl, Anna. We were both secretaries, and my desk was directly behind hers. I'd look up from my typewriter and admire her long black shiny hair. I didn't have any friends. Furman was the only one I spoke to besides my sister, Donna. Somehow, liking Anna made me ache with loneliness. When she told me stories about her Italian immigrant grandparents who lived with her and her parents, it reminded me of what it was like to have a best friend again.

DOREEN BIRDSELL

One night after dinner, the phone rang.

"Doreen, please."

"This is Doreen."

"Hello, Doreen. ... This is Hal Mezzer."

"Yeah?"

"I'm sorry that you left so abruptly. I meant no harm. I'm calling because I have a proposition for you. I know you live at home and would probably like a place of your own. I want someone that I can be with from time to time. ... There's a lot I can give you ... a lot you can learn from our relationship. You know ... the gal that was in your position before you ... she had this type of relationship with me. She's now married to a judge in Maryland and has a very good life."

"How would this work?" I asked.

"You look in the paper and find an apartment near the office. You sign the lease, and I'll pay the rent. Give me a key so I can meet you there sometimes during lunch; or maybe occasionally when I go out for a while in the evening, we can get together."

This sounded like a situation I could live with and a way to see Furman. What an opportunity. New York City was one of the most liberal places I knew. If there was any place in the world that I could walk down the street with a guy who was black without being sneered at, it was New York City.

WITHOUT FAITH

Chapter 19

A Proposal

Wow — I'm twenty-one. Old enough to sign a contract, I thought as I affixed my signature to the lease at 8 East 48th Street. I gave Hal a key, but only to the bottom lock, not the top.

He never showed up unannounced, but I wanted to be sure that he wouldn't. He came over only once or twice a week, but there was the rare occasion when I'd spend the night with him at his place or on a business trip.

Hal sent his wife on a Mississippi riverboat vacation and asked me to stay over at his apartment at the Hampshire House on Central Park South.

Geez, a whole night. Oh, well. Maybe I'll get something out of it. I can't say no.

"We'll have a nice dinner in the Hampshire House restaurant. Go upstairs to my place. I'll show you my paintings and drawings — and I have a great collection of wines and liqueurs. We'll have a great time," he said.

He was always trying to make me a connoisseur.

"When you arrive, tell the concierge you're my niece and that I'm expecting you. I'll have to come down and meet you in the lobby."

"Can't I just tell him that I'm your interior designer and I work for you?"

"No. No, that won't work … you're spending the night."

"Oh, yeah, but I hate saying I'm your niece. I know they know."

Hal had begun taking me with him on out-of-town business trips, mostly to Miami, where he was designing a hospital. It was great getting out of the City in the winter and getting some sun. I especially liked the clothes shopping. What I didn't like was checking in at the Fontainebleau hotel and being registered as his niece and then being his escort at business luncheons and dinners under the pretense of being his interior designer.

I couldn't deny that I was his mistress, but it bothered me that his associates must have known. What was a twenty-one-year-old like me doing with an overweight, balding, white-haired, goateed man of about sixty? I could live with the idea only when I was high. I told myself that it was the only way to be on my own and be able to be with Furman.

The man in the lobby called upstairs to Mr. Mezzer, and within moments Hal was escorting me to the restaurant adjacent to the expansive lobby. I could sense the concierge's eyes following me. Hal would have to tip him good, I thought.

"Good evening, Mr. Mezzer," the waiter said.

"I'll have the usual, and the lady will have a sloe gin fizz."

"Are you hungry? They make a wonderful veal osso buco."

"A little. Don't they have fish?"

"You always eat fish. Try the osso buco."

"All right. I'll try it."

After the waiter brought our drinks, I said, "Hal ... I want more. I want to make my own money, have my own career. You always promise to send me to school and help me with my career, but the only thing you keep insisting on is charm school, and there's no way I'm going to charm school."

"They'll teach you how to walk. How to speak intelligently about current events, so you can carry on a conversation at cocktail parties. What you should read, so you'll be informed. And how to dress. ... A lady wears gloves and her skirts at mid-calf," he said.

"There's no way I'm wearing gloves. And skirts at mid-calf! That's not the way you dress today. Times have changed. Women wear pants ... and jeans are cool ... and miniskirts are 'in.' You bought me this outfit. The skirt's short because that's how they wear them now. I want to go to school, but not charm school."

"What kind of school? What do you want to do?" he asked, clinking the ice cubes in his glass of scotch.

"I want to be a stockbroker. I like Wall Street. I worked there once. Why can't you buy me a seat on the exchange?" I asked.

"A seat on the exchange is about $75,000. You don't know the first thing about it," he said, laughing.

WITHOUT FAITH

"OK. Then what about a real estate broker? Maybe I'd like to manage commercial property. You know plenty of people in real estate."

"You need at least two years' experience in sales or property management to get a broker's license," he said, sucking on his Parliament cigarette.

"You can say I worked for you."

"You said you wanted to be a photographer. I gave you a Rolleiflex. What happened to that?"

"I still want to be a photographer, but I need to make enough money to open my own studio."

"OK. You find out about the schools, and we'll go from there."

After two glasses of Sambuca and a chocolate mousse, we were ready to go upstairs.

"I own half the floor, and if you look out this window you can see Central Park."

After showing me around the living and dining rooms and explaining where every painting and sculpture had come from, he demonstrated all the new appliances in the kitchen.

The bedroom was the last place I wanted to see, so I pretended to be very interested.

We then went to his office.

"I've got my own bathroom and drafting table in here, so I can work at home if I need to."

"The shower has eight spray heads along the sides, and the toilet has a bidet. How do you like it?"

"I love the bidet thing, but why do you need all that water shooting at you in the shower?"

"It massages you, I suppose," he said.

Then it was time. There was nothing left to show me but the bedroom. I hoped it wouldn't take long, so I quickly got undressed and jumped under the covers. Hal was pretty easy, but he always overdid it with Aramis. He used it like it was deodorant, especially between his legs. So not only did I have to resurrect this tiny little penis hiding behind two bulging testicles, but I had to smell Aramis in the process. I groaned as though I was enjoying myself and getting pleasure out of this mostly unpleasant experience.

After he was, at last, finally satisfied, he said, "You know, my wife has been having a problem that really concerns me. She keeps getting dizzy spells. The doctors are concerned. More than once, I've gotten phone calls that she's fallen down. She says everything around her starts spinning. That's why I thought this trip would be good for her. I think she needs to relax. She's with a friend, and there's a doctor on the boat if anything happens. I'm telling you all this because I want to know, if anything ever happened to my wife, … would you marry me and live here with me?"

"You better get her well! There's no way I could do that," I said.

Hal didn't say anything. He just nodded, and we watched TV.

WITHOUT FAITH

Chapter 20

A Baling Hooker

I hadn't shot dope for about six months. I didn't like to drink, but the methadone blocked my getting high on heroin, and that was the whole idea. Living on East 48th Street in my first apartment was really lonely. Furman was a dope fiend again, and I didn't want to be with him anymore. I had met a guy who I thought was a real straight arrow when I was temping as a secretary. Ramon worked in the mailroom, and after many drinks at the company Christmas party, I took him home and we slept together. I liked Ramon, but I knew if I hung out with him he'd want more.

I hadn't seen Linda for years, so when she called I was shocked. "How did you get my number?" I asked.
"I saw Eddy. He told me you moved to the City, so I looked you up."
"How are you? I heard you're married."
"Yeah. I'm still with Robbie. Hey, I've been thinking about you a lot ... and about when we were kids. Do you still feel the same way?"
"Uh ... well ... I ... I ..."

I couldn't believe what she was asking. My words couldn't keep up with my heart that pulsed in my throat. Did I still feel the same way! It took everything to forget about her and stop thinking that something was wrong with me — that I might be a homosexual. I hated that word.

"Do you still have feelings for me?" she asked again.
"Yeah ... I do, but I ..."
"Where do you live? Why don't I come over?"
"All right. Sure. I'm at 8 East 48th Street, between Fifth and Madison."
"I can be there in an hour. Is that OK?"
The room was spinning around me. Was this real?
"OK. Great. I'm in 2C. Take the elevator up."
I looked around the apartment and didn't know what to do.

DOREEN BIRDSELL

I didn't know what to expect when she got there.

She still looked the same. Long blond waves touching her shoulder, flushed cheeks that accentuated her blue eyes. She put down her bag, said hello — and then kissed me.

She pushed me back into my living room and onto my couch. We spent the night together. I had told her about Hal and Furman and that Hal was paying all my bills — and then she was gone. It was the best day and the worst day I ever had. I felt spread wide open and more alone than before. I didn't hear from her again, and I didn't have the nerve to call her, even when I was stoned.

✼✼✼✼✼✼✼

I was twenty-one and itching for somewhere to go, someone to be with, and to get out of my crawling skin. What was I going to do? I couldn't get stoned, so I did the next best thing: I drank. Aunt Hazel and Uncle Ted always drank beer or rye and ginger. I didn't like beer — it only made me pee. Whiskey was strong, and it hit me faster.

When I was a little girl, Uncle Ted would take me to the gin mill and order a rye and ginger for him and a Shirley Temple for me. When he wasn't looking, I'd steal a sip. "Hey. You wanna get the bartender in trouble? Wait till you're old enough."

He dunked my Shirley Temple cherry in his whiskey mix with fingers that were grease-stained no matter how much Borax he scrubbed them with. "Here you go. That's enough for now."

He always seemed to be having the best time when he was at the gin mill or at the baseball field with his grandsons, watching them play. I wished that I could be more like them — Teddy and Michael. "They were naturals," he said.

When I was growing up, he told me that I would be good at whatever I decided to do, but I needed to find a special talent for one thing. "Don't be like me: a jack-of-all-trades and a master of none," he said. His favorite saying was "I taught you everything I know and you still don't know nothin'." It took me

121

WITHOUT FAITH

awhile to understand what he meant. When I did, I got that it wasn't good for either one of us.

Now I was 21 and old enough to drink or do whatever else I liked in my own apartment. The only signs of life in my kitchen were a silver toaster, a box of raisin bran, and a fifth of Seagram's 7. The refrigerator contained a quart of milk, a bottle of Canada Dry, Cremora, and a jar of Taster's Choice instant coffee. If I needed anything else, Gristede's market was right next door.

Standing in the small, narrow kitchen, I poured Seagram's into a Welch's jelly glass, adding a few ice cubes and almost-flat ginger ale. The first sip made me cringe. After the first glass, I felt a little warmer and a little calmer. I moved to the dining alcove with my concoction and settled down to drink whatever it took to still my body and quiet my head. The traffic outside the casement windows seemed to fade away after a few more drinks. I turned on the new seventeen-inch black and white Panasonic TV that Aunt Hazel and Uncle Ted had bought for my new apartment.

I didn't have a separate bedroom, but the studio had a large L shape with a living and dining alcove, a separate kitchen, and a yellow-and-black- tiled bathroom with what the rental agent called a dressing room. It was huge compared with the bedroom I had in Aunt Hazel and Uncle Ted's four-room apartment in Ridgewood. My new place had thick brown wall-to-wall carpeting. Aunt Hazel and Uncle Ted always wanted wall-to-wall, but they had to settle for remnants; the wood floor edges that the carpet didn't cover, Uncle Ted sanded and shellacked.

I had never had this much space all to myself before. Finally I had a place that was all my own, and no one could tell me what to do or threaten that if I wasn't good they'd pack me up and send me back to my father in Port Chester. The TV in the living room gave me company, as the voices on the six o'clock news were familiar and became my drinking buddies until I could get up the courage to go outside and feel a part of something. I could go to the bar — find someone to talk to. Nemo's was directly across the street, and the downstairs bar was open until 3 a.m. That was one of the things I loved about living at 48th and Fifth —everything I wanted or needed was right there. Rockefeller

Center was a block away. May's Department Store, where Aunt Hazel and Uncle Ted had bought my TV, was just around the corner. I never saw anyone in the building I could call a neighbor, and when I hit the street the faces were always different. I was an invisible part of everything that moved.

The voices on TV and the Seagram's were no longer enough. I didn't want to be alone, and I was itching for something to do. When I walked across the street to Nemo's, it was closing time and there was no way I was going to stay in my empty apartment.

I thought: Hey, what about Grand Central Station? That's always open. Maybe I could get a drink at the Oyster Bar.

I put on my faded jeans and stepped into a pair of bone leather strapped heels. I loved shoes and always had at least half a dozen pairs to choose from. No matter how stoned I got when I was wearing heels or six-inch platforms, even if I staggered, I rarely fell. I had a great sense of balance.

It was a warm, still night in early summer, with barely any traffic except for the occasional Yellow Cab looking for a fare, as I walked down Madison Avenue to 42nd Street.

When I got to Grand Central, it was empty except for two or three men who may have been conductors. I was still pretty high, but I wanted another drink — really what I wanted was someone to talk to — so I walked over to the Oyster Bar. It was closed too. It had to be after four in the morning. The steely click of my heels on the shiny marble floor was the only sound.

The only other people in Grand Central were two black girls. They stood under an arched hallway next to the palatial marble staircase that led to Vanderbilt Avenue and the Commodore Hotel. One wore high red patent leather stiletto boots that ended just beneath the hem of her white vinyl miniskirt. The other had on black fishnets and white platform heels. When I walked by, I said, "Hi. How ya doing?"

The fishnet girl just looked the other way, like I wasn't even there, but the taller one in the patent leather boots looked at me with a big kind of bucktoothed smile and said, "Hey, girl. You workin'?"

"No," I said. "I live around here. I'm just hangin' out."

WITHOUT FAITH

The girl in the vinyl skirt turned around, cocked her head, and, with her hand on her hip, said, "Hangin' out! You gotta be kiddin'. ... Nobody hangs out here unless they're lookin' for something. ... What you lookin' for, girl?"

"Nothin'!" I said. "Everything's closed, so I'm just hangin' out."

"Well, nobody just hangs out here. ... This is our place, and we're workin'," she said.

I had never talked to hookers before, and I couldn't believe they could work in Grand Central. "I just wanted to see if the Oyster Bar was open."

"Well, it ain't!"

I said, "How do you work here? There's nobody here."

The taller one said, "When these conductors and engineers get off work, they like to spend their money, and we take care of 'em."

"Where?" I asked.

"On the trains. Sometimes in the engineer's booth."

Suddenly I saw a whole other life going on at Grand Central Station, and the men I had seen walking through the hallways were customers, not conductors.

I realized the only place I was going to get another drink was back at my place, so I told the girls I wasn't trying to get in on their scene and I left.

The walk back up Madison Avenue was even quieter than before. The sidewalks were deserted, and the traffic lights changing from green to yellow to red flashed for no one. Then, all of a sudden, a long, light blue car pulled up next to me at the curb.

"Hey, you gotta cigarette?" the driver asked.

He looked like he was in his late twenties, and when I leaned over to look inside, the guy in the passenger seat asked, "You got one for me?" The driver had dark, wavy hair and longish trimmed sideburns. He was good-looking in a tough, cool kind of way, sort of like a Latino Marlboro Man. The passenger had a thicker mustache that draped around the corners of his mouth. He was scruffy-looking, unshaven, not at all like the one at the wheel.

I reached into my bag and pulled out a pack of Kools and gave them both a cigarette.

"What you doing out here so late?" the driver asked.

"I live around here. What are *you* doing here?"

The scrappy-looking one leaned over and said, "We work on the docks. We just got off."

"You want a ride?" he asked.

"It's only a few blocks," I said.

"So what … we'll take you."

This could be fun. They're probably looking for a good time too, I thought.

For a second, I thought: Those girls at Grand Central seemed to do all right. They're with strangers all the time.

"OK," I said, and jumped in the back seat.

The guy at the wheel told me his name was Tony and the little guy was Joe.

We drove a couple of blocks and turned left onto 48th Street. We were there in less than a minute.

The little guy asked, "How long you living here?"

"Just about a month. I don't know that many people yet."

"Why don't we come up?" he asked. "You can show us your place."

"Sure. OK," I said.

The three of us stepped onto the elevator to my new apartment. The driver was tall and well-built. They were both in jeans and heavy work boots. I was taller than the other guy in my heels. I figured he was about five-foot-five. His crooked, brown-stained teeth were partly camouflaged by the thick mustache that grew over his lip. If it weren't for the smooth, bronzed face of the driver, I wouldn't have gotten in the car. I looked forward to showing off my place and having someone to hang out with. I opened the door and told them to sit at the table and I'd make us a drink.

In the kitchen, I opened the tan metal cabinet door to get out three jelly glasses and make us Seagram's 7's with ginger ale. I walked into the dining area balancing the three glasses — ice clinking — between my hands, but only the little guy was sitting at the table. He glanced up at me with a dirty grin. As I set the glasses down, I heard the door to the dressing room open; but before I could turn around, I was grabbed from behind and locked in the arms of the other one. Lifting me off the floor, he threw me onto the Castro convertible that I had left open in the living room.

WITHOUT FAITH

I screamed, "What the fuck are you doing?"

He threw me facedown on the mattress and said, "Shut the fuck up! Where's your money? I know you got money here. All you hookers got money."

"I'm not a hooker! I'll give you what I got!"

"Where do you hide it? Don't fuck with me, you bitch."

"It's … it's in the kitchen," I said. "I'll get it. You … you can have it. Just let me up."

He pulled me off the bed and pushed me into the kitchen.

He was holding me with my arms behind my back and said, "OK! Get me the money."

"I have to get it … under the sink."

"Go ahead, you bitch. Get it." He shoved me toward the sink, and I caught myself from falling.

Any cash I had I kept taped under the kitchen sink in case of a robbery or something. I also kept a long butcher knife taped under the sink, right next to the money. It was a small kitchen, so only the bigger guy stood over me, while the little skanky one stayed outside the doorway next to the dining room table.

I bent over and opened the cabinet doors beneath the sink. Furman had once told me that it was a good place to hide money in case of a robbery, but it was my idea to tape a butcher knife next to the money in case of something like this.

All I thought was: Once I get the knife, I can get them out of my apartment and I'll be safe.

I reached under the sink and tore off the tape around the handle of the knife and ripped it out from under the sink. I lunged at the bigger guy with the knife in my hand, shouting, "If you don't get the fuck out of here, I'll stick you with this, you motherfucker!"

I swung the knife wildly to push him out of the kitchen. He jumped backward, arms in the air through the kitchen doorway and around to the other side of the dining room table. I slashed the air between us, left and right, back and forth … first at him and then at the other guy, yelling, "Get the fuck out of here … both of you, or I'll stick you, motherfuckers!"

The skanky guy was in front of the door across the table from me. The taller one was on my right near the dressing room. I faced the one in front of me. ... I had to keep swinging the knife back and forth to keep it in front of both of them. ... They had their hands up in the air. ... When I slashed the air with the knife back toward the skank, hoping to get him out the door, the other one grabbed my arm and twisted it until the pain made me drop the knife. It happened so fast. I knew it was over. I immediately started pleading, "I'm sorry, I'm sorry, I'm sorry. I didn't mean it."

In a split second, I was a little girl again, and Uncle Ted was hitting me for something I did wrong, and I was screaming and crying, "I'm sorry, I'm sorry. I didn't mean it."

The bigger guy threw me back on the mattress facedown and pushed my face into the pillow, yelling, "You motherfucker ... you fuckin' motherfucker."

I was pinned facedown with his knee pressed between my shoulder blades. The springs flattened my chest through the mattress. Then he pulled my head up by my hair. I was still crying and pleading, "I'm sorry, I'm sorry. I didn't mean it."

"Open your mouth, you bitch!" Metal pushing past my teeth slid into my mouth, and what felt like a hook pulled my cheek from the inside out.

"Do you know I'll rip your fuckin' face out with this."

I could taste metal. His knee dug into my back, keeping me pinned. He slid the hook back out of my mouth. From the corner of my eye, I could see a baling hook sticking out from the middle of his fist. He raised his fist above me with the hook toward the ceiling ready to come down on me. He was going to kill me. I needed to know that I was going to heaven ... that I was forgiven for all the bad things I'd done before I had a chance to make things right between me and God ... that's all that mattered ... not him ... not that baling hook ... not how I was going to get out from under him ... but how would God take me back?

In that instant, I prayed what I remembered from second grade in Catholic school to be an act of perfect contrition. If I confessed, I would be forgiven. In a millisecond, each word completely formed in my consciousness flashed through my mind. "O my God, I am heartily sorry for having offended Thee, and I detest all my sins because of Thy just punishments, but most of all because they offend Thee, my God, Who art all-good and deserving of all my love. I firmly resolve, with the help of Thy grace, to sin no more and to avoid the near occasion of sin. Amen."

The baling hook came down swiftly, barely missing my cheek, and with a thud ripped into the mattress. He furiously tore the bedsheets into shredded strips from top to bottom. The skank tore the phone out of the wall and used the wire to tie up my feet. The bastard with the baling hook used the pieces of torn sheets to bind my wrists and gag my mouth. They were headed toward the door when the slimy little one turned around and pulled my TV out of the wall to take it with him. Oh, no. Not my TV, I thought.

When I was sure they were gone, I squirmed to get out of the wires and sheets, but I couldn't undo the knots. I rolled out of the bed and fell onto the floor. The door seemed so far away. I crawled to the wall and supported myself enough to get on my feet and then hopped to the door, which was left partially open. I wedged my chin and then my shoulder in the opening so I could squeeze through to the hallway. Hopping to my neighbor's doorway, I banged on the door with my forehead, hoping for someone to answer. A thin, elderly, gray-haired lady in a nightgown opened the door. When I saw her face and her shocked expression, I fell over inside her doorway at her feet. She kneeled down and pulled the gag out of my mouth. "I was robbed. I live next door. Call the cops."

By the time the police arrived, it was daylight. I told them I had fallen asleep and woke up with these guys in my apartment. I told them the whole story except for the part about me bringing them home.

The detective said, "There are no signs of forced entry, and it doesn't look like anyone was on the fire escape." I could tell they didn't believe me.

I stuck to my story, and they said they'd look into it.

I asked, "What are the chances of getting my TV back?"

Chapter 21

48th Street to Flushing

All I wanted to do was go home, but there was no home to go home to. I called my cousin Billy, who had opened a real estate agency in Glendale. He had molested me when I was four years old, the first day Aunt Hazel and Uncle Ted took me to live with them in Queens. I knew that he liked me and would want to help me. The first place he showed me I rented. A one-bedroom apartment in a six-family building that was a few blocks from Aunt Hazel and Uncle Ted, who had moved to Glendale from nearby Ridgewood. I felt like I'd be safe there.

My new apartment was clean and quiet. I was on the ground floor and never noticed my neighbors or the German-born landlady, who lived two flights up. I bought a hamster and a Habitrail kit to give it a home and to keep me company. The hamster, whom I never gave a name, lived on the kitchen floor next to the dining room set that Aunt Hazel and Uncle Ted had bought when I moved to the City. My Castro convertible that I slept on in the living room and the formica dresser that I had had since I was twelve years old were all the furniture I needed. The front room that overlooked the street was a bedroom. I didn't have a bed, so I kept the door closed, shut the blinds tight, and decided to use it for storage.

During the week, I'd go into the City to meet Hal for lunch. I had no friends, so when I came home I'd feed the hamster, drink wine, and sometimes go to the local bar and go home with Jimmy, who was a regular customer. Although Jimmy was in his twenties, he still lived with his parents near the Von Westernhagen Restaurant, a few blocks from where I lived. We drank, passed time, and I'd pass out at his house. The only thing we had in common was the bar. On weekends, he'd hunt deer with a bow and arrow and I'd stick close to home until Monday and lunch with Hal.

I'd visit my aunt and uncle once a week and tell them about my dreams of becoming a photographer.

WITHOUT FAITH

"How can you make money doing that?" Aunt Hazel asked.
"Photographers make good money," I insisted.
"When are you going to meet someone and settle down?"
"I'm not interested in that. I want to make it on my own."
Uncle Ted shook his head and returned to his newspaper. I knew he didn't believe me. He never did — even when it was the truth.

At the liquor store, I bought a bottle of Blue Nun, and then went home to my hamster.
Halfway through the bottle, I got the urge to find out how Linda was doing. I called her mother whose number was engraved in my memory.
"Hi, Carmel. It's Doreen. I'm looking for Linda."
"She's got her own place now. Her and Robbie are separated. That fat bastard Gerald, who thinks he's an artist, got in between them — even though she won't admit it."

Linda had her own place! This was great, I thought.
She invited me to see her new apartment on Franklin Avenue in Flushing. I couldn't believe what a great place she had. Large multicolored painted canvases hung on the brown stucco wall over a naugahyde leather couch. A tan leather steamship trunk was centered beneath a row of windows with dark-stained shutters. Laura, a macaw parrot, was perched on top of her cage and squawking, "Play ball!"
"I know that bird!" I said. "I used to hear that squawk when I rode my bike past Kennelly's bar."
"Yeah … Kennelly died and left her to my mother, and then I took her," Linda said.

A burnt orange shag rug covered the floor, and a basket chair hung by a chain from the ceiling. I could never have a place like this, I thought.
Saloon-style doors led to a small kitchen from a dining room with billiard hall lights over a round wooden table.
"This is really cool. How'd you do it?" I asked.
"I always had a flair for decorating. Oh yeah, and Gerald helped me put it together.

"How are you? Are you still with that guy Hal?" she asked.
"Yeah."
"Does he still pay all the bills and give you money?"
"Yep."
"Wow. You should move in with me. You think he'd pay the bills here?"
"Yeah. Of course! Why not?"

A dream come true! I couldn't move fast enough.

The only thing I wanted to keep was my formica dresser. It contained the only personal belongings I had: my scrapbook from grammar school and the photo album of my mother and father and Donna. Carmel, Linda's mom, let me store it in her garage in Maspeth. Gerald took my couch and dining room set for his apartment.

Within a week, I was living with Linda. All I needed to move in were my clothes.

I loved Linda so much, and I knew she loved me, but she let down her guard only when she was stoned. She'd kiss me and ask me if I still felt the same as when we were kids. (Of course, I did. It's all I thought about.) She never kissed me otherwise.

One summer night, we drove her red MGB to the Village. It was 1974, and women's lib was in full swing. I thought: This is our time to be whoever we want to be.

"Let's find a gay bar," she said.

My heart leapt in my throat. "OK. How?"

"Let's call the gay hot line."

"How do you know about that?" I asked.

"I read about it in The Village Voice."

She pulled over to the curb at Sheridan Square. I got out of the car and walked to the nearby phone booth and dialed information.

It was thrilling to say the words, "Can I have the number for the gay hot line?"

This was great. The operator can't see who I am, and she probably never

WITHOUT FAITH

knew there was a gay hot line, I thought.
   A male voice answered: "Can I help you?"
   "Hi. I'm looking for a girls' gay bar."
   "Where are you?"
   "Oh. On Sheridan Square in the Village."
   "Well. Let's see. There's Bonnie & Clyde's on West Third Street."

Linda walked right up to the bar and ordered a Seven and Seven like she was in Kennelly's back in Maspeth.
   "Put a quarter on the pool table," she said.
   "No way," I said. "Those are guys, and they really look tough."
   The bartender overheard and said, "Those are women!"

We drove back to the telephone booth on Sheridan Square and again I dialed the gay hot line. The same male voice answered.
   "Hi. I called earlier looking for a girls' gay bar. ... You sent me to Bonnie & Clyde's. Are there any other bars where the girls look like girls?"
   "Well, let's see. There is the Duchess."

Girls in bell-bottom jeans and some with halter tops lined the bar.
This was more like it.
Linda drank, danced, and talked to strangers easily.
   I couldn't understand how she fit in so well and I was the one who always liked girls and still felt so nervous around them.
   I was more at ease uptown at Maxwell's Plum in a straight crowd than in a lesbian bar.
   I didn't know how to play the game or what the game was. In a straight bar, I knew that all a guy wanted was to get me to have sex with him. Now I was on the other side and I was confused. I didn't want to have sex with these women. I wanted to be with Linda. At least in a straight bar, there was no competition.

Like it or not, this was still better than Maxwell's Plum and pretending to be straight.
   We made new friends, and the Duchess became my new hangout. I didn't

have a car, so on the nights Linda hung out with Gerald I took a cab to the City by myself.

I hailed a Yellow Cab on the way to a new club for women on the East Side that I heard had a great sound system and huge dance floor. Flushing was the home to many cab companies, so I could always catch a cab for the half-hour, non-rush-hour, ride into the city. Sometimes I would get into a cab and totally make up a new identity. I'd put on a British accent and make up stories about visiting the U.S. and being an interior designer, or whatever. I slipped into the back seat behind the driver's Afro. Noticing the name on the cabby's license, Phillip Gladstone, I realized it was a Jewfro.

Leaning over the back seat, I gave him my destination without the accent. He had deep-set brown eyes and a strong angular face, with a five o'clock shadow. I thought I knew my way around the City as well as the best cabbies and would always give the directions for the best and fastest routes. This guy wouldn't follow my directions and said that if his way wasn't faster the fare would be on him.

I told him I was on my way to a gay club for women to go dancing and it was too bad he couldn't join me.

He was a night-shift cabby and had more than a few stories to tell me about his night-shift experiences. I used to like to combine words to make up vocabulary, and it turned out so did he. We had fun "commingulating" our own words. He was obviously well-educated, had a good sense of humor, and was definitely not intimidated by my sexuality.

I asked him for his phone number when I paid the fare. He handed it to me with my change, and we said good night.

The club was jammed with women dancing to Don't Rock the Boat. After a few drinks I was confident enough to make my way alone onto the crowded dance floor, squeezing my way to the middle while moving to the beat. I became oblivious to the people, to the music, and somehow made my way back to Flushing.

A few days later, I called the cabby, Phil, and invited him to play handball

WITHOUT FAITH

in the park a few blocks away, off Main Street in Flushing. When he laughed at my suggestion, I thought I'd made a mistake calling him, even though he agreed.

I served up the first ball, and he walloped it hard and low. I couldn't return. I served up another, and he killed me for another quick point. Every serve, he returned a bullet. I ran into the fence trying to volley, and then it dawned on me. No wonder he laughed.

"What do you do? Play every day?" I asked.

"Something like that. ... I'm a four-wall handball competitor. When I told my friend you asked me to play, he couldn't believe it and neither could I."

I invited him back to my apartment to take a shower and have some lunch. He suggested we shower together. A month later, I didn't get my period. I was pregnant. It was the summer of 1974, and a song titled (You're) Having My Baby by Paul Anka had just been released. I liked Phil, but I wasn't having his baby. Phil said he'd be there, no matter what I decided. When that damn song came on the radio, he dared to pat my belly. I knew there was one thing I was not — and that was a mother.

When I was a little girl, Aunt Hazel always said, "You wait until you grow up and have kids of your own."

I always shot back: "I'm not going to have kids."

My mother died after having a baby. The whole idea of me and a baby made me dizzy to even think about, and besides I was in love with Linda. Phil was a fun guy, a good friend, but that was it.

After the abortion, the doctor told me to go home and to rest. Instead, I got on my bike, adjusted my crotch with the giant Kotex between my legs, and rode a couple of miles to my friend Sharon's house, so I could get a ride with her into the City to hang out at the Duchess.

Chapter 22

Womyn

No matter what happened, I knew I'd wake up in Linda's bed with her lying next to me, even if we were just "friends."

"It's a beach day!" I said as soon as my eyes opened to the summer sunshine. With beach towels and baby oil and the red MGB's top down, we sped off to Riis Park in Rockaway. I'd meet Hal for lunch once or twice a week. My bills were paid, and Linda's too. Twenty dollars was enough to go out for a night at the Duchess, drink, dance, and hope for another beach day.

"Don't you ever worry?" Linda asked one morning.
"No. Why? Should I?"
"You get your bills paid and anything else you want. I don't. I have to worry."
"No, you don't, Linda. ... Hal gives me enough for the both of us."
"That's not true. It's not enough. I need more."
"Like what?"
"I've been thinking ... and I've decided ... I'm going back to Robbie."
I was stunned, then felt the crush of my heart folding inward, collapsing inside me.
"Why? Why? I can ask Hal for more."
"I made up my mind. You can stay here. Hal will pay the rent. I'll keep the furniture here until I see how things work out with Robbie."

She didn't care that going back to him was leaving me. I was so hurt and felt so betrayed that I didn't pay the rent for three months. I spent the money on going out and getting high. When the eviction notice was posted on the apartment door, I asked the superintendent what would happen to all the furniture. He said the city marshal would pack it up and put it in storage until it was claimed. What a relief, I thought. I could just walk away, say nothing to Linda, and not do a thing. I was stuck in Flushing alone. No Linda. No car. No more summer.

WITHOUT FAITH

I took a taxi to the City and went back to the first gay bar Linda and I had ever gone to, Bonnie & Clyde's. I had hung out in gay bars long enough that I was no longer afraid of girls who dressed like men.

It was a weeknight, and only a few people were drinking at the bar. A foursome was at the pool table. The shooter had dark hair with one long blond curl that dangled in the middle of her forehead while she leaned over the pool table and broke the rack hard. The balls scattered, and one fell in the corner pocket. "Way to go, Jen!" one of the others said, raising her beer bottle. I put up a quarter to play. Jen won.

I bought her one drink and then another. She invited me back to her place, where she was rooming with a friend, on East Eighth Street. We started seeing each other almost every day. Jen was a tennis player from Florida, where her mother was the mayor of a small town outside Miami. She had graduated from college in Bogota, Colombia, where she had majored in Spanish. While at college in South America, she learned how to smuggle cocaine back to the States by taping it to the pages of magazines and sending it through the mail. Jen was the first person I ever met that called herself a lesbian. I didn't like the word. It sounded like a disease, but Jen said it like it was something to be proud of.

She liked to get high as much as I did, maybe even more. Although I didn't like cocaine as much as she did. Sometimes it made me paranoid. And the quaaludes Jen popped in my mouth only made me pass out. She purchased pot by the kilo and made a living dealing by the ounce and sometimes by the pound, which she delivered all over the Village on her bike, even in the snow.

All she wanted to do was make a lot of money and get high, and all I wanted was to fit in. She was also the first girl I had ever known to call herself a "woman."
"I'm only twenty-three. I'm not old enough to be a woman yet," I said.
"Haven't you ever heard of Gloria Steinem or Bella Abzug? Where have you been?"

DOREEN BIRDSELL

Jen taught me about smuggling, women's rights, and a book about the female erogenous zones. "If you're going to be with me, you have to know these things," she said.

Eviction day came, and the city marshal emptied Linda's apartment.
Hal wanted to put me up in the Wyndham House, a resident hotel at 56th Street and Fifth Avenue that was completely furnished. The silver-blue-haired woman who showed me the apartment didn't try to hide her estimating my character by scanning me from my high-heeled shoes and skirt to white collared blouse.

"You're rather young. Are you sure you can afford this?" she asked.

I gave her my letter of reference on Hal's architectural firm letterhead that said I was an interior designer at his company with a salary of $500 per week.

"Well … very nice," she said. "We also have a concierge."

I wasn't quite sure what that meant, although I knew that Hal had one in his lobby, so I just smiled and said, "Oh. That's great."

"Why don't you move to the Chelsea Hotel? It's a real cool place. Did you know Jimi Hendrix used to live there?" Jen asked when I told her about moving to the Wyndham.

There were no musicians living at the Chelsea when we moved in. It was 1974, and the only people we met who lived on our floor were drug dealers and professional shoplifters who were always trying to sell us stolen shoes or stereos. After a few visits, Hal refused to continue to pay the rent if I didn't move.

Jen thought a reasonable compromise would be Greenwich Village. 65 East 11th Street was our next address, and I started hanging out in Washington Square Park. I told Hal that I was interested in studying music, so I bought my own Latin Percussion conga. I'd cart it to the park in a duffel bag slung over my shoulder to play with the other percussionists who jammed there.

After a few months, Jen moved back to Florida, and I was alone again in the duplex apartment. I didn't like sleeping alone. I dragged the mattress downstairs and slept on the living room floor in front of the fireplace with my metallic red conga. After Jen left, I stopped paying the rent there too.

WITHOUT FAITH

When the eviction notice was posted, I found another apartment.

I hadn't spoken to Linda since the eviction, so I called her mother with the excuse that I wanted my dresser I had stored in her garage.

"Oh, it's not here," she said. "After you got Linda evicted, she made sure your stuff got thrown out."

It contained my fifth-grade scrapbook and the only photos of my mother I had. I couldn't believe that Linda could be so mean. She knew that was all I had of my mother's.

"Why … why would she do that?" I asked her mother.

Linda lost all of her baby pictures. The super of the building said he threw them down the incinerator chute after the apartment was cleared out.

We were even, I thought.

Chapter 23

New Building, New Me

February 1976

A brand new high-rise cut into the Village skyline south of Eighth Street. Just four short blocks from 11th Street and University Place, Eighth Street and Mercer was a world away, and it was very unlikely that I'd ever run into the super or landlord from my old apartment.

The lobby smelled of fresh-poured concrete. It was still a construction site, but a uniformed doorman in a brass-buttoned jacket and cap was already stationed at a tall mahogany desk on the other side of the revolving door.

"I'm looking for the rental office."

"Fourteenth floor. Elevators to the right, miss."

Stepping off the elevator onto a bare, concrete floor, I followed a string of bare bulbs that led to the rental office. One of the two women agents greeted me and handed me an application.

I settled on the 17th floor. It was just high enough to peer over the rooftops, with a view all the way to the Hudson River.

This time it would be different. I wouldn't blow all my money on dope. I was going to change — new building, new me.

All I had on 11th Street was a bed, a table and chairs, and a bad relationship with Jen, who wound up leaving me anyway.

I called Ramon, whom I usually hung out with when I wasn't getting stoned, which wasn't too often. He was the only person I knew who was my age and didn't use drugs. We met when I had taken a temp job as a secretary for the Aluminum Association, where he worked in the mailroom. He was a photo enthusiast. When I had seen his slide show of the New York City skyline, I was blown away — crimson-red factory walls, deep blue cloudless skies, bridges spanning the river. I couldn't believe that it was Ramon who took those pictures — the guy who worked in the mailroom! Suddenly, the thought occurred

WITHOUT FAITH

to me: If he could do this, why can't I? After all, he was no different from me.

He lent me his 35mm Pentax. I asked for the zoom lens. He taught me how to use it, and I biked off to Central Park to shoot my first roll of black and white film. I found something that I loved.

Ramon was a compact version of Ricky Ricardo with a camera instead of a conga. When I wanted to get straight, I always hung out with him. We'd discuss photography and art and music. Hal had always tried to get me interested in these things, but Ramon made it sound exciting — not like a lecture. Taking pictures took my mind away from everything else. I knew I'd never be able to be with a woman anyway, so I settled for Ramon.

"You could make good money doing this," I said.

"I'll do it — if you do it with me," he said.

He believed me, and for the first time I had a dream that I thought could become real.

Ramon was always there to help me make a new start. So he helped me fix up my new apartment. We bought plaster from the hardware store around the corner on Greene Street, and the guy behind the counter lent us his dolly so we could wheel the two 35-pound cans of plaster back to my apartment. We smeared the walls to look like stucco, making circular swirls for the design. For $200, I got an orange, black, and brown overstuffed futon couch; we hung the pictures Hal had given me from his office, and shellacked my dining room table to try to match the finish on the arms of the couch. I dropped a newspaper on the table before it was dry, and small pieces of it became permanently part of the table. Wandering Jews, philodendrons, and ferns in macramé baskets hung from the ceiling in front of the picture window that overlooked the West Village. Hal gave me his old stereo, and I went around the corner to Sam Goody to buy albums by Bob Marley, Tavares, and Earth, Wind and Fire. I blasted the stereo and played my conga to Jose Feliciano and Tito Puente during the day when no one was home to complain about the noise. It was great — until the thought of getting high began to play over and over again in my head. The only way to turn it off was to get high just one more time.

I was still on methadone, but I knew that if I stopped for a few days there would be no chemical block to prevent me from getting high on heroin. I could get high just once — that's all, just one more time. Then I'd get off methadone for good. I could do it and still be OK.

I knew I could call Johnny. He was Jen's connection to the drug dealers on the Lower East Side. I still had his phone number. He was a skinny Puerto Rican who lived with his mother in the South Bronx. His sunken cheeks and dark-circled eye sockets were framed by long black greasy hair. He had no upper front teeth, only a red gumline. Johnny had the best smack on the Lower East Side and never got ripped off. He walked into the worst neighborhoods in Alphabet City with his trained Doberman by his side.
"Hey. Como estas Johnny? You comin' downtown?" I asked.
"Why, man? You off meth again?" he asked.
"Yeah. I just wanna taste. You got works?"
I knew Johnny liked me and he'd get me off.

One score became once a week until it was every day again. I started going with Johnny to cop my own drugs. The dealers saw me with Johnny so often they started speaking to me in Spanish.
Even though he wanted to get it on with me, I didn't care once I was stoned. He'd get what he wanted and I'd get what I wanted.
He started following me and would show up at my apartment unannounced. When I decided that I was going to get straight, I cut him loose but he wouldn't go away. He kept coming to my apartment building, and when the doorman rang I wouldn't allow him up. I felt safe because I had a doorman and a security system.

I was heading uptown to meet Hal for lunch when I ran into Johnny on the corner, where he was waiting for me.
"What the fuck is up with you, man?" he said, pushing me so hard I had to catch myself not to fall.
"Who the fuck do you think you are!" I said and pushed him right back.
He punched me in the arm, and I started to scream. "You motherfucker. I'll call the cops if you touch me again."

WITHOUT FAITH

"We'll see, you bitch," he said, and I ran to catch a cab.

From then on, I wouldn't leave my apartment until I looked out the window to see if Johnny was down the street or on the corner somewhere. If I saw him, I'd sneak out the rear of the building through the garage to Broadway. I thought he'd just give up and go away after a while. I told the doorman not to ring me if he came into the lobby. The building had security and I had a burglar alarm, thank God.

About a week went by, and I hadn't seen Johnny anywhere. I rode my bike out the back of the building to Broadway just to be safe and took cabs everywhere if I wasn't riding my bike.

On my way to meet Hal for lunch, I checked out the window overlooking Mercer Street one more time just to make sure there was no Johnny. I flipped the deadbolt lock to open the door. It swung open in my face and knocked me to the floor.

"Oh, God! Johnny. Don't. I'm sorry!" I was screaming.

He pummeled my body with his fists, yelling, "You motherfuckin' puta! You fuckin' bitch!"

Somehow I was under the dining room table curled in a ball and screaming, "I love you, Johnny. I love you." I thought that would make him stop — and suddenly he was gone.

I crawled out from under the table and knew I'd be black and blue all over.

Oh, man. How am I going to explain this to Hal? I thought. I'll tell him I fell off my bike.

After that, I didn't open the door without the security chain and looking out the peephole. I was afraid to call the cops. They might find out I was using and that Johnny was my dealer.

One day I noticed him on the corner outside Hal's office at 59th and Madison, but he didn't dare come near me when I was with Hal.

I stopped using dope and stayed on methadone.

A couple of months passed. I felt something wet on my nipple. It was leaking. This is weird, I thought. My breast was big enough for me to pull up to my mouth and reach with my tongue. The liquid was clear and tasted almost sweet.

Could I be pregnant? I thought. Oh, shit. I had been getting my period. How could that be? Maybe I was just a little late.

I looked in the Yellow Pages and found a gynecologist uptown on Park Avenue. He must be good to have a Park Avenue address, I thought.

While in the waiting room at the doctor's Park Avenue office, I picked up a pamphlet about pregnancy and abortion. I read that serious complications occur in less than 1 out of 100 early abortions.

I lay on the table with my feet in the cold metal stirrups. The doctor pushed his finger inside and pressed down on my belly.
"When did you have your last period?"
"About six weeks ago at the most."
"Are you sure?"
"Yes. Why?"
"I think you're pregnant. The test will confirm it."
Oh, no. Who could it be? I thought.
Hal told me that his sperm count wasn't high enough to get me pregnant. It had to be Johnny. Oh, shit.

I was pregnant, and I scheduled an abortion for the following week.

WITHOUT FAITH

Chapter 24

Donna Visits the City

If the phone hadn't rung, I probably would have slept until noon. It was my sister, Donna. After I was arrested and her ex, Lucky, went to jail on the same day, we didn't speak as often. I wasn't sure if it was because neither one of us wanted to remember those days or because I had started hanging out in gay bars — maybe both — but we spoke less and less. It was hard to talk to her about being gay. I could hardly accept it myself, especially since she'd become a Jehovah's Witness and started feeding me Bible verses whenever we spoke. So when she called that morning, I was really surprised to hear from her after a couple of years of not speaking to her much except for "Happy birthday" and "Merry Christmas."

"Hey, Reenie. I'm in the City with Stanley. We thought we'd visit you."
"In the City? Great. Is Sherman with you?" I asked.
"No. I left the bastard in Port Chester."
"What did he do now?" I asked.
"I can't stand it, Reenie. I just needed to get out for a while."

Sherman was Donna's husband and Stanley's stepdad. Donna was never married to Stanley's father, Lucky. The last time he got arrested, she never heard from him again. Even though Lucky was black, Stanley was very light-skinned with beautiful, light brown curly locks. I was glad Lucky got busted, because he always beat Stanley, and Donna would sit there and try to justify it by telling me that it was because Stanley didn't listen. He was only three years old then. I hated Lucky, and I thought Donna was just too weak to stand up to him.

"Donna, where are you?" I asked.
"McDonald's. I think it's Ninth Avenue in the 40s."
"I know where it is. Get a cab and tell him to take you to Eighth and Mercer. I'll meet you on the corner and pay for the cab."
"OK, Reenie. I'll see you in a little while."

"Great! Leave now!" I said as I hung up my new Princess phone.

Donna was very thin. She was always small, petite, but now it seemed her skin just draped over the bones of her face. Her blond dull hair hung limp at her shoulders. I took her rainbow straw shoulder bag, and little Stanley insisted on carrying his little blue vinyl bag.
"Hey, man. Can you high-five?" I asked him.
He held up his hand and we connected.
"You're smart for five years old," I said.
"I'm going to be six tomorrow."

We crossed the lobby, and I picked up Stanley to let him press the elevator door to open.
First I showed them the roof. It was February and there was no water in the pool, but I knew they'd be impressed with the view.
When we got downstairs to my apartment, I pointed to the TV and said, "Stanley, check it out. We got Home Box Office. You can watch movies anytime you want."
"Wow," he said, wide eyes fixed on the black screen.
"Donna, take your coat off. Hang out a while. What were you doing uptown at McDonald's? Why didn't you call me when you got to Grand Central?"
She just stared out the window.
Stanley answered. "Mommy kept telling me to go to the bathroom, but I didn't have to. She say, 'Go to the bathroom, Stanley.' 'I don't have to go, Mommy,' I say to her. 'Go to the bathroom, Stanley.' 'I try and nothing can come out,' I tell her. 'I don't have to go, Mommy.' But she don't listen and she make me go back to the bathroom again and again!"

Donna sat on my couch fidgeting in her straw bag until she pulled out a pack of Newports while Stanley answered my question.
"Are you sure, Stanley?" I asked.
"Yeah. We're on line in McDonald's and she keep telling me, 'Go to the bathroom.'"
It didn't make any sense, and Donna wasn't denying what Stanley said.

WITHOUT FAITH

"Donna, why'd you keep saying that?" I asked.

"I knew he had to go."

"But he said he did and nothing could come out."

"He had to go!" she insisted.

"All right. All right. It's cool. So, Stanley, are you hungry? Did you eat something at McDonald's?"

"No. We just left after Mommy called you."

"All right. Let's go out and get some pizza, and I'll show you my neighborhood."

I wasn't worried about Johnny as long as I was with other people.

I went down the hall to the storage room and got my Peugeot bike so Stanley could ride with me while Donna walked alongside down Eighth Street. It wasn't far, but I used my bike wherever I went and thought it would be fun to sit him on the bar while we rode together. I wanted to show them all the stores on Eighth Street. Donna loved to shop. We had Wrangler Ranch, Gap, and all kinds of shoe stores and music shops.

"We'll get pizza and bring it back to my place," I said.

"OK," Donna said, but she didn't smile or seem interested in anything. I barely pedaled; instead I kept pushing off the curb so Donna could keep up with us on the busy sidewalk.

When we got to the pizza place, I turned to look for Donna. Just seconds before, I had seen her among a few other people on the street, and now she was gone.

I looked up and down the street and didn't see her anywhere. I turned back and rode down the street, shouting her name. There was no answer.

I knew she was gone. She took off and left me with Stanley. Alone ... his birthday tomorrow ... how could she do that? I thought.

"Where's Mommy?" Stanley asked.

"It's OK. It's just for a little while. She took a walk. She'll be back. She always comes back. Are you hungry? Let's get that pizza."

It had suddenly gotten much colder, and the sky was lead gray. My knuckles were red against the white tape on my handlebars. I pedaled back up to Mercer Street with Stanley between my arms.

I called the police and told them that my sister, who was visiting from Port Chester with her son, had just disappeared on Eighth Street.

"She's got to be missing at least forty-eight hours for us to report a missing person," the officer said.

"She's all alone, and I know something's wrong. She runs away sometimes and winds up in the hospital not knowing who she is."

"Sorry, ma'am. We can't do anything for forty-eight hours. You can try the hospitals."

Ever since that day the nuns found the penis I carved in my school desk and everyone believed what I had been saying about Uncle Frank having sex with Donna and me, she was never the sister I knew again. Every so often, she'd drift away in her mind and she'd run away. When she was sixteen, she went missing for weeks and wound up in a hospital in Puerto Rico, telling people she was Marilyn Monroe. But that was ten years ago, and I thought she was fine now.

"OK, Stanley. We're gonna wait to hear from Donna. Guess what! Remember I told you I got HBO? It's brand new in the City. It's any movie you want to see without commercials."

"I wanna see Bruce Lee!" he said.

"Bruce Lee? I don't think they'll have Bruce Lee, but let's see what's on."

I couldn't believe it. I switched the cable box to HBO, and there was a Bruce Lee movie playing. Wow, man. This is a miracle, I thought.

We curled up on the couch together as the city lights grew brighter against the darkening sky.

****

After calling all the hospitals, we waited. Every time the phone rang, I hoped it was Donna. When forty-eight hours had passed, I again called the police, who then listed her as a missing person.

On the third day, I got a phone call from Bellevue. "We admitted someone

WITHOUT FAITH

that fits your sister's description," the woman's voice said. She said her name was Donna but gave a different last name from Birdsell.

When the woman described her as wearing jeans and carrying a colored straw bag, I knew it was her.

"I'll be right over. Where do I go?"

"I'm sorry, but she left without being released."

"Why was she there?" I asked.

"It says here that she was attacked by someone with an iron pipe. We treated her for bruises and abrasions and then she checked herself out. I'm sorry."

There was nothing I could do but take Stanley wherever I went until Donna showed up.

✶✶✶✶✶✶✶

The day came for my abortion, and I had no choice but to take Stanley. The procedure was to take place at the doctor's office on Park Avenue. His nurse assured me that I'd be out in a couple of hours. My friend Ramon was meeting me there, so he could sit with Stanley until I came out.

Because Ramon was the only guy I knew who didn't drink to get drunk or do drugs, I could depend on him. I had told Ramon that it was Hal who got me pregnant.

Stanley had already put on his coat and hat and was waiting for me to say it was OK to leave. I had to look out the window before we could walk out the door to make sure Johnny wasn't lurking outside.

"Stanley, I gotta see this doctor for a little while, so my friend Ramon will sit with you while I'm with him. OK? You need to be good. OK?"

"OK, Reenie," he said as I reached for his hand. We went to the back of the building and slipped out of the garage onto Broadway.

It was morning, and all the cabs were full. Stanley and I walked hand in hand over to Fourth Avenue past Astor Place to get a cab heading uptown.

Suddenly, green glass shattered at our feet, and as I turned around, I felt a hot sting on my cheek. It was Johnny's bare hand slapping my face. The blow knocked me to my knees, and as I drew my hand to my cheek I thought: Thank God it was just a slap and not his fist, which could have really hurt me.

He stepped backward, yelling something in Spanish I couldn't understand. Stanley ran up to him, kicking his shins and screaming, "You don't hurt my aunt. You don't hurt my aunt!"

"Stanley! Get over here! Get away from him!" I yelled.

I grabbed him by the hand and pulled him into the street.

God was with us, and a taxi came to a halt to let us in.

"Uptown. Fast! Please! This crazy guy is after us!"

I hoped we had enough time to get away. As I turned to look out the rear window, Johnny was in a garbage can pulling out a bottle, which he hurled at our cab. It crashed in the street just before reaching the bumper as we sped away.

"Do you know that guy? Are you all right? Should I take you to the police?"

"No. No. We're fine. I have to be at a doctor's appointment on 65th and Park. Please. I'll be all right once I'm there."

The nurse checked me in. I put on the gown, lay on the table, and counted back from 100 while the sodium pentothal dripped into my veins.

I woke in an ambulance with the doctor alongside me saying, "I'm sorry. I'm sorry. Your uterus was like butter. Don't worry — the hospital won't cost you anything. I'll be paying for it."

I was still stoned from the anesthetic and said, "It's all right, but where's my nephew? Where's Stanley?"

"He's with your friend. They'll meet us at the hospital. I have to operate. I perforated your uterus. You should be fine in a few days. You'll still be able to have children. You'll just have a bikini scar that you'll hardly notice after time."

When I woke up, I was in a large room all by myself. A shaft of fluorescent light streamed through the doorway, and voices seemed far off down the corridor. It felt like knives were piercing me from the inside. Oh, God. I was desperate for relief and rang the call button. The nurse bounced in smiling and announced, "Everything went very well. You'll be fine. You just need rest now."

WITHOUT FAITH

"Rest! How can I rest? Fine …? Why am I in so much pain? What's hurting me so bad? Can't you give me something for the pain?" I pleaded.

"It's only air in your belly," she said.

"Air! How can air hurt so bad?"

"There's no way to avoid it. When they sew you up, there's always some air that gets in, but it will pass."

It was the worst pain I had ever had in my life, and I could barely move without making it worse.

I lay there in the dark until Ramon appeared at my bedside.

"How are you feeling?" he said.

I clutched the metal rail, squeezing it as though it would help relieve the pain.

"Where's Stanley? Call his Aunt and Uncle. The last name is Burnell. In Norwalk. That's Sherman's sister and her husband. Donna always told me they were good people. Someone has to come and get him. I know he can't stay with you."

I was in Lenox Hill Hospital, and it would be almost a week before I would be well enough to leave.

Ramon offered to let me stay at his place, where he could take care of me and I'd be safe from that freak Johnny.

It was Sunday when we left the hospital. I was so glad to get out into the cold fresh air of the street.

"Ramon, get us a Checker. It'll probably be an easier ride."

He hailed a cab, and it felt like the cabby hit every pothole on Lexington Avenue.

"Slow fuckin' down! I just got out of the hospital. Forget trying to make the lights," I yelled.

Ramon lived at 30th and Third in a ground-floor studio. It was large enough with his daybed that pulled out to two twin beds for us both to be comfortable.

It was a good idea, and I knew I'd be safe there. We ordered takeout almost every night. Tuesday night was the best because of a new TV show, *Laverne*

& Shirley. They reminded me of what it was like to have a best friend. In my laughter, I was also deeply sad for what I had and for what I had lost with Linda.

I didn't know how, but one Saturday I heard Johnny outside the ground-floor apartment window. "Hey, Birdsell! I know you're in there. I'm going to kick your fuckin' ass when you come out!"

Ramon peeked carefully through the thin slats of the drawn blinds to the street to find Johnny looking up at the building, not knowing exactly what apartment I was in.

"How does he know you're here?" Ramon asked.

"I don't know. He probably followed me here once and figures I might be here but doesn't know for sure. Don't answer him," I said, pulling the covers tight around my chin.

"Maybe I should call the cops."

"No. Let somebody else call the cops. He can yell all he wants as long as he doesn't know we're in here."

"Ramon, you punk ass. I know you've got her. She'll fuck you up too."

"Don't answer!" I said in a loud whisper, hoping for Johnny to just go away.

Ramon stayed inside the rest of the day, and we ordered Chinese that night.

I couldn't stand it anymore, and I knew I couldn't go back to Hilary Gardens, where I lived, and ever be safe with Johnny out there.

I called Hal and said that I was afraid to go home, Johnny was stalking me, and he attacked me on the street. I even told him that I was staying with Ramon, who was helping me get better, but that he was just a friend and nothing more. Hal didn't know about the abortion or the perforated uterus. I covered up with a story that I had a cyst that had to be removed, and he never asked any other questions.

Hal said, "Don't worry. Just call me if you see him again."

A couple of days went by, and again there was Johnny . "Hey, Birdsell! I know you're in there."

I didn't hesitate. I picked up the phone and dialed Hal.

"He's here. He's here right now. ... Right outside the window!"

"OK. OK. Don't worry. I'll call Tony," Hal said, taking deep breaths between sentences as though drawing long drags from one of his Parliaments. "He won't

WITHOUT FAITH

bother you again. Get some rest."

"Thanks, Hal. I'm sorry."

"Don't be sorry. We'll take care of it."

Part of me wasn't sure if Hal or Tony would or could do anything at all. I just wanted Johnny to go away and leave me alone. Tony was a professional wrestler, the last of the legitimate ones. Maybe he'd threaten Johnny enough that he'd go away.

Another week went by, and we hadn't heard from Johnny. I was able to walk without pain, but it still hurt a little when I laughed. I was enjoying staying with Ramon. We talked, watched TV, and dreamed about what the future would be like with new technology.

I said, "I bet one day realtors will have TVs on their desk and they'll be able to show people houses right from their offices and not have to take them out to show them."

"Yeah, but how could we get in on that?" he asked.

"We could take the pictures," I piped back.

We were always dreaming and scheming about new ways to be part of what would be new.

Ramon was teaching me more and more about photography and f-stops and film speeds. I knew how to see a photo, but getting what I wanted to see was a different story. Ramon helped me to learn so I could understand photography.

"Look, the aperture is just like the pupil of your eye. Dark room, big pupil, because you need to take in more light. Bright sunlight, little pupil. You get it?" he asked.

"I got it. Finally, I got it. It's just like my eye. Wow — God made the first camera. We just duplicated it in a box," I said.

"I'm going to Spain this summer," Ramon said. "If you can come up with the money, why don't you come? We'll shoot a lot, and you'll learn that the world is a lot more than what you think."

"OK. I can do that. I'll get Hal to pay my way. We can shoot great stuff and sell the slides to a travel agency."

152

"You think so?" Ramon asked.
"Yeah, sure. Like the airlines. They need pictures."
"So you'll go?" he asked.
"For sure, I'll go."

He started planning a trip to Madrid and the south of Spain and Morocco. We'd return right before the Fourth of July, so we wouldn't miss Operation Sail in lower Manhattan and the big Bicentennial celebration.

With Ramon and photography, I had something to look forward to and things that I could dream about that could be real. I was almost ready to go back to Hilary Gardens. I was on methadone regularly, so I didn't have to worry about copping drugs or needing Johnny to get them.

I was back at home on Mercer Street. Still no Donna — until one day I got a call.

"Do you know a Donna Birdsell?"
"Yes. Yes. I do. That's my sister. Who's this?"
"This is Bellevue Hospital. Donna's been here for a while."
"She's been missing for almost three months!"
"She gave a different name when she was admitted. Donna only told the doctor yesterday that she had a sister here and that her last name is Birdsell."

She was in a locked psych ward. When the door opened, five or six expressionless people, like zombies, shuffled toward me. Among them was Donna. Her hair was limp, and her complexion was ashen gray. She was on Thorazine to keep her calm and to protect her from hurting herself.

At least she was safe, I thought.

WITHOUT FAITH

Chapter 25

Chumley's

Because of the new call forwarding feature that New York Telephone now provided, I received all my calls at Ramon's place when I knew I was going to be there and answered his phone like it was mine.

One day when the phone rang, I was shocked to hear Linda's voice on the other end. It had been at least two years since the city marshal eviction at her Flushing apartment.

"Hi, Doreen? Is this you? It's me. Linda," she said in a cheery voice.

"Hey. What's happenin'?" I said.

"You want to play racquetball?"

"I don't have a racquet," I said, not even thinking about my bikini scar from the surgery that was still healing.

"I have an extra one. Why don't we meet somewhere in the City?"

"OK. How about Chumley's, in the Village? It's a cool place. They say it used to be a speak-easy during Prohibition."

"Sounds perfect."

"Go to Barrow and Bedford, and open the wood door at 86 Bedford Street. It looks like a private house, but it's not."

"OK. How about noon?"

"Great," I said and hung up the phone.

(On a Tuesday night when I was convalescing at Ramon's, we were watching Laverne & Shirley. In the midst of the program, I began to sob.

"Why are you crying? It's a comedy," Ramon said.

"I miss having a friend. I miss Linda." He knew that we were childhood friends, and I had told him about the day she came to my apartment on 48th Street.)

I couldn't wait to see Linda. I downplayed my excitement so Ramon wouldn't notice how thrilling this was for me and perhaps get jealous.

Linda got to Chumley's first and was sitting at a table with her back to the wall and sipping a glass of white wine. Wearing a sleeveless, tight-fitting navy blue halanka lace top and white dress shorts, she seemed a little overdressed for racquetball, I thought. She lifted her glass to acknowledge me as I walked across the creaky barroom floor to her table.

From the day Linda left me in Flushing to go back to Robbie until now, nothing existed except this moment on this June day at Chumley's in the West Village.

"Hey, Linda. You found it!" I said.

"Oh, sure. I just did what you said. It was easy."

As the waiter poured me a drink from the carafe, my fingers traced the outline of one of the names carved deep into the tabletop of our dark wooden booth. I didn't want to speak. I just wanted to be with her in that moment uninterrupted.

Linda's cheeks were flushed red like she'd just been outdoors. She leaned across the table, gently putting her hand over mine. "How've you been?"

"I'm great. I was at my friend Ramon's when you called. I have call forwarding, so I picked up when his phone rang. Most of the calls he gets are for me anyway. It's great, and no one knows I'm not at home — especially Hal."

"You still see Hal?" she asked.

"Oh, sure. He still pays my rent and gives me spending money. Hey. I just moved into a new apartment. You want to see?"

"Sure. ... How is Ramon? You see him much?"

"Pretty much. We go out shooting a lot together. He's got a darkroom, and he taught me how to make my own prints. We're going to Spain at the end of June. We're going to shoot slides and sell them to travel agencies or the airlines."

"Spain? Who's paying for that?" she asked.

"Well, Ramon laid out the money, but I'm going to pay him back. He put it on his credit card. It's only 600 bucks each. He's been there before and knows his way around."

"Hmm ... sounds pretty good," she said.

"How are you doing? You and Robbie ... still in Maspeth?" I asked.

"Robbie and I are getting separated. He doesn't want the same things I do.

WITHOUT FAITH

He doesn't understand. I want to go back to school. I want a house. I want to get out of Maspeth. We live in the same building with his parents upstairs. He's got a good job for the railroad, but that's all he wants. He says he really loves me, but I need to change."

"Wow, that's really cool," I said.

We both took another sip of our wine. Then Linda leaned forward and said, "Look, Doreen … I still have feelings for you."

I was stunned. I didn't know what to say. I was expecting to play racquetball and maybe have a friendship again. I thought this was all over between us. All those feelings I buried … they were alive again.

"Well? How do you feel?" she said, breaking the silence.

For a moment, the intense throbbing of my heart pulsing in my throat left me speechless.

I took a deep breath and said, "I feel the same way, Linda."

"Whew. … I didn't know what you'd say. I just had to tell you."

"Why don't you show me your apartment?" she asked.

Her words came to me like slow motion, and everything else around me faded away. My feet were taking me down Bedford Street, but I didn't feel them touching the ground. We came to Grove Street, where Linda had parked her green, four-speed Mercury Capri convertible. She loved driving a stick.

We crossed Bleecker Street, winding our way to my garage entrance on Broadway, where the attendant took her car.

The apartment was filled with the warmth of late afternoon light.

"What a great view. This could really be nice," she said.

"What do you mean? It is nice."

"Well, you know … nicer than it already is."

She turned to me, smiled, and we kissed. After all the times I'd imagined a moment just like this. This wasn't like the time she came to me on 48th Street. I was ready for this.

She slipped her hand in mine and pointed to the hallway, "Is this the bedroom?"

I nodded and followed her through the doorway.

I'd follow her anywhere.

We lay down and caressed and kissed, and slowly we each got undressed. Her skin smelled clean and fresh, like when we were kids at Candlewood Lake, hiding in the woods, stealing kisses, hoping no one would find us.

We lay there until nightfall in the dim light of the city skyline.
"Linda, can you stay over?" I asked.
"I don't have to leave," she whispered.
"I'm leaving for Spain with Ramon soon. It's all paid for. I have to go."
"I'll be here when you get back," she said.
I still couldn't believe it.

I was slowly detoxing off methadone, down from 100 milligrams a day, and would be down to zero by the time Ramon and I left for Madrid. I thought it would be easier to kick meth far away from New York and the drug dealers. When I got back, I would be clean.

I knew I just had to go through with this trip, get back to Linda, and then explain to Ramon how I felt about her. He'd have to understand that it had nothing to do with him. The way I felt about Linda was so ingrained that denying it would be like cutting out my soul.

The hotel in Madrid was palatial. Our bathroom was bigger than my living room on Mercer Street, and everything was marble. Although the bed was small, and I did whatever it took to keep Ramon from getting romantic.

There wasn't enough sangria in all of Madrid to put me to sleep. I spent every night tossing and turning as my body went through the insomnia of withdrawal.

We would tour all day, shooting rolls and rolls of film. At lunch, I'd drink a carafe of sangria. Ramon had the nerve one evening to say he thought I had had enough, but it was never enough.

He tried to impress me with the beauty and history of Spain. It became daily lectures on the Moors' invasion, their influence on architecture, the landscape, the Romans, and on and on. I tried to be interested, and for some moments I actually was — especially when we were taking pictures. Composing a

WITHOUT FAITH

photograph was the only thing that kept me in the moment.

"Why can't you just be here now? You're always somewhere else. There's so much to appreciate here." His words grated on me like a whining child.

"But I always remember it later. ... And I always enjoy it when I look back."

"But that's too late. It's over by then."

I felt sorry for him. I liked him and what he knew, but I couldn't be whoever it was he wanted me to be.

I couldn't wait to get back to New York — to see Linda and move on. I couldn't sit still, and I couldn't be comfortable anywhere in the world.

When we got off the boat in Morocco, two dark-skinned guys in their twenties who looked like they were locals approached us on the dock. "You wanna buy hashish?"

Before I could answer, Ramon said, "NO! Go away."

Oh, man! Real Moroccan hash ... in Morocco! I thought.

There would be no way I could cop drugs having Ramon with me.

"You buy drugs from those guys and they take your money and then they turn you in and get paid again by the cops."

"Yeah, right! How do you know that?" I asked.

"I read about it. It's true. Forget about it. I thought you're off that stuff anyway."

"Yeah, OK. I am. I'm hungry."

We walked into town and found a fruit stand. When I tried to pay the merchant, our tour guide stepped in and said, "You never pay what they ask. You always haggle."

"I just want a fucking banana," I said.

I didn't like Morocco. It was poor, and the people were distant. I tried to take a shoemaker's photograph, and he ran down the street after me waving a shoe and yelling something about his soul being stolen.

Walking down a narrow stone alleyway with rough stone walls on either side, we came upon a window. I glanced in and saw an old man and a woman with three little children all in one room, sitting on the floor. I thought: Oh, my God. They all live in there? In that one tiny place where anyone can see?

I was so glad we were there for only the day.

The trip back to the Costa del Sol would be another day closer to getting back to New York and to Linda.

It was time to leave the coast and head back to Madrid. I had begun to sleep a couple of hours a night but was up in the early morning light, half due to the excitement about returning and half from still withdrawing from methadone.

I took a walk down the coastal street of Malaga, and a dark, bearded man on a moped motored by. Suddenly, he and his moped crashed into the back of a stopped bus — splattered into the advertisement pasted on the back of the bus. He didn't know the bus had stopped because his eyes were on me and not on the road. He fell listless to the pavement.

I kept walking. I would have kept walking all the way to New York if I had to.

On the flight back, all I could think of was that now I had been clean for almost two weeks. I could get high on heroin now that the methadone was completely out of my system.

Just one more time. After that I'll be clean — especially now that I have Linda, I thought.

It was still daylight when I got back to Mercer Street.

I could bike over to Ninth Street and Avenue D to find out who is selling, I thought.

A familiar face nodded to me from a vacant tenement doorway.

"I got Mexican, man," he said.

"OK. How much?"

"Ten a bag ... fifty a bundle."

"One bag, man," I said.

In one pass, the money and bag were exchanged, and I pedaled back to 300 Mercer Street.

I cooked up the dope and put the needle in the easiest vein to hit in my right arm. My body and my mind were finally at rest. There wasn't anything I wanted, and there was nothing I needed.

WITHOUT FAITH

Just this one last time, I thought as I nodded out.

Linda met me at my apartment the next day and began to move in. She quickly made herself at home, surrounding us with her antique clocks and paintings.

I wouldn't answer Ramon's phone calls. The doorman rang my intercom, but I wouldn't answer, fearing it was Ramon. Seventeen floors from the street, I heard "Doreen! I know you're up there. You owe me money. I want my money. I'll get it from you or I'll go to Hal's office. I know where he is."

"Shit, shit, shit!" I said under my breath.

"What's going on?" Linda asked.

"Ramon ... it's fuckin' Ramon. He laid out $600 for my hotel and airfare. I told him that Hal would give me the money and I'd pay him back, but Hal's not handing me 600 bucks for a trip I took with Ramon. I told Hal it was for my photography, but he just sucked on his Parliament and said, 'No.'"

"What are you going to tell Ramon?"

"I don't know. I don't care. I just want him to go away. It's just an excuse to talk to me."

I felt trapped. I couldn't get out of the apartment with him outside on the street, and he knew about the Broadway entrance from the garage.

I just wanted to get high.

I'll sneak out on my bike, I thought.

"Linda, I'm going to go talk to Ramon ... to tell him to leave me the hell alone. I'll be back."

I got my bike and pedaled through the garage. The traffic on Broadway was stopped for a red light. I flew and didn't know if Ramon was there or not. He'd never catch me on my bike anyway. I raced across Broadway and Astor Place back to Ninth Street and Avenue D.

When I got back to the apartment, I told Linda that I couldn't find Ramon. I said I had waited, but he must have given up and gone home.

I was hoping that she'd get distracted with a TV show or find some decorating project to get involved with. I needed to get in the foyer closet, to the top shelf, where I hid my works behind some old books and sweaters. When I thought she was busy in the bedroom, I reached up to the closet shelf and slid my hand under a pile of sweaters. Linda walked out of the bedroom.

Oh, shit! I thought.

She was holding the blue cotton neckerchief that held my glass eyedropper, needle, and bottle cap cooker.

"Are you looking for these?" she said calmly.

I was busted.

"How much are you shooting?" she asked.

"Not much. … Just once in a while. Maybe once a week. That's all. I'm not hooked. I'm clean. Really."

"We're moving. The only way you'll stop using drugs is if we get out of the City. That's it."

I breathed deep and said, "OK. We'll look for another place." I knew she was right. I'd never stop.

"Where is it?" she asked.

I reached in my pocket and pulled out the glassine bag with white powder.

"Let's get rid of it," she said.

"OK. All right. I'll flush it."

We both stood over the bowl and watched as the toilet sucked down my dope.

The next day, Linda said, "I always wanted to live in Bayside."

"We could probably rent a house for the same amount of rent Hal pays here."

We drove to Gerald's house in Maspeth. She treated Gerald like he was her guru. I really didn't like him, but I wasn't getting Linda without Gerald. He was always after her. I thought she only liked his attention. Every diet there was, he tried, but to no use. Whenever he bent over, the crack of his ass spilled over the top of his jeans. He had wiry reddish-blond hair that hung over his ears and a scraggly beard. Maybe Linda liked his mind. He painted abstracts and tried to sell his work, but with no success.

I sat in Gerald's living room while he and Linda went out on some errand. I finally gave up looking for apartments in the New York Times classifieds and thought: I just want a place where I can move in and put on a pot of coffee.

I grabbed the Queens phone book and thumbed to Realtors and called one in Bayside.

WITHOUT FAITH

I told the woman who answered that Linda and I were interior designers from Manhattan and that we wanted a private house in a good neighborhood in Bayside with a yard, and furnished if possible.

"I might just have something like that here in my drawer. Furnished; one family; fireplace; even a piano. The woman who owned it died, and her son, who was raised there, doesn't want to sell it."

"Really! Is it in a good neighborhood?"

"Well, I would hope so. It's just across the street from where I live. I've been holding out for just the right tenants. You'll have to pass an interview and application process with the owner."

"Great! When can we see it?"

"How about this afternoon … around 2 p.m.?"

"We can do that."

To me it was the most beautiful of all the Cape style houses on the block, with evergreen hedges bordering the front lawn. We pulled into the driveway and walked up the steps onto the porch.

All we had to do was move whatever furniture we didn't like into the basement and replace it with my couch, chair, stereo, Linda's clocks and artwork, and our clothes.

Linda took off with Gerald and left me to familiarize myself with the house. I checked the kitchen, found the coffeepot, and perked a cup of coffee. This was exactly what I had hoped for.

A couple of days later, a car pulled up the driveway. From my bedroom window, I recognized the slender, attractive blond through the windshield. It was Linda's ex, Robbie. He slumped over the steering wheel, crying.

When he came to the door, I was downstairs, and Linda invited him in.

"This is everything I ever dreamed of having with you," he said to her.

I had never seen a guy cry, and I didn't know what to say.

I felt really bad for Robbie, and I couldn't look him in the eye.

After all, he never could have afforded that house anyway, I thought.

It was late October. All the trees around our house were turning red and orange. With the Rolleiflex that Hal had given me, I photographed the autumn scene in our new neighborhood.

Ramon and I were finally talking again after I paid him back the $600 I owed him. We still had a dream together of being photographers with our own studio. Whenever I went to a Broadway show, I'd turn Playbill's pages and imagine being the photographer.

Linda didn't work, and neither did I. My only obligations were meeting Hal for lunch or at a nearby hotel and taking occasional business trips with him to Florida. I was clean and far enough away from the drug dealers on the Lower East Side.

Chapter 26
Private Clubs

Margaret O'Rourke was trouble — black Irish with cobalt blue eyes, high cheekbones, and a compact curved figure. She flirted with almost everyone and especially with Linda. She was one of the girls we had met at the Duchess and I often referred to her as Wonder Woman.

Linda always acted as though we were only friends when we were in a club together. I tried to play it cool and be with her only when she came on to me. It came naturally to me, and I knew deep down that she felt the same way too. We lived together, and at least I knew I'd be the one she'd be going home with.

I liked Margaret, so I didn't say anything about her flirting with Linda. I only hoped it wouldn't go further. She didn't seem to be serious about anyone. I told myself it was all a game to her.

At the end of each month, I would take all the household bills to Hal's office and sit across from him at his expansive burl wood desk and wait patiently as he opened each bill, lining them up neatly across the blotter. He penned each check for the rent, electric, and telephone, and then gave me one or two hundred dollars in spending money for clothes and going out — usually just enough that I couldn't stay away too long. We lived off the money he gave me, but it was never enough.

My friend Sharon told me that she worked for a call girl agency whenever she needed extra money.

"How'd you find one?" I asked.

"In *Hustler* magazine. They list 'em as male escort services."

I got an interview. It was in a turn-of-the-century apartment building on Central Park West. A receptionist sat at a desk in a neatly furnished converted living room with two upholstered wing chairs, a coffee table and white shade lamps. I filled out an application and was asked how soon I could start.

It was great. The agency would call me and give me an address; I'd take a cab that the client paid for, and call in when I got to the client's house. The agency would call an hour later and signal that it was time for me to leave. I got paid $100 for the hour. The agency got half, and any tips were mine.

Most of the clients the agency gave me were regulars, so I would usually know what to expect.

One afternoon I had a call in Brooklyn. The apartment was on one of the upper floors of a twin high-rise that overlooked lower Manhattan from Sheepshead Bay just off the Gowanus Parkway.

When the client opened the hallway door, he stared at me, speechless.

Still wearing a blue Brooklyn Union Gas uniform, potbellied, with thinning gray hair, he eventually spoke. "I'm sorry," he said. "I can't believe it. You look just like my deceased wife."

His wife! I thought. I'm twenty-five years old. How could I look like his wife? This guy's got to be in his sixties.

He invited me in and showed me to the dining area next to the terrace. On top of a high polished dark wood stereo console, next to some bottles of rye and vermouth, was a framed photograph.

"This is my wife, Mary," he said.

The woman must have been twice my age. The only similarity I could see is that we both had brown hair. Maybe there was a little likeness around the eyes and chin, but she was much heavier, I thought.

"You see," he said. "You remind me so much of her."

I nodded my head and asked, "When did she die?"

"Almost a year ago. She was very sick. Cancer. I took care of her until the end. We could never have kids. I only do this because I miss her so much."

I called in to the agency to start my time. He mixed a pitcher of Manhattans, which he said was his favorite drink — and it soon became mine after I discovered it was all high-proof.

After that, we spent about fifteen minutes in the three-piece, matching-set bedroom he used to share with his wife. "It's called Danish modern. Do you like it?" he asked.

"Very nice," I said while unbuttoning my blouse, knowing this would be quick because we had already spent most of the hour talking and drinking.

As I was about to leave, he asked, "Can I see you again? Without calling the agency? I'll still pay you. They must take part of what you make. It could be all yours."

"They don't allow that," I said.

"I won't tell. I don't want to see anyone else but you."

"You know what? Give me your number. I'll think about it."

Linda couldn't believe it.

"Oh, my God! He thinks you look like his wife! That's great! He's falling in love with you — you jerk! This is great! You've got to see him again. Forget the agency. You probably won't need them."

She was right. Artie was in love with me and would do anything I asked him. I quit the agency, and between Hal and Artie we were doing pretty well, I thought.

Linda and I were sitting on our patio in the garden one afternoon when she said, "You know, Margaret works for this place in the City called Club Tahiti. She makes really good money."

"Doing what?" I asked.

"It's a private club for men. Margaret says, 'A guy comes in, picks the girl he wants, and they go into a really nice room.' And … get this … some of them don't even want to have sex! They just want company. The good thing is, they have to pay no matter what. You do that already with Hal."

"Yeah. So what?"

"Well, I think if Margaret can do it, so can you."

"You think so? Margaret's really pretty, don't you think?" I asked.

"You can do it. They'll like you."

"Why don't you do it?" I asked.

"No. I can't. I wouldn't be any good at it. Anyway, I'm too fat."

"Oh, cut that shit out! You're always saying you're fat. It's because you're German. You have those big cheeks, so you think you're fat."

"Anyway, I'm eventually going back to school. I want to major in psychology. C'mon, Doreen. You can do it. Why don't you try?"

It felt like a real opportunity. If Margaret could do it, as good-looking as she was, it would be great if I could too. Linda would be proud of me, I thought.

"All right. What do I have to do?"

"I'll call Margaret and ask her."

Club Tahiti was on the Upper East Side — Lexington Avenue in the 70s. It was a long narrow apartment above a storefront. An Asian girl, her hair pulled back tightly in a long ponytail, was stationed at a tiki hut reception desk. Polynesian music played in the background. A flowered cushioned wicker bench was the only other furniture against the straw-covered wall. Another Asian girl was hunched over a newspaper there. Both girls were dressed in flowered tights and jade green bikini bathing suit tops. The one sitting on the bench had black blunt-cut shiny hair that masked her face.

"Can I help you?" the tiny young girl said from behind the desk.

"I'm here for a job. My friend Margaret works here. She sent me."

The newspaper crinkled and slid to the floor as the girl with the doll-head hair got up and ordered, "Follow me."

Incense burned, and the music was now disco. There were no windows, only straw-covered walls. We entered another hallway, passing more beaded doorways on either side. The only furnishings were Oriental rugs and oversized, stuffed pillows in dark muted colors.

The girl stopped at a doorway and motioned by pointing with her chin for me to enter.

Facing me squarely, she asked, "You have done this before?"

"No, but I did for an escort service."

"OK. Take off your clothes. I have to see if your body has any marks or scars."

I quickly stepped out of my skirt and unbuttoned my blouse. She examined me front and back.

"OK. Get dressed. You have to get a bikini and sarong to work here. You can choose color."

"Where do I get it?" I asked.

"Jennifer at the desk will give you the address of tailor. You pay for outfit. We pay you sixty dollars for every one-hour client, thirty dollars for half-hour. Tips are yours. You have to work four days a week and start on graveyard: 10 p.m. to

WITHOUT FAITH

5 a.m. with two half-hour breaks. Tailor takes about three days to make suit. You come back then."

I was elated. I ran past the lunchtime crowd on Lexington Avenue and hailed a cab to take me back to Bayside.

"Linda, I got it! I got the job!"
"I knew you would! I just knew you would!"
"I wasn't so sure. I never did anything like that before."
"When do you start?"
"I have to go to their tailor in the City and get a special bikini made."
"Let's go tomorrow. I'll go with you."
"You will? That's great! ... Let's celebrate and have a drink," I said.

I could tell Linda was proud of me, and I think my having this new job turned her on.

"I have to work nights. Until 5 a.m."
"That's great, Doreen. You'll have all day! You can still see Hal for lunch. We can spend days at the beach. This is great!"

Three days later, I picked up my mint green G-string bikini with matching sarong and was ready to start work.

The first night, I had four sessions and went home with $300, including tips. I hailed a cab on the quiet, twilight city street and climbed in the back seat.

"Did you have a good night?" the driver asked while checking me out in his rearview mirror.

"Yeah, it was pretty good. How about you?" I asked.

"Not bad," he said.

I always tipped the cab driver more than enough. The money came easy and left just as easy. One of the girls had told me that cabbies loved working girls because they were heavy tippers.

I got used to the hours and the work. The money was so good that I would forget where I hid my cash. One day I was winding one of Linda's antique clocks above the fireplace and felt paper under the clock's iron weights. It was five hundred-dollar bills crumpled up. I must have been stoned when I hid them and didn't remember.

Margaret was on a different shift, so I never saw her at the club. I was doing all right on my own.

All I wanted was to open my own photography studio in the City, but I didn't know how I'd ever get enough money for space and equipment. Gerald had a great idea. There was a vacant lot for lease in Maspeth on the corner of Fresh Pond Road and Flushing Avenue where the three of us could open a newsstand together. He knew a guy who had put a trailer on Fresh Pond Road and Metropolitan Avenue who was making good money. Fresh Pond Road and Flushing Avenue was a busy corner with bus stops on both corners. The only catch was getting the money.

"Why don't you ask Artie to invest?" Gerald asked.

"Yeah. We could make enough money that you could open that studio you want," Linda said.

I thought about it and realized that Hal could help if we needed any special permits because he was an architect. It sounded like a good idea.

After spending the night with Artie and a few more Manhattans, I got the courage to ask him.

He knew the corner and the other newsstand on Metropolitan Avenue and agreed to put up the cash. We bought used trailers and, with Hal's help, got special permits from the building department for temporary structures. We were in business. I told Hal that Gerald had put up part of the money, Linda had borrowed from her grandmother, and I had some of my own savings.

We went to a lawyer and got incorporated as L.G.D. (Linda, Gerald, Doreen) Inc. Gerald and Linda convinced me that they could run the newsstand while I continued to work at the club.

Seven days a week, twenty-four hours a day, Gerald's niece, Linda's mother, and a couple of guys from the neighborhood worked at our newsstand. We even sold Italian ice we bought from the Lemon Ice King of Corona and made a good profit.

One of the other working girls on my shift told me about a place downtown where the clientele was better and so was the money.

"You gotta be really good to get in there. My friend pulls down about five bills a night, and she hardly works."

"What's it called?" I asked.

"Gramercy East."

A wrought iron door had a small sign overhead that read "Gramercy East." I rang the buzzer on the intercom.

"Who is it?"

"I have an interview with Gino. My name's Doreen."

The slate gray concrete staircase led to an underground club. Cigar smoke mixed with whiskey and disco music.

I was met by a man who looked like a wrestler stuffed into an undersized business suit. He led me down a hall and up a few steps into a wood-paneled room.

"This is Gino's office," he said as he knocked once and opened the door.

Gino didn't look up from the papers on his desk.

He was about thirty or so with dark wavy hair and a mustache. For a moment, I wondered if I would have to have sex with him.

At least he's good-looking, I thought.

"You have experience?" he asked.

"Uptown — at Club Tahiti."

"Why do you wanna work here?"

"I hear it's a good club. One of the girls at Tahiti has a friend that works here."

"OK. Let's see. Take off your clothes."

"Right now?" I asked and turned around to see if the wrestler in the business suit was gone.

"C'mon. Right now. I have to see what you look like."

I unbuttoned my blouse and put it on his desk, and then undid my bra, unzipped my skirt, and slid down my pantyhose while I slipped off my shoes. He sat back with his hands folded on his desk, twirling his thumbs, while he surveyed me from head to toe and back again while I stood there naked.

"Hmm. You need to lose ten pounds to work here."

"I do? Really?"
"Yeah. To work here you need to lose ten pounds."
"OK. I'll come back in two weeks," I said.
"When you lose ten pounds. Then you'll come back."

    I always thought I needed to be thinner. That's why I did amphetamines. But no one had ever told me to lose weight — not even Linda.

WITHOUT FAITH

Chapter 27

The Fat Farm and the Model

I went home and told Linda that I could have the job if I lost ten pounds.
"That's so great! We'll go to a fat farm," she said.
"What's a fat farm?" I asked.
"One of those places you fast to lose weight."
"You know about those places?"
"Don't worry. I'll find out, and we'll go."
Linda was excited to go just so she could lose weight too.
By Monday we were on our way to Pawling Health Manor in Hyde Park, New York, where we would juice-fast for a week. We got a room outside the main house in a motel-like building with two double beds. The only stipulation I had was that we have a private room.

When we arrived, the woman who checked us in told us that we might have to have a roommate but would do that only if there was nowhere else to house another guest.

I figured this was my chance to get really healthy. I'd drink fruit and vegetable juices for a week, but most of all I'd be with Linda in a room all to ourselves.

Our room was one of the units in the motel-like section at the bottom of a sloping hill beneath the manor. When I drew open the curtains, a woman with a suitcase in hand was walking down the hill.

"Oh, shit! There's someone coming. I hope they're not coming here," I said.
"Let me see," Linda said, pushing me to the side. "No, she's probably going to another room."
"She's still coming this way. Damn! They said we'd have a private room," I said.

Then came the knock.
"Hi. My name's Debbie. I guess we'll be roommates."
Oh, well. At least Linda and I will be sleeping in the same bed. There's no way I'm sleeping in a rollaway, I thought.

Debbie was a tall brunette with high cheekbones accentuated by dark shiny hair pulled tightly back in a ponytail. Her slender facial features did not match her pear-shaped physique. She put down her bags and noticed my camera bag under the nightstand next to the bed.

"Whose is that?" she asked, pointing to the camera bag.

"Mine," I said.

"Are you a photographer?"

"Well, yeah."

"What do you shoot?"

"I work with another photographer who shoots product, but I want to shoot theater. You know — like the shots you see in the Playbills. That's what I want to do. Right now, Linda and I own a newsstand-grocery, but that's only to get enough money to open my own studio in the City."

"You'd love fashion," she said.

"Oh, really?"

"Definitely. You could photograph me. I work for Ford Models."

"You're a model?" I asked.

"Yes. I'm in their Ford Classics division. I'm an oversize model. I've just gotten a little too oversized. ... That's why I'm here. I need new pictures. You could photograph me for your portfolio ... and mine, couldn't you? That's how it works, you know. ... You take the photos and get to build your portfolio. And you give prints to the hair and makeup people, who get to build their portfolio. It's called a test."

"Yeah. I guess I could do that."

I couldn't wait to call Ramon.

"Ramon. It's Doreen. I met a Ford model. She wants us to photograph her."

"What do you mean us? You mean she wants you to photograph her, don't you?" he asked.

"No. No, Ramon. I told her that I work with you and that we'd photograph her."

"What is this for? Do we get paid?"

"It's called a test. We get pictures, and we give pictures to hair and makeup people and to her. We can shoot fashion!"

"Where would this happen? Why do you need me?" he asked.

WITHOUT FAITH

"We'd do it in the City at different locations. You're really good at that. ... Maybe some in the studio. ... You do the lighting. I'll shoot, and you can shoot too. What do you think?"

"All right. When are you coming back?"

"In about a week. We'll set something up then."

I could tell that Ramon was still angry that I had left him and was living with Linda. He said he tried to understand how I felt about her. I told him it wasn't him — that I just wasn't into guys.

"I'll call you when I get back. OK?"

"All right. I'll think about some places we can shoot."

"Great. See ya."

As each day went by, my energy got less and less from drinking only fruit and vegetable juices. There was a workout room there, so I thought I'd get in shape. It took all my energy just to walk across the lawn to the workout room. I looked at the barbells and said, "No freakin' way."

I couldn't wait until Saturday. The week would be over, and I'd get real food.

A banquet was to be served in the main house. This was better than drugs. Real food — but we couldn't eat until we listened to a lecture about how to cook some of these special vegetarian dishes and make better choices.

All I wanted to do was eat and get on the scale to see how much weight I'd lost.

Finally, we ate. It was the most delicious meal I had ever had, and I couldn't believe it was vegetables. The scale weighed me in at 118. I had lost nine pounds, and my jeans fit great.

We hopped in my orange Karmann Ghia and sped back to Bayside.

Chapter 28

Cherry Grove

It was a hot, muggy August night in 1977. The only thing in my life that I kept impeccable was my 1972 orange Karmann Ghia. Although it was five years old, it had only 22,000 miles on it and looked brand new. It was the summer of Son of Sam. Many of his victims were in Queens, and one of the girls was attacked at a club on Northern Boulevard, not far from where I lived in Bayside.

Linda started going out with this woman, Anna, whom she had met at the Duchess. Nothing I said would change her mind. She didn't want to be with me and was ready to move on without me. There was no way I was going to stay in Bayside alone in that house. I leased an apartment on East 89th Street with Margaret, who thought we'd be great roommates and I'd forget about Linda and Bayside.

Margaret invited me to Cherry Grove on Fire Island with her friend for the weekend to help me get away until I could move out on the first of the month. Margaret usually knew where the best parties were. The girls liked her.

The day before I left, Linda's sister Sally called to borrow my car. I liked Sally. I had known her since she was four years old. She was all grown up now, all eighteen years old of her, and she loved my car.

"Oh, man, Sally. If you mess up my car, I swear I'll …"

"Don't worry. Don't worry. I'm a good driver. I know how much you love that car — I'll be careful. C'mon, you can't use a car on Fire Island," she said.

"OK, OK. But you better call me when you bring it back so I know it's OK."

I was hanging out in Cherry Grove, having a few drinks at Uncle Charlie's, a one-room bar with dance floor between the ocean and the bay.

Linda's away for the weekend with this chick Anna, and I'm drowning on Fire Island, I thought.

There wasn't much going on in the bar. It was still too early for the dance crowd. I took a walk out to the phone booth on the boardwalk and called my

WITHOUT FAITH

answering service. There was a message from Linda's mother that Sally had been in a car accident and she and her girlfriend were in the hospital.

"Oh, shit. My fucking car," I said aloud as I dialed.

"Hello, Carmel, Mrs. Meehan? It's me, Doreen. What happened?"

"Oh, those poor kids," she moaned. "They had an accident. Sally will be all right, but her friend hurt her knee. They sent them both home. Sally said it happened so fast they didn't see the other car."

"What about my car?" I said.

"Oh, pretty bad. Sally said she thinks it's totaled."

Shit, shit, shit. My fucking car! I thought. The one thing I had left. Now that was gone too.

Whatever buzz I had from the wine I was drinking was definitely gone. What else could I do but go back to Uncle Charlie's?

My friend Diane danced into the bar all revved up for Saturday night. I told her about Linda dumping me for this fat bitch and her sister totaling my car.

"You'll feel a lot better. Open your mouth."

She popped in some pills, and I swallowed them down with my white wine.

"Hey, Diane. What was that you gave me?"

"Oh — Tuinals."

"How many?"

"Three."

"Oh, shit! THREE! I've been drinking wine all fucking day. What do you want to do — give me barbiturate poisoning?"

"You better stay with me tonight so you don't pass out," she said.

"OK, OK. But don't leave me."

Time suddenly grinded to a slushy blur. I could see with only one eye open. Diane left the bar, and I fell off the bar stool to follow her. All I could see was her red underwear — or was it a bathing suit? Whatever, I needed to follow it. She moved so fast I kept falling off the boardwalk into the brush. I climbed back up again and caught sight of that red underwear, and then I was in the weeds again. Next thing I knew I was down at the dock where the ferry comes in — the only place in town that was concrete and not boardwalk. I took a dive right on my chin. My red-bottomed friend thought she should take me to the doctor.

The doctor's office was nearby, on a street called Doctor's Walk, plainly marked in big white letters. He bandaged my chin, and Diane must have left me there because it was just he and I now.

"Where are you staying?" he asked.

Thank God the house where I was a guest was on the bay side and I didn't have to remember a street name.

I didn't even know who Margaret's friend was.

I finally spotted what looked like might be the house. It was as gray as the early morning sunless sky.

"Oh, yeah! Up there — that's it."

We walked up the stairs to the second floor. The doctor slid the door open. It was just one big open room with a bed in the back separated by an old couch in the middle. Margaret was crashed out on the bed with her friend lying next to her. They were both on their backs naked. Margaret's friend had a dildo strapped on that was sticking straight up in the air.

"Excuse me, but do you know this person?" the doctor asked.

They both screamed when they saw him, then jumped out of bed and dived behind the couch.

"Who the fuck are you?" Margaret yelled.

"I'm the doctor. Your friend here fell and got hurt. I'm just bringing her home."

"We'll take her. Just put her on the couch."

I was still staggering. I just wanted to stop — to go unconscious.

"OK. Go. Go. She's fine now," Margaret yelled over the back of the couch.

They went back to bed and pulled a curtain across the room for some privacy.

After a few moments, Margaret yelled, "Get the fuck out of here, you pervert! What do you think you're doing? We'll take care of her."

The doctor hadn't left. He was helping me get undressed.

He couldn't get out fast enough, and I heard him stumbling down the wooden stairs.

WITHOUT FAITH

I passed out for a few undisturbed hours.

On the way home that afternoon, I met Emma on the ferry back to Sayville. A white gauze bandage covered my chin, and I was black and blue everywhere you could see skin but I was glad that the bandage was under my chin and wouldn't leave a tan line.

She sat across from me on the sunny upper deck. Her legs crossed with one foot swinging back and forth staring at me, smiling.

"Looks like you've had a good time," she said

I told her about the night before. My ex, her sister, my car. Moving to 89th and Lexington, and that I couldn't wait to get out of Bayside.

She gave me her name and phone number. I gave her mine. I think the bandage and bruises turned her on.

Chapter 29

After Dark

At the end of the bar, Emma sported a cigarette in one hand and waved a bottle of beer in the other. She turned her head in short, quick motions, her hair fanning the air. When she spoke, she pointed her chin downward and long-lashed eyes peered from behind sun-bleached bangs.

This intrigued me, and so did her tall male friend, with the sailor-boy crew cut. He was an uncommon sight in this predominantly women's bar. When she called to tell me she'd be at the Duchess, I thought she'd be alone. I sat at the other end of the bar, hoping to draw her attention. As she walked toward me, I hopped off the bar stool to face her.

"How about a date?" I asked. I was fueled by the anger of Linda leaving me for someone else.

I had never been this forward with a woman I hardly knew and was caught off guard when she replied, "How about tonight?"

I felt my confidence beginning to weaken, but I kept up the pretense and said, "OK. What about now?"

"I came into the City to hang out with my friend John. I can't just ditch him. Why don't you meet me at the Anvil at midnight on 14th Street near the river?"

The wine, the dark smoke-filled bar, the slow music, and her smile dared me to take her up on it.

"That's in the meat district. Are women even allowed in the Anvil?" I asked. She cocked her head and said, "Oh, sure. If you go with a guy, it's cool. Just tell the bouncer you're lookin' for John and Emma."

I wondered what she was into, hanging out with gay leather boys.

"OK. Look for me at midnight," I said.

I parked on 15th Street and walked to the six-story triangular building, which was primarily a sleazy hotel with the Anvil on the ground floor.

A few leather boys were on the street outside the entrance, and I wasn't sure if they were bouncers or customers. I was really nervous about going in by myself. It would probably be pretty easy to find Emma in a gay men's bar, I thought.

I bit my lip, took a deep breath, and thought: It'll be OK. She's just a little young and likes hanging out with gay boys.

No one stopped me at the door. The smoky saloon was overcome with a mixed stench of sweat, beer, and poppers. Men in leather chaps baring skin were everywhere in pairs or small groups, moving in one motion to the beat of deafening disco music. I walked up to the shiny, wet bar and hoped I'd see Emma somewhere on the rail. At the other end of the bar, a young boy in a leather bikini bottom danced on top of the bar. Emma was watching him with a bottle of beer near her lips, laughing and moving to the music. I made my way through the crowd as though she was a safe harbor in a sweaty sea of strange men.

"Hey, babe," she said, grabbing my hand to dance.

When we were on the dance floor, she asked, "You wanna get stoned?"

"Sure, on what?"

She handed me two quaaludes and a bottle of Lite beer, and I chugged them down.

"I gotta get rid of John, but I just can't dump him. Give me a minute."

Parading to the end of the bar where he was waiting, she whispered something in his ear, kissed his cheek, then turned to catch my eye and quickly motioned to the door for me to follow.

****

"I just signed a lease on my new apartment uptown. It's not furnished yet, but I have the keys. We can stop somewhere and I'll buy some towels so we can shower," I said.

"Maybe we can buy an air mattress — you know, like a beach thing to lay on," she said.

I felt caught up in a wave since I had met her on the ferry and that I had no choice but to just keep riding, so I said, "Sure, it's morning. There's got to be some stores open. We'll find one of those 'Everything' stores."

We drove uptown in the MGB that I had borrowed. Margaret needed money, so I agreed to pay her garage bill if she let me use her car. She was breaking up with her girlfriend, and we had decided to move in together. She needed the money for the garage and I needed a car. At least it was an MGB. I missed my Karmann Ghia.

When we got uptown and turned down East 89th Street, the sun had already risen well above the trees of Central Park. I got a parking spot just a few feet from the front entrance to the new Beta North Apartments, where I was leasing. I was always lucky when it came to parking spots.

I was about to step out of the car when Emma said, "I gotta tell you something before we go upstairs."

Oh, geez. What now? I thought.

"I'm a diabetic and I need to take my insulin."

"Oh, is that all?" I said, smiling with relief.

"Not really. I have to give myself an injection — now."

"An injection? ... That's great. Can I do it?"

"You know how?"

"Yeah, I used to use needles. I don't anymore. Not in a long time. But I'm really good at skin-popping. I'll do it for you."

"OK. Cool!"

She pulled a maroon cloth bag out of her jacket pocket. It contained a disposable syringe with a blue plastic-covered needle in a plastic wrapper and two tiny bottles of insulin. She took the blue plastic cover off with her teeth and pushed the needle through the rubber top of each insulin bottle and drew it back.

"Five milligrams of N and five milligrams of R. I take more if I've had sugar or too much to drink."

"Wow, that's great. I can do it. Where do you want it?" I asked.

Lifting up her red-and-black-striped polo shirt and unbuttoning the top of her slacks, she pointed to her thin waistline and said, "Here."

I pinched her waist and popped in the needle with a snap of my wrist, being careful to push the plunger slowly to inject the insulin under her skin.

"You see. You didn't feel a thing, right?"

"No, I didn't. You're good. Now let's see your apartment."

The black mini-venetian blinds had been left drawn all the way to the top of the sliding glass door, and I was blinded by the morning light that penetrated the long living room and kitchen combination. I dropped our new purchases on the floor, drew the blinds, and closed the door to the empty bedroom.

"Nice place. Cool view," Emma said, hopping onto the kitchen counter bar.

"Yeah, I'm moving in soon."

"You have much stuff?" she asked.

"Not really. I'm leaving most of it behind."

"My friend Margaret needs a place to stay, and she's got furniture, so I'll use her stuff and just buy a bed. She's going to sleep in the living room."

"Wanna take a shower?" she asked.

"Together?"

"Yeah. C'mon. It'll be fun."

I hadn't thought about how I looked until we got in the shower.

"You're black and blue everywhere!" she said.

"It's from falling in Cherry Grove the other night. Remember? I told you about it on the ferry. I was so fucked up. I kept falling off the boardwalk."

"Oh, shit! Well, I don't mind. Can I kiss you? Will it hurt?" she asked.

"No, it doesn't hurt."

We kissed and held each other under the hot running water. The water splashed off our bodies all over the bathroom floor and walls because there was no shower curtain. I didn't care. It didn't matter that I was black and blue all over, and I loved that Emma didn't care either.

We dried ourselves off and went into the living room to lie down on the wood floor with only our towels and the box containing the air mattress.

It had an air valve with a pin like a bicycle tube. I was determined to get it blown up. I used my mouth to cover the pin and blew — desperately hoping it would take air.

"Why didn't they tell us this would need a pump! I would have bought a pump!"

"Forget it. It's not going to work. It's really OK," Emma said.

"All right, all right. We'll lie on it. It will still be better than using towels," I said.

We lay on the flat canvas mattress against the hard wood floor, and I pretended that my bruised body didn't hurt.

When I wasn't thinking about Emma, I thought about that flat mattress and how much better it would be if I could only get some air into it.

****

The insurance company paid me $5,000 for the Karmann Ghia that Artie had given me $2,200 to buy. What a deal! I thought. I got top dollar because the adjustor said it had been kept in mint condition and had low mileage.

I drove to Briarcliff Manor with Emma and made a deal for exactly $5,000 for a refurbished 1969 hardtop convertible Corvette. I persuaded Artie to give me another $2,000 for the custom paint job — dark metallic blue with an iridescent white stripe that fanned out across the rear. Finished off with a chrome covered carburetor, mother-of-pearl shift stick, and mag wheels, it overwhelmed me every time I stepped on the pedal.

****

Oh, God. It's another shitty morning. When the hell's it gonna be a beach day again? I can't hack this, I thought, seeing only gray through the black slats of the partially closed blinds. My head pounded when I leaned over the side of the bed, groping to find the clock on the floor to give me a clue what time of day it was.

Margaret and her furniture had not moved in yet. I had only a bed and a couple of wooden stools from Hal's drafting room, but at least I had a car.

I slowly got up and grabbed my jeans and T-shirt that lay in a heap on the floor from the night before. Barefoot, I walked out to the living room and onto the standing-room-only terrace to try to wake up. Usually, I could see all the way to the World Trade Center, but today the towers were lost in the clouds and the only sounds were faint, muted horns from the traffic below, signaling

WITHOUT FAITH

that it must be a weekday.

Oh, yeah, that's right. Last night was Sunday, and I had been out since early afternoon at Bonnie & Clyde's, I remembered.

The bar had recently opened a restaurant serving brunch for women only that included unlimited bloody marys and mimosas, of which I had an unlimited amount.

I wish the damn phone was installed so I didn't have to go outside. I can't even order breakfast, I thought.

I had no memory of getting back to the apartment the night before — only being alone on a dance floor at an after-hours club somewhere in SoHo.

There's a telephone on Lex and 90th across from the diner. I'll call Emma and then get some breakfast, I thought.

The fog turned to a mist, and I tried squeezing my body under the aluminum overhang of the public phone to protect myself from the weather and the world.

Where's my change? I know I had change. Maybe I can bill the call to Hal's number, I thought.

"Hello, Emma. It's me. I can't fuckin' believe it …"

"Believe what?" she asked.

"I can't find my fuckin' car. I can't remember where I parked it."

"Don't worry. You'll find it. Where are you?" she asked.

"90th and Lexington. … Oh, maaan," I moaned.

"What's the matter?"

"I look like shit."

"What are you looking at yourself in?" she asked.

"You know, the mirror reflection on the telephone box?"

"Oh, don't worry. Everybody looks like shit in that thing," she said.

"Just walk around — you'll find Baby. She's hard to miss."

"I gotta find it and get it in the garage before alternate-side-of-the-street parking kicks in. Hey, what if I come out there and pick you up?"

Emma still lived at home with her parents in Bayshore, Long Island, only minutes from the Sayville ferry that went to Fire Island, where we had met.

✷✷✷✷✷✷✷

After a couple of months, Emma and I were still seeing each other. It was really loose, and she liked to party and slept over often. I think Margaret was jealous, because she picked up this chick, Sherry, whom she didn't really like, but she didn't want to be alone. Sherry was not the type to want to get serious either — only drink, smoke pot, and party. She was all legs with long blond crinkled hair from a bad permanent. Whenever she spoke, she'd blow a puff to get the hair out of her face first.

One night after leaving the bar, we were blasting the Pretenders through speakers that hung by chains from the ceiling and doing shots of tequila. There was a loud banging on our apartment door.

Before I could open it, Margaret said, "Wait! *Who the fuck could that be?*"

"Maybe somebody got in the building and wants to break in!" Sherry said.

"Get your gun," Emma yelled.

I stood in the hallway motionless. There was a shot and a loud ping.

I opened the door and saw a man running down the hall to the staircase. He didn't look back.

"I think he heard the shot and got scared," I said.

We were laughing and screaming when Margaret said, "The fucking gun went off by accident. It ricocheted off the fucking stove and hit me in the chest. Look! Mother of God. It left a red mark."

"You shot the fuckin' stove. Oh, man. That's a brand new stove. If they see that, they'll deduct it from my security," I said.

"We can cover it up with white-out or something," Emma said.

"I think you should leave it. It looks cool. If anybody asks why there's a dent in the stove, you can tell them you shot it," Sherry said.

✳✳✳✳✳✳✳

More than a year later, I was at Emma's parents' house celebrating her birthday.

"I can't believe you're nineteen," her mother said, waving the cake knife.

"Nineteen!" I said. "I can't believe you told me you were twenty when we met! You lied about your age! That makes me eleven years older than you!"

WITHOUT FAITH

"So what! I'll be twenty next year," she said, laughing.

We were more like roommates who occasionally had sex. She didn't get in the way of anything I did, and I didn't get in the way of her going out with guys.

✳✳✳✳✳✳✳

By 1981, the economy began to affect Hal's business and he had to tighten his spending. "I'm worth more dead than alive," he said.

There was no way I was going to get a job. I wanted to make a living as a photographer, but jobs were few and far between. The Corvette was too expensive to garage, and I kept getting tickets on the street, so I gave it to my mechanic for some quick cash.

Emma agreed to work as a temp, and we moved downtown into a tenement on East 25th Street off First Avenue — one room with a kitchen sink, stove, refrigerator, and bathroom. But I didn't have to work. It was all Hal said he could afford.

The building was so infested with roaches that no matter how much Emma or I sprayed Raid or set Roach Motel traps, they came back. One afternoon I got so drunk that when the roaches crawled up the wall, I ran down to the basement, where the superintendent had his office.

"I'm going to get a fucking gun and shoot you if you don't get rid of those fuckin' roaches right now," I yelled.

He slammed the metal grate door shut and locked it to separate us. I shook it, screaming, "I'm going to get a fuckin' gun and shoot you!"

The next day I called the AA hot line and went to a meeting at the McBurney YMCA on West 23rd Street. I quietly opened the back door. People were standing around talking at the front of the room at what seemed to be a very far distance. I figured the meeting was over and it wasn't where I belonged, so I backed out the door after only a minute or two. I felt great after that — like I was ready to do something to help myself and not get so drunk anymore.

I wanted a new life. Hal came up with $1,500 for me to move if I promised to get a job, and I left the roaches for a newly renovated brownstone on West 24th Street across from London Terrace Towers. He finally agreed to buy me furniture. Using his charge account, I bought a Henredon sofa and a roll-top desk. Artie gave me his Danish modern bedroom set, and I hung my photography of City nightscapes on the living room wall.

After waiting up all night for Emma, who never came home, I took a drive to my friends Moe and Cindy's house in Maspeth, Queens, to get out of the City.

A young woman in her late twenties was curled up in a sleeping bag, resting peacefully on their living room floor, which gave me an opportunity to study her appearance — short blond hair, long eyelashes, full deep pink lips, and round cheeks.

"You never told me you had any good-looking friends," I said to Moe.

"That's Lydia. She's friends with Cindy. Lives in Jersey."

"Why is she here?" I asked.

"Her lover is in Portugal visiting her mother. We're going on a picnic today. Wanna come?"

"Yeah. Sure," I said.

After the picnic, we all went to the Duchess. I asked Lydia to dance to a slow song, and we kissed.

Lydia was fresh and innocent, compared with the women I had known.

When I told Emma about Lydia, she knew it was time to move out and didn't put up a fight.

✷✷✷✷✷✷✷

If Andrea could have given herself a title, it probably would have been Mayor of the Duchess. She knew everyone and invited me to her twenty-first birthday party.

"Hey, Dor. Check this out!" she said, handing me a star filter she had been given for her camera.

"What a cool gift. You know you can smear the edge with Vaseline and get some really great effects," I said.

Marching toward me with long, quick strides was a little Italian with black curly hair and tight black leather pants. Grabbing the filter from my hand, she said, "It's my gift. I'll tell her how to use it."

"Well, I'm just telling her what else she can use it for. I'm a photographer," I said.

"I majored in photography at the San Francisco Art Institute, and it's my gift. Get your own."

"Whoa, Carol. Be cool. It's OK. This is my friend Doreen. She's just tryin' to be nice," Andrea said.

After a few drinks, we all became friends and started hanging out together.

Carol's girlfriend, Maureen, was a tall Irish girl with light brown wavy hair and a much quieter disposition. I noticed her pull a bottle of vodka out of her shoulder bag and knew I'd met someone who liked to get high as much as I did. We had different styles but were the same in many ways. Maureen liked off-track betting and liquor stores. I liked dance clubs and bars.

Chapter 30

Parallels

It was November 1983. We were still laughing long after we had sped away from the old man who had given us directions to Route 9W so we could find Parallels, the dance bar in the woods of Rockland County. Carol did the best imitation of the old man's crackling voice: "Ya seee that road? Yah take dat road till ya can't take it anymore. ..."

Cars overflowed the parking lot, and we had to find a spot in the lot on the other side of Route 9W. The customers were three deep at the bar, and the dance floor was packed. I ordered doubles so I wouldn't have to go back to the bar as often, but nothing I drank or smoked got me high. We drank, we danced, we drank some more, and I still felt straight.

When the bar was thinning out, the music was a drag, and the party was going somewhere else, we decided to leave. The fog glowed around the streetlights that dotted the wide, winding highway. Carol and Maureen were already waiting for us across the street in the dirt parking lot when Lydia and I stepped onto the pavement hand in hand. To our right, in the distance, headlights were coming through the fog down the highway on the other side of the double yellow line. I pulled my hand from Lydia's and sprinted across the road to the parking lot.

I was almost to the other side of the road when the front bumper must have caught my leg. The impact thrust my body over the hood. The next thing I knew, I was laid out on the highway with excruciating pain in my leg. I entered another reality. A different world from the club I had just walked away from was going on above me. People were milling over me. Carol bent over and made a pillow of her black cape to put under my head. She was waving her arms and pushing people and telling them to step away. It seemed like only seconds later that the police were asking me questions.

"What's your name? Do you know what day it is?" the cop said.
"Doreen. Saturday. Where's Lydia?"

WITHOUT FAITH

Where the hell is she? I thought.

All around me were pant legs, and indiscernible voices were above me. I was laid flat out on the damp, black asphalt pavement of Route 9W. A man in a uniform stood over me talking to people as though I weren't even there.

"Hey! You're standing on my fucking arm!" I yelled up at him.

Carol kneeled down and said, "Calm down, Doreen. There's no one standing on your arm."

"Yes, there is! This fuckin' cop won't get off my arm."

"No, he's not Doreen. I swear."

I had just become aware of the piercing pain in my twisted arm, and I thought it was from this cop standing on it.

A woman who said she was a paramedic straddled my body and with scissors began to cut through my new sweater. I said, "Hey. I just bought these clothes, even the bra!"

She said, "Don't worry, dear. I have to get it off to get to your arm."

All I could think about just then was my brand new outfit.

I was lifted onto a stretcher, and Carol said, "I'm going to come with you. Lydia and Maureen will follow." We were on our way to Nyack Hospital.

Carol waited by my side and said, "They'll probably just put your arm in a cast, and then we can take you home."

They rushed me into the emergency room and then right in to be X-rayed. I kept complaining about my leg because it hurt as much as my shoulder did, but no one seemed to pay attention.

It was around 3 a.m. when the doctor finally got there to examine me.

He said, "You smell like you've been drinking. ... How much have you had?" He sounded more like a cop than a doctor.

"Not much. I was just hanging out with my friends. Maybe I had a couple glasses of wine, but not that much."

I wish I *was* stoned — maybe I wouldn't be feeling so much pain. Maybe this wouldn't have happened at all, I thought.

"Where were you that you wound up here like this?" he asked.

"We were at a club ... Parallels. We were there to see a band we like."

I hoped he didn't know it was a gay bar.

"What about my arm? It's killing me. Can't you give me something?"

He looked at the X-rays and said, "Your humerus is severed. It's completely broken right below the shoulder."

Carol held the hand attached to my uninjured arm. "The humerus is the long bone that connects your shoulder to your elbow," she said.

The doctor turned to Carol with a raised eyebrow and asked, "And who are you?"

"I'm her friend, and I want to make sure she's going to be all right and that she understands what's going on."

Oh, no, Carol. This is no time to be confrontational, I thought.

"If you get in the way, you're going to have to leave if you're not a relative," the doctor said.

"When will I be able to go home?" I asked.

"You're not going home. Hopefully we can do a closed reduction. We'll manipulate the bone to put it back together and hope it holds without open surgery. We need your consent."

"OK. You have my consent."

A nurse shoved some papers over me to sign.

"Wait a minute. You mean it might not work?" Carol asked.

The nurse tapped Carol's shoulder and said, "Miss, you'll have to leave. You can see her after the procedure."

"I'll be here, Doreen. Don't worry," Carol said.

"Carol, wait. Call my cousin Ann for me. Tell her what happened. I can't go tomorrow. I'll call her when I can."

Ann had called me that morning to tell me that Aunt Hazel's cancer was no longer in remission and that she probably didn't have much time left. Although I could not face that this might be true, that Tazel could die, I had promised to visit her at Calvary Hospital in the Bronx the next day.

The doctor was hurriedly pushing my gurney down the hall with one hand and putting on a green operating room gown with the other when the gurney bounced off the wall. I screamed in pain: "My arm. Please! Be careful."

WITHOUT FAITH

He said nothing and gave the gurney another shove to push it through the operating room doors. I felt like trash in a wheelbarrow.

An anesthesiologist gave me oxygen, then an injection that put me to sleep.

"Don't worry. I'll be here the whole time to make sure you don't wake up," he said.

I went from brutal alertness to black; then suddenly, sharp stabs of pain like a railroad spike pierced my shoulder. I could see the masked doctor standing over me, his hands pressing on my shoulder. The raw broken bones moved violently under my skin. I tried to scream, but I could not. Why couldn't they see that my eyes were open? No one heard my silent screams. Then everything went black again.

My eyes sprung open under a fluorescent frosted panel of glass. A television hung suspended at the foot of my bed, while moans drifted through a drawn curtain alongside my bed.

My arm had been stretched out over the side of the bed in an open metal contraption that curved at the elbow. I could barely reach the call button with my good arm to summon a nurse for help. I pushed the gray button again and again.

The bell rang just down the hall, but no one answered. Finally, there were footsteps.

"Please help me. I can't stand it."

The frumpy middle-aged woman resembled a waitress more than a nurse. Nothing felt real.

"Oh, I can't believe you're awake already. We just brought you here from surgery."

"Awake! I woke up while I was in the operating room!"

"Oh, no," she said in a calm voice. "That couldn't be. You were under anesthesia."

"No way! I was awake. They didn't even see I was awake."

"Please give me something. I can't stand it. And my leg — I think it's broken."

"You've torn all the ligaments. Sometimes that hurts as bad as a break."

"It's killin' me."

"I can't give you anything else for three hours."
"Can't you call someone to give me something?"
"I could get you some juice."
"Juice! I need something to kill the pain. Please. Please!"
"I'm sorry. We'll give you pain medication when we can."

Agonizing moans from the other side of the curtain in my room grew louder.
"Are you all right? Can you hear me?" I asked.
Whoever it was only moaned louder, and the moans made me hurt even more.
I could think of nothing else but the piercing, stabbing pain in my shoulder. In my mind, I saw an image of Jesus on the cross with nails piercing His hands and feet. His face was not one of pain but of a deep, heartbroken sadness. This wasn't like what the nuns taught. This was real.
"Oh, Jesus. How did you stand it? This is just my shoulder. Help me get through this," I prayed.

I didn't know if it was day or night. The doorway to the yellow hallway was mostly vacant, and the light never changed. I listened for footsteps, but they rarely came.
I stared at the door, hoping Lydia would come, or the nurse to relieve my pain, or the doctor with some news — anyone or anything for relief.
Light footsteps from the hall drew nearer. It was Lydia in her new black leather jacket and jeans. She couldn't kiss me or touch me. She stood by my bedside rocking back and forth, shaking her head, biting her lower lip.
"Look. My mom's coming in from California tomorrow for Thanksgiving weekend. I don't think it's a good idea for her to meet you like this."
"I don't either, but can't you leave her for just a little while to come see me?"
"I don't know. It takes an hour to get here without traffic, and I really don't want to leave her alone. I'll try."
"Lydia, I just want to get the hell out of here. I want to go home."
"Don't worry. You will. Listen — I gotta go. I got a lot to do. I'll call you later."
I kept the phone by my side, where I could quickly reach it with my good

arm. The phone and the call button were my lifelines.
I called Ann to get Aunt Hazel's number.

"Hi, Aunt Hazel? It's me, Reenie. How are you?"
"In a lot of pain, Reenie. How are *you*? Ann told me what happened."
"I'm in a lot of pain too. I don't think they know what they're doing here. I just wanted to let you know that I'll see you when I get out."
"Oh. ... OK, Reenie. Make sure you keep in touch."

The next day, the phone woke me from a semiconscious state.
"Hi. It's me, Carol. I'm at my mother's, and she made a great dinner. I'm bringing you leftovers so you can have a real Thanksgiving meal. That hospital food sucks."

She bounced through the door dressed head to toe in black leather, swinging a bag of turkey and trimmings stuffed in Tupperware.
I wasn't hungry, but I was starving for company, and Carol knew what I needed without my having to ask.
"When are you getting out of here?"
"They're taking me to St. Vincent's tomorrow by ambulance to do another operation. My operation didn't work, and they said I probably need pins to hold the bone together. I told them I want to get back to the City ... I want to go to St. Vincent's. I don't trust this doctor."
"Yeah, he's an asshole. I think he hates women. Is Lydia going with you?" Carol asked.
"She'll be here in the morning. She'll follow behind the ambulance."
"I can go too ... if you want."
"No, that's OK, Carol. Thanks anyway, but Lydia will be right behind me."

✶✶✶✶✶✶✶

It was 9 a.m. and Lydia still hadn't arrived.
"I'm giving you an extra dose of Dilaudid for the ambulance ride. It should help the pain when we have to move you," the nurse said.

The more the better, I thought. And thank God I'm getting the hell out of here.

"The attendants are here. We're going to move you in a few minutes."

"No, I can't go yet. ... My friend's not here!"

"You can't wait. We've got to move you now."

"No. Wait a minute. ... Did she call? She said she'd be here. I can't go. What'll happen if I leave and she comes? She's gonna ride behind me. I need her to be here."

"Look, the ambulance is here and we cannot wait," the nurse said.

There was nothing I could do or say to make her change her mind. I was in the ambulance on my way to New York and felt every painful ripple in the road.

Tall bare trees and telephone poles one after the other blurred by in the side windows of the ambulance.

The two attendants in the front seat had my life in their hands.

"Hey, this van stinks like beer. What do you guys do — drink in here?" I yelled.

"No way!" came a voice from the passenger seat.

"Hey, listen. Do you know how to get to the City from 9W?" he asked.

"You mean, you don't know how to get to the City?"

"We never did this trip. But we have a map."

"I don't know. I can't see where you are."

We hit a bump, and the pain pierced through my arm like a sword pushing from the inside out.

"Take it easy! I'm in a lot of pain," I yelled.

Then we hit what felt like a crater pothole. My stretcher bounced out of the steel hook that kept it secured to the side wall of the ambulance. My stretcher was rolling. I was petrified that my shoulder was going to slam into the wall of the van.

"The stretcher's loose! Help! Slow down. Please, STOP!"

Without a word, they pulled over and hooked me back in.

I didn't trust them. I swore they drank in that van. They kept making turns and stops on wooded streets. Where was the highway? Were they going to rape me? How could they? I'm all bandaged up, I thought.

I lay frozen with my fists clenched. "Please God, please just get me to

WITHOUT FAITH

St. Vincent's," I prayed, hoping they wouldn't hurt me.

My heart raced with hope when I saw the tall buildings. The ambulance came to a stop, and I was lifted out onto Seventh Avenue.

Men in sparkling white uniforms took over and pushed me into a hall and said someone would be back for me.

I wondered how Aunt Hazel was. She was lying in a hospital bed too, waiting to hear from me.

It was only minutes later that Carol walked down the hall toward my stretcher. She gently put her hand on mine and asked, "Are you all right?"

I told her about the ambulance ride … that Lydia never showed up … and how glad I was to see her.

"You'll be all right now," she said, patting my hand.

My room was in a new wing that overlooked the West Village. Its warm peach-colored walls, pleasant pictures, and kindhearted nurses made it feel more like a hotel.

I got settled and was given some medication that finally eased the pain.

Lydia eventually showed up. "Our car broke down, and I couldn't get in touch with you. You were gone when I called. I'm sorry, I'm really sorry."

I had never really needed her before this. If I were dying, this would not be the person I would want to be with, I thought.

When she left, I reached for the phone to call Aunt Hazel.

"Hi, Aunt Hazel. It's me, Reenie."

"Oh, Reenie! How are you, sweetie?"

"I'm fine, Aunt Hazel. I'll be fine. I have a good doctor who's going to operate tomorrow. I'll be out of here in a couple of weeks and come see you."

"Oh, that's good news."

"How are you? Are you all right? Isn't it something — we're both in the hospital?"

She laughed a little and said, "Yeah. Who'd ever want that?"

"You're going to be all right. I know you are, Aunt Hazel."

"Oh, I'm OK, I suppose. Ann told me I'd go home soon. They just don't know when yet. I'll see you soon, OK? You take care. Call me."

✷✷✷✷✷✷✷

The next day, I had open reduction surgery and Dr. Boland inserted a pin that successfully held the bone together. I made him promise that he would cut me where the scar would not be obvious when I wore a bathing suit.

In a matter of days, I was walking again and closer to getting out of the hospital.

I had a good surgeon whom I trusted, and days filled with phone calls and visits from friends. I talked to Aunt Hazel on the phone every day. "I'll see you as soon as I get out," I promised.

Two weeks later, I was home and getting disability checks. I thought how lucky I was that the driver had good insurance.

I bought two slings — one gray for every day and a red plaid one for when I wanted to dress up a little bit.

I was finally able to go and see Aunt Hazel in the hospice. I was afraid to go by myself on the subway. My arm was still very fragile and healing. I couldn't drive yet, and Lydia told me she couldn't get out of work. Carol, who knew the Bronx well, said she would drive me.

Aunt Hazel was in a private room. Her face was taut and drawn, but she attempted a smile and then grimaced in pain. I gently kissed her cheek.

"Reenie, could you help me? My leg hurts so bad. Maybe it'd help if you put it on a pillow for me."

She had never asked me for anything ever until now.

I had only one good arm to help her, but I managed to lift her heavy, swollen leg. When I rested her leg on the pillow, she said, "Reenie, dying's a bitch."

My whole life, I rarely heard her curse or ever complain.

Ann called me a few days later and said, "Reenie, you need to get to the hospital. She wants to see you before she goes."

WITHOUT FAITH

When I arrived, Ann and her kids were there. I held Aunt Hazel's hand and squeezed it.

Ann whispered in her ear, "Mom, Reenie's here."

Aunt Hazel woke for a moment, and her blue-gray eyes met mine. Her lips parted, and she went back to sleep.

The nurse put her hand on my shoulder and said, "She's gone."

"She waited for you, Reenie," Ann said.

There would be a two-day wake and then the funeral in Glendale.

I bought two bottles of white wine and put on the stereo.

I played the same song over and over: "Ain't nothing gonna break my stride. Nobody's gonna slow me down."

I couldn't cry, and I couldn't get high.

Lydia drove me to my friend Moe's house in Maspeth so I could go to the funeral home with my friends who had known Aunt Hazel.

I was wearing a gray and burgundy pinstriped suit for the wake.

My belly began to get very itchy, and I thought it was the wool suit. I lifted my blouse to look at my waist. I had welts all over, like somebody was writing on my stomach from the inside out.

"Oh, my God. You've got shingles," Moe said.

"Shingles! That's what my Aunt Marion always used to get. I'm too young to get shingles."

"It's not how old you are. It's from nerves," Moe said.

"Oh, shit. Now what do I do?"

"Have a drink and calm down. Maybe it'll go away."

I lifted the gallon bottle of Almaden and poured another glass of wine, and then another, and another, but nothing helped and nothing changed.

I didn't know what I was feeling. I was crawling inside. I paced around the dining room table until it was time to leave.

As soon as I walked into the funeral home, the smell of flowers was overwhelming. It was a disgustingly sweet fragrance, an overpowering floral stench. I wanted to leave, but there was no way I could. This wasn't like when

Uncle Ted had died of a heart attack five years earlier. I was high on heroin then, and nothing penetrated.

Someone was leading me through an archway to a red-carpeted room lined with those awful flowers. There was Aunt Hazel in a beautiful powder blue dress with a pink corsage.

The pain of cancer was erased from her face, and she was as I had remembered her.

I was empty. Aunt Hazel was gone. Nothing would ever be the same. There was no going back and no one left to prove anything to and no one to blame.

WITHOUT FAITH

Chapter 31

Blue Nun and Harleys

My life felt like a barren desert, and the only water that trickled through came out of a glass at a bar. It had been four months since Aunt Hazel died. The only thing I was proud of was that I was thirty-two years old and still got proofed at the bars. The money I was getting from Hal was less and less, as he complained that the economy hurt his business and he was probably worth more dead than alive.

The changing seasons only meant coat or no coat.

It was a Monday night in mid-May. Margaret, whom I still thought of as Wonder Woman, invited Lydia and me to a see a movie at her apartment in Sheepshead Bay. Monday was the only day of the week I did not drink, unless I was going out. Lydia popped open a can of beer, and I emptied a bottle of Blue Nun into my glass.

Lydia drove our new used Datsun 280ZX through the Battery Tunnel into Brooklyn, where Margaret was sharing an apartment with her old high school friend Julie the pothead. We smoked a joint and had a few more drinks. Then Margaret announced that we were going to watch the movie *Caligula*.

"What's *Caligula*? A gladiator movie?" I asked.

"No, man. ... It's a really cool porn flick," Margaret said.

"I don't want to see that!" I said.

I thought that only perverted men watched porn. It made me sick to think of it. My own memories of Uncle Frank flashed back. I had to get out of there.

"Oh, c'mon. It'll be fun," Lydia said.

"I'll drive Lydia home if you want to go," Margaret said.

Margaret looked like a cheap hooker with overdone red lipstick. I knew there was something going on between them. I didn't care. I just wanted to get out of there.

"OK. I'll drive myself home. I'll see you later," I said.

Nobody seemed to care.

My fractured left shoulder had healed well enough with the help of the pins in my arm. I no longer needed a sling, and I was able to steer and shift well enough. Back on the Belt Parkway, I pressed the buttons for the windows to roll down, pushed my foot to the floor, and shifted to fifth gear. It was late, and only a few cars were on the road as I wound my way alongside the bay under the Verrazano Bridge, whipping past each car.

A roar of motorcycle engines drew near, and suddenly motorcycles were all around me. A guy with a long black and gray streaked beard blowing in the wind and a swastika on his helmet cruised by, revving his engine. "You wanna race?" he yelled into my open window.

Another guy on a Harley was on my passenger side looking in my window, and another cruised just behind my rear bumper. I clutched, downshifted, and pushed my foot to the floor for more power. We took the turn around the river onto the Gowanus toward the Battery Tunnel. As fast as they had appeared, they were now gone. My car was no contest. I was alone and felt empty and desolate.

I wasn't used to feeling like this. I wasn't used to feeling anything at all. Kelly, one of our friends who rented the apartment across the hall, had been bugging me to see her mother, who was a therapist. One morning after one of my drunken rampages, Kelly had asked: "Do you know you're an alcoholic?"

The next day would be the third Tuesday of seeing her mother, Rosalyn, who had become my therapist. Tuesday was a good day for me, because I usually didn't have a hangover.

But tonight I didn't care if tomorrow was Tuesday or any other day. When I got home, I made another drink and still felt like shit. I couldn't get high and I couldn't sleep, so I just drank until I passed out on the couch.

I was startled by a knock at the door. The morning light shone through the grate of the ground-floor living room window. The knock got louder.

"Who is it?" I yelled.

"It's me. Julie."

I stumbled to the door. Julie stood there, leaning against her old, rusty bicycle.

WITHOUT FAITH

"You rode here from Brooklyn! Don't you still feel stoned from last night?" I asked.

She smiled, and her grin revealed a big pot seed stuck between her two front teeth.

"C'mon. Let's get high. I got some really good weed," she said.

"No thanks, Julie. I just got up. Not today. I have a therapy appointment at 11 o'clock. What the hell time is it? What are you doing here so early?"

"I don't know. About eight? I took my bike on the subway and rode the rest of the way to hang out with you. Lydia's still in Brooklyn with Margaret. Wait a minute. ... Therapy! Why the hell are you going to therapy?" she asked.

"I don't know. Kelly told me she thinks I'm an alcoholic and maybe I should see her mother, who's a therapist," I said.

"Oh, yeah. That's right. She's a shrink. You don't need that shit."

"I don't think so either, but I'm going to prove it to Kelly," I said.

Although it was less than a mile from my apartment in Chelsea to Horatio Street, where Rosalyn had her office, I drove. I felt safer knowing my car was outside.

I got a parking spot just a few doors from her building, and I had about ten minutes before our appointment.

I gripped the steering wheel with both hands and thought about the night before on the Belt Parkway. I was bored, lifeless, and sick and tired of every day melting into the next.

"I could actually go on living like this." The thought startled me.

"Oh, God. You can't, you can't," voiced another thought, sounding other than myself.

"I could stop drinking," I answered.

"What would I do with my life without drinking?"

"I don't know, but it would be better than this," the unfamiliar voice said.

"What about Friday nights?"

"You'll be fine."

"What about my friends? ... Who am I gonna hang out with?"

The other voice said, "You're tired of this. You *can* live without drinking."

202

"No, I can't."
"Yes, you can!" said the louder voice.

My hands clutched the steering wheel even tighter. I squeezed my eyes shut; every muscle tensed. It was as if a huge wall that split me in half came crashing down.

I let go of the wheel, opened my eyes, and whispered, "I'm not going to drink anymore."

It was as easy as that. It was gone. The contrary voice and the desire to drink were gone.

I felt elated. I had the answer, and I knew what to do.

It was time for my appointment with Rosalyn. I rushed to the doorway of her lobby. I couldn't wait to tell her.

Her living room doubled as an office that overlooked uptown Manhattan. Everything looked different, brighter. Even Rosalyn's horsy, masculine features appeared softer.

I took my usual place on the shiny brown leather couch across from her.

Legs crossed, she swiveled back and forth in her chair and asked, "So, how are you today?"

"I'm fine. I'm really, really good. I've decided that I'm not going to drink anymore."

Rosalyn smiled and nodded her head slowly and asked, "How are you going to do that?"

"I'm just not going to. You don't understand. Something just happened to me downstairs while I was waiting to come up here. It was like a battle in my head. Then it was finally over. Believe me, Rosalyn. I know I'm not going to drink anymore."

"Well, what about Lydia, whom you live with? Doesn't she drink?"

"Yeah, but that's OK. It doesn't matter what she does. I'm not going to."

"What about all your friends? Don't they drink?"

"Yeah, but that's OK. I'm not going to drink with them. Julie came over today and offered me a joint and I told her, 'No.' That was easy."

"I'm really glad that you've decided not to drink anymore, but I really think

WITHOUT FAITH

you would do well with the support of a program. You've heard of Alcoholics Anonymous, right?" she asked.

"Oh, yeah. I went to one of their meetings a few years ago after a really bad night. I was really upset, and there were all these roaches in my apartment that the super wasn't doing anything about … no matter how many times I told him. I was wasted and told him that I'd get a gun and shoot him if he didn't get rid of the roaches. The next day when I woke up, my girlfriend, Laurie, threatened to leave me if I didn't do something. I knew that was bad and that I was in trouble. Even my side hurt. I thought that maybe my liver was swollen. I called Information and found a meeting at the McBurney Y on West 23rd."

"What was that like?" she asked.

"All I remember were the backs of people's heads in this big room and somebody talking up at the front. I stood at the back of the room for a little while. The only thing I remember was people saying what their name was and that they were an alcoholic. I felt bad for them. I knew for me that I just needed to stop drinking by myself during the week."

"What's different now?" she asked.

"I know I'm not going to drink anymore. I just know it. It's gone. I can't wait to tell Lydia and Kelly too. I don't need a program. I'm going to do it this time. This is different. I felt the wall come down."

"Doreen, I'm really glad for you and I believe you, but I think you'll do so much better if you just go to AA."

She leaned over in her chair with both feet firmly planted. Her dark eyes locked with mine as if this were a plea. I felt so bad for her because I knew that she thought she was right and that AA was what I needed.

"Rosalyn, look. I'm not going to drink anymore. I really appreciate you thinking that I need AA, but I know that I'm not going to drink anymore. I don't need to go there."

Leaning back, she said, "All right, Doreen. But remember, it's always there when you need it. Will I see you next week?"

"OK, sure."

I felt really bad for Rosalyn. She tried so hard to get me to that AA. In the hallway outside her apartment, I was about to push the call button for the elevator when I turned around and rang her doorbell instead.

When she opened the door, I said, "Look, Rosalyn. I'll do this if you really want me to. I'll go to AA if you go with me, but you have to meet me before the meeting and come with me."

"That would be great. There's a meeting I can take you to this Friday at the seminary on Ninth Avenue and 20th Street. Meet me on the northwest corner at quarter past six. And if you think you're going to drink before then, call me first," she said.

"I'm not going to drink, Rosalyn. I'm serious. I'll meet you on the corner Friday."

"OK. I'll see you then." She smiled and closed the door.

WITHOUT FAITH

Chapter 32

First Days Sober

I didn't know what to do first. I had had clothes at the dry cleaner for a really long time — maybe they were still there, I thought. It would be like getting new clothes. I went to D'Agostino for groceries and filled the refrigerator, then cleaned the apartment. My new life was already better than ever.

Thoughts raced. What else do I need to do? I can't remember the last time I had my teeth cleaned. I'll make an appointment with the dentist.

Lydia would be home from her job at UPS around 5:30 p.m. She was well-suited for the work with a trim figure, bulging biceps, and an easygoing personality.

I had the table set and a meatloaf cooking in the oven. I never cooked. Meatloaf was the only dish I remembered Aunt Hazel teaching me to make.

"This is great," Lydia said while attacking the meatloaf. "How was your day? Did you see Kelly's mom?"

"Yeah, I did."

"How'd it go?" she asked.

"Well, Lydia. ... I decided that I'm not going to drink anymore. Rosalyn wants me to go to AA. I don't need AA, but I promised to go because she insisted. I felt bad for her. So I said I'd go."

"AA! You're kidding! You're not going to drink anymore? I mean, sometimes you drink too much ... but it's just for fun. Maybe you can cut down a little, but geez, you're not an alcoholic, for God's sake."

"Every time I drink I get stoned. I can't do it anymore. I really thought about it. I feel great knowing that I'm not going to drink anymore. Something happened, Lydia. I can't explain it."

"But you're not an alcoholic!"

"I thought you'd be glad about this! You always told me I drank too much — that I better slow down or I'd hurt myself again."

"Yeah ... slow down ... not stop completely. ... You can control it."

"Lydia, my mind's made up. I'm going to do this."
We ate the rest of the meal in silence.

✸✸✸✸✸✸✸

It was Friday, May 18, 1984, and I hadn't had a drink or a joint, or even an aspirin, since Monday night. It had been three days since my therapy appointment with Rosalyn. While I waited for her on the corner of Ninth Avenue and 21st Street, I caught my reflection in the corner store window. Rosalyn had said in one of our sessions, "Think of all the money you'll save not drinking," so the money I would have spent drinking that weekend I had already spent on new pants, a blouse, and a vest. I wanted to make sure I looked good for this meeting and for Rosalyn.

Wow — this is the first Friday night that I'm not going to get high, I thought. Everything felt new. The light was golden; the sky, a pastel blue.

Rosalyn was right on time but didn't even stop to exchange hellos and barely smiled.

"I'm glad you came," she said.

She touched my elbow and pointed toward the seminary across the street to hurry me along. We passed the lobby and entered a beautiful garden in pink spring bloom that was enclosed by an entire block of two-story brownstone buildings partially covered in ivy. I had never thought something this beautiful could exist behind the cold, tenement exterior of Ninth Avenue. The garden path led to a doorway, where several groups of men and women hovered, talking and smoking cigarettes. One by one, they entered the building into a ground-floor classroom. More than a few nodded and said hello to Rosalyn as we made our way inside. I felt safe in her company.

The room was filling up quickly. I took a seat at one of the school desks near the door where we entered, while Rosalyn moved closer to the front across the aisle.

A pudgy guy in his early twenties wearing a white T-shirt tucked into his jeans stood at the front of the room next to a woman who sat at a desk facing the classroom. She was a little older than he was, with short, curly Irish red hair and a rosy complexion.

WITHOUT FAITH

When he introduced her as "Our speaker tonight ...," I lit a cigarette to settle down.

She began with her childhood, when she lived in the back of a candy store that was owned by her mom and dad. She said, "It wasn't all ice cream soda for me, although it was fun when my friends came in. Every afternoon, my father would find a reason to send my mother out to run an errand or something. He would lock the door and turn the 'Open' sign to 'Closed' and send me to the back of the store, behind the curtain. I knew he would follow me and make me take off my clothes."

I couldn't believe it! She said that in front of all these people! I looked around the room to see if other people were as shocked as I was. I expected people to be talking to each other about what they had just heard. I looked at Rosalyn for some kind of acknowledgment, but she and everyone else continued listening to the speaker like nothing had happened, munching their snacks, flicking their cigarettes in tin ashtrays, and puffing away. I lit another cigarette, and my spine stiffened.

She said, "I hated having to work in the store after school, and every day I hoped my mother wouldn't leave because I knew what he would do."

Oh, my God! I thought.

She went on to talk about her drinking and then drugging, and by the time she was finished speaking, I felt like I had come home — that at last I fit in somewhere.

At the break, a very thin guy about twenty-five years old gave me a small brown manila envelope and said, "This is a beginner's packet." He opened it and took out a little phone book and a pencil and wrote his phone number and told me I could call him anytime. Then another took the book and the small yellow pencil, scribbled her name and number, and said, "You can call me too. This is how it works."

Rosalyn asked, "How'd you like the meeting?"

"I can't believe it. I wish I would have known about this when I got out of Odyssey House."

"You're not ready till you're ready," she said.

Chapter 33

No Will of My Own

When I stopped drinking and using drugs, I could no longer hide from myself.

Lydia moved out. Soon after, Carol moved into my Chelsea apartment but still kept her East Side studio. All it took was admitting to Lydia that Carol and I had kissed, and she was gone.

Carol was a film editor. I loved photography. She hated men, was fiercely independent, and encouraged me to stand on my own two feet.

I had to stop living as though somebody owed me something because I was betrayed as a little girl. No one could give me back my childhood and its innocence. I had to stop relying on the things and people who kept me from being me.

I couldn't stay sober and keep seeing Hal. I just stopped calling and answering his phone calls.

Although he was overtaken by illness, I couldn't bring myself to see him when he was hospitalized for liver disease. I had always felt as though I was indebted to him. I couldn't be the person I was trying to become and visit the darkness of my past by seeing him again.

"I really need to see you," he said when I finally answered one of his calls.

"I can't, Hal. I can't see you anymore. I'm sober now, and what we did all these years is wrong."

"No, it isn't. I loved you. I took care of you. It's not wrong."

"Yes, it is, Hal. If it were your daughter, would you let it be OK for her to do what I was doing?" I asked.

There was silence.

"Goodbye, Hal."

The next thing I had to do was let go of Artie. I went to Silver Springs, Florida, where he had moved when he retired. I had to face him to say goodbye.

I thought Artie would understand because he always said he wanted what was best for me. I felt like he was just a nice guy I took advantage of to get what I wanted. He had lost his wife and was vulnerable. I could rationalize his behavior, but not mine and not Hal's.

At every opportunity, Artie would ask me to marry him. I had finally told him that I was gay and it would be impossible. His argument was that I needed to be taken care of and that I'd be his legal beneficiary, entitled to his home and stocks and eligible to collect his Social Security benefits when he died.

I couldn't do it. I had little to hold onto but my name. Somehow, I knew or felt that I could never erase a marriage.

When I told Artie that I was leaving him, he argued: "But I've left you everything in my will. Everything's yours."

"I don't want anything from you, Artie. Take me out of your will. I'm sorry."

Chapter 34

Personal Development

I had gotten a job as a freelance secretary at Broadway and Ninth Street. It was perfect. The dress code was relaxed, and it was in the Village. It seemed that most of the freelancers who were pounding the keys for a paycheck were actors, writers, designers, and artists of one sort or another.

A woman who worked there introduced me to Actualizations workshops, a spinoff of EST, the Erhard Seminars Training. I got hooked. I became completely immersed in this new thing called personal development.

I was introduced to men and women I would have otherwise never known. They were a mix of corporate executives, actors, doctors, secretaries, business owners, and others all looking for something more. My friends were still spending their time and their money in the Greenwich Village bars. I didn't drink, and I didn't want anything to do with my old life.

The people I now spent most of my time with were involved in Actualizations. We bonded, sharing our histories, hanging out in coffee shops, and becoming friends.

I talked a lot about my Uncle Frank, the sexual violation, and my early childhood. I longed for someone who would finally listen to me and hear my story. I wanted to purge the sickness that I felt Uncle Frank left on me. I was impatient to catch up with the life that I had missed for the past twenty years.

More than two years passed. I put all my enthusiasm and ambition into completing what the Actualizations founders called the leadership development program. I was determined to finish, although many who tried could not. It required commitment to continue what was called "inner work" by participating in advanced workshops and facilitating workshops for beginners. But mostly the measurement of success came from selling the workshop to others. Basically it was a lot of sales training in how to enroll people in the workshops — without which there would be no Actualizations.

I was completely ripe for this — guilt-ridden for never finishing anything, for being a disappointment to my aunt and uncle for failing to graduate from high school on time, and getting discharged from Odyssey House for breaking a cardinal rule by having sex. I had been a disgrace and a loser. I heard my aunt's voice: "Reenie, what's wrong with you? Why can't you finish the things you get started?"

I had a chance now, I thought, to prove that I could finish something worthwhile.

After completing the program, I still felt an unquenchable emptiness — like eating cotton candy for dinner. It felt safe for me to be vulnerable in the supervised cocoon of a workshop, but it would soon evaporate when I was confronted with my fears that I had to contend with on a daily basis — the responsibility of work, paying bills, flat tires, dodging traffic, the horns in the street, the noise in my head. Blissful peace was quickly eclipsed by the need to survive and, beyond that, to achieve something I wasn't yet sure of.

Chapter 35

Oracles and Addictions

Super 8 film cameras were replaced by camcorders. VCR and Beta were the new technology now available to the consumer. One day while baking in baby oil on the beach in Riis Park, I had an idea.

"C'mon, Carol. You're a film editor. I'm a photographer. That equals video, don't you think?" I said.

"Yeah. Maybe. Why?"

"We should start a business together — doing something with video."

Carol began the research, and we used her credit cards to buy equipment to start a business transferring 8mm film to videotape.

Carol and I had given up my Chelsea apartment to save money and moved into her studio on East 21st Street. In 1984, there wasn't even a heading in the Yellow Pages for video. We worked diligently together and made a success of it, but now, three years later, something inside gnawed at me with dissatisfaction. I no longer depended on drugs or alcohol but felt that I needed to be on my own. I had never done anything on my own.

Stacey, whom I had met at Actualizations, was the owner of a career consulting service. She had straight fine wisps of short light blond hair and blue eyes. Most often she came to workshops dressed smartly in designer business suits and pumps, and she walked with an air of self-importance. She was unlike any gay woman I had met. She was admittedly attracted to me but always kept me at a distance. We would spend time together, and then I wouldn't hear from her or she wouldn't return my calls. Being with her was almost like being alone. After being with Carol for the past three years, I cheated on her with Stacey.

I didn't care that Carol and I had started a video business together, that she was a better friend to me than anyone I had ever known, and that leaving her would be devastating to her and any possibility of a future friendship. I was obsessed with Stacey, and my feelings for her drove me to her in the same way that heroin drove me to the dealers no matter how dangerous the neighborhood or the dose.

WITHOUT FAITH

Down the street from where Carol and I lived and ran our business together, I had seen a sign, "Furnished Apartment for Rent."

My new home was right next door to the 13th Police Precinct and the NYC Police Academy. I was living alone for the first time without a bottle, a needle, or a pill to fill the emptiness.

The furnished sublet apartment was in a 1920s tenement brownstone. Six blood-brown stone steps with an iron railing, thick with decades of repainted black glossy paint, led to my first-floor apartment.

The heavy brown metal door opened, leaving just enough room to clear an iron railing and black spiral staircase that led to a downstairs bedroom. The only furniture was a raw wooden platform bed with a bookshelf headboard and a black dusty clock radio. The floor was covered with a grayish shag rug that looked like a towel made from the shedding of a worn clothesline. The taste of stale cigarette smoke coated my tongue. A bamboo shade partially covered a narrow cellar window. Passing by were the white-spoked wheels of a baby carriage, followed by a group of heavy shiny black shoes, obviously the cadets from the Police Academy next door. The upstairs living room was large enough only for the overstuffed tweed and corduroy couch that was plopped in front of the exposed brick wall. The north-facing front wall was consumed by an iron-caged window that overlooked 21st Street and the Police Equipment storefront displaying uniforms on headless mannequins. I had no dishes or pots and pans. The deli down the block was the only kitchen I needed.

I was running out of money and ways to earn it. I could no longer pick up the phone and call Hal or Artie to bail me out and pay my rent. I was at my end. Stacey wasn't returning my phone calls, so I kept checking to see if there was a dial tone.

Each day I searched for answers and direction using crystals for healing, tarot cards for love and success, the book *I Ching* for its ancient Chinese wisdom, and the Nordic runes just in case one of the other oracles didn't give me the answer I wanted to hear.

Although these means of divination offered no clear-cut "yes" or "no," every day I would ask the same question, sometimes more than once a day: "Will Stacey and I have a relationship?" The answers never seemed to be in my favor.

DOREEN BIRDSELL

So I'd shake the bag of Nordic rune stones again, reshuffle the deck of tarot cards, hold the amethyst crystal that I wore around my neck, and try again.

Sesame noodles from the Chinese restaurant on Third Avenue would make me feel better, I thought. When I returned, the red light on my answering machine was blinking.

"Doreen. ... Hi. Uh ... it's Stacey. Listen, I wish you were there. ... Maybe this is better ... that we don't talk. We can't see each other anymore. It's not good. It's not good for me. My therapist told me that I use you like I used to use alcohol, and I'll never get better if we keep seeing each other. ... I'm sorry, Doreen. Please. Don't call me back."

I clenched my fists and dug my nails into my sweating palms. Everything felt cold, damp, and empty. I couldn't argue with what she said. I could only hope it wasn't true. I didn't know what to do. I felt crazy with frenetic, desperate energy that I couldn't contain and couldn't express. It wasn't sorrow. I had no tears. It was desperation ... like when I couldn't get high. I knew I couldn't drink or do drugs. What else could I do?

The answer came in a low, quiet voice. "Suicide." I entertained the answer and thought, "How would I do it? I don't do drugs, so it can't be an overdose. It has to be quick and painless." I didn't like the idea of a pistol. Somehow it felt too involved, too obviously suicidal. "No, a rifle would be better." I imagined myself at the edge of my bed with my back to the narrow street window facing the back wall of the basement bedroom. The wooden stock of the rifle resting on the floor, the gun barrel leaning on my temple, and my finger close enough to gently press the trigger. This was acceptable. It felt casual, almost accidental.

Another voice betrayed this idea and said, "You better call Lillian."

****

A few months earlier, I had biked to an AA meeting uptown that I found out about from my friend Kathleen, whom I'd met in Actualizations. I was confused and distressed and would wake before daylight to pedal my way to Central Park in high gear, screaming when I reached the top of Heartbreak Hill. One morning, I circled the park six times, and still there was no relief,

WITHOUT FAITH

no exhaustion that could give me rest. I tried to pedal away from the past and the rage that I felt whenever the face of my Uncle Frank flashed before me and began to torture me. I didn't know how, but I knew I needed to change. I had decided to leave Carol and the business we started together. I didn't know what I was heading toward — just that I needed to go.

I sat in a circle among a dozen or so strangers in this new meeting place. When it was my turn to speak, I said my name and sobbed, my body heaving. I was unable to speak without hiccups in broken sentences about my ending a relationship, careful not to mention it was with a woman. The touch of a hand on my back was like a warm blanket that radiated from her palm to my heart.

When the meeting was over, I spoke to a tanned, thick-mustached older man whose name and face I came to recognize as the meeting had progressed.

"Were you ever in Odyssey House?" I asked.

"Yeah, I was. So was Lillian," he said.

"Lillian? Lillian … from the Adolescent Unit in the Bronx? Wow. She made me go to the adult house in Newark when she was the supervisor there. That was like … almost eighteen years ago. Can you believe it? Which one is she?" I asked.

"She's the one that was sitting next to you. The one who put her hand on your back."

****

Lillian answered the phone, and when I told her what I was thinking, she laughed. "You're feeling loneliness. Haven't you ever felt lonely before?" she asked.

This was a revelation. I had never known this feeling before and could have never named it.

"What do I do?" I asked.

"Don't drink, and go to meetings; and don't think, and go to movies."

"You gotta be kidding. It's much too deep for that!"

"Keep it simple, stupid," she said.

"I don't understand."

"Don't analyze, utilize."

Everything I said had a slogan for an answer.
"Thank God I like movies," I said.

My bike was my city steed that brought me to AA meetings every day. Every morning, I biked uptown to the 7:30 meeting, where Lillian and I became reacquainted.

This day something different happened. I got on my bike and tuned into a radio station: love song. Switched the station: another love song. This time, there was no one for me to put in the place of the lover. Although I was alone, I wasn't feeling lonely. When the lyric of the song had someone's name, I sang "God": " 'God,' I love you. 'God,' I worship and adore you. You'll never let me go."

It was God. … I got it. … It was all about God. That was all I needed. I only needed to put God where the pain was. Wait a minute. Maybe that was just that one song, I thought as I continued pedaling up Third Avenue. Then another love song came on the air. I tried it again: " 'God,' you're my everything, you're my everything. … You're all that I need to get by."

"Oh, my God!" I was startled by my own pun.

I couldn't wait to get to the meeting, to tell Lillian what had happened. I was so happy.

Lillian put her hand on my shoulder and said, "Whatever works, kid."

She didn't get how important this was, but that was OK. I knew how special it was. This was the beginning of a new love that no one could ever take away.

WITHOUT FAITH

Chapter 36

Pain and Suffering

Not long after I had moved next door to the police department on East 21st Street, I received a court date for the lawsuit I had begun almost four years earlier against the insurance company of the driver who hit me that night in Nyack on Route 9W.

It was difficult to sit on the stand and be questioned about that night. My attorney, Alan Schnurman, was well-prepared and assured me that we had a good case. I was not afraid to answer any questions about that night except for one when I looked at the jury of mostly men and a few women.

My attorney did a fine job of questioning and made me feel at ease. Then the insurance company's attorney rose and approached me in the witness stand.

"Where were you that night?" he asked.

"I went out with my friends to this club to see a band that we heard was good."

"What was the name of the club?" the attorney asked.

"Parallels," I answered.

"Isn't that a gay bar?" he asked.

"Yes, but we went to hear the band," I said, turning to glance at the jury members, hoping I wasn't judged. Their expressions were blank. A dark-haired Hispanic woman looked into her lap when our eyes met.

"No more questions," the attorney said.

The jury found in the insurance company's favor.

"We'd like to appeal," said my attorney.

My hopes evaporated, until a month later when I got a phone call from my attorney's office.

"We heard from the insurance company's attorney. They want to settle out of court."

"I can't believe it! I thought it was done with," I said.

"I can't believe it myself. They said they're willing to settle for $50,000. If you say yes, we can cut you a check for $33,000."

Thirty-three thousand dollars! The words made me dizzy.

I had no doubt that I was going to rent a loft and open a photo studio in a building at 23rd Street and Third Avenue that Carol and I had dreamed of having our business in but couldn't afford.

I was on my own now, although I had left a broken heart in my wake. I had to go it alone, but still I needed Ramon and his expertise as a photographer. At least I thought there would be no strings attached, but there were always strings.

WITHOUT FAITH

Chapter 37

Alternate-Side-of-the-Street

"Me and my friends are going to that new club, Private Eyes. You wanna go?" Ginny asked.

It was the first time I was going out by myself as a single woman to a gay dance club. I was three years sober. I put on an oversized T-shirt, tied at the waist with a thick brown leather metal-studded belt, and slipped on a pair of ash gray leather lace-up ankle boot stilettos that I hoped I could dance in. There was no one to reassure me about how I looked. It was just me and the mirror. I was very nervous about going out alone but grateful knowing that I was meeting someone I could connect with.

My friend Kathleen had gone out of town for the weekend and asked if I'd move her car so she wouldn't get a ticket when it was alternate-side-of-the-street parking. It was parked on the Upper East Side, where she lived, but I didn't think she'd mind if I used it while she was away as long as I didn't get a ticket. The club was within walking distance of my loft at 23rd and Third, but I felt more confident taking her car and not walking the streets alone.

After a few Diet Cokes and sweating until my hair was matted to the back of my neck, I said good night to Ginny and her friends.

The sidewalk of West 20th Street was almost as hot and steamy as the club. It was one of those late spring days when a blast of heat overcame the City as a reminder of what summer would be like. Not even the darkness of night cooled off the heat of the day.

I left the club heading west toward Sixth Avenue, trying to remember where I parked the car. I began to worry after I circled the entire block and found myself back in front of the club again.

I circled the block again — and still no car. Voices behind me were drawing closer as I approached the corner of Fifth Avenue. Their laughter was getting louder, and I hoped I would make the light before they caught up. The light turned red. Damn, I thought as I stood at the curb.

"Where you headed?" asked one of them. She was younger than the other two, maybe in her mid-twenties. Ringlets of dark brown curls framed long-lashed root beer eyes. She was not like her two swaying companions, who could barely focus. One was like a blond rag doll, whose knees buckled while standing at the crosswalk. Her stodgy Italian girlfriend hoisted her back to her feet.

"I'm looking for my car," I said.

"Where'd you park?"

"I don't remember … somewhere around here. I circled the block so many times when I was looking for a spot, I forgot what avenues I parked between."

"What kind of car is it?"

"It's a white Chevy, and it doesn't belong to me. It belongs to my friend."

"I'll help you look. These two don't need me anymore."

The one who was more coherent said, "Good night, Rachel," and stumbled away with the blonde.

I thought I'd never find the car now that I was distracted by trying to make conversation with a stranger. I was relieved that she did most of the talking, asking me questions requiring mostly one-word answers.

"What's your name? You were at Private Eyes, right? You live in the City? Where?"

When I answered, "Twenty-third and Third," that's when it got a little more complicated and she became more inquisitive.

"Who drives when they only have to go five or six blocks in the City?" she asked, laughing.

"I don't know. I like to drive … and I didn't have to walk."

"You're walking now," she said laughing.

Where the hell's my car? I thought, while we crossed another street.

When we found the Chevy, she asked for my phone number.

"Do you need a ride?" I asked.

"Oh, no, thanks. I have a car — and I know where it is," she said, smiling.

We met for dinner at Joe's on West Fourth Street. When we sat down, I ordered a Diet Coke and she ordered the same. So far, so good, I thought.

WITHOUT FAITH

Before we had finished our meal, I found out that Rachel was a Jewish girl who was raised in Belle Harbor out in Rockaway, taught special ed at Jamaica High School, coached the tennis and bowling teams, and had no history of drug or alcohol abuse. She never smoked cigarettes, she played tennis with her parents, and the only woman she had ever been with was her college professor who dumped her for someone else.

Our stories were nothing alike except that we had been in love with other women.
When I told my new therapist about Rachel and that I had absolutely nothing in common with her, she perked up.
"Give this a try. This might be a good experience for you, Doreen."

Within a month, I had keys to Rachel's apartment in Kew Gardens and spent almost every night at her place.
When I didn't eat, she got worried. If I didn't have money, she worried. That part was OK. I'd let her help me with that.
When my bike got stolen, she showed up at my loft the next morning with her brand new red road bike.
"You're using this till we get you another one."
"I don't want your bike," I yelled down the staircase.
It was futile. She was already climbing the staircase with the bike slung on her shoulder.

That night, I rode the bike to my AA meeting and locked it to a pole at the bus stop at 79th Street and First Avenue in front of St. Monica's Church. When I came out a little past 7:30 p.m., the only thing left was the red frame of the bike, still locked to the pole.
At least ten people were standing there, waiting for the bus. I asked, "Did any of you see who did this?"
"Oh, yes," a woman said. "A young man came over with tools. ... He really looked like he knew what he was doing ... so I thought it was his bike."
"*His* bike! It wasn't even *my* bike," I yelled, as though it were her fault.
The parts cost more than the bike to replace, and I didn't have the money.

When I told Rachel, she said, "Don't worry. I'll tell my father that it happened to me. He'll take care of it."

The next day, Rachel was at my door again. This time with running shoes strung together around her neck.
"Oh, no," I said. "I'm not running."
One of the things I loved about biking was that my feet didn't have to touch the ground. I hated even the idea of my feet pounding the pavement.
"You're gonna love it!" Rachel said. "Here — try these on."
They were ugly, gray waffle-like running shoes, but they were comfortable and they fit.
"OK. OK. I'll give it a try."

I had had one good running experience in my life. A couple of weeks before I had met Rachel, I attended a women's retreat on the south shore of Essex, Massachusetts. "Finding Your Power in the Feminine Greek Archetypes" was the theme. The participants were to find their identification with a goddess archetype. I chose Artemis, the archetypal figure for the young independent and unmarried woman.

After a long day of workshops, I enjoyed a well-prepared meal in a cafeteria-style setting where I was served with the eight other women workshop members. We were served Haagen-Dazs for dessert that night. After the dining room cleared out and I was alone, I helped myself to more ice cream. I finished off a whole pint of chocolate and felt awful. I didn't know what to do about feeling stuffed, and my premenstrual bloat made me feel even worse.

I could run! I thought. After all, that's what Artemis would do.

Wearing khaki shorts and white Reebok sneakers, I busted out of the dining room. The screen door reverberated against the cedar shakes of the retreat house. I ran up the hill on a dirt path that led out of the retreat compound and onto the smooth pavement of a quiet yellow-lined country road that wound its way through the marshland. In rhythm with my steps, a chant formed in my mind: "Longer, stronger, further, faster. ... Longer, stronger, further, faster."

The recollection of this recent experience enabled me to give in to Rachel's

WITHOUT FAITH

insistence. I surrendered to running and the ugly shoes.

Rachel and I went to Central Park, where she coached me like one of her students and taught me how to pace myself and run longer distances.

"This is really boring and purposeless. Let's at least have a goal. Did you ever run in any races?" I asked.

"I ran some 5 and 10K's and the Long Island Half Marathon once," she said.

Now that excited me. "Let's run the New York City Marathon!" I said.

"That requires a lot of training. And it helps to have other people to run with," she said.

"I'll get my friend Ellen to do it. We'll have someone else to train with." I knew Ellen was so competitive that she'd go for it.

"OK. I'll get the applications, and we'll start training," Rachel said.

In the sixth mile of a ten-mile training run, we came to a corner with a gas station where I knew we would be turning. I headed for the gas pumps to cut through to the other street. Rachel grabbed my arm and pulled me back. "You can't cut corners," she said. The words penetrated deeply, and I realized that training was teaching me much more than the endurance to run long distances.

We were one of the 24,000 in the lottery to get a place in the 1988 NYC Marathon. Six days a week, we ran and we ran and we ran — longer, stronger, further, and faster.

I had given up on ever getting anything more from my father than a telephone call on my birthday, so I was really surprised to hear from him the day after I finished the race. "Donna told me you ran the marathon. I watched it on TV, but I couldn't find you."

"Well, there were a lot of people in that crowd," I said.

"Yeah, I know, but I watched anyway. Did you finish?" he asked.

"Yeah, I did."

"Atta girl!" he said.

I never expected that from my father. All my life, I wanted some bit of encouragement, a sign that he was proud of me, that he loved me. When I felt as though it no longer mattered and I let go of any expectation of him, that was when I finally received it.

224

Chapter 38

Anthony Quinones

The doorbell rang. Must be my appointment, I thought with nervous expectation.

My rent was overdue, the bills were late, and I needed any business I could possibly get. I had spent most of the money from the lawsuit on renovating the loft and the rest writing $2,000 rent checks for six months. By now, I had borrowed $6,000 from Ramon with a promise that we would become business partners and I'd pay him back from every job I booked. It was one thing to owe him money, but now I felt like I had sold my career as well.

I opened the door to my loft-studio. The fragrance of sweet cologne was followed by a fresh-shaven, dark-haired, slender young man of about twenty years old, who walked in for our consultation. He was dressed completely in black, including the buttons on his stiff-collared shirt.
"Hello. I'm Anthony Quinones," he said extending his hand.
I invited him to sit on the couch while I pulled over a chair and let him review my portfolio.
"A good friend of mine told me I should try modeling," he said.
"Have you been photographed professionally before?" I asked.
"No, but I'm told I'm very photogenic."
"What do you do now?" I asked.
"Nothing yet. I just left the seminary. Turned out it wasn't my calling. I'm trying to figure out what to do next. In the meantime, I need to make a living."
He needed a portfolio, and I needed the business.
"How tall are you?" I asked.
"Five-ten."
"That's a little short for fashion, but there are agencies that use all types of models."
I knew I would have to do some convincing to get him to hire me.
"Because you've never done this before, you need to hire a photographer

WITHOUT FAITH

you can trust and have a connection with. It's really kind of spiritual," I said.

"How do you mean spiritual?" he asked.

"When you're being photographed, you have to let go completely — to trust that your photographer knows exactly when to push the shutter button. It's a dance with you, the camera, and being in the moment."

He nodded in silent agreement, but I still didn't think I had gotten through to him. So I opened up with him.

"It's like these Twelve Promises I learned. ..."

"Oh! You mean like the over 900 promises in God's Word, the Bible?" he said before I could finish.

"Over 900? No, I'm talking about *Twelve* Promises. Twelve — the ones they teach in AA. I'm in AA."

"Over 900?" I asked again. "Wait a minute." I went into another room and emerged with a pocket-sized green Gideon Bible someone had handed me on 23rd Street one day. "I tried reading this. This Bible is Greek to me. I don't understand. Show me."

Anthony smiled and said, "Actually, part of the Bible was written in Greek."

He reached into his briefcase on the floor next to him and pulled out a black book. It was a Bible much larger than mine.

Flipping through the pages, he stopped. "Here's one. ... 'Beloved, I wish above all things that you prosper and be in health, even as your soul prospers.' "And quickly turning back some more pages, he said: "Here's another one. .... 'I have come that you may have life and have it more abundantly.' "

"I want that," I said. "Show me where it says that in my Bible. It can't be the same book."

He thumbed through my little green book and pointed to the very same words.

Why didn't I see this before? I wondered.

"My mother took this course she really liked called the Power for Abundant Living. Would you be interested?" he asked.

"Sure. If it's got the word 'abundant' in it, I want it."

Meditating while holding the amethyst crystal I religiously wore around my

226

neck, tossing *I Ching* coins, reading *A Course in Miracles* and tarot cards, and going to workshops and retreats weren't helping me pay the rent, I thought.

"So it's OK if I give my mother your phone number?" he asked.
"Like I said, I'll try anything with the word 'abundant' in it."
Anthony thanked me for my time and said he'd call me to make an appointment to shoot his portfolio. I never heard from him again. I didn't hear from his mother either.
I still had no steady work coming in, but running to train for the marathon every day gave me a purpose and kept me somewhat calm. My 7:30 a.m. meeting was a three-mile run uptown. Afterward, I'd do the 6.2-mile loop around Central Park once or twice depending on the marathon training schedule. I always carried a token for the bus or subway in case I couldn't make it back, but I always did.

It was a few weeks later in early September when I got back to my loft and listened to the one message on my answering machine. "Hi. My name's Steve Budlong, and I hear from your outgoing message that we're in the same business. I'm the vice president of the audio/visual department at Equitable Life. I'm calling to invite you to an orientation for the Power for Abundant Living workshop. Give me a call. I'd love to hear about what you do. Maybe we could work together sometime."
Vice president … work together. Before my thoughts could mesh, I was dialing his number.

I went to the orientation, which was held in a small apartment uptown. There were about ten people, men and women mostly in their thirties like me. Steve gave me a warm and genuine smile and held my hand to say hello. I was convinced that he was someone I could trust and felt safe with him.
"It's so nice to finally meet you. What do you think about doing the workshop?" he asked.
"I have to wait until after the marathon. I've trained all summer. It's a lot of hours running. Do you do these workshops often?"
"We'll call you when we do the next one. I was serious about work when I called

WITHOUT FAITH

you. Why don't you call my office tomorrow?" he said, handing me his card.

After I finished the 1988 Marathon in early November, I took the next workshop which started later that month. It turned out to be a thirty-five-hour, two-week study of the Bible from Genesis to Revelation. I showed up because I wanted to be successful in my career and be financially independent. That's what I considered abundance.

I was never very good at memorization, but during one of the sessions the commentator recited a verse that he said was from Proverbs: "Trust in the Lord with all your heart and lean not on your own understanding. In all your ways acknowledge Him and He will direct your path."

The words entered my hearing and burned into the memory of my heart. It was as though the words became absorbed within me. I thought my life was turning upside down, but I realized it was turning right side up.

My relationship with Rachel was always tumultuous, and I knew we had gone as far as we could go together. I'd argue that we had to break up because she was a Jew who didn't want to believe in Jesus, and when that didn't work I argued that it was because she was straight and I was gay. It wasn't that Rachel was a Jew and that she struggled with her sexuality. I knew that this was not the best for me, and I was sure it couldn't be the best for her either. It was still so hard to let go of what had become painfully comfortable because it was familiar. I was beginning to learn that letting go meant having faith in trusting that God would show me the way and I would not come to harm.

In the coming months, Steve introduced me to someone at Equitable who gave me a job photographing the interiors of their beautiful new executive floors on Sixth Avenue. They paid me $10,000 to shoot the space. Standing at the elevator, admiring the sky-high view of Manhattan, I thought I had finally made it.

Chapter 39

Within My Means

A new life and a new family of friends. Francois was a young Frenchman who was sweet and intellectual. Beth and Glen exhibited their musical gifts in song, and serious Chris strummed the guitar. Leah, a beautiful, tall Haitian woman who was also new to the group, befriended me as another newcomer. Steve and his wife, Terry, were loving and generous with their home, where they held weekly groups for Bible study, at Lexington and 25th Street, only three blocks from my loft. Their sincere love for God was contagious, and their confidence in the constant presence of a Holy Spirit was magnetic.

It was 1989, and just when I thought I was on my way, Wall Street took another tumble. Advertising and corporate budgets shrank to nothing, and I couldn't get work.

The rent was late again, and my landlord, Mr. Wong, was starting to pressure me.

"Like you run marathon ... you pay rent!" he said.

He would not let me out of my lease until a new tenant replaced me.

I prayed. I fell to my knees under one of the large skylights and opened my hands and my heart to heaven: "God, thank you for this space and that so much healing has happened here. Please continue to make this a place of healing where many will be blessed. If it is not me who can stay here, then please, please, God, bring a renter for Mr. Wong."

Not many days later there was a knock at my door.
"Doreen!"
Oh, no. It's Mr. Wong again, looking for the rent, I thought.
"Doreen. What is yoga?" he asked.
"It's ... you know ... it's stretching," I said, opening my arms to demonstrate.
"Oh. Oh. ..."
I knew he didn't understand.

WITHOUT FAITH

"Why do you want to know about yoga?"
"Someone call me to rent loft. Says he wants it for yoga."
"That's great! That'll be perfect for here."

When I confided this to Steve, he told me about his friend Doug, who was moving to Minnesota with his family and had a share in a studio on West 22nd Street.

I went from paying (or not paying) $2,000 a month to $500 for an office with studio privileges in a 3,000-square-foot space. My new landlord, Brian, was a successful commercial photographer who let me take Doug's place and gave me the privilege of using any of the photo equipment or props in the studio. It was ideal. Brian was married, with two young children, and generous with his time and professional experience. It was what I called a miracle.

Ramon was incensed by my broken promise to pay him back. I couldn't pay him, and I couldn't tolerate the endless daily phone calls. A friend of mine who was an attorney helped negotiate a repayment plan with interest for $242 a month. Ramon had to agree to stop calling me and not try to see me. For the first time, I was committed to paying my debt and to living within my means.

Chapter 40

Moving On

I didn't know where I was going to live. Brian's studio share was a great deal for my business, but it didn't include a place to live. I also knew that I couldn't continue depending on Rachel.

Carol and I were on speaking terms again, and when I asked, she agreed that I could sleep at her apartment from time to time until I figured things out. She never told me I had to leave, but I knew that I robbed her of her privacy.

As often as I could, without Brian becoming suspicious, I would sleep on the couch in the office I rented and leave before he arrived for work so he wouldn't know that I had spent the night. My office had a closet large enough for me to store my clothes and my photo equipment. I never told Brian that I didn't have a place to live, and he never asked.

One morning, my sister, Donna, called frantic. "That son of a bitch — I'm going to kill him," she yelled.

Charice, my twelve-year-old niece, had been sexually abused by her father's friend.

I felt like it was me all over again, and I couldn't control my feelings of pain and rage at having been abused myself.

"Where is he? Have him arrested so he doesn't hurt somebody else!" I said.

"Sherman won't believe Charice. It's his best friend, and he swears he wouldn't do something like that. 'Charice doesn't know what she's talking about,' he says."

It was futile. The best Donna could do was to be there for Charice and keep the bastard away from her.

Oh, my God. Poor Charice. Poor Donna. That asshole Sherman. What the fuck is wrong with him, I thought.

Because Charice was developmentally disabled, I thought he didn't believe her … or because it was his friend … or just because he couldn't believe this could be true.

I was raw, I was tender, and I was reeling from not being able to tell the

WITHOUT FAITH

difference between what happened to Charice and what happened to me as a child. All the feelings flooded back from my childhood.

I needed help. I made an appointment with a therapist in the West Village whom a friend referred.

Donna and I would often experience the same feelings or have a crisis simultaneously. Donna always had a sixth sense about what was happening with me. Very often when I would have a nightmare about being sexually abused, Donna would call the next day to ask me if I was all right. She said she had had a premonition. "Are you thinking about Frank?" she would ask. It would always amaze me that she knew.

I had such rage that I felt responsible for the car alarms that would go off when I walked by.

I was really nervous about going to therapy. I felt like I would erupt. Donna offered to take the train to the City from Waterbury, Connecticut, to be with me, and I took her up on it. We sat on a stoop of a brownstone on West 10th Street, down the block from Dr. Greenberg's office, before my appointment.

"I never felt like this, Donna. I don't know what's wrong with me."

Sitting two steps above me, she reached down to rest her hand on my shoulder. "You'll be OK, Reenie. It's what happened to us as kids — that's all."

I knew she understood, and her presence comforted me.

"Will you wait for me when I go in for therapy?"

"Sure. I'll read something."

The intercom buzzed us in, and we sat in a tiny room that contained three chairs.

I heard a door close, and then the waiting room intercom came alive: "You can come in now."

I sat across from a woman with dark wavy hair, full-bosomed and wearing a low-cut black-and-white flowered cotton dress.

She smiled and asked, "What brings you here, Doreen?"

"Do you deal with sexual abuse?" I asked.

"It's my specialty."

I was a river of tears falling over a cliff. I told her everything about my uncle,

Charice, and Donna and me as kids. I never stopped crying, and she gave me permission to scream if I wanted to. I didn't hesitate.

We scheduled three visits a week. I also agreed to check out the Karen Horney Clinic, which had just begun group therapy sessions for women who had been sexually abused.

I was exhausted and had found hope.

"Donna, did you hear me screaming in there?"

She looked up from her magazine, oblivious. "I didn't hear a thing."

I rode my bike every day to Central Park and pedaled the 6.2-mile loop over and over. I took Heartbreak Hill in high gear, and when I reached the top I screamed. I screamed for Charice, I screamed for Donna, and I screamed for me. The years of sexual abuse that bound me began to unravel.

WITHOUT FAITH

Chapter 41

Loving and Available

Leah knew about my past relationship with Rachel. She and Steve were the only ones I confided in that I was gay.

Steve and his wife, Terry, moved to Westchester, and Bible study moved to Beth and Leah's small two-bedroom apartment on 25th Street between Second and Third avenues. Seven, eight, and sometimes more of us were crammed into the tiny living room-kitchen every Thursday night.

When I told Leah that I was looking for an apartment, she said,

"I'm gonna need a roommate! Move in with me! Praise God — it'll be perfect! Beth's getting married and moving upstate."

I agreed that it was a good decision, but everything inside me resisted. She worked as a fashion model and was also pursuing a career designing and selling costume jewelry. I knew she thought that I was really straight and that getting closer to God would be the answer. Secretly, I hoped she was right. Being straight would be an easier life, I thought. I believed Leah loved me and accepted me in spite of my sexuality.

Even though I had a plan and slept on the couch in my office and sometimes at Carol's apartment until Beth would move out, something still gnawed at me. I searched the real estate classified section every week and knew that if I found a place it would be a sign from God not to move in with Leah.

No matter how much I asked around and checked bulletin boards and newspapers, nothing was as good a deal as I was going to get with Leah for $700 a month with my own bedroom.

When I brought Barb to Bible study — she was a gay rock musician from my Greenwich Village AA group — Beth asked if I could stick around until everyone left so she could talk to me.

"Doreen, are you a lesbian?" she asked.

"I am," I said, "But if I have to be labeled I prefer to be gay. Listen, Beth - I love God. I believe in Jesus. But I believe that people misinterpret the Bible about gay people being sinners."

"Would you be willing to sit down with me and go through the Scriptures and see what the Word says?" she asked.

It still didn't make sense to me that the same God who loved me would disown me. I wanted to believe that God loved me for who I was.

Although Beth and I had different and strong beliefs about God's view on homosexuality, she still asked me to photograph her wedding. Maybe that meant she didn't think I was a sinner after all, I hoped.

Leah was going to be my roommate. She loved men, wasn't an alcoholic, and never abused drugs. She was a lover of God and saw everything as an opportunity to recognize God's presence. Her enthusiasm for Bible study and worship was effervescent, and she loved meeting new people and sharing her faith.

The apartment had a homey Caribbean flair with baskets and bright colors. The wicker screen in Leah's bedroom offset her bed from the desk where she created ornamental bracelets and earrings. My bedroom was small, but it had a window in the airshaft with an air conditioner.

I paid $179 for the least expensive bed I could find at Kleinsleep. It was the first bed I owned that wasn't a convertible sofa. The salesman kept trying to upgrade me to a more expensive bed but finally gave up when I said, "Look, I really have a good back. This will be perfect for me. I don't need any of those special pillow tops or that extra firmness. It only has to be a double." I wasn't settling for a twin — I deserved better.

A heavy cherry-wood chest of drawers that once was my Great-Aunt Annie's was the only piece of furniture I held onto. Her furniture had been passed on to my father; but when he moved into a senior housing project in Port Chester a few years earlier, he had to scale down, so I claimed it. It was practical and I thought quite beautiful. I considered it an inheritance that gave me a family connection.

The morning after I had moved in the aroma of fresh brewed coffee drew me into the summer bright kitchen. Leah had already left for work and my new Braun coffee maker was filled with fresh, hot coffee. I thought, Leah doesn't

WITHOUT FAITH

drink coffee. ... She made that for me? I would have never thought of doing something like that.

There were a lot of things that didn't come naturally to me. God knew I needed to be taught, and I didn't take well to being told what to do. Leah was someone I could learn from by her example.

On Saturday, we shared the responsibility of cleaning the apartment. I got the bathroom, Leah took the kitchen, and we split the hallway and living room.

"When I clean, I imagine that Jesus is coming over and that's all I need to know to make it right," Leah said.

I scrubbed each black and white tile on the floor with cleanser one by one, scoured the tub, and didn't miss an inch on the commode.

I continued to run every day even though I didn't have Rachel to prod me on. If I didn't make progress anywhere else in my day, I felt like I had at least one success under my belt if I ran. I discovered a great running route through East River Park, alongside the river, and under the Williamsburg Bridge and back.

A few days after moving in I was jogging down East River Park below 14th Street on the pedestrian path that bordered a fenced baseball field. A big black dog lunged onto the fence, barking, its teeth snapping at the chain links that separated us.

"Good dog. ... What a good pup," I said to be friendly.

He ran alongside me, the fence between us. I kept repeating, "Yeah, that's a good dog. ... What a good dog."

A few yards ahead of us, the fence and the field came to an end. "Bye, pup!" I said. The dog found a hole in the fence, jumped through and was suddenly running by my side.

"Good dog. ... What a good dog!" I said again, trying not to show fear and hoping I wouldn't get bitten.

He was thigh-high to my stride and didn't lag behind or pull ahead, remaining in perfect step. My new short-haired companion was mostly black with a white chest and four white-stockinged legs sprinkled with black polka dots. He followed me almost two miles farther to the Williamsburg Bridge and back up the river again.

I noticed that "he" was really a "she" and was wearing a black leather silver-studded collar but had no tags. "OK. If you follow me all the way home, I'll give you breakfast," I said.

When Beth lived with Leah, I knew there was a very firm "no dogs" rule.

Sweating and still panting from the run, I hid my new friend in the stairwell and rang the bell to the apartment. When Leah opened the door, I said, "I know you're wondering why I rang the bell, but I found something ..."

Before I finished, Leah poked her head into the hallway. "OK. Where is it? ... It's a dog, right?"

I couldn't believe it! "How'd you know I have a dog?"

"I knew it! Just by the look on your face."

"She's in the stairwell."

When I opened the door to the stairwell, she ran up to Leah like they were old friends.

"You're not allowed on the couch," Leah said, kneeling down and holding her head by scrunching up the furry fleshy part of her neck.

"And you're not allowed on my bed either," I added.

I called her Roxanne. She got her name from the song *Roxanne* by The Police.

That night, Roxanne slept on the throw rug alongside my bed; but when I woke up, she was on the couch. I got her down before Leah got up.

Quickly getting dressed, I went out for a run with Roxanne. She ran six miles by my side off leash and followed me all the way through the river park and back.

I hoped that no one would see her and claim to be her owner. I figured that somebody had just let her go.

I took Roxanne to the studio and introduced her to Brian. He liked dogs and had no problem with me bringing her to work. We got home that night, and before my key could finish turning the lock, Leah opened the door.

She had a big grin on her face and asked, "Guess what I found today?"

"Not another dog?"

"No. Not a dog. A cat!"

"A cat. ... How? ... Where? What are the odds I'd find a dog and the next day you'd find a cat?"

"It's all right. ... Let's see how they get along."

"OK. C'mon, Roxanne."

The hair on the back of her neck was standing up, and I gripped her leash. A velvet black cat sat on the ledge in the hallway, seeming very at home. Slowly I gave Roxanne some slack to sniff her new roommate. After the first swipe of the cat's claw on Roxanne's nose, Leah yelled, "No, Cyrano!"

"Cyrano! How'd you come up with Cyrano?" I asked.

"You know. ... Roxanne and Cyrano — the opera?"

"No, I don't, but if you say so. Where'd you find the cat?"

"For the last few days, I would see this cat under the stairs of an apartment building and he looked abandoned; and today he came out when I passed by and let me pick him up. I figured since you got a dog and now that Beth's gone, we could both have pets. Isn't it great how God works!"

"Well, I guess we'll all get along. Anyway, I've got to get Roxanne to a vet and make sure she's got her shots and all."

I took her to Bideawee and the vet told me she was about six years old and he'd have to take some blood tests to make sure she didn't have worms. The test revealed that she had heartworm. "I've never seen a case so bad. We weren't even testing for heartworm, but there's so many that it shows up in a single drop of blood," he said and showed me the heartworm cells under the microscope.

"Can you cure it?" I asked.

"We have a remedy, but it's expensive."

"How expensive?"

"It can run about $700. We need to do arsenic treatments. She'd have to stay in the hospital to be monitored."

"Seven hundred dollars! Isn't there some kind of fund or scholarship for stray dogs that have found homes?"

"No, not that I'm aware of, but you can call around and see if someone will do it for less. This will eventually kill her if it's not treated."

Then it occurred to me that somebody might have dumped her who couldn't afford to treat her.

I went back to the Yellow Pages and called the Humane Society. I took her to East 59th Street next to the Queensborough Bridge to a small brownstone, where the vet at the Humane Society concurred that she was six years old. "How can they know that?" I said to Roxanne. "You're much younger than that."

The Humane Society wasn't giving anything away either and I knew I'd have to pay, but I felt better about giving the money to the Humane Society. I nicknamed Roxanne "One-month's-rent."

I asked the vet about the cost and if there was any way I could possibly get a discount because I had found her.

"How did you find her?" she asked.

I told her the truth, hoping the vet would give me a break.

"Well, I was running down the East River like I usually do in the morning, and I was praying. I had just gotten out of a bad relationship, and I asked God to send me someone who was loving and available. It was just then that this dog started following alongside me from behind a fence in a ball field. This was God's answer, I thought: She's loving and she's available, and this is all you can handle right now."

I didn't get a discount, but I got Roxanne. She survived the treatment and ran with me every day.

WITHOUT FAITH

Chapter 42

You Call Yourselves Christians?

Leah and I had a great opportunity to rent an apartment in Stuyvesant Town. It was on the top floor in one of the buildings of a seven-story brick development that lined the East River from 23rd Street south to 13th. Our new apartment number was 7-H — 7th Heaven, I thought.

For only $100 more a month, I took the larger of the two bedrooms. Two windows with double exposure — I was sure it was an unbelievable luxury for a bedroom in a Manhattan apartment. There was room to spare after carefully situating everything I owned — my double bed, Aunt Annie's dresser, a weight bench that Rachel gave me, and a desk made from black plastic horses holding two polished planks of thick finished oak for the tabletop. There was even room for my bike.

When the elevator doors opened, a middle-aged gray-haired woman who was about to enter reared back when she spotted Roxanne. I tightened the leash and moved to the side.

"Do you know there's no dogs allowed in this building?" she asked.

Sidestepping her question, I said, "She stays in my studio across town. ... She doesn't actually live here."

Damn. The girl who sublet us the apartment told me that a dog wouldn't be a problem. What am I going to do? It's too late, I thought. I'm already moved in, and Roxanne is family.

Thank God I was a long-distance runner. No matter what the weather, every morning at 6 a.m. Roxanne and I ran down six flights of stairs, snuck out the front door, and jogged through East River Park to lower Manhattan and back. I stashed her in the back seat of my ten-year-old, beat-up gray Honda Civic, got ready for work, and drove to the West Side to my studio.

I'd meet friends in the Village at 6 or 7 p.m. and then head back home at night with a pint of chocolate peanut butter Tasti-D-Lite. I surveyed the street to make sure we could enter the building undetected. A woman appeared from the small south-side lobby wearing a large wool overcoat. After crossing the street into the darkness of the industrial south side of East 13th Street, she stopped, turned, and looked in both directions. Reaching under her coat, she pulled out a tiny squirming furry dog and set him down for a quick evening pee. I discovered there was a secret society of dog owners in Stuyvesant Town pretending to be invisible to one another. When the doorway was clear, we ran inside and up the stairwell to safety.

✳✳✳✳✳✳✳

I made it back to the apartment just a few minutes before Bible fellowship was to begin. Leah, who loved the ritual of preparing the living room for Bible study, was engaged in conversation with a young woman.

"This is Lisa. She's a friend of Lee's," Leah said.

Lisa, dressed in worn blue jeans and a white turtleneck, was a tall, very attractive woman in her late twenties.

"When Lee told me about you guys and that she was studying the Bible, I couldn't believe it," Lisa said.

"Why? Because you think Lee seems so unlikely?" I asked.

"No. Not just that. A couple of months ago, we got a new car salesman where I work. ... And I noticed that he was always *happy* — *even when there was no business* — and he was always reading the same book. I couldn't stand it anymore, so when I asked him what he was reading, he showed me a Bible. *Could you believe it?*"

Leah and I gave each other a knowing glance, and I nodded my head, smiling.

The doorbell rang. It was Lee.

"Hey ... Lisa," she said, almost singing her name. "You made it!" Lee was so short she stood on tiptoes to give Lisa a hug.

People began to arrive one after the other - Glen, Francois with his mother, Elva, her boyfriend Phil; and our leader, Chris. After the hellos, we took our seats. Chris began by thanking God for our gathering, and, as usual, we picked up our songbooks and waited for our cue from Chris.

WITHOUT FAITH

In the middle of singing "Count your blessings, name them one by one …," the floor beneath our feet began to vibrate from the hammering of what could have been a broomstick. It was Mr. Freedman, our downstairs neighbor, banging on his ceiling and yelling, "Be quiet up there!"

We took it down a notch with a more somber hymn. Mr. Freedman took it up a notch, blaring the evening news from his apartment below. Lisa lifted her eyes from her songbook, and when our eyes met I politely nodded to encourage her to just keep singing.

Chris said, "Let's open with a word of prayer! Lord, we pray for Mr. Freedman. We pray that your Spirit of peace be on him and his home … that his heart soften to our gathering here in your name, Jesus, and we thank you for this time together."

Saying a prayer in the moment was a new way of dealing with adversity for me. I'd come a long way from the day I threatened to get a rifle and shoot the superintendent if he didn't do something about the cockroaches that swarmed my apartment.

Lisa drove from Armonk each week to our fellowship. She forgot her Bible one night, and as I leaned over to let her read from mine, I had a shocking thought: Oh, my God. She's gay and she's single.

Instantly, I shook off the very idea to refocus and regain my place in the worship setting. I knew that I had a responsibility that was far greater than my social life.

✶✶✶✶✶✶✶

My photography business was gaining momentum, and the daily things of life took on a steady, predictable routine. I kept track of my daily spending and had a financial plan. I was so proud of the way I kept my numbers. I had a spreadsheet, a savings account, and no outstanding bills.

I was able to visualize my life beyond the next month of bills and believed that my dream of having a successful life could come true. My feet were planted on solid ground, and I had faith that God loved me and gave me the opportunity to have an abundant life.

I was happy. This is what happy was. I had a home, a photo studio, and my old Honda Civic that took Roxanne and me back and forth to work and to be with friends I loved every day.

Run, go to work, get a free parking spot, see clients, shoot a job, hang out with my friends, go to Tasti-D-Lite and get my pint of chocolate peanut butter, head home with Roxanne, study God's Word, brush my teeth, and go to bed.

Everything was going great until the day my car died in front of Carol's apartment on East 21st Street. My old, reliable Honda was double-parked on a police precinct block with no clutch.

I went upstairs to Carol's apartment and called Lisa, who worked for Toyota in Mount Kisco.

"How much can you spend?" she asked.

"Three thousand dollars."

"What are you looking for?"

"A Jeep or a Saab," I said.

"For three thousand dollars!"

"Why not?"

"I can get you a nice Honda CRX with 92,000 miles on it. It's in great shape."

"Can you look around for a Jeep or a Saab?" I asked.

"I doubt I'll find one, but I'll call you back."

"Hurry up, OK? My car is dead outside, and I need something right away," I insisted.

I sat there for an hour, and she didn't call back. I couldn't believe it!

I had $3,000 and fully expected her to find me a Jeep or a Saab within that time.

My Honda sat outside still double-parked with a note I put on it: "Won't Start — Went for Help." I had paid $300 for that Honda almost a year before, and it had lasted much longer than I ever expected. The mechanic at the Gulf station on 23rd Street at the river said he'd tow it away for no charge if I gave him the title.

Meanwhile, I thought: Where is Lisa?

The Honda was gone, but I was still in Carol's apartment, not willing to

WITHOUT FAITH

leave until I heard that Lisa had solved my problem and found me a Jeep or a Saab for the $3,000 I was willing to spend. I was grateful that Carol was busy doing her work, didn't offer me any advice, or tell me that I had to go.

I called Lisa again, and this time I got a voice recording.

"Lisa, I really need something right away. I just had my Honda towed away. Call me back."

Three hours later, she called. "I checked around and found a Jeep for $6,000. You know they're not good on gas."

"What about a Saab?"

"Saabs aren't cheap. How much more can you spend?"

"I've got $3,000 to spend and that's it."

"How's your credit?"

"I don't want credit. I want to pay cash, and I only want to spend $3,000."

"One of my guys has a Honda CRX in great shape. It's got high mileage and I can probably get it for you for $3,000."

"I really want a Jeep or a Saab."

"Doreen, you're going to have to take the Honda CRX or you're going to have to wait."

"All right. I'll wait. Thanks, Lisa."

When Lisa came to Bible study a couple of days later, I asked her, "So, what's new? What do you have? Did you find a car for me?"

"The Honda CRX. That's it! And you're lucky if it's still there."

"OK, OK. I'll take it. What should I do?"

"I'll check tomorrow to see if it hasn't been sold and if it's still there. Can you come tomorrow?"

"OK. I'll make sure I can."

"Let me know what train you'll be on, and I'll pick you up at the station."

The next day, I boarded the Hudson Line with thirty-one hundred-dollar bills folded securely in the inside pocket of my leather jacket.

The bare trees, snow-spotted woods, and overflowing streams of Westchester County soon replaced the concrete and asphalt city landscape.

"Mount Kisco — next stop," the conductor shouted.

DOREEN BIRDSELL

The storefront shops and country setting of Mount Kisco made New York City seem even farther than it actually was. A horn tooted. It was Lisa in her new black Sentra SER that she had recently purchased from the Nissan dealership next door to where she worked at Toyota. She said, "It was a much better deal - faster and sportier than the Tercel that my boss offered me."

She was smartly dressed, wearing a gray skirt and magenta blouse. I wasn't accustomed to seeing her in business attire and had never seen her in a skirt. She had beautiful long legs that were most often covered in blue jeans.

"Are you hungry? I know a nice place for lunch. It's just a few blocks away."

"Sure, I can eat," I said.

As we stood before a lunch counter to place our order in a busy café, I didn't know what to talk about. Most of my conversations with women usually began with "What clubs do you like?" or "Where do you go dancing?"

Then I realized that Lisa and I had something much more substantial in common. We could talk about our faith.

When we sat down with our sandwiches, I asked, "What's your favorite Scripture?"

"Psalm 18:33 — 'He makes my feet like hinds' feet.' It gives me comfort. I know that God is there with me, and no matter what, I can be like a deer that's sure-footed. What's yours?" she asked.

"Proverbs 3, verses 5 and 6 — 'Trust in the Lord with all your heart and lean not on your own understanding. In all your ways acknowledge Him and He will direct your path.' I love that one. It was the first verse I was ever able to remember. It just burned into my heart when I first heard it, and it stayed there."

The other diners around us seemed to fade away, and time escaped us.

"We'd better look at that car," Lisa said.

The two-tone silver Honda CRX was parked in front, waiting for its new owner. It was a five-speed, with power windows and air conditioning, and handled like a little sports car. It cost exactly $3,000 cash, tax included. I loved that car.

WITHOUT FAITH

Lisa and I started spending more time together. She loved to walk and I loved to run.

We had a special New Year's Eve Bible fellowship, and Lisa asked if she and her dog, Alice, could sleep over.

"If it's OK with Leah," I said.

Leah loved Lisa — she loved her hunger to know God.

"Of course you can sleep over! It'll be a great time," Leah said.

We had fellowship, sang, and ate a pasta dinner together. And when the ball dropped, we kissed, hugged, and tooted our horns for 1994. Roxanne and Alice started to bark, and Lisa and I quickly grabbed our dogs' snouts to conceal their presence.

When it was time for bed and I was in the bathroom with Lisa sharing a tube of toothpaste, we suddenly heard a voice that sounded as though someone was in the same room with us. The source was the apartment below. It was Mr. Freedman.

"I know you have dogs up there! I know you do! And you call yourselves *Christians!*" he said.

It took all of our strength not to burst into laughter and make the situation even worse.

Lisa and I really enjoyed each other's company. She lived in a little cottage in Armonk with her dog, Alice, and cats, Snowy and Ringlet. I loved getting out of the City and meeting her to jog after work. During one of our outings, I asked if she'd like to shoot some hoops. Although she was six feet tall and had at least six inches over me, I thought I'd still have a chance playing H-O-R-S-E. I did not know that she had gone to Fairleigh Dickinson University on a basketball scholarship. I'm sure it was only because of her generous spirit and love for the underdog that she spotted me closer to the basket.

It was a Sunday morning after a long run when we had brunch at a nearby diner. We sat across from each other in a booth at a corner of the diner. I had begun to feel uncomfortable about seeing her so much. Every day with her was like a new beginning. I had to clear the air with her, because I didn't want to allow any feelings I had for her that weren't appropriate to get in the way. I believed that I had to overcome my feelings for her for a higher purpose and I had to tell the truth to make it go away.

I folded my hands on the table and steeled myself to say what I knew needed to be said: "Lisa, I have to tell you something. I've got to get this out of the way so it doesn't affect our friendship. I really want us to remain friends, and I don't want anything to come between us."

She leaned across the table, arms folded in front of her, and gave me her full attention.

I took a deep breath and said, "I'm attracted to you. I don't want to do anything about it. I just want to tell you so I can get it out of the way and we can move on to have a friendship."

I felt a weight lift. We can move on now, I thought.

Lisa leaned even closer.

"I feel the same way," she said almost in a whisper.

The red vinyl seat squeaked as I squirmed. My heart raced and my mind went blank.

"I wasn't prepared for that answer. I … I don't know what to say. Like I said, I don't want to do anything about it. Let's just move on the way things are — and we'll see where it goes. OK?"

"All right," Lisa said as casually as ordering pancakes.

WITHOUT FAITH

Chapter 43

Peekskill

The Perlmans, clients whom Lisa had helped with the financing of their new Toyota, asked if she'd be interested in housesitting and caring for their three cats in their Peekskill home for the winter.

The large old home rose up at the end of a long tree-lined driveway. On the crest of the hill, in the clearing, was a fenced-in swimming pool covered by a thick blanket of snow. The only other dwelling was a small cottage at the edge of the tree line that was occupied by a renter we never saw.

Lisa asked if I'd sleep over so she didn't have to be alone in that big house, and it easily became a way of life. We dined in the local restaurants at night and jogged together around the nearby frozen Lake Mohegan at daybreak. Roxanne and I commuted back to the City every morning when Lisa left for work in Mount Kisco, and on Thursday nights we attended Bible study at my apartment.

Leah was the only one from our study group whom I wanted to know about my feelings for Lisa. I knew that the others in our group believed that homosexuality was a sin because of the way the Scriptures referring to sexual immorality were interpreted, but I knew in my heart that could not be true. I continued to be a part of this study group for the rich spiritual relationship and because I was continually amazed, the more I learned, about the power and love of God. I told myself that it didn't matter that I couldn't be open about my sexuality.

Leah knew me. She knew my heart, and she had taught me about love by her selfless example and always how she saw God working in her life. When we had become roommates, she always woke before me and brewed my coffee even though she didn't drink coffee herself. At night she loaded my toothbrush with toothpaste, leaving it on the sink ready for me. She helped accessorize my wardrobe with earring and bracelet combinations that she had made. I'd pass her bedroom doorway on the way to work in the morning, and she'd often stop me to let me know how a particular Scripture had just opened her heart.

One morning it was the Gospel of John, Chapter 17 — Jesus' prayer to the Father the night before he was crucified. Leah read it to me and with tears in her eyes she said, "He prayed for us that night. For you, and for me."

I never had a friend like Leah.

✷✷✷✷✷✷✷

Traffic was light for a Thursday night as Lisa and I made our way down the Taconic State Parkway from Peekskill to the City. Bible study was at 7:30, but we had arrived an hour early. Leah was putting on makeup at her desk when I peeked into her room to talk to her privately.

"Leah, I need to talk to you. You know I've been spending a lot of time with Lisa, and I know you think that homosexuality is wrong, but it can't be. I want you to know how much I love her and how much we both love God. Leah, it's so important for me that you understand," I said.

She got up from her desk to face me. "You know I love you. I love Lisa too, but I believe that if you pray wholeheartedly God will relieve you of your attraction to women, Doreen."

Her deep and soulful eyes shifted, searching mine, pleading for understanding of her truth.

"You don't understand, Leah. It would be like asking God to change your skin from black to white," I insisted.

"I'm going to love you anyway, Doreen, and I'm going to pray for you both, no matter what," she said.

She reached out to hug me, but I felt so sad and so separated. I wanted her to understand, to accept us. I felt like I had put the weight of the promise of God's unconditional love and acceptance upon her. It was too much for either one of us to bare. Her approval wasn't coming, and the truth of my own convictions had to be enough. I still had doubts that were faint whispers from Catholic school nuns and biblical interpretations that said homosexuals could not enter the kingdom of heaven.

It broke my heart that Leah could not embrace my feelings for Lisa. How

WITHOUT FAITH

could she think that it was something that needed to be fixed? I feared that this would affect Lisa in her search for the truth to do what's right. I was afraid she would be shaken. After all, I was shaken. I had to trust that no matter what happened, it would be OK, and that if I had to let go of Lisa, I could. For the first time in my forty-one years of dying and living, I was in love with a woman who knew and understood God as I did. How could our God not want this for us? I thought.

I was so torn. I loved Lisa. She was new in Bible study, and I was supposed to be a good example for her. She was 28. I was 41. I had to be the mature one, even though at times it seemed that Lisa was far wiser in her years than I.

Later that evening, after everyone had gone home and Leah had left to be with her boyfriend, Chris, Lisa and I sat on the couch in the quiet, dimly lit living room. I faced her squarely, placing the palm of my hand to rest on her heart.

"Lisa, I know that we can't be married and we're certainly not virgins, but I love you so much and want you so much that I don't want us to make a mistake. I want to wait until we are sure we can commit our lives to each other in the eyes of God. We can't have marriage as we know it, but we can have it in our hearts. Will you do this?" I asked.

Lisa's eyes filled with tears. She gently cupped her hand over mine on her heart and said, "Yes, I can."

We kissed and sealed our love and our promise.

✶✶✶✶✶✶✶

On a clear, crisp winter morning with a sky so blue and air so fresh that my nostrils quivered trying to breathe the frozen air, I followed Lisa's brand new black Nissan heading for the Taconic Parkway with my window rolled down and heat on high after spending another wonderful night with her in Peekskill. We entered the two-lane entrance ramp simultaneously. Lisa's passenger window rolled down, and she smiled and shouted across the lane, "I'm going to live with you!"

My heart nearly flipped out of my chest. I couldn't respond with more than a smile and a wave goodbye as I inhaled her words and exhaled with a knowing "Yes" deep in my soul.

I knew this beautiful, tender woman was the one I would spend all of my life with, and it was time for us to fulfill our promise to each other and to put our trust in God, no matter what others believed.

WITHOUT FAITH

Chapter 44

Westport

Wednesday was Lisa's day off from the dealership. We rounded up our dogs, Alice and Roxanne, who were finally getting the idea that they had to get along with each other. Alice, a mischievously curious beagle-terrier mix, was half the size of Roxanne. They both had been strays, and Lisa and I did as little as possible to discipline them except if they were a bother to someone else.

Roxanne was a cranky, sometimes unpredictable dog who was always biting someone, except for Lisa or me. And if the door was open a second too long, Alice would take off until we could corner her or bribe her back with a delicacy like a can of cat food. Food was Alice's motivation for everything.

Northern Westchester to Connecticut is a beautiful drive on a clear blue-sky day after a snowfall. I was so happy to be with Lisa searching for a home that we could afford to rent and begin our new lives together. We had been back and forth from Peekskill to Westport every Wednesday and Sunday for the past three weeks.

We rounded the water's edge on Harbor Road and turned down a road that was no wider than a driveway. The tires crunched the gravel beneath us as we made our way down the beachside street to a two-story house. Three concrete steps led to an aluminum storm door that opened to a mudroom. A narrow white and beige kitchen connected the newly carpeted living room with a glassed-in porch at the rear.

Upstairs were three more rooms that the realtor said qualified as bedrooms. Only one of the rooms could barely fit a queen-size bed. There was no dishwasher. More than a washer and dryer, I at least hoped for a dishwasher. I could bring clothes to the laundromat, but there was nowhere I could bring dirty dishes.

"Hey, Lisa! You can see the water from here," I said, peering out the window of the low-ceilinged living room.

Alan, the balding realtor, who was standing in a sandy puddle in the kitchen from the snow melting off his galoshes, said, "Oh, that won't be for long.

They're rebuilding the house on the corner that was destroyed by the nor'easter that came through here."

"Oh, well, you can see it now," I said.

The three of us huddled on the new linoleum floor in the kitchen, studying the listing to compare what we read with what we saw.

"So, what do you say?" the realtor asked.

"We'll take it!" Lisa said.

I couldn't believe it. She didn't even ask me. I wouldn't have even tried to talk her into this place. But I trusted her instincts, shrugged my shoulders, and was happy to move on to moving in.

We were sure our new landlord would like us, and even though the listing said one small dog was allowed, why would anyone mind if we had two dogs — and I really didn't think cats counted as pets.

WITHOUT FAITH

Chapter 45

Meeting Mary

The distant whir of a motor woke me from a dream. The sunlight permeated every corner and crevice in the plastered ceiling of our bedroom. Fully awakened by the realization that this was our new home, our cottage by the sea, I perched myself up on both elbows, careful not to wake Lisa.

The grassy alleyway between the two houses on Harbor Road allowed for a precious glimpse of the Saugatuck Inlet. Craning my neck toward the window at the head of our bed, I felt like a little girl on Christmas morning. With eager anticipation I waited. It *was* a motorboat and a water-skier streaking across the wake in tow. This was our new home and my new life beginning with Lisa.

✶✶✶✶✶✶✶✶

Lisa couldn't get another day off from work, so my sister, Donna, was helping me unload the few pieces of furniture and boxes we had in the U-Haul van.

We took a break and rested on the bench of an old wooden picnic table between the back of the garage and the house.

"Donna, can you believe it? After all these years, we live within ten miles of each other?"

"I knew someday we'd be close, Reenie," she said.

Donna had managed to go back to school and graduate from the State University of New York with a bachelor's degree in social work. She was working for a local health agency.

Five years earlier, she had been in a psychiatric ward, again having relapsed. Her ex-husband, Sherman, had taken custody of Charice until Donna was well enough to care for her. Donna was finally properly diagnosed as bipolar, manic-depressive, and able to regain custody of Charice. Without lithium, she became another person and a threat to herself, but she had been taking her medication regularly now for five years, was a good mother, and was able to provide a home for both of them in nearby Bridgeport, where Charice had started high school.

DOREEN BIRDSELL

Although Charice was a mentally challenged child, she was happy, and she and Donna were the center of each other's life. Charice was a child who laughed easily, and her joy was exuberant and contagious.

✲✲✲✲✲✲✲✲

A white-haired man in his early seventies who lived in the run-down, paint-worn Cape next door was repairing his gray weathered fence, installing new posts. When I passed by carrying a box from the van, he said, "Hope you like peace and quiet."

"I love peace and quiet," I said.

"Well, that's all you're gonna get here. It's like livin' in a cemetery."

"That's just fine with me. My name's Doreen. You live here long?"

"Forty-five years. Moved here after the war."

"What's your name?"

"Larry Schaffer," he said while wrangling with his fence.

"This is my sister, Donna. She's helping me move in."

"You see that picnic table you're sittin' at? I built it over twenty years ago for Erna and her husband when he was alive."

"Wow — nice work," I said.

"Yeah, I build doghouses too. I sell them to the pet stores. They're not like those cheap things that don't last. I shingle 'em and put in a wood floor too. You need a doghouse?"

"No, I don't think so, but I'll ask Lisa. She lives with me."

"Who lives over there?" I asked, pointing to the mustard-colored bungalow on the other side of our house.

"Oh, that's Mary. She's my sister, but we don't talk."

It was then that I felt as though we were being watched. The closed white blinds on the bungalow window next door rattled, and whoever it was didn't want us to know they were there.

✲✲✲✲✲✲✲✲

A long orange extension cord was connected to a lawn mower being pushed by a woman wearing yellow rubber rain boots. This was the first we had seen of Mary.

I wondered how safe it was to mow a lawn wired to an electrical outlet. What do I know? I've never even owned a lawn mower, I thought.

Blondish-gray hair was mostly concealed under a faded pink baseball cap. A long-sleeved cotton shirt was neatly tucked into the elastic waistband of her black stretch pants. Mary appeared to be in her late seventies, but her smooth, thin-skinned, flushed complexion and petite figure were those of a woman who had once been very attractive.

She commandeered the lawn mower, making deliberate rows with a military-like precision. I made a few trips back and forth to my car to unload groceries, each time waiting for a chance to make conversation, but it never came. Mary continued marching behind that lawn mower with an unwavering determination.

****

Each morning when Lisa and I woke, our dogs, Roxanne and Alice, ran to the front door, barking and pawing the storm door incessantly until they were released to storm the neighborhood. They'd chase each other down the gravel street, turning over garbage cans, discovering their new surroundings.

Now this is how a dog's life ought to be, I thought — until the day Lisa and I came home and found a clear plastic bag on our front steps. When I picked it up, I discovered it was dog poop.

"Yuck! Who would do something like this?" Lisa yelled.

Simultaneously, we scanned the seven houses in our immediate vicinity as though we could discern who it was. I examined the bag more closely for a clue. Was it a baggie with a tie or a zip lock? Which one of our neighbors was missing this very bag? And who would be so disgustingly cunning to pick up poop, put it in a bag, zip it up, and sneak over to our house when we weren't home and put it in our doorway?

The pebble walkway crunched behind us. It was Mary.

"I can tell you who did it. I saw her. She didn't know I was home … that I could see her prance across the street and creep up to your house holding that bag out between her fingers," Mary said, imitating the suspect's steps while pretending to hold a bag ever so delicately with her pinky in the air.

"I wondered what was in that bag until I heard you just now," she continued.

Lisa and I were frozen with our mouths gaping wide. We registered much more information about this woman, Mary, than about who brought the poop.

"Well ... who did it?" Lisa asked.

"You don't know? You can't guess?" Mary asked with her hands on her hips and head cocked, provocatively blinking her eyes slowly once or twice, compelling us to guess.

"I don't know. ... It wouldn't be Sarah across the street, or your brother, Larry; not the lady in that pencil house. They're never home. Jim and Carol would never. They're nice people." I said.

"Oh, you don't know these people. You can't put anything past any one of them. It was that little snively one who's always running around in those short shorts, thinking she's some kind of athlete."

"You gotta be kidding! We don't even know her. I've maybe only seen her once," Lisa said.

"Why would she do that?" I asked.

"Because Roxanne did her business in her yard. I saw her do it," Mary said.

"Oh, my God! So why didn't she just *tell* us?" Lisa asked.

"Cuz that's just the way she is. Ever since she moved here, she thinks she owns the neighborhood. You gotta watch out for that one."

It was that bag of poop that first brought us together. Mary continued to be aloof, letting us in only when *she* decided there was something to say and it usually had something to do with not getting our weed wacker too close to her fence or parking too close to her property line. Mary had a white 1972 Datsun and two overturned dinghies that she used to protect the parking spaces in front of her house.

We warned her that there would be more cars than usual at our house on Wednesday nights when we had Bible study and took it as an opportunity to invite her to join us.

WITHOUT FAITH

"I don't need that. I go to church every Saturday for Mass."
"Well, you're always welcome, Mary." Lisa said.
With a wrinkled nose and pursed lips, she shook her head and walked away.
There were ten of us who faithfully gathered every week, including my sister, Donna, and niece, Charice. We always began our fellowship together by singing at least three old-time hymns.

It was summertime, and the song *To God Be the Glory* resounded through Mary's open windows. Although she wouldn't hesitate to knock on our door if we dared to park too close to her dinghy, Mary never bothered us about our enthusiastic singing or the cars that often parked over her coveted property line on our Wednesday Bible study nights.

A few weeks later, at about 10 p.m. on a Thursday night, Lisa and I were driving home from Norwalk. Only a few miles away, we heard thunder. Lisa sped as fast as she safely could to get home. We had nicknamed Roxanne "Jack Nicholson" because her eyes would resemble his crazed expression in *The Shining* whenever there was a storm, and she would destroy everything in her path to find safety. Her paws were like chain saws that could tear through any wall or door.

When we arrived in our driveway, we found Roxanne in the bushes next to the garage.
"Oh, my God! How did she get out?" I said.
"Roxanne, Roxanne!" Lisa cried from the car. Usually she would run up to us, tail wagging and barking, but she only lay there, heavily panting.
Her front leg was swollen and disfigured.
The tiny second-floor bedroom at the front of the house was where we kept Roxanne and Alice when we were out. The screen was now broken through and hanging from the sill.
Apparently, Roxanne had broken through the screen, gotten out onto the roof that covered the mudroom entryway, and jumped from the second floor.
Lisa was screaming: "Oh, my God! Oh, my God!"
Out of nowhere came Mary in a Burberry flannel bathrobe and moccasins. She rushed to Roxanne, her hair in two long braids, and she quickly took charge.

She put Roxanne's paw in her hand and said, "She needs a doctor. Do you have a vet?"

"Yeah … but how are we going to move her?" I said.

"We'll put her on a board and lift her into your car."

We moved quickly and got Roxanne to the vet.

This was the only time we ever saw Mary let her guard down and show compassion.

The next day we brought Roxanne home. Her broken leg was in a plaster cast covered with a pink sock. As much as Roxanne resisted, we had to keep her in the strongest crate we could find so she could heal.

Mary didn't come out of her house when we lifted Roxanne out of the car, but we knew that she saw every move we made and that she cared.

WITHOUT FAITH

Chapter 46

Saugatuck Shores

For Sale, Boston Advance Rowing Shell with Oars — $50. Not a tab was missing, and to be sure no one else would beat me to it, I ripped off the flier taped to the window at Peter's Bridge Market, hoping to guarantee my acquisition. What a deal! I thought.

Sitting on the small cup-like seat of the scull, I gripped the oar handles, and Lisa gave me a push offshore. The boat glided like a hockey puck on ice. I thought this would be so easy, but it was more like being on a tightrope. The shore was only fifty feet away, but I didn't know how to navigate my way back using the unwieldy ten-foot-long oars and almost capsized.

I took a lesson at the local boat shop, traded running for rowing, and dollied the boat down to the shore every morning at dawn.

A few weeks later, on the Fourth of July morning of 1994, I rowed east toward the sunrise. A full moon was setting over my shoulder. Boats rocked on their moorings in the distance, and the world felt still asleep. It was the most beautiful morning on the water I had ever known. I held the oars perpendicular to the narrow boat, dropping them into the mirror-smooth water, and came to a sudden stop. A line of honking geese glided inches off the surface of Long Island Sound.

My thoughts drifted to a summer afternoon when I was eight years old, sitting in the back seat of Uncle Ted's old 1954 forest green Pontiac. A drive in the country was a weekly escape from the heat of the city. A team of rowers on the Housatonic River cut its way through the water, almost keeping pace with our car. Jumping from the back seat, I wedged myself between Aunt Hazel and Uncle Ted.

"That's what I want to do!" I said.

Aunt Hazel laughed and said, "Reenie, you got a champagne appetite and a beer pocketbook. You better marry somebody rich."

DOREEN BIRDSELL

Houses on Saugatuck Shores were so close that conversations could be overheard when the windows were open, and comings and goings on the water were obvious to everyone on Harbor Road. Our lawn cutters from the neighborhood, Battista, ten years old, and Alberto, twelve, were enterprising brothers who were selling a twenty-year-old powerboat that their father had given them. I loved to row but wanted to share my love for boating with Lisa. The powerboat would be good for our relationship, I thought, and $400 was a good deal for a boat with a motor.

On a Saturday in summer, Long Island Sound was like an amusement park filled with water-skiers, sailors, and fishermen. I had persuaded Lisa to take a ride on our newly overhauled seventeen-foot Lone Star. She didn't share the same affection for boating but agreed to go if she could drive.

We headed toward the open water of Long Island Sound at full throttle, bouncing over the wake of other boats near the channel between Compo Beach and the Cedar Point Yacht Club.

We almost collided with a passing sailboat, and I yelled from the stern, "Turn the boat!"

"I'm trying! Nothing's happening!" Lisa yelled, spinning the wheel.

The steering cable had snapped.

I threw my arms around the old Evinrude 75 horsepower motor and used the weight of my torso to steer the boat away from shore and the other boats.

Cruising by on a catamaran were Alberto and Battista, enjoying a fast ride. Alberto hollered to his brother, "Why's Doreen hugging the motor?"

Sailing had to be better than this, I thought. I sold the Lone Star to two fishermen and purchased a twenty-two-foot O'Day sailboat that was advertised in the Bargain News.

Our boating mishaps and antics on the water didn't go unnoticed by Mary. She saw everything.

"You girls better watch your mooring. You gotta watch these men around here. They think they own the water," she warned us.

WITHOUT FAITH

When her dinghies weren't being used to block the parking spots in front of her house, she moored them offshore at the end of the block to maintain her mooring rights. In the five years we lived on the Shores, I saw Mary rowing a boat twice: once after I started sculling, because I believe she was competitive, and once to inspect her moorings.

Whenever Lisa and I invited her to join us to go sailing, she would never accept. Every day she made her neighborhood rounds, which she called jogging, taking a two-mile walk down Harbor Road to the yacht club and back with a yellowed-white earphone dangling from one ear connected to her transistor radio. A Nantucket pink baseball cap always concealed her blond bun, and her recreational attire was black stretch pants, sweater, and spotless white sneakers.

One day she'd be icy, and the next she'd stop to tell us stories about her life.
"My father was a piano player, you know. … My sister Coleen and I used to sing and dance when he performed in Norwalk. We were quite an act," she said, sashaying back and forth to demonstrate.
It seemed that Rowland Place, the pebble beach road on which we lived, was now her stage and Lisa and I her audience for her to animate the activities that consumed her day. Most often she was preoccupied with who was trying to get her to sell her brother Larry's house.
Mary and Larry never spoke and were so secretive that we never knew Larry was sick until Mary and Coleen knocked on our door on Easter morning.
Coleen, who was quiet and soft-spoken, said, "We wanted to let you know that Larry died and if Mary and I ever sell his house we want you and Lisa to buy it."
"Yeah, we like you girls," Mary said, "and we know you'd like to live down here. Rentin' is like throwin' your money in the river."
"I'm so sorry," Lisa said.
"We didn't know. We would have visited. Gone to the funeral … " I said.
"He didn't want nothin' like that," Mary said. "That family of ours. Those nieces and nephews tried to get their hands on Larry's house. We had to buy them out. That's why we didn't say anything. All the trouble they caused."
Mary was cautious about everything and suspicious of everyone. "You

know," she said, flinging her arms back toward the road, "If a strange vehicle comes down this street, I write down the license number. You *never* know who these people are — comin' down here snooping around. You know somebody stole my license plate? I used to see a white Datsun hatchback — the only one I ever seen just like mine — in the Pathmark parking lot over in Norwalk. I liked those marker numbers "777" — had 'em for years — and wasn't gonna lose 'em. Sure enough — it took two weeks but I found him! Had to borrow a screwdriver from a guy with a truck. But I got 'em!"

I admired Mary's persistence and the courage it took for her to stand her ground in spite of people's opinions. She had strong convictions, and I counted that as an asset even though she tried my patience with her stubbornness. The more stubborn and cranky she was, the more friendly and patient I became.

✷✷✷✷✷✷✷

The late November morning we moved in 1999, Mary didn't show herself. We knew she didn't like goodbyes. She didn't like hellos either. We would miss her and Saugatuck Shores, but our friends Jane and Jennifer, who lived in Stuyvesant Town, where I had lived, were eager to rent our "cottage by the sea."

After saving enough money for a down payment, Lisa and I had finally purchased our first home. We couldn't afford being close to the water and were farther inland on Long Lots Road, but we were still in Westport, the town we came to love and call home. We took comfort knowing that our friends would keep us connected to Saugatuck Shores and that we would be back often.

WITHOUT FAITH

Chapter 47

Mary's Ageless Birthday – 9/14/00

"Let's take a ride," I said to Lisa.

It had been almost two years since we moved inland. Thoughts ceased and my heart swelled whenever we rounded the bend at Harbor Road. I was always overwhelmed by the same sudden appearing of the Saugatuck Inlet that opened to Long Island Sound just as the road turned to parallel the water's edge.

We parked in the driveway at our old house on Rowland Place and walked down the gravel road to the water, silently gazing at the horizon as the day turned to dusk. Moments later, Mary appeared alongside us.

"Hi, girls. You visiting your friends?" Mary asked.
"Yeah. We love coming down here," I said.
"How are you doing, Mary?" Lisa asked.
"Oh, oh, I'm just fine … I think I'm fine."
She sidestepped a little bit, shuffling while looking at the ground, and said, "Look, can I ask you girls a favor?"
A "favor"? I thought.

The only time Mary had asked me for anything was when she noticed how well I had fiberglassed the hole in my dinghy one summer and asked if I would repair hers too. I was flattered that she asked and proud of myself for having taught myself how to do it. I had to walk away from her while she chased me down the street with a hundred-dollar bill because she wouldn't accept my fixing her dinghy as a gift. So, asking us for a "favor" really got Lisa's and my attention.

"I've never been sick, you know, because I'm so healthy. The only doctor I ever needed was a dentist and once an orthopedic when I broke my wrist. I'll have nothing to do with those doctors otherwise. Anyway, there's something wrong with my breast — I think I pulled a muscle when I lifted the lawn mower out of the trunk of my car. I called my sister-in-law, Pauline, to ask if she'd go with me. You know what she said?... "

Mary's voice raised an octave. She looked over her shoulder and changed personalities to imitate her. "Ohhhh. Well. ... I don't know. I'll have to look in my appointment book," she said in a soprano voice. "An appointment book! Huh!!! Since when does she have an appointment book? She hasn't had anywhere to go in years!"

By now Mary was prancing up and down Harbor Road, her arms flapping at her sides. "I'll have to look in my appointment book? ... Oh. Sure!"

Lisa and I shot a quick glance at each other. We knew that this was not a casual favor. Mary wouldn't ask us if she wasn't afraid, but she would never admit it. The stillness of the evening and our own agenda was suddenly eclipsed. Lisa and I recognized without speaking that this was a spiritual moment calling us to a greater commitment.

Lisa reached out her hand to touch Mary's arm, but she flinched and withdrew.

"You meet me here tomorrow, and we'll go together. The three of us, right?" Mary asked, "Oh. And tomorrow's my birthday.

"Wow - September 14th! – Happy Birthday!" I said.

"No - No celebrating....And don't go getting me a card or anything...That's not why I said it...It just happens to be – that's all.

At the doctor's office, Mary decided that it would be best if I filled out the paperwork.

"These girls are with me, and they're going to be in the room with me the whole time," she told the doctor.

"OK, then, but let me be in charge of the examination — all right?" he asked, smiling.

Mary turned to us, then the doctor, and agreed with a nod.

"I need to ask you a few questions," he said.

"First of all: How old are you?"

"Why do you need to know that?"

"It's a simple question. Please?"

WITHOUT FAITH

"Does a year or two matter?"
"Please."
"All right."
"Girls, cover your ears," she said and whispered in his ear.

When the nurse asked Mary to undress for the exam, she adamantly refused.
"I'm not taking off my pants for anyone! And that's final."
"Mary, they need to do a thorough exam. It's all right," Lisa said.
"When is the last time you had a gynecological exam?" the doctor asked.
"Never! Never needed to!"
"Never? Well, we should take a look."
"I'm here for my breast. You don't need to go down there."
"If I'm going to be your doctor, I need to fully examine you and at least do a pap smear."
"No way! Who says you're my doctor? I'm just here for this one thing."
This man had no idea what he was in for, and neither did we.
"All right, all right. But you have to let me examine your breast. Can you take off your sweater and put on the examination gown?"
"I don't need that thing. I'll let you lift up my sweater."
She held her body perfectly straight with her eyes squeezed tight while he probed.

He became quite serious and had his nurse order a mammogram immediately.

Chapter 48

Our Primary Purpose

Perhaps the gynecologist had warned Dr. Meinke about Mary's disposition, but her cantankerous personality seemed to charm him. He was respectful of her privacy and demand to be fully dressed when he examined her, as well as her need to have us with her at all times. He was painstakingly patient in describing to her how any cancerous cells in her breast could multiply and attack the rest of her organs and that surgery was crucial.

"No way. I'll take my chances," she said.

"You can't do that, Mary," I said.

"Look, Mary. I think you should listen," Lisa added.

"Mary, can I hold your hand?" the doctor asked.

Sitting at the edge of the examination table, Mary studied Dr. Meinke closely, eyes squinty, hands clutching her knees. There was nothing pretentious or official about him. Instead of being cloaked in a doctor's gown like the previous physician we had seen, Dr. Meinke wore a crisp white shirt and burgundy tie, tucked into cuffed navy blue dress pants. He was balding, in his 40s, with a flushed complexion as though he had recently worked out. His lips turned naturally upward as he held her gaze. She momentarily surrendered, turning over her hand, palm up, for him to hold.

"Mary. I see that these girls have given up their time to be here for you. If you trust them, then trust them to help you with this decision, and listen to them," he said.

The urgency of the situation made us all very nervous. The only solution I knew to this anxiety was to pray for Mary's healing, to pray that God would be with us, no matter what.

I looked Mary square in the eyes and said, "Mary, we have to trust God and to believe. I promise that we will be there for every doctor visit, no matter what. You will not go through any of this alone."

"You'll come to the hospital? You'll wait and be there when it's over?" she asked.

"We'll be there," Lisa said, touching her shoulder.

WITHOUT FAITH

Mary lifted her chin to the doctor, who was still holding her hand cupped between his own gentle, skillful hands. The fear in her eyes was replaced by a bashful, girlish grin I never would have expected from Mary.

"I'll do it — only if it's OK for the girls to be there," she said.

****

The surgery was scheduled for the day after Thanksgiving. As we turned off Harbor Road to Rowland Place, Mary was ready and waiting, standing on the other side of her bungalow's sliding glass door. She stepped out onto the concrete patio that overlooked the water just down the street and had a clear view of all the neighborhood goings-on. She had taken great care to put on lipstick, pinken her cheeks, and wear a camel turtleneck cashmere sweater, black stirrup pants, and leather pumps.

Mary often surprised me with her expansive wardrobe. She was outfitted for everything, from yellow rubber waders on rainy days to beautiful suits and dresses for church. She was never married and never spoke of a boyfriend.

Before the procedure, the nurses had to agree to a compromise that would allow Mary to leave on her pantyhose if they were to continue. Dr. Meinke met us in the Norwalk Hospital lounge immediately after the surgery, still wearing green scrubs and O.R. cap. He took a deep breath and said, "I'm sorry. It's gotten into her lymph nodes."

"What's that mean?" I asked.

"She may only have two years. She probably had this for quite some time before saying anything about it."

****

We didn't know what to do first. Mary had no one but us. Her sister, Coleen, had died suddenly of an embolism only days after we had moved to Long Lots Road two years earlier, leaving her with a sister-in-law, and nieces and nephews whom she said she wanted nothing to do with.

I couldn't look that far ahead, trying to imagine what to expect. We needed to take Mary home and make sure she had what she needed while the wound from the lumpectomy drained.

Dr. Meinke referred us to an oncologist. Persuading Mary to get chemo was almost impossible. Her stubborn resistance pushed Dr. Meinke to become as frank as possible.

"Mary, if you don't get treated you will die sooner," he said.

A few days after the first chemo treatment, I stopped by her house while Lisa was at work to see how she was doing.

"That's it! If the cancer doesn't kill me, the chemo will," she said, almost staggering.

There was no further arguing. Radiation and daily doses of tamoxifen were the only treatment she would accept. Mary was the most proud and independent woman I had ever known.

At lunchtime the next day, Mary pulled into our driveway on Long Lots Road in what had been her brother Larry's old Dodge, white-capped pickup truck.

"I just need you to wait here while I take my pill," she said. "I've never taken anything stronger than an aspirin."

"Come in the house, Mary."

"Nope. I got my water. You just stay out here while I do this. … OK. Here it goes."

One gulp, and a moment later Mary was backing down the driveway in a hurry to be somewhere else.

We followed up with the doctors regularly and met Mary at the Whittingham Cancer Center weekly for her radiation treatments for the next six months.

About a year later, Roxanne had broken another window screen during a thunder and lightning storm, but this time she had also pawed through a door and the wooden frame. I was between explaining what happened to the repairman and holding back Roxanne from jumping on him when the phone rang.

WITHOUT FAITH

"Doreen, are you busy? Can you come over here?" Mary asked.
"Yeah. Sure. I have a guy here doing some work. Is everything OK?"
"I'm all right. But come when you can, OK?"
When I arrived fifteen minutes later, she was lying on the floor with the telephone next to her.
"Mary! Why didn't you tell me you fell?"
"I didn't want you to worry and maybe have an accident driving over here."
"I could have gotten here faster, Mary!" I said, helping her to the couch. "We've got to get you to the hospital."
"I'm fine. I just got dizzy. I'll be all right."
The swollen lump on her forehead had already turned purple.
"Mary, you gotta let somebody look at this. You might have a concussion or maybe you might have broke something."
"That's enough! I've had enough of them doctors!"
"We need to get you help. You can't be alone anymore," I said.

Lisa and I took turns going to her house every day and again at night before bedtime. We finally persuaded her to let the Visiting Nurse Service check on her once a week.

****

I had never cared for anyone in my life. My father and I hadn't spoken for three years after Donna told me that he had molested Charice. I was never sure if it was true. My father denied it. Donna wasn't always reliable because of her manic-depressive episodes; but because my father drank and blacked out, I believed that he couldn't be sure either.

I couldn't talk to him anymore, and I told him not to call because I had to figure things out.

The day he called me to ask for help, I knew he was in trouble. I picked up Donna and went to the senior housing residence in Port Chester. I turned off the engine, and we sat in silence for a moment.

"It's Wednesday. And there's a man up there who needs our help," I said. "That's how we have to look at it — that's how we'll get through it."

He was frail and undernourished. Donna arranged for him to have Meals on Wheels deliver daily, and I did the paperwork to get him into the Port Chester Nursing Home. On the day he was to be moved, he was so thin that Lisa was able to lift him into our car.

I visited him often over the next few months, keeping him stocked with his favorite Werther's butterscotch candies, and I bought him a Bible that he kept on his TV.

I'd read to him and encouraged him to pray. I never asked anything of him except to believe in God and read the Bible. I wanted more than anything to have a relationship with him that I could trust. I wanted him to be my encourager, to be my father, to love me.

I had a great opportunity to photograph temples in Italy and Greece. I thought that when I told him I was going, he'd be happy for me and proud. Instead, he said flatly, "Don't go."

"It'll only be three weeks." I assured him he'd be fine.

On the eighth day of my trip, I was in Sicily and made a call home to check in with Lisa.

"I'm sorry, Doreen. We didn't know how to reach you. Your father died," she said.

I couldn't speak. I sobbed uncontrollably. I stayed in Italy and finished my work, pretending that was what he would have wanted me to do. I couldn't believe he died while I was gone. I was so torn between my unexpected grief and the thought that my leaving him may have accelerated his death. He had abandoned me for the last time, and my heart was broken open to the final loss of my father.

Donna and I scattered his ashes in Candlewood Lake, where as children we had family picnics and rare moments of being together.

WITHOUT FAITH

Chapter 49

What a Predicament

I didn't know where the drive and compassion to care for Mary came from. I only followed and found the next thing to do as it occurred. It seemed all so unnaturally natural.

Mary fought the doctors and Lisa and me every step of the way. Her illness took over, and she insisted on being at home and having Lisa and me be the only ones to care for her. She made sure we knew where all her important papers were, and where and how she wanted to be buried.

"I want to show you where Coleen and Johnny are buried. I bought four plots," she said. "I want my funeral to be just like the one I had for my sister, Coleen. You tell them that at Collins Funeral Home. ... Oh ... and no flowers. I don't like flowers — they're a waste of money. And nothing in the newspaper. You understand?"

"I got it, Mary. I understand," I said.

Mary never ceased to amaze me with her bluntness and ability to face anything head-on — especially her death.

Lisa and I divided our time based upon the immediate need and our threshold for different situations. Upon Mary's determination to make sure everything would be exactly as she planned, I volunteered to take her to the cemetery, visit the plot where she would be buried, and handle the funeral arrangements. Mary dressed for the occasion in full makeup, red blazer, and colorful silk scarf to visit the places that signified her impending death.

"This is one of the best plots. I like the stream and the woods in the back. I knew Coleen would like it. I want a stone right there next to Coleen's — with my name only and no date. You got it?" she asked, pointing to the earth beneath the family headstone.

I nodded in agreement.

"I own four plots here. That leaves only one more. It's not enough for both you and Lisa, but I'm giving it to you both. And I want you to use it."

"That's all right, Mary. Lisa and I are going to be cremated. That'll be plenty of room."

To be certain Lisa and I could be buried in her additional plot, Mary had me check with the office at the cemetery's entrance.

"We allow six urns per plot," the woman at the desk informed us.

I prayed and I prayed my way through that day. I kept asking, "God, please get me through this. Please give me what I need to be here for Mary the way she needs me."

****

On good days, Mary would have us doing all types of projects. We were her hands and feet.

"I'd like you to get up in the attic with some of these clothes I'm not going to wear," she said one day.

Garment bags were hung on metal poles on either side of the attic that ran the full length of the floor. The attic consisted of nothing but clothes — enough wardrobe to stock a boutique.

"Mary! What are you doing with all these clothes? Most of them still have price tags on them," Lisa said.

"When I liked something, I bought two," Mary said.

It was unusually hot that summer, and Mary had no air conditioning. I had my cell phone to my ear, talking to a client, because I had to do whatever it took to keep my business going, and at the same time I was putting medicine on Mary's bottom for bedsores. I was so hot I thought I was burning from the inside out. When I got off the phone, Mary said, "You know, you girls better treat me right. I'm leaving everything to you two," pointing a finger at my sweaty face.

"Mary, you don't have enough to make me show up here every day and do what I do for you! I'll see my reward in heaven," I said.

The words came to my ears as though someone else had spoken them, and without saying it, looking into each other's eyes, we both knew that it was our love for each other that held us together.

This woman came into my life, let me love her, care for her, and she was

WITHOUT FAITH

going to die. She had given us power of attorney to handle her affairs, pay her bills, and have access to medical information.

Lisa and I began spending every free moment with Mary. The telephone was our lifeline when we had to be apart.

Mary was not happy with our new, but necessary, arrangement. Norma, a large, muscular, redheaded woman from the Sisters of Poland, whom we found through a church in Bridgeport, helped us care for Mary when she could no longer get out of bed.

Norma was the first person we had met on this journey who was able to take charge of Mary. She bathed her, cleaned under her fingernails, pinned up her hair, and would conveniently forget how to speak English when Mary would try to convince her that she could get out of bed.

It was September 14, 2002, Mary's 80th birthday — although she told us she was 79 years old.

Two years had passed since our first doctor's visit together. Norma had the day off. Mary was almost giddy knowing that Lisa and I were sleeping over. Usually, we would take turns when one of us had to stay. Donna and Charice watched our dogs, allowing Lisa and me to spend the day and night with Mary.

We bought Mary balloons, a new radio, and lottery tickets to celebrate her birthday.

"Thank you, girls, but I like my old radio."

"This is better. It's lighter. You can't even lift the other one," I said.

"I can too. It's just fine. ... I'll keep this one though. Just in case."

We all laughed, knowing that Mary would have her way.

After lunch, Mary was feeling well enough for a drive in the car around Compo Beach. When we got home, she was tired but a good kind of tired. Our friends Jane and Jennifer came by about 4 o'clock with a birthday card and a box of chocolate. After they left, we scratched lotto tickets. Mary won one free ticket.

She enjoyed a coconut candy and we got ready for bed, and all agreed that we had had one of the best days of our lives.

Even in her last days, Mary was strong-willed and alert. "I hope you girls never have to go through anything like this. How did I ever get in this predicament?" she asked.

As she grew weaker and quietly drifted in and out of consciousness, I took her hand in mine and whispered, "I love you, Mary. God loves you too."

I wanted, above all else, for her to know that there was an amazing life beyond all this and that she did not have to be afraid.

****

Autumn had swallowed up the remains of summer, and the night had become cold and damp. I relieved Lisa so she could go home and get some sleep.

There were longer silent spaces between each dragging breath until finally there was only silence — October 18, 2002, 3:15 a.m.

The pain ended. Her spirit was free.

When the hospice nurse arrived, she asked for a basin of warm water and soap. Mary loved Ivory soap. She would have approved.

****

The arrangements had been made. Mary made sure nothing was left to decide. We were to have a morning wake at the funeral home and take her to her chosen resting spot immediately following.

When her coffin was lifted into the hearse, my legs lost feeling and I had to catch myself. The pain of Mary's dying bore through me like a hot iron spike. With heaving sobs, I cried. I didn't recognize the pain — I could only surrender to it.

I loved her. She allowed me to love her and be with her when her spirit left to go home. I cried for her. I cried for Tazel. I cried for the mother I never knew until now.

WITHOUT FAITH

Chapter 50

Probate

Lisa and I were drained. I was so weak, and my heart ached. I was overcome with having lost Mary. Suddenly there was nothing left to do except to clean up Mary's house.

It was a mild October afternoon when we drove down the pebble beach road to her house. Through the sliding glass doors, we saw the stripped, empty hospital bed in the living room.

"I can't go in there yet. Let's take a walk," Lisa said.

We walked down the quiet, empty street without another word between us.

Turning the corner again back toward Mary's house, we noticed an unfamiliar pickup truck parked in front. A husky, broad-shouldered, white-haired man in his mid- to late 50s began walking in our direction, a piece of paper in his hand, his eyes focused on us.

"I'm Andrew. Mary's nephew," he said.

"Oh, I've heard of you," I said, reaching out my hand to greet him.

He flinched, pulling his arm back with an exaggerated jerk.

"You see that house?" he said, pointing to the empty gray house that had once belonged to Mary's brother, Larry. "It's not yours! … And you see that house?" he said, pointing to Mary's. "It's not yours either! And you're not allowed to step in either one of them! I got a court order right here!"

I was so raw and vulnerable I couldn't respond. Lisa took a step toward him and snapped back, "Who the hell are you? I've been here for almost ten years and never saw you once!"

"I've been here! I used to come and try to help Mary, but she'd never let me."

"Because she knew all you wanted was her house!" Lisa shot back.

"I got a court order. You stay out of that house and don't dare talk to me!"

I grabbed Lisa's arm to hold her back. The rage in his eyes terrified me, and I was reeling. We couldn't even have the closure of putting Mary's house in order.

We were barred from Mary's house the day after we buried her. The nephew had gone to Probate Court with a court order that said we "unduly influenced" his aunt.

"How did they know Mary died? Mary asked us specifically not to put a notice in the paper," I told the woman at Probate Court.
"He said that he saw the grave open," she said, looking up from her desk.
"Her grave open! They were watching her grave?"
"We have nothing to hide," I said. "I came here with a list of all the relatives to be notified."
"He was very angry. He came here to make a claim and went through the roof when he found out about the will that was filed," she said.

Before Mary's diagnosis, she had been in a feud with her next-door neighbor who refused to trim his hedges. Mary's repeated requests turned into resentment as the hedges slowly eroded Mary's view of the water and her peace of mind.
Mary was never happier than the day Jed and his wife, Cheryl, bought the house and uprooted the hedges that the previous owner had allowed to become overgrown. Jed promised Mary that he would never plant or build anything to ruin her view. When Mary became ill, he mowed her lawn whenever it was necessary. Jed knew that we were her caregivers; and when she confided in him that she wanted nothing to do with her relatives, he offered her his legal services if ever she needed him. A few months before she passed, Mary had Jed draw up a Last Will and Testament making Lisa and me her sole heirs.

Exhausted, we left for Provincetown and spent three days at a bed-and-breakfast to get away from everything and renew our strength.
Until now, I hadn't had rosary beads since I was in grammar school. But because they were Mary's, I clung to them throughout the weekend and I prayed: "God, you brought Lisa and me so far … through so much. I know we'll be OK. There's nothing these people can do to harm us. Whatever they say, God, I know you know our hearts and you'll protect us."

We arrived at Probate Court with an attorney for the reading of the will and faced a conference room filled with fourteen people, not including the judge

WITHOUT FAITH

and attorneys. All but one on the list Mary had given us showed up to contest the will. Mary knew there would be trouble.

Under oath, and during several court appearances, Lisa and I recounted the past two years with Mary and told the same truth over and over.

Our attorney told us that the case might go to Superior Court and be tied up for years.

We prayed and asked other people to pray for us. Five months later, I was sitting at my desk at home when the phone rang. It was Jackie Conlon, our attorney. This case was so personal that she had come to know us quite well by now.

"Doreen, it appears that they're dropping the case."

"You're kidding! I can't believe it. Really! What happened?"

"I think they knew that it would be a long time, cost a lot of money, and maybe never win after they heard our case."

It was done, and Mary's Last Will and Testament would stand as she wished. Lisa and I were depleted and finally able to begin absorbing all that we had been through with Mary and then with her relatives.

****

Two years later, while on vacation in Provincetown, Lisa and I were biking down Commercial Street in the west end and stopped in a plaza that had a beautiful view of Cape Cod Bay. One of the buildings on the perimeter of the brick-paved courtyard was a real estate office. The bed-and-breakfast we had stayed in after Mary had died was listed for sale in the window.

We both knew without a doubt and without conversation that this was to be ours. The vision we once had to own a B&B, but put on hold after Mary became ill, God had not forgotten. Because of Mary's gift to us, it was now possible and became a reality.

****

When I was three years old, I asked my Aunt Hazel to tell me why my daddy and Donna had to go away.

DOREEN BIRDSELL

"When a mother dies, the family falls apart," she said.

Life has given me a different answer -- Faith, the mother who gave me birth, Aunt Hazel who fought to give me a home, the unexpected mother I found in Mary, Lisa who has always been by my side, and to so many others, I give thanks for giving my life purpose and a family where death no longer has a grip.

I know that God has always loved me, and I believe loves us all. I also believe that healing will never find a reason to cease as painful memories sometimes reoccur. Because of it I am grateful for the gift of compassion that my life's experience has given me to help others. How amazing God is to have given me a mother named Faith.

"Without faith it is impossible to please God. Anyone who comes to God must believe that he is real and that he rewards those who truly want to find him."
Hebrews 11:6